THE DEVIL'S OWN GAME

A SOMEBODY'S BOUND TO WIND UP DEAD MYSTERY

ANNIE HOGSETT

Poisoned Pen
PRESS

Published by Poisoned Pen Press, an imprint of Sourcebooks
P.O. Box 4410, Naperville, Illinois 60567-4410
(630) 961-3900
sourcebooks.com

Library of Congress Cataloging-in-Publication Data

Names: Hogsett, Annie, author.
Title: The devil's own game : a somebody's bound to wind up dead mystery/Annie Hogsett.
Identifiers: LCCN 2019023948 | (trade paperback)
Subjects: LCSH: Man-woman relationships--Fiction. | GSAFD: Mystery fiction.
Classification: LCC PS3608.O4827 D48 2019 | DDC 813/.6--dc23
LC record available at https://lccn.loc.gov/2019023948

Printed and bound in the United States of America.
SB 10 9 8 7 6 5 4 3 2 1

Praise for Annie Hogsett

MURDER TO THE METAL
The Second Somebody's Bound to
Wind Up Dead Mystery

"The bittersweet mystery, with the open-ended threat of a villain-ous mastermind, is reminiscent of P.J. Tracy's early Monkeewrench novels."

—*Library Journal*

"What are a newly and wildly rich couple to do? Why not start the T&A Detective Agency? They are handed their first case when Loretta Coates, a librarian friend of Allie's, asks Allie to find her boyfriend, Lloyd Bunker, who has vanished without a trace, as has his classic 1967 GTO. As Allie and Tom investigate, they discover that Lloyd's disappearance is connected to a web of other misdeeds that could spell trouble for themselves."

—*Publishers Weekly*

TOO LUCKY TO LIVE
The First Somebody's Bound to
Wind Up Dead Mystery

2018 nominee for the Salt Lake County Reader's Choice Award

"In this entertaining, sexy debut, Allie is a sharp Stephanie Plum paired up with a hot partner. She quickly learns how adept a blind man can be in dealing with trouble. The original voice, humor, and unusual premise will appeal to Janet Evanovich readers."

—*Library Journal*, Starred Review

"As the plot zigs and zags, readers will enjoy hanging out with Tom and Allie, whose quirkiness will remind some readers of Janey Mack's Maisie McGrane."

—*Publishers Weekly*

"Fast pacing, multiple plot twists, and humor, including a Stephanie Plum-like main character, enliven the story and keep the pages turning."

—*Booklist*

THE DEVIL'S OWN GAME

Books by Annie Hogsett

The Somebody's Bound to Wind Up Dead Mysteries
Too Lucky to Live
Murder to the Metal

For my Shore Acres Neighborhood.
Inspiration, support,
and the joy of your friendship.

"Love looks not with the eyes, but with the mind,
And therefore is winged Cupid painted blind."

—William Shakespeare,
A Midsummer Night's Dream

PROLOGUE

WEDNESDAY, FEBRUARY 28
UNIVERSITY CIRCLE, CLEVELAND, OHIO

7:45 P.M.

Darkness was no threat to the blind man. Night was his second nature. He thrived in it. Was part of it. For him, navigation was a reflex. Without calculating, he knew how far he'd walked the path he'd been told to take.

"Wait there ten minutes," the man said. "Then walk along the water. There's a bench. I'll meet you. We need to be careful."

His feet knew the way. He wasn't there yet, but he was right on time.

Just now he was aware, without being diverted or even interested, night had fallen, turned colder, and spawned a rising wind. He smelled open water close by, felt the moisture of it on his face, noted muffled traffic sounds and a spatter of voices. Moved quickly.

What seized the blind man's attention in his final moments was an unanticipated buzz of panic. The tap of his cane, the crunch of the rubber soles of his Brunello Cucinellis on the recently salted sidewalk, the rattle of ice in the branches of the trees bordering the lagoon, all were amplified by the sudden, terrified clench in his chest. The hammer of his heart. The voice in his head.

What have I done?

"No. *Think.*" He urged himself. "This will work—I'm *not*—"

The bullet found him. He died between one step and the next, without any idea of what was lost or why. Gone before the cane slipped from his hand and clattered onto stone, his body, young and fit, following it down with instinctive grace.

He lay warm on the freezing sidewalk, his blood soaking into a patch of ice, glinting in shifts of light from a streetlamp. The trees shuddered in the wind. From a distance came the sound of sirens.

Chapter One

WEDNESDAY, FEBRUARY 28

7:00 P.M.

A standoff between two tall, good-looking blind guys at the front door of a world-renowned art museum is a battle of the bands. I'm a peacemaker. Truly. I am. I prefer my people well-behaved, but right then I was rooting for Tom to clobber this guy. Figuratively speaking, of course. A small, hypothetical smackdown.

Tom, Otis, and I were heading through the glass north entrance of the Cleveland Museum of Art. Tom, pushing his way in. Other blind guy pushing his way out. The standard two-step goes, "Oh, you first."

"No, no. You come right on ahead."

But this man barged forward, thrusting out his cane like a fencer, missing my ankle by centimeters. I jumped back.

"You want to get out of my way, whoever you are?"

Tom stepped aside and held the door open. "Kip? Kip Wade? It's Tom Bennington. How've you been? You here for the Touch Tour?"

A sneer and a snarl. "Tom *Ben*nington? I'm leaving specifically so I don't have to be anywhere near your damn tour." A pause. "Or you."

Okay. Tall, handsome, blind, and an asshat.

Tom abandoned the pleasantries. He held the door open wider and waited, silent, for this Kip to come on out. This Kip, however, stopped dead in the middle of the doorway and unleashed a blast of vitriol that sounded to me like a lifetime supply of pent-up rage.

"What are you doing here, anyway, Bennington? *Touch Tour?* You loser. Why don't you contribute something to the museum instead of using it for your playground? Make a damn difference for a change? How come you're not a big philanthropist, you sorry son of a bitch? With your ridiculous Lotto win. How many people have you killed with your money so far? Why don't you make some good come out of it? Ditch your Allie…*cat* and do something worthwhile for a change. Go back to work. Teach a few of your classes, even."

Crap. The number of Tom's sore spots in that tirade was at least three notches past his tipping point. "Allie-Cat" sounded cute and sassy to me, but I would never confuse it with an expression of esteem. Otis and I exchanged glances. *Who is this jerk?* I shivered. Icy wind and a dash of wintery mix were getting sucked in around us and in through the open door. Inside was grand, welcoming, and warm. This was no-man's land, cross-hatched by white canes.

Museum-goers, now wisely choosing other, less obstructed, doors, started noticing and slowing up the in and out. Tom and Kip were an attention-grabbing traffic jam. For one thing they were both shockingly good-looking. Both well-dressed. Both lean and fit. But the planes of Tom's face were gentle and relaxed most of the time. His mouth tended toward smiling. His signature dimple, always a heart-stopping surprise—*Chill. Out. Allie Harper.*

Anyway. He was the charming, affable version of tall, blind, and handsome. Every single thing about him was irresistible. *Chill. Out, Alice Jane.*

The other guy was the disagreeable and aggressively rude version. His smile was turned upside down and twisted into a glower. Obviously, his mom never told him his face would freeze like that. Too late now. I liked his shoes, though. They looked crazy expensive. Becoming suddenly, unexpectedly jackpot-rich raises one's shoe-awareness quotient.

I put what I hoped felt like a supportive hand on Tom's shoulder. I was within shin-kicking distance of Kip, and in the mood. Booted up for it too. My new Louboutin "mad-spiked quilted leather ankle boots" cost more than a not-totally-junked used car. "Spiked" felt like the operative choice for this occasion.

I raised half an eyebrow at Otis.

C'mon, just this once?

He shook his head. Slowly…side to side… No…

Right. I got it.

Butt out, Alice Jane.

Tom valued his independence like nobody's business. He'd be royally bent out of shape if I kicked the shins of this apparent archrival with my fancy boots. Besides, I figured the no-shin-kicking rule of museum decorum applied to the environs of the front door. With the jerk-quotient already so high, assault charges would no doubt be involved, and I had no time for that. Also, Tom might not bail me out. Otis either. I settled for giving Tom's shoulder a small encouraging squeeze I hoped didn't signal, "Go git'im."

Tom slipped out from under my hand and moved in on Kip Wade. Now they were almost touching, face-to-face, dark glasses to dark glasses. Formidable adversaries, radiating hostility. I couldn't see Tom's face, but I knew he was mad because his handsome neck was handsomely flushed. What he murmured was for Kip's ears only, but I was right there, maintaining my proximity to this exchange. For solidarity's sake. Also for soaking up the testosterone.

I knew Otis would stop anybody from getting hurt. I might as well relax and enjoy the throwdown. I couldn't hear all of what Tom said to Kip but it concluded with a two-word combo. Second word "you." First word sounded like it maybe started with an "F."

I was watching Otis. Otis was watching Tom. Tom and Kip were linked into the Blind Vulcan Hate Meld. Authentic rubbernecking was happening among the patrons of the arts jamming their own doorways. Tension. Embarrassment. Curiosity. Checking out the escalation. Building, building more—

Kip pulled the plug. Repeated back to Tom what Tom said to him, layering an extra smidgen of emphasis onto the "you." Shrugged. Bullied his way past Tom and out the door into the dead dark of a last day of February in Cleveland, Ohio. Head down. Cane stabbing.

Gone.

It was 7:07 p.m.

Chapter Two

Not a minute too soon, the doors closed behind us and the welcome hush of the museum gathered us in. A short stroll and we'd shucked off the chilly night, the disagreeable company, and our coats. Inside the glass-and-marble elegance of the atrium, we collapsed onto a bench in the bamboo grove. Quiet. Sheltered. Adrenalin levels returning to high-normal.

Time to move on.

"You guys don't hustle, you're going to be late for that Touch Tour."

Otis Johnson, Voice of Reason. Shifting into bodyguard-standing-down mode but, as usual, scoping out everything around us. Otis and Tom shared a keen awareness of any space they entered. Otis had all the advantages of 20/20 vision and the full-complement of his military/cop/security/PI experience. Not to mention several decades of black guy self-preservation.

Tom had all the advantages of his formidable intelligence, his Grade A PhD, and every one of his enhanced senses that were not sight. On top of those, he could access what he called his Blind Spidey Sense, which worked well for him. Sometimes not so much for me. My sneaky, self-serving side was always at risk of exposure by Blind Spidey intuition.

Between Otis and Tom, not much got by.

My own extra-fine-tuned Tom radar was telling me Tom was not quite done being mad. Sitting as close to him as museum decorum allowed, I felt the hum of his agitation. Kip Wade had ticked him off every which way. Ridiculed Tom's blindness with his sneer about the Touch Tour. Stabbed him in the sensitive spot of his completely unintentional $550-million lottery win and the chaos it had unleashed all around town. The jackpot death toll over the past couple of years had totaled approximately sixteen. Bad guys, good guys, stupid guys, men, women, poison, gunshot, fall from high building, innocent bystanders, righteous self-defense—the works. The number was approximate because we hadn't located bodies for all of them. The MondoMegaJackpot was a mashup of lucky/unlucky ticket meets death and destruction.

Tom was obsessed with his commitment to give away a major chunk of the money. Which now, after taxes and savvy investing, added up to $250 million. And growing like a weed.

"Like kudzu," Tom said. Spoken like a man from Georgia, where coiling kudzu vines overran and choked out any growing thing within their reach. The money had strangled Tom's career as an associate professor of English literature at Case Western Reserve University. Another sore point Kip had skewered.

The "Allie-Cat" rudeness splashed gasoline on the fire. Smoldering, I could tell.

Otis cleared his throat to communicate, *Let's buck up and move along.*

In the Tom/Allie/Otis Alliance, Tom was the brilliant one, I was the unpredictable one, and Otis was the glue that held our whole enterprise together. At the moment he was working at getting the night back on track.

"Touch Tour? Tom? Allie?"

Tom shook his head and pressed the face of his watch. Mickey Mouse chirped, "It's seven-twenty-eight. Have a great night!" He exhaled his pent-up aggravation. "No. It's too late to wander in there now. I'm going for a walk."

A walk. Terrific. I knew that walk. It circled the long way around the museum's gardens, offered steps down to a path alongside its deep, wide lagoon—a site so picturesque it was featured in wedding albums all over town. No happy brides and grooms were getting their photos shot out there tonight. Sure, it was lovely, even in darkest February, but the operative word would be "darkest." Likewise, "spookiest."

I avoided the ridicule I'd invite by whining "But it's *dark* out there" to Tom. The first time I'd said that he'd dismissed me with a grin. "In here too."

Tonight, I paused for two seconds, recalculating, before I went ahead and whined, "But it's *horrible* out there. It's *Cleveland* out there, Tom. February. Raining. Sleeting. Snowing. All at the same time. Let me check my app—um. Yeah. Uh huh. I thought so. Wind rising too."

Tom smiled for real now. "I'll be fine."

"Would you like me to come along?"

"Out into horrible Cleveland? February. Raining, sleeting, snowing. And, the ever-popular 'rising wind'? Why ever would you want to?"

Some things don't have to get spoken out loud.

To keep you safe. To bear witness to your continued safety and the well-being of my—everything.

He read my mind. "I'll be fine, Allie. You were planning to skip the tour anyway. Go sit on your favorite bench in your favorite gallery with that Buddha you love so much. Practice mindfulness." A grin. "Meditate on nonviolence, while you're at it."

Tom Bennington, you know me too well.

He stood up, flipped open his white cane, a practiced gesture that dismissed all protest. "I'll be back in a half hour. I'll come find you. Besides, we both know—although he has considerately made no comment at all—Otis will be a discreet distance behind me the whole way. The usual five yards, Otis?"

"That's about right, Tom. Don't mind me."

"Or me either," I sulked. "I just hope you don't run into that Kip again."

Tom was over it now, I could tell. "I'm not afraid of R. Kipling Wade. I think I could take him. If Otis helps."

"Does the R. stand for *Rudyard*? That explains a lot."

Otis stood up. "Let us make a point of never asking him. You ready, Tom?"

"Yep. Let's get going." He leaned in close to me and murmured so only I could hear, "See you later, Allie Cat."

All was decided. I walked them to coat check, followed them to the entrance, and watched them go out the door. Peered after them until they vanished out of my sight. Tom walking briskly, his cane a confident sweep. Otis following at the measured distance he could cover in seconds if anything went wrong. Anything that wasn't a tree branch falling or a motorcycle jumping the curb— *Cut it out, Allie.*

I peered some more at the empty sidewalk. As promised, the night was despicable. Naked trees across the street in the Oval quaked in the gusts of wind. Floodlights all along the walkway freeze-framed individual raindrops into long filaments of silver. It made my neck cringe to look at them. Outside those perimeters of light, darkness ruled. I stopped myself from peering. Went back inside.

It was 7:35 p.m.

Chapter Three

I herded my worried, twitchy self up to Gallery 241-B, "Arts of Ancient China." My favorite gallery. My favorite bench. My favorite Buddha. Serenity guaranteed.

Tonight, however, the joint was hopping. 241-B's next-door neighbor, 241-C was hosting this evening's Touch Tour.

The tours were created, in a brilliant stroke of outreach, to invite blind and visually impaired visitors in for the purpose of breaking the most sacred rule of museums everywhere: HANDS OFF THE ART!

A select number of works in the museum's collection could stand up to respectful handling, and the participants, whose sensitive fingers were trained for skills most people's eyes couldn't match—reading braille, for example—got a chance to enjoy the dimension ordinary sighted museumgoers would not comprehend. Museum experts were present to narrate the fine points of the works and supply details about the history of the pieces and the artists.

With Tom to vouch for me, I'd tried it several times. Closed my eyes and felt my fingers looking at art. Even through thin, non-latex-y gloves, with my untutored touch, it was magical to put my hands on a stone sculpture more than three thousand years old and realize this was a boy I could have passed on the street without noticing, if he hadn't been made of stone. Time is an illusion every which way.

This evening the magical tour was lively. Laughing, exclaiming, commenting, asking questions, talking to the docents and among themselves, the attendees made happy waves of sound that rose and fell throughout the big, airy spaces of the neighboring galleries.

Not peaceful, but heartwarming. I could deal. I sank down onto my bench and made eye contact with Amitāyus, the Buddha of Infinite Life. Centerpiece of the Asian Art collection of the museum.

Amitāyus was not the most user-friendly Buddha I'd ever seen. His expression always struck me as distant—and a tinge long-suffering. Eyebrows arched, eyelids drooping, the downward turn of his mouth suggesting possible disdain. All in all, he looked a little fed up, a little tired, a little like my mom.

Why was this Buddha my Buddha? I guess I felt a certain kinship with him. For one thing, he'd sat with his legs pretzeled up for centuries. His nose was busted and his hands had been destroyed somewhere along the way. Hard knocks. When I looked him up on Wikipedia, it said his most important enlightenment technique was "the visualization of the surrounding world as a paradise." An order so tall it inspired me.

Sometimes when I sat down, shut up, and met my Buddha's droopy eyes, the icy chunk of fear I'd locked inside would thaw. And a voice who lived in there too, would whisper, "I'm right here, Alice Jane. You're fine."

Who knew? Maybe I was fine. I reminded my ever-vigilant self it had been a full six months since anything halfway threatening had fallen into, risen out of, or wrapped itself hungrily around Tom's jackpot of murder and mayhem. We lived in a different sort of house now. Drove different cars. Kept the security tuned up and our heads down, the way crazily, undeservingly, notoriously wealthy folk are supposed to do. Tonight's minor run-in at the museum's front door was the first seriously confrontational moment we'd experienced since July.

I checked my watch. 7:43. In another four hours and seventeen minutes it would be March. Perhaps I should go ahead and enjoy a deep breath.

I closed my eyes and let my shoulders cascade down from around my ears. Inhaled. Exhaled. Heard a footstep right next to me. And the light tap of a cane.

Yes.

A rush of relief. "Tom?" I opened my eyes—

A blind woman I'd never seen before was standing in the space between me and the Buddha. A sari of elaborately patterned gray fabric draped her thin body. A matching scarf concealed her hair. Her expression, masked by a pair of huge dark glasses, was indecipherable.

Alrighty. The creepy harbinger of impending death from a bunch of movies I now extra-regretted having seen was bending over me. Bringing her pale face disconcertingly close to mine. "You're…Allie Harper?"

Maybe. Maybe not.

"Uh. Yes. But how—?"

She shrugged like a normal, non-harbinger human being. "I have a little sight. I have to be up close but—And I know all about Tom and you from, you know. Around. We're a small community. Tom was signed up for tonight, but—A man gave me a message for him. For you, too, I hope.

"Tom never showed and I have to catch a bus to get home. The tour people told me you come here and sit. I thought if you weren't here, I'd prop it up in this Buddha's hands where someone was bound to see it and make sure he got it." She turned to lean in closer to the stone. "Good thing you're here, though. This Buddha doesn't even have hands. Handicapped." A harsh, mocking bark of a laugh.

"Somebody whacked him good. Got his nose too. Do you know when that happened?"

I shook my head and then, to be on the safe side, said, "No."

She fished in the folds of her sari. "Here. This is all working out. I can give the note to you now. For Tom."

Okay.

When she handed me the thick, cream-colored envelope with "Thomas Bennington III" written on it in calligraphy—like a wedding invitation—I was startled to see she was still wearing the special gloves. Being me, I couldn't stop myself from asking. "You're still wearing the—?"

"Museum's gloves?" Her grimace made her look older than I'd first supposed. The corners of her mouth were bracketed by lines. Gouged deeper by the frown, they underscored the bitterness of her tone. "No. These are mine. As if it's not enough being blind. I have severe skin allergies. I touch the wrong thing, it's blisters all over the place. I thought I could do the tour in spite of it, but that was overly optimistic. Doesn't matter. You have the envelope. Don't forget to give it to Tom."

With that, the woman turned and navigated out of the room, her cane leading the way.

At that moment, while my unnerved feet were standing me up to chase after her and find out who exactly gave the envelope to her for Tom, my phone went off in my purse. "The Heart of Rock & Roll." Huey Lewis and the News. Nine thousand decibels, bouncing off the gallery walls. I jumped about a foot and fumbled in my purse to grab it and shut it up before Museum Etiquette could tackle me.

Huey Lewis meant Lisa Cole. Intrepid "Don't-Call-Me-Girl-Reporter" from Channel 16, *It's News to You!!!* The exact same Lisa Cole, who, summer before last, delivered Tom and his killer lottery ticket out of my fantasies and into my life by being a total out-of-control, jerk-journalist-on-the-hunt-for-a-story—a.k.a. HummerWoman. The one who honked at a blind man in a crosswalk. Froze him right there, where I could step on up and pick him off. Lisa was mostly forgiven now. Friend and sometimes fellow very-amateur-detective.

My answer was on the sharp side.

"Lisa. What's up?"

"Allie. What's wrong?"

"Nothing. You just set Huey off full-blast in Gallery 241-B of the Cleveland Museum of Art.

"Oh. Sure. Hey."

Usually Lisa was all perky banter when she called. Right now, her tone felt off. It flashed through my mind, as it did from time to time when I wasn't fast enough to suppress it, that a woman who would honk at a blind man in the street, regardless of any extenuating circumstances, might not be entirely trustworthy. I suppressed the thought.

"Lisa? What's wrong?"

I could hear her breathing and the wind scuffling with her phone. In the lull, my ears picked up on the distant sound of sirens from wherever Lisa was calling. Some sexy crime scene, I figured. Ye olde *News to You!!!* The wailing was seeping into my awareness from the background of her call. Rising and falling. Where was she? So many sirens. So many. So—

"Lisa. Has something terrible happened?"

"No. *No.* Well. Just—Allie, is Tom with you?"

"No, he's not, Lisa. But where are you right now? With all those sirens?"

"I'm outside the art museum, Allie. On the sidewalk east of the lagoon. Severance side, close to the Euclid intersection. There's been—a shooting."

The sirens screamed all the way into me now. Bleeding through marble walls, breaching wide expanses of glass. Soaking into tapestry and canvas, careening off polished stone, and penetrating all the suits of armor. Not loud yet, but undeniable.

"Allie," she asked again. *"Allie, where's Tom?"*

I clicked off my phone and looked at my watch.

It was 7:55 p.m. and the sirens were howling inside my chest.

Chapter Four

I needed a glass box.

The museum boasted two dazzling "glass box" galleries—one on either side of its second floor—striking showcases for special exhibits. The one on the east side of the building would give me a view of the walkways around the park, the lagoon, down toward Severance Hall, "home of the internationally renowned Cleveland Orchestra." Lisa Cole's call came from somewhere down there.

I had to see what was happening. I was afraid to look.

At that hour of a Wednesday night at the end of February, the museum wasn't packed, but as I rushed through 241-A into the hall, people spilled out onto my walkway, hurrying along with me at a brisk but orderly pace. Murmuring their concerns. Clutching their phones. Frowning at their phones. I checked mine. No bars. The walkway overlooked the wide open space of the atrium and a growing, milling crowd.

I headed for my glass box as fast as I could without getting tackled by a guard. Speed-walking. Museum staff people shook their heads at me, but they could hear the sirens too. I kept repeating, "Sorry! Sorry! Emergency! Sorry!" Moving as slowly as my panicked heart would permit. Trying again to call Tom. No signal. Again and again. No signal. No signal.

A PA announcement droned instructions. Guests were to please move calmly to the atrium and please remain inside the building "for the next few minutes." *Move calmly* as a word combo is not a confidence-enhancer. Someone had popped open an alarmed exit and now that door was screeching at us too. Terror buzzed in my throat. I clenched my jaw to trap it there and kept going.

The PA continued to drone. "Please move calmly—Please remain—"

Please, *God.*

The clear glass walls of the box strobed a rainbow. Police cars, ambulances, and fire trucks flared color onto white marble. The sirens were dying out as, one by one, the vehicles slotted themselves into place. Walkie-talkies and bullhorns were dominating now, and the revolving lights gave me my first look at what was happening outside.

Peering out and down over the bank, I could see the scope of the emergency. Cops in protective gear. Running. Heads down. Spotlights sweeping. The cycling of garish red and blue painting it all. I had a view of much too much, but nothing of what I most needed to see. I pressed my face against the cold expanse.

Whatever was happening out there was big.

Please, God. Not Tom.

I backed out of the box and found an outside door. It opened onto a balcony planted with stiff, frozen plants. Alarmed but not locked. One more shriek wouldn't register in that din. I pressed through. Freezing wind and icy rain slapped my face and bare arms. *Bad. Cold. Freezing.* The memory of my coat, safely checked downstairs, skipped into my mind and back out again. Vaporized by the flaring terror of the night.

In the white glare of a streetlight, I saw a Cleveland cop running up over the frozen grass, making his own path toward the museum. Toward *me?* I hollered and waved. He saw me. Stopped, looking up, his expression blank.

Tony?

The first summer of jackpot disaster, Anthony Valerio was the officer of the Cleveland Police Department with a boatload of questions for me. By the end of last summer—with its own relentless string of calamities—he'd progressed to quasi-friend and quasi-consultant for our quasi-amateur detective agency.

More than anything on earth, I wanted Tony Valerio to not be coming up the hill to break some bad news.

Please, God.

He saw me now, too, both of us washed in dancing colors. I still couldn't read his face. Or his lips. He was yelling but the roar of engines and the clamor of shouting drowned him out.

"What?" I screamed. "*Tom? Otis?*"

He stopped cold. Our eyes met. He shook his head in frustration and gestured to our right, along the side of the museum, in the direction of the Oval and the glass doors. I focused on his face. He shouted through cupped hands. I could read his lips and hear him now too. Loud and clear.

MEET ME...DOOR!

He turned away and ran, low to the ground, along the side of the building.

I screamed at him.

Tony! Tom?

He turned back, touched his ear, shook his head again. Ran away.

Chapter Five

Faltering feet. Rubber knees.

I shoved myself through the crush of people getting herded by security off the escalator into the atrium. Milling about. Checking their phones. In the middle of the space, a young woman, trim and professional, holding a microphone, was climbing onto a chair to address the crowd.

I didn't want to hear what she had to say. Tony was bringing me my answer. *Dead or alive?* I needed to hear it from him.

I stopped apologizing for stepping on people. I stopped caring whether I was stepping on people. I bulldozed through the crowd. I could see Valerio, waiting for me by the front door.

Nothing on his face.

The words of the woman trailed after me. Bits and pieces, drifting from inside the open space under the arc of glass that sheltered the bamboo grove where Tom and Otis and I—I smothered the memory as her words broke through.

"—however, I have some hard news. At approximately 7:45 this evening, a man—who had been here at the museum earlier to attend our Touch Tour event for blind guests—was shot and killed, while walking on the path by the lagoon."

A blind man walking by the lagoon.

The room echoed shock and dismay. I stopped walking.

A blind man. A blind man walking by the lagoon.

Tony heard her too. He read my face. I read his. His looked like mine felt. Frozen. He was shaking his head no. *No?* I walked, holding myself together, breathing Tom back into his life for a last handful of seconds until—Tony was standing right in front of me.

"Tony?"

"I'm sorry, Allie. I'm an idiot. I thought you'd know. I forgot the phones aren't—Tom's fine. He's perfectly fine. Freezing his ass off but fine. Otis sent me to get you. He told me yesterday you guys were coming here tonight. So when I heard…hey!"

Relief will knock you over. The rush of gratitude to my head made sparkles in front of my eyes, and, for a long five seconds, I sagged against Tony and leaned on him. Breathing "Tom is fine" into my own paralyzed lungs. After a couple more seconds, I got a grip and straightened up. Lost the grip and hugged him some more. Didn't bother to apologize.

He unhugged himself and frowned at me from under his signature unibrow in a way that made me want to hug him all over again.

"It was a totally different blind man, Allie. Although—he must have looked a lot like—hell. I should have stayed when I saw you standing out there and told you, but I thought—I'm an idiot. Are you crying? Don't cry. Everything's fine. Well, not fine, but you know—"

I used my entire stock of diminished mental capacity to stop myself from hugging him again.

"It's okay, Tony. I'm fine. I'll be totally fine in a minute. Everybody in here clearly thinks it was a terrorist attack."

"No terrorist attack. Although causing people to wonder if something is a terrorist attack is a form of terrorism. Head game."

He looked me over as if assessing my overall stability. Started pulling his coat off. He had an armored vest on under the coat and he pulled that off too. Dropped it over my head and started fastening it around me. It fell on me like lead but also kind of like a hug.

"Tony. You can't give me your vest. What if you get shot?"

"Alice Jane Harper. I'd rather get shot about six times than explain to Otis L. Johnson I let you get shot. *Holy shit.* I'd have to shoot *myself* before I could tell Tom. Here. Put on my jacket and come on."

"I have my coat checked right back in there. We could—"

"You don't want to get in that line. It'll be there until tomorrow morning."

I glanced behind me. He was right. I shrugged into his coat and followed him out the door.

I'd watched three guys go out through that door this evening. I was pretty sure one of them would not be coming back.

Chapter Six

Here's a thing I'd learned in the last couple of years.

Watching about a billion episodes of *CSI: Wherever* from the comfort of your own couch, in your own safe, warm, lakeside cottage, does zip to prepare you for an actual crime scene. Before tonight, I'd been up close to—even in the middle of—several of those. Trust me. A couch, a bowl of popcorn, and a wooly afghan your grandma knitted for you back in the day seriously dilutes the crime-scene experience.

Here and now, it was in my face.

The rain had slacked off and Tom and I were huddled together on one of a trio of benches up against a low stone wall. This bench was wet, cold, and well back from the perimeter staked out by yellow tape and the barrier surrounding that perimeter. A pop-up shelter hid the body I was 99.5 percent sure was Rudyard Kipling Wade. A guy walked by, carrying—among other things—a white cane folded into an evidence bag. The immediacy of Kip's murder was rocketing all over me. I did not mention this to Tom.

When Valerio and I were close enough for me to pick out Tom and Otis, I'd run on ahead. By the time Valerio caught up, he'd resumed his customary stone-faced cop demeanor. He fled the emotional reunion as fast as he could. I tried to get control of my joy.

Otis, at least, submitted to a sensible amount of my sobbing and hugging before he went to join Tony—outside the perimeter but closer to the action. Tom and I had assured ourselves that we were both alive and unharmed with the kiss I'd believed would never happen again. After a bit, he said, "This is lovely. I never kissed a girl in a bulletproof vest before. Quite the obstacle to romance, huh?"

I only said "I told you not to go out there" once. Possibly twice. And kissed him again.

"Tom, where were you when—?"

"Oh—close. But not—" He gave up. "Yeah, Allie. Much too close. It was weird, though. We stopped when we came around the corner of the building to argue about—discuss—whether the sleety mess would be worse if we came in this direction. Or around on the other side. We almost bagged it then. But the wind backed off so—"

"I need to hear this too, Dr. Bennington."

I'd been focusing on Tom and choking back my reaction to "much too close," so I'd failed to notice Tony, Otis, and a woman I'd never seen before, approaching our freezing wall. I hoped Tony wasn't here to ask for his coat back.

Tom stood up, offered his hand, and said, "Hi. I'm Tom Bennington."

She shook his hand. "Lieutenant Olivia Wood, Homicide," and produced a badge which she flashed at me and pressed into Tom's palm. "My badge. Does this work for you?'

He slipped off his glove and ran his fingers over the shiny metal. "Works great, Lieutenant Wood. Nice badge." He grinned, "Nice move too. Nobody ever handed me a badge before. What would you like me to tell you?"

"Sit down, Tom. I sure am ready to."

He sat and she squeezed in with us. Otis and Tony stayed standing where they were. Cop-like.

"Tell me what you heard," she began. "Or sensed. In any way. Anything that stood out for you. As far as I can tell, you and Otis were the only eyewitnesses—witnesses—to this shooting. I need to know what he saw, but you have insights—" She smiled. "There are a lot of those tricky sight words, I'm noticing. But you know what I mean."

I'd met all kinds of cops in the post-MondoMegaJackpot Era. Understatement. My first homicide detective showed up a year and a half ago and flashed his badge at our hotel room peephole. This one was different. For one thing, this one was a woman of about my age.

Go us.

A young female detective with brown skin.

Go Cleveland PD.

I gave Lieutenant Wood the once-over on behalf of the sisterhood. She was my height. Had my basic unruly hair. Hers was under tighter control than mine, pulled back into one of those chic, trendy little buns with a few darling wisps escaping here and there. Her keen, intimidating gaze communicated "No. Nonsense."

Dressed for police business too. Khakis. More sensible boots than mine, which I assumed were cowering in tonight's weather. Smartly cinched trench coat. Although there was no way to tell for certain at the moment, I didn't figure her for any of that breathtaking Lady CSI cleavage. She passed the Allie Harper inspection.

Tom was smiling back at the woman he was hearing her to be.

"Yeah, it's tricky for sighted people. But not for me. Don't fear the sight words. I have a friend who, first time I met her, said, 'Let's just agree to bulldoze over that one.' It's fine. What would you like to know? Where should I start?"

"As we walked up here, I heard you say the wind had died down, so you came this way."

"Yes."

"That sort of thing." She frowned. "This is not for the public, and not for sure yet in any case, but it's pretty clear to us that this was a sniper. To that person, a drop in wind speed might signal the optimum time to fire."

A sniper?

She gestured to the steep slope behind us. With its abundant ground cover and artfully placed trees, it sheltered us from the street, while providing a glimpse of the celebrated concert hall. Guys were stringing crime-scene tape around there, too, draping the stately balustrade in yellow plastic.

"He would have planned to shoot down here from inside a low wall, up there at Severance Hall. Not a tough shot for a pro."

"Severance *Hall*?" Outrage saturated every syllable. "*Jesus.*"

Tom's delight in the Cleveland Orchestra was untouched by his blindness. "Everybody hears better in the dark," he said. I'd close my eyes to listen too.

All through the winter, Tom, Otis, and I sat in that splendid space—savoring the music and the freedom to hear it there. For Tom, a shooter taking aim at Kip Wade from there was a desecration. In the lights illuminating the scene he'd gone pale. "When we get this son of a bitch, Lieutenant," he said, "I want to be there."

She nodded. "We'll see what we can do about that. We plan to get your son of a bitch, Tom. Tell me more about what you noticed as you came down here."

"Sorry, I—" He rubbed at his jaw, collecting himself, recreating the moment. "Otis and I were walking together at that point. I was hearing our footsteps. Not actually thinking about it. But I can hear them now. And my cane makes a specific sound on that kind of sidewalk. I was listening for sounds of cars, up on the boulevard. That's automatic. An orientation thing. Spatial. There weren't many cars. Out on Euclid Avenue, yeah. A steady hum. A handful of people besides Otis and me, as far as I could hear. Far away. The sleet was stinging my face. Rain mixed in too.

"Kip couldn't have been very far in front of us, but I didn't hear him. Maybe he stopped for a minute. Or maybe the rain covered his footsteps—I heard the shot. I guess. But—you know. You'd notice, but not be—interested, unless you knew—It was muffled and from a little distance. I would never have imagined—But Otis put his hand on my shoulder. Stopped me."

"So a single, surgical shot. And then?"

"We stood there for, maybe, twenty seconds before all hell broke loose."

All hell?

"All hell." Lieutenant Wood. Unsurprised.

"Yeah. The response was fast. Crazy fast. A squad car. Then a bunch—two and three at a time." He was concentrating hard. Reliving. "One. And then before that one was completely stopped, another one. And right after that, more. Canine unit? I know it's funny, but I believe I heard a dog after a bit. Big. Maybe just a regular dog—An ambulance. Same thing. Another right behind, I think. A firetruck. Another firetruck. Doors slamming. A lot of running. Yelling.

"Otis took us both onto the ground." Tom was back in that scene, facedown on freezing stone. "But the sirens. All—They—" He stopped. Collecting himself. "Lieutenant Wood, sound like that. Noise. It takes away my hearing. And I can't—"

I leaned into him, wrestling with my memory of a different night of pure terror. On a scale of one to ten, that night and this night were both beyond tens. A person can survive and still be lost forever. Tom deaf would be Tom lost for a very long time.

Otis and Tony stepped in closer, filling the gap Tom and I made when we disappeared into our shared nightmare. Olivia Wood saw it too. Nodded to Otis.

"Otis? Your take?"

"Response time was crazy. A shooting like that one? Accurate and quick? A single shot, as far as anybody can tell. A hidden gunman, at a short distance, so probably suppressed. Certainly sounded suppressed to me.

"Like Tom said. Could have been anything to a civilian

bystander—if there'd been bystanders. No fuss. Not much muss. One victim on the ground, shielded from the street by shrubs and trees. A damn dark, secluded place on a crappy night? Cleveland cops are fast when they need to be, but they're not psychic-fast—Were there a ton of 911 calls? All at once? There must have been. And timed. Somehow. Because—"

"Fifteen calls. 'Shots fired.' 'Fire at Severance Hall.' Timed to hit after the shooting. One call right after another. Except for the ones that were concurrent. Threw everybody off. Scrambled the troops."

Valerio caught my eye, "What I meant when I said causing people to wonder if something is a terrorist attack is a form of terrorism, Allie."

"Yes. And then you said, 'Head game.' But what kind of head game? How does it all—?"

I lost my place in my own question. A tussle was breaking out at the bottom of a stairway that led down to us from the street.

"Oh, *stop it*. You have to let me through. I'm a mile from your scene. Let me in. My friends are right over there. C'mon.

"Allie! Tom!"

Lisa Cole, Ace Reporter. Uniquely herself. Cute, blond, chasing her story. The officer backed up a step and she advanced six. Around him. Taking a couple more. Waving her arms. The cop made an end-run and stole back his step advantage. She kept waving at me over his shoulder. Backing him up again. Invading his official and personal space.

"Look. Officer. *Look*, dammit." She turned her pockets out. "Nothing in my hands either. See? No microphone. I'm completely harmless. *Clearly* no gun. Look in my teeny purse." She popped it open with a snap of her fingers. Held it under the cop's nose where he could have confirmed the absence of a gun. If he hadn't backed up another foot.

"All I got is lipstick and my goddam press pass. Look. My camera dude is not in there, either. I'm off the clock. Please. Be nice. Those are my goddam friends over there. Let me go sit on that perfectly innocuous *bench*. And see if they're all right. *What.* What's with the face? You never heard a woman swear before? Or say 'innocuous'? Dammit. Get a life."

Lisa Cole. Never at a loss for a bad word.

I was impressed. The officer was not. He hustled Lisa back up the steps. She made the "call me" sign in my direction and huffed out of sight.

Even if you're a homicide detective, spunky little Lisa Cole, born Lisa Čebulj in my former Collinwood neighborhood—irreverent, ambitious, and generally unstoppable—could pry a wee chuckle out of you. Lieutenant Wood shook her head. "That Cole. Pain in the collective butt of the CPD. But she's a good, honest reporter, even working at 16. How do you know her?"

Tonight was not opportune for the long-version Hummer explanation.

"She introduced me to Tom."

Time for "We're done here." For one thing, the rain which had piddled away to scattered sleet as we talked was morphing back to 100 percent rain. More appalling than the 50/50 drizzle/sleet duo. For another, the Medical Examiner's van was on the street above us, beeping in to park.

"Lieutenant Wood? Can we wrap this up? Officer Valerio, I need to give you your coat and your vest back."

"I'll pick them up later, Allie. I'm fine tonight. I feel better knowing you have a vest."

Lieutenant Wood, who I was already secretly calling "Olivia" in my mind, smiled. "That's not necessarily standard operating procedure, but it's kind of sweet."

"Take my word for it, ma-am. It's a cleverly disguised insult. But I forgive him."

She focused back on Tom, the smile still warming her tone. "Tom, thank you. You helped me clarify what happened here.

You bring a different dimension to a scene. Anything else your senses are telling you? Before you go?"

He took off his dark glasses and put his head back to let the rain fall onto his closed eyes, listened to the idling engines and radio chatter. Footsteps and low voices. Exhaled the tension of an evening none of us could have imagined when we arrived at the museum's door. I shivered and checked my watch. It still wasn't March.

They were going remove a body bag soon. I did not want to see that.

Tom inhaled. Long and deep. A catch in the breath. The anger was back.

"Yes, Lieutenant Wood. From here. Close by. I smell Kip's blood."

"So do I, Tom." She wasn't smiling anymore either. "I'm very sorry. So do I."

Chapter Seven

THURSDAY, MARCH 1

The lakeside cottage of your dreams.
"Oh, my! What a cottage!"

    This Tudor Revival cottage, with its extraordinary cedar-shingle roof is the jewel of a prestigious gated community! Magnificent windows provide remarkable vistas. Expansive scenes of Lake Erie. Here to be enjoyed from patios, decks, and pool. Lovely meandering woods and gardens enhance the expansive grounds. High ceilings capture light. Everywhere, you'll find handcrafted moldings, hardwood floors, handmade tile, quarried stone, and graceful ironwork. Artisan-carved mantels embellish the five fireplaces. Stunning, below-window cabinets open the kitchen to the lake view. Wolf®, and SubZero® appliances—a chef's dream. A charming butler's pantry supports gracious dining and entertaining for your family and friends. Master suite features his and hers dressing rooms, sybaritic spa bath, and library/study. Each of four guest rooms on the second floor has its own bath. Balconies open to the lake view through French doors from both living room and bedrooms. The full lower level provides additional living space, complete with bedroom, bath, and kitchen, plus gym, billiards room, and wine cellar. For longer-term guests or visiting in-laws, a fully-finished, fully-equipped suite over the four-car garage. The ultimate amenity? Your own private beach.

Our new lakeside residence was a little bit Tudor revival. A whole lot Hobbit Hole. Nestled under its overhanging roof of steam-bent cedar shingles, it even had one of those cute round windows over its massive, yet friendly, front door. Chimney pots right out of Mary Poppins. You could look at it and say, "That is one sweet little house."

Except for the seven thousand square feet.

At midnight-and-change a.m. on the first nasty cold day of a brand new month, Otis drove the family Escalade down and around the long, curving driveway, past small glades of snow-encrusted pines, to our new lakeside mansion. I approved of this house. Right off the bat, it didn't loom. It nestled. Was it big? Oh, you bet, but unlike our nine-thousand-plus-square-foot hacker-death-trap former mansion, this one said, "Cottage." Not, "Versailles."

Margo Gallucci, my former landlady and best friend forever, liked to refer to our former residence as "your real mansion" or more informally as "that fucking mansion-y mansion." All of us had been in awe of it. Afraid of it too. Beautiful and gracious as it was, I never felt safe during those days and nights. For good reason: It was a carefully devised trap.

Our new house had a much less threatening vibe. On a night like this, I felt welcomed. As opposed to dismissed with a disapproving sniff. The only thing historic about it was the trust fund that paid to get it built in 2013, but whatever it lacked in snobby landmark status, it made up for with a serious reduction in menace. The former owners were poised to move up to a bigger, juicier-pedigreed mansion at the exact moment we were poised to flee to a smaller, less scary one. Fresh starts come in all sizes.

Our new place was ridiculously too big, but even at seven thousand-plus square feet it was more home than museum. To be perfectly candid, it did not trigger my well-established "check shoe for dog doo before entering" reflex.

Here's the deal: If you're wearing a sign on your back that says, *550-million- dollar-jackpot-winner. Rob me. Kill me. Whatever comes to mind,* a house that throws open its unceremonious mudroom door and says "Get in here, you. You're cold, damp, and scared to death" is the answer to an accidental lottery winner's prayers.

Why, thank you, house. How very kind.

Otis pulled into Stall Number Two of the used-to-be four-stall garage and waved to the security guy who came out of the new security room which now occupied Stall Number One. We disembarked. Guard guy nodded, said, "Hi and goodnight." Went back in and closed the door. Efficient. Sensible. Awake. I like that in a security guard. We had a couple of them in the garage room twenty-four/seven, three shifts. Two guns per shift.

The garage door slipped quietly into place.

Good night.

My wonderful moment of "That was quite the day, but all will be well as soon as I'm fast asleep and things get back to normal" lasted the four and a half minutes before I saw headlights slide across the ceiling.

Incoming.

A car door slammed. I peeked out a "magnificent window" at the "vista" of our ice-covered driveway—*Oh, hell...o.*

A City of Cleveland squad car. And who disembarked

from this car and came crunching up to our friendly front
door? Officer Anthony Valerio of the CPD. Back for his vest,
I presumed.

I cracked the door—four-and-a-half-inches-but-who's-
counting—and stuck my nose out. An icy wind tossed in a
couple handfuls of sleet. I gave up and yanked the door the
rest of the way open.

"Didn't we already say goodbye? Not nearly long enough ago?"

"Yeah, I don't want me to be here right now, either. Can I
come in?"

———

Another twenty minutes and all four of us were stationed around
the island in the stone and granite, lavishly applianced, Tuscan-
ambianced kitchen, enjoying Otis's special, high-test hot choco-
laty beverage of a recipe nobody ever gave my brother Justin and
me to warm us up after our snowball fights.

I skootched as close to Tom as two separate barstools would
permit. He slipped an arm around me. I leaned closer, right up
to the point of teetering, put my head on his excellent shoulder,
breathed in his manly Thomas Bennington goodness, and had
another sip of my bourbon-spiked drink. Then another.

Steaming hot. The beverage and the man.

"Otis," I chirped. "No marshmallows?"

"Allie." He shook his head. "You know marshmallows and
bourbon don't mix. Especially an excellent bourbon like this
one. Keep sittin' there and get quiet for a minute. You're jigglin'."

Otis grew up in Cleveland with a big extended family of expa-
triate, racially endangered Southerners. I grew up in a tiny West
Virginia town, barely enough south of the Mason-Dixon to soften
our vowels. Otis and I now had about the same dollop of The
South in our speech. Mine drifted back in when I talked to my
mother on the phone. Tom, who hailed from Atlanta, was steeped
in it. Hard to shake that sweet music.

I sat there. As soon as the jigglin' started dyin' down, the yawnin' stepped up. We all shared a yawn and polished off our hot chocolate. It was almost one a.m. by the time Tony got down to officially talking.

My relationship with Anthony Valerio was still evolving. I pictured this as the type of evolution that takes two steps forward, three steps back, and ends up making a chicken. Some days he trusted me. Some days he thought I was—in his own words—a "force for crazy." Most days, however, I believed he secretly liked me and grudgingly approved of maybe forty percent of what I did and said. I could handle that. I secretly loved Tony almost all the time. He'd taken a bullet for me and Tom once. I had to make sure it never happened again.

Just now he was frowning at me as if I had Force For Crazy embroidered on all my hankies.

"We need to meet."

"What do you call this, Tony?" Tom's expression was quizzical. "Slumber party?"

"No. This is the meeting about the meeting. At the museum tomorrow. They sent me to—" He stopped, waiting for the perfect word combination to manifest itself.

My eyelids were drooping. My patience was dead. "They sent you to keep us awake until we give up and agree to whatever you and they want? I'm there, Tony. Spit it out."

Wait a second.

I paused to let a question drift into my brain and raised a finger to signal I had a point to make. Just in time, I recalled how finger-pointing was the danger-sign of alcohol. Stir an "excellent bourbon" into "shocked, terrified, and sleep-deprived." Recipe for stupid. I recalibrated my head.

"Except, Tony. One thing. Why you? How come you're involved? Last time I checked you're Third District of the Cleveland Police Department and the museum is in the jurisdiction of the First. And they've got boodles of University Circle cops too. It's a damn cop-a-thon around there."

"That's the thing."

I planted my elbow on the island, propped my chin up with my hand, and squinted. "Tony? Could you be a teensy, weensy bit more specific? What part of any of this is 'the thing'?"

If my chin-hand had been free I'd have made finger quotes, but I couldn't do that without smashing my face onto the granite, so I merely raised my brows to communicate suspicion. We were about a foot apart. He lowered his brow to signal "Back off, missy." He needed his space, but he held his ground. Missing his vest a lot right then, I bet.

"Tony. No kidding. I am so tired and sleepy and—*whatever*. I'm falling off this stool. Plus, I'm so freaked out I'm dangerous. It's been a long, damn, scary-crazy evening—night—*morning*. A blind man got shot. The Museum of Art got locked down. Also, batshit crazy. Not the way it's programed to go in there. So? Tony? Would you please fish or cut bait about—?

"Allie. The 'thing' is the T&A."

Here's a piece of advice: Never name your hypothetical detective agency using the initials of you and the guy you recently shared most of two bottles of very nice champagne with. Not to mention a, shall-we-say, very long, satisfactory romantic interlude. Or two. In the Presidential Suite of a Ritz-Carlton.

Forethought was not operating right then, but at least I should have listened to Tom and put my initial first.

Too late now.

Time passed. The name stuck. We deduced that our investigative services would be sufficiently informal as to not require a business card or its name lettered on one of those noir-detective, frosted-glass office doors. "Spade & Archer" we were not. And we didn't need to turn a profit at any time in the foreseeable future. Thus, no need to advertise.

What I had in mind that evening a year and a half ago, was helping people get answers for those nagging personal questions that demolish their peace of mind. Mysteries that didn't necessarily require any official law enforcement involvement. Or a gun.

Okay. Sure.

Right out of the box, our first case was a murder. I didn't have a gun yet, however. I was more than happy to hide behind the guns of Otis and his security guys. And they were, no question, happy to not supply Inexperience and Unpredictability—a.k.a. me—with a weapon. We still didn't have a business card and in spite of a reasonable outcome and a satisfied, if sad, client last summer, we were still so unofficial as to be almost invisible.

Now it looked like our cloak of invisibility was about to get vaporized.

"The T&A?" Tom's horrific night was unraveling in bourbon and fatigue, same as mine. "The T&A Detective Agency, Tony? Such as it is—" He veered off again. I could tell he was wondering, *And what IS the T&A, exactly?* But he rallied. "What does the T&A have to do with any of this? Whatever this is? Which we don't know yet—"

Tony nodded. "That's the thing— Oh. Hell. They—We— Even *I* believe there's a role in this—what's happened tonight. A role for the T&A. Small. Temporary. Unofficial. Just for tomorrow, maybe. They sent me to convince you three to show up at the museum tomorrow morning. Ten-ish?"

"Did you explain to the folks at the *CMA* that 'T&A' stands for Tom and Allie? Because if you didn't, we're not coming."

"I did, Tom. I explained that we—you guys and Otis. And me, sometimes—I figured it was best, Tom, to not involve Margo right now. And Lisa's excluded herself by being one of the reporters covering the story. And swearing like a lumberjack. Or like Margo—never mind. Lieutenant Wood now knows a little of what you guys do. Tom, she's all about your—uncanny, she called it—abilities. And, of course, what you bring to the table because of your Mondo—thing."

"Because of the T&A's exceptionally robust operating budget?"

"That too, in any case, they—we—would like to talk with you. Maybe ask for your help. Ten o'clock tomorrow? Ish?

"Okay, ten-ish o'clock." Tom nodded.

"Yeah, ten-ish," I agreed. "Good night, Tony. Now."

Otis sealed the deal. "Tony? Would you like to sleep over in one of our assorted palatial guest rooms?"

"Uh huh. Trying to convince the Bratenahl PD I'm not a walking talking DWI would be a bad start for tomorrow."

We adjourned so fast we were almost running, and by two a.m. nobody was stirring but the couple of security guys in the garage.

Chapter Eight

The three of us arrived back at the Cleveland Museum of Art on Thursday morning. Given the givens, I would have preferred to be hiding out in a tent on the north ridge of K-2.

We straggled in from the parking garage at the "ish" end of ten-ish. Valerio had left us a couple of hours earlier, grumbling, "Maybe a shower and a change of uniform will fix my head. See you around ten." Took his vest, jacket, and one of our coffee mugs with him as he went.

On the elevator ride up from the garage, Tom, Otis, and I huddled in silence. We were all thinking—but not saying—the same thing. A blind man, loud and disagreeably alive barely fourteen hours ago, was dead this morning. No warning. No explanation. No reprieve.

Alive and rude then. Cold and dead now.

I'd not met him before last night and—based on that one time—I hadn't liked him, but I couldn't stop imagining Kip Wade's last moments. Walking in darkness the way Tom walked. His senses tuned to the night. The richness of sounds and smells all around him. His cane scanning the path. Cold rain on his face. Cast out of this world by a bullet he didn't hear coming. Into whatever waited for him at the end.

Light. I hoped there was light.

In my unsettled state of mind, the museum's vestibule, buffed to its usual shine this morning, still reverberated with Tom and Kip's doorway confrontation. Nightmare *déjà vu.*

The entrance hall, already well-stocked with museum-goers, echoed with talk and smelled like art. At least I didn't need to check my coat. I picked it out, still hanging all by itself on a rack. Unclaimed. Abandoned. Forlorn. I sent it a telepathic message. It sent me a telepathic sniff.

I hadn't checked my purse last night. It was considerably under the thirteen-by-seventeen-by-six-inch size limit. Nobody would ever catch me lugging around something that hefty unless I was on my way to France. A friendly woman behind the visitors' desk told us our meeting was set up in the banquet area off the restaurant. No Tony in sight. The "other members of our party" hadn't arrived yet either.

Some party.

We stood around for thirty seconds. I ran out of patience at fifteen. "Let's go visit my Buddha. I could use a shot of not-freaked-out." We went. I left my phone number at the desk for the stragglers.

In the golden glow of Gallery 241-B, a well-groomed and reassuring-looking young guard—fair-haired, rosy-cheeked, attired in the traditional dark slacks, nice jacket, tie, and name tag—was stationed next to my Buddha. I estimated this guy had been there long enough to attain a state of blissful boredom. His eyes and the Buddha's were at the same degree of half-mast. They looked good together.

The guard woke up when he spotted Tom and his cane. I followed his sleepy train of thought until logic ruled out any possibility that this blind man could be the much-discussed blind man of the evening before.

"You're not—" he began. And stopped, having decided, "*You're not the dead blind guy; you're a different one,*" wasn't a felicitous choice. "Uh. Sorry. I'm afraid you all aren't allowed to be in here right now. They're tidying up after an event next door last night."

He paused. Back in the soup. "Not tidying up the—you know, the—What happened with the bl—that was outside. Completely—This was next door to in here—"

I rescued him. "No, of course not. We understand. We're here for a meeting about all that. Thought we'd stop in to—Compose ourselves a bit. Maybe?" I ended on a pathetically hopeful note and offered him my wistful face.

He nodded and resumed his relaxed stance. Tom and I sat on the bench. I dropped my purse onto the floor at my feet. Otis crossed the room and placed his body between us and the rest of the world. Our museum guard shifted from foot to foot and cleared his throat.

"The bli—The guy last night didn't spend any time in here, you know. Passed through. The room for the Tour, 241-C, to your right, is a dead end." He heard himself say the death word. Shifted from foot to foot. "A—er—sort of—*cul-de-sac.*"

"Thanks for telling us," Tom said. "You seem to be guarding the—Is this the Amitāyus Buddha?"

The guard glanced at the plaque and nodded. Then he caught himself and said, "Yes." After that, he stared at Tom as if he'd never seen a blind man up close before. He cleared his throat. Took the leap. "Can you see me, sir? At all? I mean, I don't—"

"No. Not at all." Tom smiled. "But I'm reasonably sure you're about five-ten." He hesitated. Considering. Breathing. "Somebody in your household smokes. Not you. But you want them to quit. So they go outside, maybe? You yourself quit, a long time ago? And I know this Buddha. I come here a lot. By the way, my name is Tom. Tom Bennington." He held up his hand to exactly the right spot.

The guy's jaw sagged toward disbelief. "How'd you—?" He cut himself off, shook Tom's hand, and said, "Chad. Chad Collins. That was—How did—?"

"Sound, for the most part. I'm fortunate to have my hearing. Many blind people don't—I can guess how tall you are, Chad, by where your voice is coming from in relation to where I'm sitting. You and Allie are about the same height."

Chad's attention swiveled to me and our eyes met. I grinned. Offered up my hand. "Allie Harper, Chad. Good to meet you."

I overcame the urge to add, *Look out, Chad. He can locate your lips by listening to you breathe.*

You can't always say what comes to mind.

"And the smoking thing. That I quit?"

"It's in your voice. A bit. You've done great. Keep bugging her."

Watching Chad, I could see how psychics astound, dismay, and get paid the big bucks.

At least we'd earned his confidence. At the same time, something about me had grabbed his attention. "You. Allie?"

I nodded.

"You were sitting right there last night. On the bench. A few minutes before—"

All hell broke loose. I nodded again. "Were you here, too, Chad?"

"No. But they showed us the tape from last night. You were on it. Here. With your eyes closed."

My neck prickled. A phantom from my past hissed, *Your privacy is dead.* The invasion of being observed, tracked, and targeted fades but lurks. Forever, perhaps. I shook it off, but another ghostly memory jabbed at me. Something—something I'd dismissed in the wild, flurry of the alarms and lost to the insanity that came after was—.

Nagging.

"You saw me on the tape? Why were you looking at the tape?"

"The blin—The guy who got shot only passed through here. Like I mentioned before. To 241-C. And back. Before he left the museum and went—outside. The cops and our security people wanted to see—Well, truth is, they are looking at every scrap of tape there is from yesterday and last night and there is a crap-ton—Oh, sorry." He glanced around. Nobody else there, but Otis, and Otis didn't appear dismayed.

"I bet it's amazing how many hours—" I soothed him. With half my attention.

Something nagging.

He sighed, relieved not to be shocking a patron. "You would not believe. But they looked at these galleries first and there you were, where you're sitting now until—

Until I heard the tapping of a cane. And opened my eyes.

Critical information. Sidelined by my scrambled brain. Lost to the chaos of last night. Deleted by the four hours of sleep—

It poured back in. All of it. *The woman in gray. Harbinger of death. For real.*

"Until a blind woman wearing a gray sari handed me—"

Chad filled in my last blank, "Yeah! She gave you a white envelope. Do you have it? The cops were looking for it. And for you."

A white envelope.

The wedding invitation.

I'd had it in my hand when Lisa called. The sirens—Had I dropped it onto this immaculate floor, where it would now be standing out like a large white sore thumb—with Tom's name written on it in calligraphy? Obviously not.

Had I dropped it on the way to the glass box? Or, total worst case, on the floor of that freezing wet and windy balcony?

I snatched my purse up off the floor. Unzipped it. Peered in.

Uh oh.

Holy *crap.* Literally. Totally. By definition.

If museum security had a clue about the contents of this modest-sized purse when I breezed through this morning, they'd have confiscated it on the spot and called the CDC.

Never mind. Based on the urgency of the circumstances, I overcame my embarrassment, dispensed with museum etiquette, and dumped my clattering junk collection onto the polished floor. Directly in front of the Buddha of Infinite Life.

Buck up, dude.

Tom moved his feet.

Ignoring my warming face, I pawed through functional and non-functional pens, wallet, congealed mints, tissues, sunglasses, sunglass case, gum wrappers, gum wrapper wrapped around used gum, loose change, credit card receipts, including one used as a gum wrapper, and a napkin-swaddled chocolate cupcake with no paper baking thingie. On the bright side, it still had most of its icing and some of its sprinkles.

On the other bright side, the envelope's thick paper and graceful cursive script stood apart from the rest of my collection.

Thomas Bennington III

I grabbed the pack of tissues from the pile on the floor, plucked one out, and used it to lift my prize out of the debris.

Otis had abandoned his doorway and was standing looking down at this operation, phone to ear. Tom was standing next to him, his face a careful blank. I was fairly sure his heightened senses had warned him of the cupcake. The gum and mints too, for all I knew.

Otis murmured something to somebody and brought his attention back to me. "Allie, you're doing great. Why don't you lay the envelope down here on the bench?" He indicated the spot. "Tony is in the building. He's bringing somebody with him to take care of this."

I collapsed back onto the non-envelope end of my bench, releasing all hope of the moment of peace and calm I'd dragged us up here for. My quiet oasis of not-murder-and-mayhem was getting more blown up for me by the minute. I always believe I'm about to get my life handled and I never do. That didn't stop me from making a silent vow to do a more respectable job of organizing my purse.

The Buddha's countenance was placid as ever. He didn't seem to be disturbed about any of the turmoil I'd brought him. I figured he was working on visualizing the junk from my purse as a paradise. He still looked slightly amused.

Tony came through the door from 241-A with a man I identified as "crime scene guy." He was wearing the gloves but not the booties. This Non-TV-CSI came over and commandeered the wedding invite. And my purse. And its contents. If my worst fears were realized, he would individually photograph and bag every item in it. And put it in a report. From which it would be leaked. And show up on Instagram.

Our man Chad was now looking at us expectantly. Gratified to be a player in the investigation, I could tell. "We saw something else, too, Allie. On the tape. Before your part." He waited.

I bit. "And?"

"It was in 241-C. The dead guy? He was in there before he— earlier. He gave the envelope to your blind woman."

Chad was waiting. I was staring back at Chad. Speechless.

If we could place the envelope, the blind woman, and Kip Wade in the same room, at the same moment, less than an hour before Kip's murder—tie them together to make a picture, what would that picture be?

Not one I would *ever* want to see.

I cleared my throat. "Chad. I think that's important. We'll need to—just—thank you." He suppressed a satisfied grin, but flushed a happy shade of red. In those few disoriented seconds, I decided I liked Chad Collins. Liked his guileless face, the big hands he probably had to be constantly reminding not to touch the art. His sandy hair and serious brown eyes.

Time to go. Otis, Tony, and Lieutenant Wood were waiting.

Tom and I both thanked Chad, and the three of us executed smooth handshakes all around. Otis shook his hand too. Chad beamed, but as we turned away, he had one more question. Troubled again, the flush of pride fading.

"Tom? Did you ever wonder if maybe they shot that blind guy by mistake? Thinking it was you?"

Chapter Nine

10:55 A.M.

Provenance, the museum's restaurant, was poised to open its doors to the early luncheon crowd, but we slipped through, doing our best not to look like a threat to priceless art. As Tom threaded his way, folks kept glancing and glancing again. Appraising the tall, handsome blind guy. Dead ringer for a dead blind guy.

The possibilities were tantalizing. And after all, how rude could it be to stare? I didn't blame them, I stared at Tom all the time. But their double takes unnerved me. Moments before, Chad had spoken my worst unspoken fear. The pesky elephant I'd been frantically trying to banish from the room inside my chest was now barging around in there.

Blind guy shot by mistake.

I was painfully grateful when the young woman at the desk shepherded us through and walked us around a corner out of sight.

The Provenance staff had set us up in a room designed for banquets. No banquet for us. Water, coffee, mints. End of story. No festive glassware laid on for a celebration. No understated floral design. We all brought our game faces. Three of the five of us brought guns.

The windows of this room overlooked a moody vista of yellowed grasses, misty trees, and lowering clouds, dominated by the golden dome of the Temple-Tifereth Israel, now the university's performing arts center. Beautiful. Atmospheric. Somber. Maybe that last part was me.

We barely got a sip of the museum's water before Deputy Director Cecilia Southgate—power-suited, and focused like a blowtorch—joined our party. Ms. Southgate was allowing us ten minutes out of the crisis-management intensity of her day. She made sure we were "comfortable and well taken care of" before she set us straight.

"We're grateful to have you all here this morning." She scanned the table. Sharp blue eyes behind fashion-forward frames searched, assessed, and approved each of us in turn. *Check. Check. Check. Check.* Her gaze lingered on Tom, and a long, thoughtful pause shadowed her expression. *Check.*

I strained to see Tom through Ms. Southgate's eyes, minus the filter of all my Thomas Bennington addictions. He was the mirror of her most commanding qualities. Comprehensively educated, fiercely competent, devoted to the arts—even after his blindness stole the lion's share of their joy from him. She was all that, but also the sort of woman who might be hearing Andrea Bocelli when she looked at Tom. I could let her off the hook on that one. Him too. Matter of principle. He couldn't help being hot.

Something else was front and center for Ms. Southgate as she sat staring at Tom. The realization triggering the distress I read in her eyes—and the fear that was rocking me now. On a dark night Tom could pass for Kip Wade.

Blind guy shot by mistake?

She shook it off. Damage control was her main job today. To be fair, nothing much had happened inside the museum. The guy showed up at the Touch Tour for mere moments, contributed to a scene of unpleasantness at the museum's door, went on his way. What Ms. Southgate was still in the dark about was the news that Kip Wade, in 241-C, handed a blind woman in gray a message. For Tom. And the woman in gray had given it to me instead. An indelible moment I'd wiped clean off my consciousness.

I can give the note to you now. For Tom.

I blinked. Came back to what Cecilia Southgate was saying. "—why you're here. All of us need this terrible crime to be solved. Explained. We'll be able to breathe better when that happens."

She was gazing at Tom again. Sadly. Behind those sharp eyes a human being.

"For Kip Wade and his family, this is a senseless tragedy. I knew Kip. He was a complicated young man but devoted to the arts and to this museum. He would want all of us to be safe and for you to help us find answers to give us all peace of mind. And bring his killer to justice, of course."

She stood up. Brisk again. "You have many things to talk about. I've given Detective Wood and Officer Valerio my number. If you have questions. If you have concerns. If you need food, coffee— Anything. *Carte blanche.* Call me. Ask anyone here for help or information.

"You have my full cooperation and that of our staff. Don't hesitate—" She left the invitation hanging.

We waited in silence until her footsteps died.

Cleveland Homicide Detective Olivia Wood took command of our round table. "Here's where we are. As of this morning, Officer Valerio is on loan from the Fifth District to Homicide. We're grateful for his help and his contribution to all our efforts last night. He is here, primarily, as our liaison with your agency, Tom and Allie. Your T&A—"

Good job, Lieutenant Wood. She only rolled her eyes maybe a quarter-roll. Her lips only twitched a slight bit.

"Let's just call it the 'arrangement' you and Allie have with

Officer Valerio. And Otis, who's ex-cop and, I understand, a licensed PI. And your other associates.

"Up to now, we've caught only glimpses, but I feel safe saying this is not a straightforward murder. Homicide is not usually this entangled. Somebody shoots somebody and we go pick up the one who's still alive. Or it's domestic—Woman hands us a gun and says, 'I've been putting up with his shit for years.'

"We need another shoe to drop." She shook her head. Rueful. "I don't think I've ever said that about a case. Not out loud."

"There's a lot we don't see yet. Connections not made. Perhaps the envelope we'll be able to open shortly will cast some light— But I do believe you four will have a role in helping us resolve it. Tom, you have skills I've not encountered before. You'll be an asset to this investigation, I'm sure." A flash of wry humor. "Maybe now we know why the "T" gets top billing."

Tom shook his head.

"Well, despite the unconventional name, I'm confident you all are not going to be a bunch of loose-cannon vigilantes, roaming around, interfering with our investigations, annoying citizens, getting yourselves hurt."

I did not dare look at Tony. I bet his eye roll was the full three-sixty. Tom could probably hear it. The hard, cold truth? On our first official case, we fledgling T&As crossed every single one of those boundaries in hot pursuit of answers. With exactly, but exactly, the results she'd enumerated. If we ever decided to ditch "T&A" as our name, we could pick up "Loose-Cannon Vigilantes" without missing a beat. Never mind. We were learning.

Fortunately for me, Lieutenant Wood was giving Tom all her attention. "I'll be frank about this too, Tom. Your money has already made a difference for us."

Refreshingly blunt, Detective Wood. No pussyfooting around the Mondo. I liked that about her too.

"I understand you would prefer not to think of it as your money, Tom, but until you give it away or someone takes it from you, the power of it is yours. In the past months, you've more or less footed the bill for some good work. You prevented a significant crime against yourselves and a whole circle of people around you, and, more important from the CPD perspective, you helped dismantle a widespread criminal operation the Fifth District was delighted to see go. And, Tom, you and the T&A—

Woo. Barely a flutter this time.

"You helped solve a premeditated murder we were all set to miss. It's safe to say there'd be no justice for Lloyd Bunker if not for you."

She refocused on the rest of us, rallying her points. "All of you are uniquely positioned to help us out now. For a number of reasons. Not the least of which is our awareness that last night's incident keeps circling back to you."

I resisted the impulse to clamp my hands over my ears. *Don't let Tom be the next victim. Don't let him be the intended first victim. Don't let somebody take a second shot.*

Too bad, Allie.

I couldn't shut out the cold certainty, coiling and twisting inside me. Like Tom's kudzu. Or a nest of snakes. Kip Wade's murder was somehow all about Tom.

A quiet tap. The door to our meeting room swung open and the sound of merrily clinking crystal and silver, dinging against china, broke into my fragile state of mind like a falling tray of glassware.

With impeccable, gut-wrenching timing, here came Chad Collins and the crime scene guy. Chad was wearing gloves like a pro, beaming like a Christmas morning, and proudly delivering, as if it were a square, paper version of the holy grail itself, an envelope.

The Envelope.

———

Chad delivered his trophy to Olivia Wood, who produced a pair of gloves of her own, and he laid my "wedding invitation" on her gloved palms.

"Ms.— Lieutenant. Wood. The woman who got this from Mr. Wade and gave it to Ms. Harper was wearing gloves."

I found my voice. Kept it level as I could. "She said, 'As if it wasn't bad enough to be blind,' she had severe skin allergies."

Chad nodded. "But Allie wasn't wearing gloves, of course. And the envelope spent the night in your purse, Allie."

He permitted himself a small disapproving grimace that suggested, "*And your purse, Allie, is the Evidence Contamination Epicenter of the Known Universe. Also the purse equivalent of a twenty-nine-dollar-an-hour motel.*"

I wanted to shoot Chad an eye-dagger but spoiling his moment of glory would be like kicking a kitten. Also, in spite of the roil of fear and confusion set off by what this envelope might contain, I couldn't un-notice the smudge of chocolate on its corner. I sucked all that up. No comment.

Olivia handed the envelope over to the crime scene specialist who also wore gloves. He took pity on me. "It probably makes no difference, Ms. Harper. The entire area was unsecured until this morning because nobody last night understood it was significant. We did our best, but those galleries were a freeway. Once we have suspects, we may get additional opportunities to find something useful as evidence. For now, we agree we should open the envelope. Carefully. And see what it says. It could be—" He pressed his lips together. "Time-sensitive."

Our homicide detective agreed. "We want to see this now. Larry, do you have what you need?"

Ah, Larry. Good to have a name. In case I had a question. And the guts to ask it.

"Yes. Here. I'll open it." Larry hesitated. "Sorry, guys. You all get to wear these."

Disposable masks. All around.

Moments freeze people. This one froze me. Especially my lungs. Trapped inside my mind, deep under icy water. Drowning. Dying for lack of my next breath and afraid to breathe it.

Breathing could kill me. Kill us all.

Larry noticed. He spoke to the table at large, but he looked straight at me. Captured my stare with his eyes. They were brown. They were warm. His eyebrows were reddish brown. I took the breath.

"I'm Mr. Abundance of Caution," he said in a reassuring, this-is-no-big-deal way.

"You can skip the masks and step away, if you'd prefer. The odds are—Listen, it will be fine. It's not going to explode or anything. This is routine. Protocol. Whoever sent it wanted to get your attention and probably scare you. Not kill you."

Of course I believed him. He'd saved my life.

We all put on our masks. If one tiny grain of anything fell out of there, we'd leave the room in an orderly way. Everyone in the building would probably go too. In an abundance of caution.

None of that happened. Larry, who I will always think of as Larry Calm & Brave, slit the envelope. The only thing big enough to be visible to the naked eye—a square of high-quality stationery—came out. A handful of words in elegant script, stood out black against the vellum. I could read it from where I was sitting.

What you don't see is what you get.

Chapter Ten

I put my hand on Tom's arm as Olivia Wood read the message aloud, and I felt the muscles tense as he clenched his fist.

"We can take our masks off now." Larry said.

We were all breathing again. But not smiling in relief. Chad was frowning bafflement. "What does it *mean*?"

"I can think of a lot of things." Tom had not unclenched his fingers.

Larry, said, "There's one more thing about this you all need to know."

We waited. He focused on me.

"Allie, it's—"

"Larry?"

"Your blind woman wasn't blind."

————

A coil within a coil.

Larry Calm & Brave told us everything he knew.

"While I was finishing up my part up in the galleries, one of the University Circle cops stopped in. He's working with museum security, reviewing the thousand miles of tape they're going through down there. He told me he kept hearing about the weird blind woman so he went and searched through the footage to figure out how she left the building. He found her, the bli—" He glanced toward Tom. "The woman in the gray dress.

"He said he could tell she—or someone who briefed her—studied where all the cameras on her route into the museum were located and where they were aimed. Said the cameras do a great job and don't miss much, but they can't cover every square inch. You can duck them if you work on it. Takes effort. And attention. You'd have to be able to see.

"She passed through at a precise angle to each one to keep them from catching her face. Looped her head scarf up close. Had her big glasses. He said she looked plenty eccentric but not blind. No cane in sight when she was in the atrium. And she left the building in a giant hurry. No tapping around—Sorry, Tom."

Tom shook him off. "Larry. No kidding. Tapping around is my freedom. You and I are fine. Somebody who steps up when there's maybe anthrax on the table is my friend for life.

"But this feels like more bad news. If she is not blind, she'll have no connection to the people at the Tour. No record of registration. Nothing. We've lost her, and anything she knew about what happened. Except everything about her—about all of this—feels like it points to—"

My elephant of dread was sitting at the table with us now.

A name I'd never wanted to hear. A face I'd hoped never to see again.

"Tom." Lieutenant Wood cut him off. "Stick with us. We haven't exhausted the possibilities. Not by half. There's CCTV everywhere on the street and the grounds here. Give us a minute to run her down. This woman didn't pop out of nowhere to casually hand you or Allie the envelope. Someone schooled her on how to pass as a blind person. Someone told her exactly what to say. She had to study the cameras, so she had to come here and look at them. At least once. Even if someone gave her a schematic or whatever. Take my word for it, Tom. People slip up. We'll find her.

"Even if she's only the messenger, she knows more than she knows she knows—" She paused, chasing her sentence around. Shrugged. "You know what I mean."

Our eyes met and I knew something else: The homicide detective and I were having the exact same thought in the exact same moment. *Only the messenger?*

Kill the messenger.

A handful of times in my life, I've met someone who gave me the electrical jolt that says, *Here is someone you are meant to know.* Tom was all that and more. At first sight. No question. Unfortunately, D.B. Harper, my reprehensible ex, was so high-voltage and blue-eyed-red-hot back in the day, he was a false positive on that one. Fried all the circuits of common sense. Too bad. Those electrical shocks can be misread. And killer painful.

In that moment with Lieutenant Olivia Wood of CPD Homicide, I was looking into the alternate universe in which I could have been her. Of my many roads-not-taken, she was one. Too late now for that path, but I would at least become a much more effective amateur detective if I could learn from the woman who was definitely not looking at me as if I were "A Force for Crazy." At all.

I answered the realization I saw on her face.

"We'd better find her soon."

She nodded without breaking eye contact. "Yes. Allie. We'd better. We'll make it a priority."

The world unfroze and we moved on.

Tom knew the messenger was in danger too, I could tell. He'd read the vibration off a high-frequency glance he couldn't see. The Blind Spidey never sleeps.

———

Larry C&B was done with us. "Okay. Chad and I are out of here. I'll take this envelope to the lab and we'll see if—" His body language said, *Don't get your hopes up.*

Before they could make it to the door, somebody knocked on it.

My vote was for coffee or maybe even lunch this time.

Nope.

A police officer in a blue uniform—the standard twenty-pound array of cop equipment, including cuffs, mace, and gun, bristling on his belt—popped the door open and walked on in. He was medium-tall, burly, with a blond crew cut that suited him perfectly.

Larry said, "Oh, hey, Jack. I was just talking about you. Chad and I are done here. Come on in. Lieutenant Wood, this is the officer from the University Circle PD who's looking at the tapes."

Officer Jack took three steps into the room, nodded to Lieutenant Wood, said, "ma-am," to her. And then to the room at large, inquired, "Ms. Harper? Mr. Johnson?"

Otis said, "That's me."

I said, "And me."

The officer said, "Ms. Harper, Mr. Johnson. I need you to come with me."

To my paranoid ears that sounded official. For three seconds I wondered whether the University Circle cops had a jail, and if it would have decent Wi-Fi.

I tilted my head at Otis. *What's up?*

He shrugged. *No idea.*

By mutual, unspoken agreement, we went.

The officer's full title was Officer Jack Zupančič. I bet he and Lisa Cole could speak Slovene to each other. I bet they had nine hundred friends and family members in common.

Maybe this guy was not here to bust up my day any worse than it already was.

Right. And maybe pigs will fly, Alice Jane.

Chapter Eleven

Officer Jack steered us out through the restaurant's bar, past a chic group partaking of a perfectly curated board of delectable-looking charcuterie. He said "Thanks, miss" to the hostess who was unable to pry her eyes off his overpopulated belt. Impressed or horrified, but professional about it.

Otis's gun was sequestered under his jacket but his "don't mess with Otis" demeanor was on full display. Next to those guys, I believed I was invisible in my anonymous gray slacks, gray sweater, and non-haute-couture shoes. Good. Hiding out was my main game. Again.

Once we were in the atrium's wide open space, the cop said, "Ms. Harper. We need you to take a look at the footage from last night for us. The woman who spoke to you in the gallery upstairs. You probably heard somebody taught her how to dodge the cameras? That's not as foolproof as you might think. We got her, square-on, a couple of times. Not that it helps any, with her all wrapped up in that kooky outfit.

"The good news is, whoever coached her didn't know that, in January, security installed a handful of new cameras—leading edge tech—on each floor. Not many of us heard about that. Now we can get big wide shots of the main spaces from overhead. Decent images. Don't bother to look up, Ms. Harper. I can't find them and I know where they are. If you'll both follow me, you can take a look. And there's something—" He opened a door.

The museum's security office was modest in size, dimly lit, and dominated by a wall of monitors. My eye was drawn to the one with a zoomed-in image of a woman, frozen on the screen. The uniformed guy at the console said, "Hi, Ms. Harper," without taking his eyes away from the display. "Name's Jeff." He patted a folding chair on his left. "Come sit next to me." I sat.

"Name's Allie."

Officer Jack grabbed a chair, dragged it over to the other side of Jeff. "Call me Jack, you guys. Let's get on with this."

Otis took up his position against the wall. I was here to look at video. He was here to watch over me. I hated every single thing about this except Otis.

Jeff hit play.

Right off the bat, I could see my blind woman wasn't being blind just then. The cane, no doubt collapsed and stuck into her bag, was not in view. Enveloped in the sari, her face hidden by the scarf, huge dark glasses goggling—the lady was bizarre as hell. The weaving dance she was doing to evade the cameras enhanced the spooky effect. Even at no more than three inches high, she creeped me out.

"Yes. That's her, no question. What else do you need to know?"

Can I go now?

"They've put together all the segments we've got so far that she's in. And there's a question—Take a look. I don't want to prejudice you. Okay?"

Jeff was whisking the video forward.

"If it will help us find her—okay."

"Great. I'll run this normal speed, but stop me whenever you want a closer look."

The woman came in through the door of our encounter with

Kip Wade. The time stamp read 6:01 p.m. When we'd arrived, she was already inside the museum. Waiting.

Damn. Of course she was. She'd arrived early to meet Kip in 241-C. So he could pass her the envelope.

What you don't see is what you get.

I must have been jigglin'. Otis came over. Put his hand on my shoulder. Leaned down. Spoke quietly.

"Allie, listen, reviewing stuff like this—Sometimes it helps to put yourself in the subject's place. Trick I picked up at the security job. Try to get an idea of what it's like to be her. See what she sees. Feel what she feels. Give it shot?"

"Okay."

He stepped away. Said, "Roll it back to the beginning, Jeff?

"Give me a second to think about how to do this, Jeff."

"Just say 'go' when you're ready, Allie."

Jeff rolled her back to the outside doors. I breathed as calmly as I could. Trying to be her, coming in the north entrance. Wearing what she wore. Seeing what she saw. Feeling what she felt. Our doorway. An hour before us. No Kip/Tom skirmish yet. No Otis. No me—"Go, Jeff."

I am standing outside the door. The handle is freezing—No. I'm wearing gloves, but—I left my coat behind. I'm freezing. Damp. My heart is beating too fast, but I'm...excited to be...here. It's a challenge. My sari is light, filmy. Can't let it get tangled and trip me up. And the glasses are ridiculous. I can't see for—Good for me. I'm supposed to be blind. Being blind now.

In through the front hall. Atrium. Right. Four steps. Stop. Left. Five. Skirt the trees and tables. Counting. Changing direction. Escalator. Relax, just stand here, head down, head down, head down. Slow, careful, pause—1-2-3 off!

At the top of the escalator I was suddenly Allie Harper again, and my personal neck was prickling. In spite of her realistic portrayal of blindness—now with cane in hand—the sari woman had stolen a glance behind her. Quick, but unmistakable.

"Jeff. Stop. I—She looked over the edge. Can we see what she saw?"

"Yeah, Allie. Good. We caught that too. There's a man there, at one of the tables. Out of range of the closer cameras. But he's definitely watching her and now she knows he's there. Any thought about who—? Want to take a closer look right now?"

No. And no.

"Not yet. Let's keep going. She'll turn in to 241-A now."

By the time she came toward us and entered the first section of the gallery, she was all blind all the time. Into the second section. Around my Buddha. On into Chad's "*cul-de-sac.*" Our camera lost her then, except for what showed through the door. Which was a big cloudy bunch of nothing.

At 6:53 Kip came out.

Had he timed his exit to confront us? He'd known Tom was registered for the tour. Or was his angry reaction to meeting Tom at the front door raw nerves, jangled by an unexpected encounter with us? Whatever he was up to last night, the Kip I was looking at didn't have a clue he'd be dead in less than an hour.

I shifted, restless in my chair. Chilled to be studying the arc of a murder.

Grateful to disappear into somebody else's perspective.

I'm coming out of the gallery, turning left—Ah!—heading into a restroom. I feel more confident now. I can stay out of sight until my next appearance—Wait. I'm—There's a—

"Jeff, she looked again. Can you back that up to where she comes out of 241? Somebody down the hall there?"

He ran it back and the not-really-blind woman came out of the bathroom, skittering in reverse, cane zipping back and forth in front of her as she moved in the wrong direction. My neck tingled again. Shadow by the wall, one door up the hall. Big, tall, and fuzzy.

"Jeff, can we see the person leaning against the wall across from…uh…242-A? Ancient India? Maybe?"

"You're right. He's there, Allie. We tried before. But he's out of—Let me do one more—C'mon. C'*mon*. No. Sorry, Allie, it's worthless. I know what you're talking about. But he's out of range of the wide shot and in the blind for that hall. I could blow it up till doomsday—Just make it grainier. Can't get him. Could be a dude waiting for his wife. Wishing he was home having a beer and watching college basketball."

I didn't think so.

"Okay." *I'm coming out of hiding for real now. Feeling more exposed than before. Tentative. Taking a second to get back into being blind. Making my way to Ancient China, glad the blind people won't be judging my performance. Jittery now. Nervous. Getting a grip. I can do this. It's showtime!"*

A clean shot of both of us. From the gallery's cam this time. Me sitting. Eyes closed. Her passing carefully, quietly, by me into the next section, cane not quite touching the floor. But she didn't find Tom. Back with me. Talking to me now, turning to peer at the Buddha's missing hands, handing me the envelope—then hurrying out. Leaving Allie Harper to toss the envelope into her public disgrace of purse and answer her phone.

I'm done! It's all done. I'm—

Another not-so-blind pause. Lightning bolt this time.

The man. That man.

"Jeff. Is that same man there? Is he waiting for me—for *her*—right outside the gallery?"

"Yeah. He's there. I've nailed him. Do you want to see?"

"No. Yes. Not—You've got him saved, right?"

"Oh, yeah."

"Let me concentrate on this." *And not know for sure yet.* "Give me a minute. He's already gone when she—when I come out, right?"

"Yes. Until—Yes. And there she goes."

I am barely steps from the top of the down escalator, and I hear a blast of sound that jars my whole body. Assaulting my ears, stealing air from my lungs. Seconds later museum visitors begin emerging from all the rooms of the west wing into the hall. All around me.

A handful, then a cautious stream, fast becoming a torrent. Bobbing heads and shoulders on the escalator.

For a moment I'm back to being Allie Harper again, trapped in that crush of bodies. Checking my phone. Fighting panic.

I shivered, remembering.

"You okay, Allie?" Otis had my back.

"Fine, Otis. Jumpy is all."

Our target was walking faster, a glimpse, here and there, getting swallowed up by the flood.

I've put the cane away, abandoned the escape route I practiced. I'm making a beeline for the door I came in through. Quick. Quick. Is that man is following me again? If I don't hurry, a guard or a cop will be blocking me. They'll say, "Sorry, ma'am, I can't let you go out there. It's not safe."

If it's not locked down already. Caught. I'll be caught.

My heart drums. It's not safe in here, either—not for me. The sound of my breathing, short bursts, in my ears. I'm dizzy. Scared. It's okay. I'm okay. No one is paying attention to anybody. Go. Go. Go.

We'd lost her in the sea of bodies. I wondered if she knew this deluge was coming. Whether she was as shocked and frightened as the rest of us. Or extra scared, because she'd been forewarned this night would go off the rails, and "off the rails" was the plan all along. And maybe, not being the least bit blind, she'd recognized the man who'd been tracking her. Watching her. Who was maybe behind her now as she hurried along. Or already waiting.

"Jeff? Do we have a shot of her leaving?"

"That's up next. She was one of the last to make it out the doors. Ditched her whole avoid-the-cameras routine. But we still didn't get a good look. Gimme a sec—Here. There she goes."

I'm running. Everything—falling apart. Hurry. Hurry! Forget this stupid—Guard coming. Guard. Guard. Don't stop. Out!

Helter-skelter down the lighted walkway. Features still hidden by the scarf. Sari billowing. Nothing frail or uncertain about her now. The guard leaning out the open door, yelling soundlessly into the sleet for her to come back inside. To be safe.

I'm hidden in the darkness and the rain. Safe.

Jeff let the scene run.

I kept watching. Calming myself. Catching my breath. So I saw it all.

This focus, unlike many of the others, was sharp, clear, and close. I was back to being Allie Harper again, shaking my head at the frantic people swarming onto the elevator. Abandoning a lovely, warm museum for a car, going nowhere, stuck in a frigid parking garage. I empathized. Tough to pick your smartest move when the world goes insane and your imagination conjures the worst.

The elevator door slid closed, leaving a man behind. The man, tall, well-dressed, unaccustomed to being thwarted, slapped angrily at the closed door and turned back to confront the guard who—civilized jacket, tie, and name tag aside—had been well-trained to deal with panic and was all about procedure now. And—

"Allie," Jeff said, "Here's your guy."

The tall man swiveled. Unperturbed by the chaos. Sought out the vestibule's camera. Gazed into it—Smiled—I knew that smile. It visited me in my most terrifying dream.

"Jeff—Stop. Freeze him."

"Do you know this man, Allie? Have you seen him before today?

The man was looking straight at me.

Allie?

By the second *"Allie?"* Otis was at my chair again. His hand back on my shoulder. "Allie. Is it—Is that... *him?*

The deadly eyes. The arrogant sneer. The only thing missing was the oppressive presence of the "world's most expensive fragrance for men." I could almost smell him. Hear his voice, delivering the threat I'd tried to erase from my memory.

I'll be back around sooner or later. I am still quite interested in your money.

"It's him, Otis. Show us the rest, Jeff."

The video started up again. Tito Ricci stepped up to the door and slugged the guard—a vicious punch to the gut—stepped back to let him fold in on himself and crumple onto the floor. Strolled out the into the night.

Chapter Twelve

If I could offer one smart rule for everyone on the planet, it would be, "Do not make a deadly enemy." This is a fantastic rule. It was not workable for Tom, Otis, and me because our deadly enemy was a self-made-done-deal before he landed on the doorstep of our lives, fully equipped with a nefarious scheme, a sociopathic henchman, and a chunky bankroll.

Tito Ricci—not his real name—was a crazy-ass nightmare in one expensively dressed, oppressively fragranced package, and he was all ours. Last summer, disguised as a social-climbing businessman, Tito masterminded a hacker-heist of the Mondo Money. It flopped. Our hacker beat his hacker, and—in an ill-considered fit of pique—Tito summarily executed his hacker-protégé right in front of Tom and me. On the concierge level of a Marriott hotel.

The T&A more or less trashed his scrapper-drug ring too.

Tito went away very, very mad.

Here's a corollary to my clever Make-No-Deadly-Enemy rule: "If you have a deadly enemy, do not let him get away."

Ours got away. Big time. Nobody last summer laid a glove on Tito. His plans fell through, at least in part because of the T&A—and he vanished. Leaving a trail of dead associates and innocent bystanders. "Skipped town" does not do justice to how brutally gone he was.

Except he wasn't. Not gone from our hearts. Or our minds. Or my nightmares. Or—in spite of my happy-dappy pretending between last July and now—maybe not even gone from Cleveland. Whether he ever got as far away as we'd been hoping, i.e., outer Tasmania or—possibly—hell, made no difference today.

He was back.

I was trying to act not-hysterical.

Otis was all business.

"Now that we know we're looking for *this* man, can you guys make another pass? And let's set up facial recognition for the CCTVs around the outside of the museum. Especially on the walk from the north entrance and down to where—down to the end of the lagoon. First priority."

Otis and I thanked Jeff and Jack. Said goodbye. Their curiosity followed us out the door. We weren't ready to talk about what we'd seen.

I wasn't ready to think about it.

We walked in silence up the stairs and out across the atrium. We were almost to the door of the restaurant when my pseudo composure buckled.

"Holy crap, girl. Are you awake finally? What have I been trying to tell you!?!"

Uh oh.

Lee. Ann. Smith.

"Otis. I need a minute. Ladies room?"

"Sure, Allie. I'll come with you."

Otis didn't mean that like it sounded.

We headed down the hall to the door with the female graphic. He popped it open and called in, "Cleaning crew."

A flurry. A short burst from a hand dryer. Two young ladies—high-school-age—rushed out, still shaking water from their hands, stifling giggles. They registered Otis as "no way janitorial," but were too busy being young and adorable—and totally unaware of the gun under his jacket—to care.

"Is that it in there, ladies?"

Another outbreak of giggles. "Yeah."

He went in. Came back in a half minute with the "all clear."

"Go ahead, Allie. Take your time. I'll be right here."

Otis would tell anyone who wanted in there, "Sorry. Out of order. Take the up escalator, turn right, you can't miss it." He was resourceful like that. And if anybody argued, he'd have Cecilia Southgate kill them. *Carte blanche is carte blanche.*

———

I scurried on in.

The lovely solid door whisked shut behind me.

Hint: If you need a place to hide, a bathroom is a decent choice. For starters, assuming conditions are reasonably stable, guys can't come in after you. Often that's fifty percent of your problem solved right there. Another helpful thing is, once inside, you can have your mini-breakdown behind a good, solid, steadfast, stainless steel door, and, if you're quiet about it, no one will know.

I sat, fully clothed, on the sparkling toilet, my blurred reflection in the polished door. Put my head below my knees. Listened for the voice who'd hustled me in here to tell me something I already knew.

"*Alice Harper. Get over yourself.*"

Let me clarify something about Lee Ann Smith. I know you're aware of that voice in your head? The one that says stuff like "I'd never do tequila shots." Or "I am never going to kiss this guy—Or steal that car."

Hurray for you, right? But what about the other voice in there that answers that wussy voice back, "Aw, shut up. We could both be dead by the time another...

"1) shot of Gran Patron Platinum...

"2) guy that smoking hot…

"3) Mercedes convertible with the keys in the ignition… comes along."

Lee Ann Smith is my "Go ahead, steal the car!" voice. Although, as best I can recall, we never stole a car. Was there some small-ish petty crime in our distant past? Yeah. And in the interest of full disclosure, "*Kiss* this guy" was both a euphemism and an understatement.

She's an escapee from my hastily buried past. I succeeded in ditching my Lee Ann side for a decade or so. More or less. I will hold her responsible for D.B. Harper, dickhead lawyer extraordinaire.

Forever.

She was the genie I let out of a bottle last summer when Otis and I needed a cover story for our investigation at a scrapyard. I'd slipped right back into her walk, her talk, and her rundown, red cowboy boots. She was a pair of washed-to-death jeans and my favorite beat-up plaid shirt from another lifetime. Naturally, she has my maiden name.

To be fair, Lee Ann seems to be a teensy bit…*more present* for me than the arguing voice in most people's heads. She's like a… um…separated-at-birth-bad-girl-twin.

When I hear her in my head, she can be loud, but she's not demon possession. Exactly. I don't have to burn incense to summon her voice. These days she merely wanted to hang out in my head, drink Otis's best bourbon, and have me wear our boots. Also, some of the stuff she begged me to suggest to Tom was plain wicked.

This wasn't about any of that.

"*Buck up, Alice Jane. He's back. You gotta accept facts: Tito Ricci's filthy paw prints are all over this.*"

Sometimes I didn't hear from her for weeks—except for the slutty Tom conversations. But whenever I started thinking she'd moved on—and especially when I was ignoring a skulking uneasiness—she'd go ahead and spit it out. Right now I was trying to calm us both down.

"Lee Ann. Shut up. His name is not even Tito Ricci."

How is that relevant? Given the givens?

"Which are? According to you..."

"According to me and probably CNN, Little-Miss-Denial-Is-Not-Just-A-River-In-Egypt. It goes like this:

"Number one. A blind man gets shot dead. Tom is also a blind man. Who looks like the dead one. A lot.

"Number two. The blind man gets shot after storming out of an event for blind people. Tom signed up for that thing months ago.

"Now. Number three? Would you like to tell me what three is, Ms. Exceedingly Amateur Sleuth?"

She was ticking off her numbers, one finger at a time. I closed my eyes and focused on remembering the name of the nail polish she was brandishing at me: Urban Decay "Oil Slick." And how she'd gotten it.

"Lee Ann. You stole that bottle of polish from Crystal's big sister. In high school."

"Well, somebody sure did. Number three, please? Alice Jane Smith Harper?"

I exhaled. It felt good to release, all the way, the breath I'd been holding since last night.

"Okay. Yes. All right. The wedding invitation."

"Like, seriously. 'What you don't see is what you get.' If that isn't a threat tailor-made for a blind guy, what is? Punctuated by the actual shooting to death of a look-alike? Who, for sure, didn't see that one coming. Give me a break. And, girl, it's ominous every which way, but it pales, purely pales, in the spotlight off that money shot of him at the museum door. What's it going to take for you to get your head out of your—?"

"Stop. I got it. I get it."

She had me. She was me.

Now I had a question. Relative to the one fear that ruled them all. "So, do we believe Tom was the target? Maybe Kip Wade was a mistake, and it's Tom who's supposed to be dead right now?"

"We don't know. Yet. But, I'll tell you what, Alice Jane. It's hard for me to believe the person who set this whole massive thing into motion—and we both now know for dead certain it's Tito Ricci, right? Even Tito Ricci would never be crazy stupid enough to shoot or have somebody else shoot the wrong guy. Tom wasn't the intended target, Not last night, anyway."

"How come you haven't mentioned this before?"

"Oh, sweetie. You're slow. You had to see his face before you could hear me talking."

She was gone again.

I got up. Opened the stall door. Peeked around. Splashed cold water on my face. Noticed, too late, this eco-conscious place had no paper towels. Washed my hands and dried them ergonomically and ecologically in twelve seconds in the hand dryer. Used the sleeve of my sweater on my face. Treated myself to a deep, cleansing breath.

The worst thing about hiding in the ladies' room is sooner or later you have to come out.

Chapter Thirteen

"Sorry. I ran into a friend."

The "imaginary" is silent.

Otis and I returned to the dining room and dropped our Tito Ricci bombshell, complete with my eyewitness account—not to mention the promise of video—to substantiate it. Nobody, including Lieutenant Wood, who barely knew of Tito, was dumbfounded by our news.

I was the only one of us who could hear Lee Ann's self-satisfied, *"Damn-skippy."*

Technically, I was the sole member of the group who'd attended The Ladies Room Conference, but they were in sync with its findings: 99.98 percent confident that:

1) Kip Wade was the designated target.

2) Kip's murder was a message—a cruel and terrible object lesson.

3) They were extra, extra sure the message was addressed to Tom "What-You-Don't-See" Bennington. 99.99 percent.

Tito was back now. For revenge and a fresh shot at two hundred million dollars. And change.

Payback and his payoff.

Tito Ricci could not have been the highly skilled, terrifyingly accurate killer of R. Kipling Wade. His alibi had smirked at me from the monitor in the security room—but he was our unanimous candidate for Devil in Charge.

Even Olivia Wood, newcomer to our story, was tuned into the logic of Tito. "I'll review what little we have on him from last year, but it sure sounds like his appearance on the video was intentional. Perhaps staged."

By him. For us. Tito Ricci, filling in the blanks of many, many of our questions.

"But you know—"

Olivia. Preoccupied now. Deliberating. "For him to let himself be seen—identified. Flaunting his involvement where you could see it, Allie—was ill-advised. Stupid. His anger is making him careless. Unfortunately, it makes him more dangerous—more unpredictable—as well."

Helpful to know, but here was the heart-stopper for me: On a low-visibility night of rain and sleet, a killer had been waiting on the parapet of Severance Hall, aiming for a tall, handsome blind man with a white cane. I could not stop recalculating the perilous timing, and confronting my mental picture of Tom in the crosshairs. How close he'd come to the line of fire last night.

Intentional or unintentional, dead is dead.

I was an experienced and intuitive reader of the pulse in Tom's throat. He was grappling with how close he'd come. Fear and impatience crackled in his voice.

"That's all interesting, Lieutenant Wood. But where exactly does the T&A fit? That's why we're here, right? Instead of hiding out in Fiji? Which has tremendous appeal for me right now. What is it you want from us? Specifically? And where do I fit? 'Moving target' sucks as a job description—"

"Tom, you're both his revenge and his reward. This Tito wants to wound you. And he wants as many of your millions as he can get his hands on. Wounding you is easy, right?"

"Right. He'd hurt—"

"Allie." Tony finished the sentence neither Tom nor Otis would touch.

"Yes." Olivia didn't want to agree, I could tell, but she wasn't going to sugarcoat it either. "And Tom, a payoff—even millions—wouldn't satisfy him."

"No. The opposite. Payoff triggers payback. The moment I give him the money, he'll kill her."

Tom clasped his hands and put them on the table and bent his head over them, like praying. After a few seconds, he sat back, took his glasses off, tossed them out in front of him, and rubbed at his eyes. His beautiful brown eyes, staring at nothing, empty of emotion. His face was wooden, but anger had him now. His voice trembled with compressed rage.

"I'm going to hazard a guess, Olivia, that we got invited to today's party, not because of our personal peril, or even because of what happened to Kip, but because last night's—drama—statement—whatever the *fuck* you want to call it, took place *here*.

"And *here!*" He struck the tabletop. Hard. Everybody jumped. "University Circle. Tito 'staged' Kip's murder as a phony terrorist attack against—everything that's here. The museum. The orchestra, everything—"

I was locked onto Tom's fear and anger, but I was watching Lieutenant Wood and Officer Anthony Valerio. She was making metal notes, but he was the one vibrating right along with Tom. When Tom stopped to catch his breath, Tony stepped into the hollowed-out silence Tom's fury had made.

"You're right, Tom. Tito—*Toto*—Whatever the fuck his name really is. Sorry. Can't—" He shrugged and waved a hand to signal *Not sorry. Not taking it back.*

"Even I can see he is just dying to be the big mastermind. Last summer, you guys and the T&A blew Tito's operation sky-high, ran him out of town, and kicked him in his ego.

"But anybody who says, 'Boy howdy. That Tito Ricci is really,

really, off-the-charts pissed at Tom Bennington, and that's what all this fiasco is about?' No. Not a goddam chance.

"It's about all of *this*." His impatient gesture swept over our table and on out the window to the view.

"This museum, plus the orchestra, the botanical gardens, the natural history museum—Hell. There's even a museum full of 'historically significant' cars. Not to mention the 'University' of University Circle. You could hit a *goddam golf ball* off the roof of this building, in any direction, and whack some priceless, irreplaceable treasure. Worst case, the radius from here to—to effectively all of it—is barely a thousand feet.

"Right now. Right goddam here. At this goddam table? We're sitting on the goddam bull's-eye." He stopped for a breath. Glaring.

"Oliva," Tom voice was calm, but steely. "I know you genuinely believe the T&A can help you get to the person behind—all of this. We can. Allie knows what Tito looks like. Otis, Tony, and—others who helped us last summer—have serious skills. But I suspect Cecelia Southgate and her counterparts are also hoping the jackpot might, if push comes to shove, solve the ransom problem. Maybe it would. Who knows? If I could heal half the damage the jackpot has done by giving it all away, it would be a blessing for me. But solving that problem will not solve ours.

"This person. This angry, unstable, evil man will not be done with us until Allie is dead, and my life is over. And I'm probably dead too. We'll help you, but we need you to help us in return. I promise to handle the payoff, if it comes to that. But I need your word that you'll do what you can to protect us from his payback. Deal?"

Olivia smiled. "Serve and protect is still our job, Tom. Especially when the stakes are high and our friends are in danger. So, yeah. T&A and the CPD. In this together. Deal. And, for the record, cops are not usually in favor of anybody paying a ransom. For so many reasons. We'll do what we can to keep the money safe too."

Tony glared tiredly at us from under the unibrow as he sat back and delivered his professional assessment of our situation. "This is the deep shit."

Chapter Fourteen

2:15 P.M.

"Ms. Harper, there's a phone call for you at the front desk."

The young woman who came to get me was the same one who'd graciously greeted us this morning. Also the one who'd been so mesmerized by Jack's duty belt. I was with her on that. The only thing missing from a cop's belt is nunchucks and a tennis racket.

Otis followed us into the bar, checked to make sure the line of sight between me and Sniperland was blocked, and positioned himself near the door. Stacey, according to the delicate silver script at her throat, who was no-doubt supporting her engineering-degree habit by playing the gracious hostess, showed me the phone.

I stood at the check-in desk of Provenance with my back to Stacey and said hello.

"Is this Allie Harper?"

The familiar voice of Gray-Sari Woman from last night.

The Messenger.

"Yes. And you're not blind."

A quiet, but palpable, disturbance-in-the-force from behind

me told me I ought to be having this conversation away from prying ears. "Are you safe where you are?"

"You want to know the truth? I don't think I'm safe anyplace in this world right now. But I've been as careful as I can. Why?"

"This"—I turned, smiled, and nodded at my frozen hostess—"is not a good place for a conversation. I'm—hogging their phone. But we do need to talk, and it sounds like you already know why. Give me your number. I'll call you back in fifteen seconds."

"I'd rather call you."

I gave her my number and passed the restaurant's receiver back to Stacey. Smiled a thank you. She smiled back. Tentative. Polite. Civilian.

My phone rang. I cleared the door of Provenance in the three seconds it took me to answer it. I sensed Otis falling in behind me.

"Okay. Now. Can you tell me your name and where you are?"

"Not so fast." Her voice quavered. "I have something else I have got to tell you first."

Here came the unintended consequence of Otis's "trick" with the camera footage: This woman, whoever she was, whatever her motivation for coming here last night, was not a complete stranger to me. I had walked through the museum with her, run with her from the alarms, shared her frisson of fear when she saw Tito Ricci sitting at a table. Saw him through her eyes before I was willing to admit it to myself he could be here again.

Tito Ricci chilled me too. This woman and I were Sisters in Tito.

I sighed. I hoped this sigh made it through the ether with all its empathy and compassion intact.

"I know. You were a pawn in somebody else's game. Believe me, I know him. He's the Pawn-Master. He convinced you it was a silly prank. You never in a million years thought anybody would get hurt, let alone shot dead. You're horrified. And you're not a bad person. He promised you a lot of money for a small favor. You only—"

A thrill of recognition lighted up my neck-tingle again. I heard the echo of my own voice saying, *It's showtime!*

"You're an actress? *Actor*. Aren't you? It's why you were so believable. So good. Last night was a role for you. It was a—a gig."

It was her turn to get the tingle. I heard it in her gasp. "Do you know about me? Do you know who I am? How—"

"No. Only what I said there. I have experience with that guy too, and the actor part makes sense. Did you meet him? I'm pretty sure what he looks like. Can you describe him?"

I waited for Tito. Tall, dark, and contemptible. Good looking if you could go for a carefully polished, expensively dressed, unregenerate, bullying, menacing thug. Which once upon a time, I had. But we weren't discussing D.B. Harper.

Not talking Tito, either, as it turned out.

"About the fittest man I've ever seen. Very blond—white-blond—hair. Like Swedish children. Pale eyes too. Gray, maybe? Almost silvery—Not super tall. Five ten, maybe? For sure not six. Very composed. Not scary. Exactly. Although I was spooked. No smile. Not fun. Not very much anything. Neutral. Like clear water. Cold, though." Her tone turned angry. "Colder than the ninth circle of hell."

Ha. The Judas Circle. She read Dante. I read Dante. I liked her already.

"He wore that outfit guys who work out all the time wear. During the three hours of the day they're not working out. Ripstop? Black. And a killer jacket. Looked like it would repel everything and be warm."

"What did he say?"

"Not much. We met in a bar. Nobody around, but no chit-chat for him. He told me what, when, where, and set up a time for 'cane training and wardrobe.' He said not to worry. He said the only people there who could figure out I was pretending to blind would be blind. And I only had to be partially blind for that role. And then there you were."

"Okay. Look. What can I call you? Doesn't have to be your real name."

"Gloria. That's my real name."

"Gloria, tell me where you are. Is your phone even half secure?"

"It should be. Trackfone®. I bought it for twenty bucks this morning."

"Good. Where are you? We'll come get you. To be upfront, I'm bringing my bodyguard and probably at least one police officer. He's a nice guy named Tony, but they'll both be armed, so if you're planning—"

"I'm planning to live at least another day or two, Allie. I'm thrilled to hear about cops with guns. Have them bring extra. I'm...I'm at a friend's place. Apartment a half block off Lee."

She gave me the address.

"Gloria. Lock the door and don't pick up your phone unless you're certain it's me. Does your new phone have my number on it now?" She thought so. I gave it to her again anyway. Safe side.

"How did you know to call me here?"

"I have a friend who works at the museum. In their restaurant. That's how I got the—gig. I called her this morning to see what was happening. I knew something went wrong—something bad. I barely made it out of there last night. It was a damn disaster movie.

"I know they're—the police—are looking for me. Sta—my friend told me you all were holed up in the banquet room today. Don't get her in trouble. Please."

"Stacey."

Daughter. I'd bet the farm.

"Yeah. Just—don't."

"I promise. She's lovely, Gloria."

"Uh huh." A whisper of tears. She clicked off.

————

I stood at the edge of the atrium, under Otis's watchful eye. Shuffling the clutter of my confusion and fear, absorbing the normalcy of today's café lunch-ers and sore feet rest-ers, squinting at their devices in the dazzle from the ceiling. The sun had come out and was streaming its light in on us, gilding everything. Last night's frantic, milling crowd might never have been here. The building was healing itself. I could use some of that.

Jeptha Wade had donated this land for a museum in 1916 "For the Benefit of All the People Forever." Was his promise being held for ransom today? By an obscene beast of a man? Would it take Tom's money to keep it safe?

I knew us. Tom would pay. I would pay. Even if the money couldn't save us, it might save this.

I veered back to "Jeptha *Wade*?" A name bound to be on a few minds around town this afternoon. Was Kip Wade one of Those Wades? They were icons in the city's history. Tito, the status-seeking social climber with his designer everything and his cloying Rich Guy Cologne, would be aware. But where would a man like Tito meet a man like Kip?

Back inside Provenance, the reception desk was unattended. We asked the bartender. Otis checked in the kitchen. Stacey was nowhere. "On her break, maybe?"

Maybe.

Maybe Gloria Somebody was in more trouble than she knew.

Chapter Fifteen

I filled everybody in on Gloria's story.

"I believed her. At least enough to go fish her out of an apartment she's hiding in up by Lee. You agree, don't you, Lieutenant?"

"She's a person of interest with information we need. And, besides that, she was involved in a scheme with your Tito. You've convinced me he tends to be a death sentence for his associates."

We exchanged that glance again.

Kill the messenger.

"Let's go get her." She stood. "All of us. Tony and Otis for security. Tom, because he's my new secret weapon."

Olivia was great. Maybe she'd keep us all alive.

Right before I got Gloria's call, we'd ordered lunch. I was getting the "goat cheese stuffed lamb burger with apricot jam, shaved fennel, and potato wedge." That one had me from "burger." Also "potato wedge." An ordinary girl with sudden, unexpected access to lottery millions will simply move upscale on the burger and fries. You can take her out of McDonald's, but—

You heard it here.

As we trailed through Provenance, I caught a glimpse of our food being delivered to our vacated room. It looked good.

———

When is an Escalade more than an Escalade? When it's a brand new Escalade ESV, built to seat seven. 4-Wheel Drive. 3-Zone Climate Control. Swarming with options and amenities. The new car's color was the inevitable black. The ultimate badge of SUV intimidation. "Black Raven" this time. "Ice Black," the shade of the Escalade we traded in for this better, roomier one, was "not available" on this model. As far as Cadillac and Otis were concerned, Black Raven was the new Ice Black. I decided to secretly think of it as "Iced Raven." Or "Raven On The Rocks."

I was unconditionally onboard with our new vehicle. It was another luxury tank.

Today was the vindication of Otis's "we gotta get us more room." On this trip, once we gathered up Gloria, there'd be six of us. Tinted windows were good too. Tailor-made for transporting Gloria No Last Name. The woman most likely to be next on Tito's hit list.

Otis drove. Valerio called shotgun. Tom and I commandeered the second row of supple, expensive-smelling, black leather bucket seats. Detective Wood was stuck back in coach. We figured on putting Gloria in the center of the third row. I'd go back with them once we had her. We weren't returning to the museum. Day would be done before we got everyone sorted.

The "not going back" was the best part of my day so far.

My shameful preoccupation, as we pulled out of Wade Oval Drive onto East Boulevard, rolling like an invasion force, was the lunch we'd abandoned in our rush to get to Gloria. The goat cheese-stuffed burger was on my mind and, by this point, I'd escalated from too nervous to be hungry to ravening wolf. My wolf was growling.

At Severance Hall crime scene tape—about a mile of it— fluttered in the bitter wind. Everyone but Tom and I turned to stare. I was studying the slope down to the plaza where Kip's body no longer lay. Shadows cast by bare branches. Yellow tape everywhere down there too. I imagined an assassin on the parapet above us, looking down, and for a split second we were driving through his line of fire.

Otis made a left onto Euclid and headed east, past the Church of the Covenant to the intersection where Mayfield and Euclid meet. Tom, Otis, and I studied a map of this intersection on the first day of the first case of the newbie T&A Detective Agency. I would always think of that map as "The "Ouija Board of Death." A spike of dread stoked my uneasiness about Gloria.

Tito had disposed of witnesses a shocking number of times. Gloria had seen him. He'd seen her right back. Face-to-face. She'd also spent face-to-face-time with his ice-cold associate, whom I was ready to designate "Tito's Sniper."

They'd never let a loose end slide.

———

Traffic up Mayfield was ugly. Otis drove as fast as he could, pushing his luck against the lights. A couple of times it worked, but when you're stuck, you're stuck. Every delightful Little Italy eatery we were creeping by was vying for my attention with pizza, pasta, and pastries. I'd lost my appetite.

My hands were sweaty from gripping the leather armrests. My foot pressed down hard on a phantom accelerator. My heart pounded as if I'd been running. Gloria would be counting the seconds until we'd show up and pull her out of there—

The hesitation I'd heard in her voice. When she told me she'd be waiting in "...a friend's place on Lee." That pause nagged at me.

Let it go, Allie.

I'd been with Gloria—*been Gloria*—last night, until the moment she'd flung herself out the door into the flashing vortex of lights. Howling with sirens. Her sirens and my sirens were the same sirens. Her night would have been a wakeful sequence of realizations about what she'd been a key part of. Worrying about Stacey. Wondering if she was okay. Afraid to call.

Her scariest moment would be counting down right now. The escape hatch to safety opening in front of her. The cavalry so close. Maybe an awareness of danger rushing toward her too.

Go, Otis, go.

Chapter Sixteen

4:10 P.M.

In the sharp, clean afternoon light, the two-story red brick apartment building, a half block around the corner from Lee, looked 100 percent normal. A crisp, white pediment framed the door. Wide picture windows stared onto the street. From the front walk, I called Gloria's new phone.

No answer.

The door opened into a small entryway, like an airlock, We stood inside for a moment. Waiting. Listening. I smelled air freshener and bacon, and my stomach turned over. Not in a hungry way. Somewhere above our heads a phone was ringing, but no one picked up.

The inner door was supposed to protect the residents from unknown visitors. To block us. Make us identify ourselves. Wait to be buzzed through.

It was ajar.

Tony and Olivia left Tom, Otis, and me in the downstairs hall and started quietly on up, hands resting on service revolvers. One of the steps groaned, loud as a slammed door in the anxious silence. They stopped, waited, listened, started again. I let the phone keep ringing. It wasn't set up to roll over for messages. She hadn't had time.

My chest was too tight for a normal breath. I tried to hear what Tony and Olivia could hear, but my ears were occupied with the droning ring and the racket my heart was making. I figured pedestrians out on Lee could hear that. After ten or fifteen seconds, Tony yelled, "Police!"

Nobody answered. A door banged against a wall. More footsteps. Olivia's "Gloria? It's us. Allie's with us. It's safe to come out," echoed down the empty stairwell. A pause. Another short walk. Another door banged. After another few seconds, the phone quit. More silence. Olivia came to the top of the stairs, wearing gloves and holding the silent phone. Our answer was on her face.

"I'm sorry."

———

It was a crime scene.

Otis, Tom, and I had to wait outside the door. As far as I was concerned, this was a blessing. I was fine with the hall. Almost the entire apartment was visible from where we stood. The kitchen and living room were small and tidy. The bedroom door was open, but Valerio had placed himself between me and anything I didn't need to see.

I examined the living room. Systematically. Like a detective. Made note of the cheery colors. The battered recliner. A quilt assembled by a beginner. Lots of books. In the kitchen, cat dishes—food and water. A pottery mug, with the teabag still in it, overturned on the counter. The only sound in the place, besides distant street noise and Tony and Olivia's hushed conversation from the bedroom, was the drops of tea hitting the floor.

I did not need to confirm that Gloria was dead. I cautioned myself not to look, but Tony stepped out of the doorway and left me alone with a moment that imprinted itself on my memory before I could turn away.

Gloria, the actor, had been trained, I was sure, to craft any gesture as an eloquent communication. Especially in a death scene. Gloria's killer had broken her and thrown her aside with such violence her lifeless body spoke only of awkward disarray. Her grace and human dignity lay in a battered heap on the floor. I staggered backwards into the hall. Tom caught me. Held me tight. Offered no words of comfort.

———

Olivia had a brief conversation with somebody at the Cleveland Heights PD and we all went outdoors to wait. When the squad car pulled up, Olivia and Tony met them, shook hands, told them what we knew, and turned the scene over to them.

Tony said, "See if you can locate the cat. Ask the neighbors."

We looked for Gloria's friend's name on the bank of mail boxes inside the hall and found "Gloria Kostas Apt. 203."

I cringed. Otis swore under his breath.

"They coulda looked her up on Whitepages.com."

Olivia called downtown and told them where to start searching for Stacey "maybe last name Kostas" and to find out what she knew. She ended the conversation with, "This is a murder investigation and that young woman is at risk. Find her. She might come here, to the apartment. Call me when you've talked to her. And, Frank, listen. Her mother is dead—Just—Be kind."

Otis drove. Shadows crept out onto the street. The sense of warmth the bright afternoon sun gave us was draining from the day. Storefronts and houses stood transfixed by the failing light. Nobody talked. Tom hadn't had anything to say since before Little Italy. I thought his mood was probably darker and more desolate than his blindness. None of us had anything to offer any of us.

Something inside me—maybe Lee Ann Smith—seized control of my dull frozenness. Wouldn't let me off the hook.

You're her witness here. Don't leave her like that.

This morning I'd believed I was looking through Gloria's eyes—She was still with me. I was still with her.

I am filling this cup with the boiling water.

I'm unwrapping the teabag, keeping my fingers steady as I can. All my attention is on this tea. The color of the tea. The smell of the tea. Spice. Citrus—breathing it. I'm so scared. They're coming to take me someplace safe. They're almost here right now. With guns. She promised. By the time this tea is brewed they'll be here. I'm ready. My things are packed. I'm fine. I'll be fine. By the time this tea is brewed, I'll be—

Otis drove us on into the dusk.

———

Tony's squad car was still in our garage. He refused our transparently insincere offer of a beer and drove away, promising to deliver Lieutenant Wood wherever she wanted to go. She wasn't talking either. Not interested in a beer. I wondered how our homicide detective would be evaluating the T&A this evening. B-minus. Maybe C+, was my guess. Early days.

The security duo in the garage greeted us. The welcome mat was still out.

Down to three, we got ourselves beers, sat at the kitchen bar, and didn't bother to drink them. We waited, not saying anything significant, until Tom's watch responded to his touch, "It's nine-oh-five!"

Said our subdued good nights.

Otis went to close up, sign off with his team in the garage, and head on down to his place. He was gone for ten minutes, during which Tom and I sat, not talking, too disheartened to move. Otis came back to us with something way more healing than beer.

Otis's home in the new residence was the man cave *par excellence* in the basement. Although calling an entire floor, only partially below grade, impeccably finished with wood, tile and stone, heavily appointed with Crate and Barrel's finest, and featuring a state-of-the-art lounging and TV area, plus a game room with video and pool table, master-size bedroom with full bath, over-stocked kitchen, and a well-equipped laundry, "the basement" was a massive understatement. It was The Otis Johnson Level of this place. He'd let us visit, kick back, enjoy his spectacular in-your-face view of lake, patios, and pool, but the power of invitation was his, and he always had the right to throw us out.

The most valuable thing in The Cave of Otis, according to him, was his complete collection of the full flavor-range of Mitchell's Ice Cream. Otis's Mitchell's was stored in a spare freezer in his personal kitchen, next to his personal workout room. Where he kept his calories paid off.

Many flavors on demand was one of the perks of sharing a house with Otis. He stocked it. Tom paid. We all shared.

"What's the point of being stupid rich?" He would ask as we sat around licking our spoons. "If you can't buy yourself some fine ice cream? In many, many flavors? And keep it close at hand?"

The Key Lime wasn't enough to make me not want to run and scream, but it helped. Otis knew it was my favorite. That he knew this about me, and brought it to me on this wretched occasion, was sweeter than the taste of lime.

In bed at last, with the house silent, and the waves outside about as shushed as waves ever get, I closed my eyes, snuggled my body against the sleeping warmth of Tom Bennington, and told all the day's voices, "Good night and shut up."

Chapter Seventeen

FRIDAY, MARCH 2

9:00 A.M.

"Tom, are you absolutely positive this sniper person didn't shoot at the wrong shoes?"

Margo Gallucci. Unedited. Unrestrained. Unapologetic.

She'd appeared in time for breakfast. About fifteen minutes after Valerio. I felt free to speculate about that in my imagination, but I didn't raise the slightest suggestion of an eyebrow. At either one of them. Survival of the discreet-est.

Margo was rolling. She barely paused for coffee and an ample helping of steel cut oats with brown sugar and fruit, before launching the Margo Interrogation Barrage.

"I talked to Lisa Cole, and Lisa said she heard the dead man was wearing Brunello Cucinellis. Those shoes holler 'rich guy'. 'Lottery winner *rich* guy. Lottery winner rich *blind* guy.'"

Margo and Lisa Cole were our brand-name shoe mavens. I could identify expensive, and even wear it sometimes, but I wasn't on first name terms with it. Yet. My fancy mad-spiked boots quit speaking to me yesterday morning because I'd slopped them through rain and slush in Wade Park the night before. They needed a shoe doctor and maybe a shoe social worker to find them a more stable home.

Margo was a looser loose cannon than me, but her sharp instincts and her willingness to throw it all out there could be a bonus. Usually, she brought an interesting mix to the party. As a semi-official member of the T&A, Margo was both my inspiration and my red flag. Smart. Lots of energy. No mouth brakes.

"Tom? Do you believe you were the target?"

"Let's all stop worrying about that. Survey Monkey says no, Margo. 99.99 percent. We have bigger fish to fry."

Margo beamed at him and shifted gears. "Ha. Fantastic. Does that mean this a case for the T&A?"

So much for keeping Margo out of the loop.

I caved. "Yes, Margo. Tony, would you care to explain how this is going to work?"

"Not really."

Tony's increasing personal interest in Margo was incrementally decreasing his enthusiasm for getting her deeper into the T&A. "Personal interest" was a euphemism.

Margo glared at Tony.

His motivation for stonewalling seemed uncharacteristically romantic, so I covered for him. "We think the murder was a message, Margo. For Tom. The fact that the dead guy was blind and resembled Tom does suggest it."

The rest of us already had a minute or two to absorb an act of such cold-blooded cruelty. Margo was horrified. Also unleashed. Zero to sixty. Three seconds or less. I braced myself.

"A message? Somebody killed a human *being* so he could be a fucking *message*?" She stopped. Simmering. I could see she was torn between demanding more information and trying to digest what she had. Or breaking something.

I waited, examining Margo's face and general body language for a clue to what might be coming next. Once she got going,

Loose Cannon Vigilante Numero Uno could swear like a sailor.
Or Lisa Cole. If those two ever joined forces with Lee Ann we'd
all be toast.

Wrapped in one of her signature scarlet shawls and flushed
with fury at Tito's callousness, my former landlady was Margo-
gorgeous. With lake and sky raging away at the windows behind
her, she could have stepped out of one of those Italian mas-
terpieces. Titian, today. Maybe. Not the really holy ones. At
fifty-something-give-or-take, Margo was in full command of her
creamy complexion, her carelessly fabulous hairdo, and her dark,
expressive eyes. Which were back to flashing again.

"You all get what this means, right? You'd have to be blind—
Crap. Sorry, Tom. Never mind. We all know who has the—the
what do we call it?—'the means, the motive, and the evil' to send
a message by killing a guy who could be mistaken for you, Tom.
I'll tell you who. Mr. Handcrafted Vodka, that's who. Mr. Fucking
Tito. He's back."

She swept us with a satisfied smile. "'Catch Fucking Tito.'
That's our next case. The T&A needs to meet. I'll cook. It'll be
pasta fagioli this time. Warm everybody up."

Margo was getting dangerously energized by the possibility
of a new case. Jumping into her leading role: Den Mother of
the T&A. I was less than gung ho. We'd tried to catch Tito once
already. Major fail. And I had news I was sure would bring her
down. And set her off again.

"Margo."

"Margo, what?"

Although I was certainly not going to ask any awkward questions about anybody's love life this morning, I could tell Tony
had sketched in a few of the events of the past two days for her.
Not all. He'd left out the "murder message" part, and the woman
bouncing at me now hadn't heard about Gloria either.

She'd heard the lump of lead in my throat, though.

"Allie. Something bad."

"Yes. The woman who pretended to be blind and brought me the note at the museum—"

"The woman in the Indian outfit?"

"Yes."

"She's dead. He killed her too?"

"It looks that way. Probably his associate—"

"That *fucking* sniper?"

Margo swore a lot when she was about to cry too.

I noticed Tony fidgeting in his chair. Steering around what Margo had and had not heard from him was getting to be a navigational challenge for all of us. Officer Anthony Valerio needed to man up and admit they were an item. So he and I could compare notes on how to contain the Margo detonations. He was almost family.

"You found her?"

"Yes. Yesterday afternoon. Her name was Gloria. She was— She wasn't a bad person, Margo. She was an actor. They tricked her. She thought it was a prank."

"*Bastards.* And you think this will scare me off."

"Margo." Tom's expression conceded the contest. *Hands up. I surrender.* "We wouldn't know where to start."

"Thanks, Tom. We're good then. I'm outta here. I need to strategize. No worries. I got this.

Behind her back, Tony rolled his eyes.

I rolled mine right back. *Coward.*

Chapter Eighteen

"We could close all the blinds."

Paranoia was back. Every square foot of our seven thousand darling, hospitable feet, plus the half acre or so of decks, patios, pool, hot tub, piney woods, lawn, and beach—all of it—was ground zero for me this afternoon.

The real estate agent who believed "Stunning below-window cabinets open the kitchen to the lake view" was a fabulous selling point wasn't standing at our sink today. I wanted our stunning views shut down for the duration. It didn't help that Otis, Tom, and I were having our strategy session in the kitchen.

Double-crossed and cranky, the me who longed to be home free and happy was crying on the inside and sulking on the outside. I'd been kidding myself. The lull in the action of "Tito's Revenge" was a fifteen-minute intermission. Not enough time for a decent box of popcorn.

Tito's return was as inevitable as a rock falling off a cliff. He was crazy-furious with us for screwing up his master heist last summer. His monstrous message Wednesday night was a preview of what he had in mind for us.

Kip was dead. Gloria was dead. What next? Who next?

My request for full-house-window-blind-deployment got

turned down flat. Otis and Tom both ganged up on my chicken-heart. I hadn't expected that from Tom.

"Cut me a little slack, you guys. We've never had a sniper before."

Otis answered my whining with sniper logic. "Allie, don't kid yourself. He's been 'our sniper' for a while. Could have been around for weeks, observing every inch of this house not hidden by trees and other obstructions. From so far away you wouldn't believe. These guys don't play.

"I feel strangely uncomforted, Otis. Do we think he used his scope to watch me undress?"

"Allie."

"Tom? You too? I'd have expected you—"

"To what? Be obsessed with how somebody might say, 'Poor Tom. He didn't see it coming?'"

"I'm sorry Tom. I—"

"Allie. I'm not dismissing your fears—"

My pride was ruffled now. "Well. It's not *fear*. Exactly—"

No, you pathetic baby. It's blubbering, wet-your-pants terror. Alice Jane's a baby. Alice Jane's a Ba—

I kicked her out. Lee Ann had a knack for showing up when I needed her least.

My phobia about being spied on was a holdover from nights my little-kid-self had to walk all alone past the dark, cold, rubbernecking windows of our old house on my way to bed. A truck out on the highway would moan or a wind-stirred branch scrape skeletal fingers along the glass. I never knew when my brother Justin, the future preacher, would pop up, yelling, and bang on the windows to send me screaming up the stairs in my footie pj's. Lee Ann mocked me back then too.

I shouldered them both out of my head. All grown up now.

"You're right. I'm scared. I need to get used to it again."

Tom sighed. "We're all scared, Allie. It's a side effect of brains. But here's a twist. If our sniper weren't a smart, well-trained, precision-oriented sniper, he might have shot me already, by mistake. And I would be dead instead of Kip. The only consolation I can think of is Tito's scheme, whatever it is, would be dead too."

"So we're lucky he's good at his job?"

"I guess I'm lucky he's not careless. The bad luck was all Kip's Wednesday night. Whatever he was up to, he didn't deserve that."

"So we can't do anything to make us more secure." Small whine.

"Never said that, Allie. There's plenty. I'm staffing up right now."

Otis had a plan. Until today our pair of security guys worked eight-hour shifts. Two at a time in the control room, watching monitors. Our floodlights—tastefully concealed—were installed outside last fall. We'd only tried them once. If not for the pine trees, the house, and the lake—and, of course, the other houses—you could have landed a 737. Anybody breaking our perimeter would set off an alarm and if the guard in the security room didn't like what he saw on the monitors, he or she would hit the lights.

They referred to the setup as "Bambi Cam." Two guards, around the clock seemed silly this winter. Overkill. Until now. The good old days.

Going forward, we'd have two extra guards on each of the shifts. Along with the duo in the security room, there'd be one in the gatehouse and one free-range on the grounds. With a dog. I was jazzed about the dog.

Otis couldn't flat out steal all his man- or woman-power from the Cleveland Police Department, but he could woo some ex-cop security guards he'd known with a fine opportunity. He was running their work histories every which way. I wouldn't want to try to sneak even a minor shoplifting charge past Otis.

Fortunately, I'd never been caught. Except by old righteous Justin. He'd scared me straight when I was fifteen or so, after he'd started walking his pain-in-the-ass path of righteousness. No doubt, I owed him one. Or Lee Ann, Miss Oil Slick Smith, did.

"Oh, hell. Get over it, Allie. It wasn't a Mercedes, or anything."

———

Early Friday evening, a new gate guy arrived at the front door with the mail. I was waiting for him under the cover of gathering shadows in our foyer, watching night fall onto our woodsy front yard, smothering the dreariness of the day.

He waved his bundle at me.

In the light from the rustic hobbit-lantern, I could see it was the usual straight-to-recycling flyers and the daily brochure exclaiming, "Yes! Viking is still offering both river and ocean cruises!"

For a few heartbeats I indulged myself in imagining that at this very moment, on this very night, a person with the means to buy a ticket—me—might be standing by a polished railing in the embrace of the sexy, handsome blind man she loves—Thomas Bennington III. A warm breeze, tangles up her carefree hair as a blood-orange slice of sun vanishes into the sea. That breeze also brings her the seductive aromas from the "Chow-down-because-you-sure-enough-paid-an-arm-and-a-leg-for-it" complementary buffet.

I won't lie. Every part of this fantasy made my knees weak with yearning.

I opened the door. Gate guy was grinning ear to ear.

"Ms. Harper, you've got an admirer." He held up a small envelope, put it to his nose, and then waved it in the air. "Mmm Mmm."

A sharp, venomous sting in my chest.

"Oh. Hey. Put that down, will you? The floor is fine."

The grin vanished. He laid the letter on the stone of the foyer. "What is it?"

I inched closer. I could read the name in elegant script above the address.

Alice Jane Harper

My heart slipped sideways.

"It's 1872, 'One of the world's most expensive colognes.'"

The smell of terror.

"The man we're supposed to be looking out for? It's from him?"

My stomach churned. My worst memory wore that fragrance. I choked on the answer. "Yes. Tito—Tito Ricci. Not his real name."

Tom burst out of the kitchen, moving swiftly along the path we all kept uncluttered for him. Molecules of that pricey cologne must have reached him two rooms away. Blind Spidey didn't need more than one or two. His arms were around me the second before I started crying.

I burrowed into the front of his shirt, as if he could keep us both safe in there, and sobbed. "He hates us, Tom. He wants us dead."

"He hates me, Allie. It's me he wants—"

"Same difference. Couldn't we box up the damn money and mail it to him?"

"Hey," He was rocking me as if the gate guy and the envelope were a hundred miles away. "Shh. Shh. We're here. We're safe. We're going to fix this."

I roused myself to make a disparaging remark, but he cut it off with another "Shhhh."

To the guy he said, "Can you get Otis? Tell him we need the crime scene folks to open this envelope." He frowned for a second. "And bring a bowl or a lid or something from the kitchen to trap that stink."

Chapter Nineteen

10:45 P.M.

The envelope had left the building.

Once the shock wore off, I was willing to bet the only weapon in there was a fragrance overdose and a nasty note. At that moment, cooling our heels, awaiting the arrival of a fresh threat or cruel jibe, we were as safe we'd ever be.

Ironically, our "competent sniper" talk had cheered me up. Helped me see the logic. Tito had no plans to kill us tonight. He'd wait. Make us cringe and beg. Sooner or later, he'd be targeting Tom's money. Then he'd do his damnedest to make sure we died in a scenario that would pay off his rage in full. Right now, tonight, he was satisfied to wound us, jerk us around, watch us suffer. Send us scary notes. He was obsessed with his game. We all said so.

I posed my next question. "And what game do we think that is?"

Since Tom and Otis had signed me onto their view that hiding was stupid and pointless, we were hanging out in the breakfast nook off our kitchen. First of all, it was not remotely "a nook." More of a fancy English greenhouse with grand aspirations. Lots of old-world flavor, not as Tudor-tastic as the house, but not so Victorian as to be out of step.

It connected to the lake side of the kitchen like a pleasant sunroom or perhaps a small, tasteful wedding chapel. Made of glass. A windowed cupola on top. Ceiling fan. No steeple. In spite of my optimism that we'd survive till morning, I wasn't perfectly relaxed. People who live in glass houses should not piss off snipers.

The former owners left us the nook's furniture when they moved on up to a bigger house, which, I'd heard the wife tell our real estate agent—when she thought I wasn't listening—was "much, much nicer." Maybe she dreamed she'd find fulfillment in another couple thousand square feet. With a grander pedigree. I could have warned her about the creepy factor of those venerable piles, but I didn't like her much.

The bronzed-wicker arrangement in our glass house was "Upscale Twenty-first Century Porch." Pottery Barn, my guess. Breakfast set, a seating area populated with a couch and comfy chairs, and—in keeping with the all glass/all the time décor—a glass-topped coffee table. In days of peace and warm weather, our view of decks, pool, lawn, and lake would be dazzling. Tonight, I had no use for it.

At least we'd all scored Coronas. With limes. Tostitos too. Also, Otis's homemade salsa. Plus, I could verify how alive Tom was. How warm and breathing. His arm was around my shoulders. The lights were low as they'd go. In the glinting blackness of the glass the three of us looked tired and vulnerable. Kinda like sitting ducks.

Stop it, Alice Jane.

I closed my eyes and felt a slow, steady pulse on the spot where Tom's wrist lay against my arm. Vital signs.

Otis knocked my lulled state of mind down a notch by saying, "It's different this time."

I opened my eyes.

Tom shook his head. "Otis. You said that last time."

"Yeah, well. A lot of the guys who went after you in your first summer were yahoos. But last summer was stage-one different. Unrelated incidents connected by a plan and a person we couldn't see. Tito, behind the scenes. And last time, it didn't feel as personal. I don't pretend to understand everything that's shifted, but this is different."

I wished I could see Otis's face better so could read it. I gave up, leaned more into Tom, and let the beer sink in. Closed my eyes back. The last traces of 1872 had dispersed. We'd let the front door stand open for a while—under guard—until the windy night blew it way. I could breathe again.

Otis was pursuing his "Tito is different this time" theory.

"Last summer was systematically vicious, but not emotional. When he killed, it was kinda surgical. Strategic. Cold. He had a plan and he worked it. Somebody got in his way? He'd take them out. Plenty awful, but not over-the-top angry, like he looks to be now."

I opened my eyes. "Except for—" I threw in.

"Yeah, Allie. Him. That last one he killed before he took off in July. Let's forget for a second it was murder. It was dumb. And Tito was smart. Right up to that last day.

I shivered. Tom rubbed my arm. First aid for frostbite of the heart.

Otis kept going. "Made no sense to wipe out that level of asset. Once-in-a-lifetime genius hacker capabilities? And we know that the dude and Tito were perfect for each other. Batman and Robin on the dark side. Two rotten peas in a nasty pod.

"Based on what you told us, Allie, Tito lost it in the moment. Bad timing. That protégé of his would be even more valuable to him now. Everything fell apart for him. Heavy losses. The millions he'd planned to get from you. The money from his very efficient scrapper/drug ring. And the one guy who could have helped him pick up the pieces and get back on track? Dead because Tito lost it. He's probably extra pissed at you guys about that."

"But we didn't—That's not—"

"Logical, Allie?" He rested his case. "And here we are. Stage Two."

I sat with that. "The opposite of logical, Otis."

"Yep. Tito is back. And this time he's not the clever dude. He's burning mad enough to go out of control. Working a plan that's already kinda stupid-elaborate. Look, Tom. If he wanted your money, all he'd have to do is get to Allie, am I right."

"Yes, Otis. You are."

"*Ow*, Otis."

Otis blew by my dismay. "And if he'd started back in January when we were relieved and careless. He'd could have her by now. Given how she—Allie, you know you tend to go a little bit—"

"Stir crazy? Off the rails?" I closed my eyes back, slunk deeper into my chair. This line of inquiry sucked.

"No future in beating yourself up." I heard him help himself to a handful of the chips. A pause for crunching. A swallow of beer. I wasn't Blind Spidey, but I was practicing. Otis clunked the beer bottle down. I judged it to be empty. "We're clear who we're dealing with. But we don't have a clue what he's going to do next. Because—"

"If you're right, Otis," I followed his line of thinking to the scariest conclusion I could come up with. It fit. "He's got no logical plan about that either."

"We're guessing, but that works," Tom agreed. "He wants to mess with us. Terrorize us. Threaten us. Demand the money—I can't see exactly what his demands will be. But I—we—have a lot to lose. I don't like this any more than you do, Allie. But I'm not delusional. We're both logical targets because he's angry about everything that didn't work out last time. Especially his dead hacker. He's bringing it straight to us.

"That's bad enough. But here's maybe the most disturbing thing. He led off with this—I don't know how to refer to it— this surrogate murder, maybe? What Margo said. 'He killed a human being as a fucking message.' Looks like it was designed to make it a bigger statement than merely '*Oh look, Tom. Be very afraid.*'"

I knew what he meant.

For the Benefit of All the People Forever.

"Yeah, Tom. The museum is the focal point so far. Maybe something about it—how people are drawn to it—sparks his anger. He could easily find out we go there, but maybe it was simply the perfect backdrop for the murder of Kip. Whether Kip was a 'Jeptha Wade' Wade or not, it would tickle Tito's sick fancy to shoot a Wade by the Wade Lagoon in Wade Park."

"That's Otis's Stage Two Tito. Again. He did a high-profile thing in a high-profile way. In a high-everything location. The elaborately orchestrated public spectacle of the killing of a guy who could be me. He picked a very large canvas. University Circle. But it's not pragmatic. It's not smart. The timing is the slightest bit different? Sniper shoots me and not Kip? Game over."

Otis's cell phone went off.

His ringtone told you one thing: "Someone is calling." It sounded like a phone. Ringing. As a fan of playful musical self-expression, I found Otis's unimaginative relationship to ringtones disappointing. Sad, even.

He picked up. "Otis Johnson." His face was set to unreadable. "Yes. Uh huh. Okay. Sure. Go ahead." He listened. "Uh huh." He clicked off.

I knew what was coming.

"They opened it," I told him.

"Yeah."

"They read it to you."

"Yeah."

"Are you going to share it with us?"

"I suppose. It doesn't mean anything."

"Tell us, Otis. C'mon. The suspense is killing me." Tom. Annoyed. Resigned.

The subdued lighting in the greenhouse was plenty bright enough to show me the shock on Otis's face.

"How did you—Tom? That's what it says."

"You're kidding. It actually *says*, 'The suspense is killing me?'"

"No. It says, *"The suspense is killing you."*

"Killing Tom?"

"No, Allie." Tom's face was set. "The envelope was addressed to you. He's saying the suspense is killing you."

"What does that even mean?"

Otis answered me. "We're guessing on dangerous ground now, but maybe he's saying that this time the suspense is about killing you. That you're his target this time."

To my surprise, Tom laughed. It wasn't the happiest sound I ever heard but it made the top ten most confusing. I was stung. "You think that's funny, Tom?"

"Oh, quit, Allie. It's a joke. A bluff. He's messing with us. You're his ace and he knows it. Even Otis's 'Stage Two Tito' would never play that one now. If he killed you, I wouldn't give a shit what else he did. This is nuts. I wish we knew how his mind works. What he's all about."

I thought I might be able to get us some answers. "Toss me your boring phone, Otis. I'm making a call."

———

I needed a shrink, but not for me this time.

In the wake of D.B. Harper, and before Tom, I'd found myself a wonderful therapist. She was a full-fledged psychiatrist too—which was probably overdoing it, but I was hoping for a prescription. Or two. Which I never got. She kept me on for a few extra months even after I couldn't afford her anymore. As a parting gift she offered me her "operating instructions for the solo flier."

"Breathe," Ruth told me. And she showed me how.

"Stop that, Allie. Don't just suck in air, blast it out, and go right back to being frantic. Do all this. The way I tell you. Do it five times. Don't be a dope about it."

It was an exercise she called, "In/Out. Deep/Slow. Calm/Ease. Smile/Release." A famous monk, Thich Nhat Hahn, taught it to children, she said. When I told her the smiling part was dumb and would make me feel silly, she told me to shut up and smile. "It's part of the practice. Stop shortchanging yourself by trying to be cool."

Then she'd told me to meditate too, and recommended an app—*An app. Holy crap*—to provide instruction. "Don't look at me like that. Pretend your little boat is sinking and I'm offering you those floaty things for your arms. I know you'd prefer a monastery in India, but sweetie, those are hard to get to and right now you don't even have the cash for therapy."

This pulled me up short. "Am I sinking? Am I that bad?"

"Allie Harper. Look at me. You're fine. You are a tough, resilient young woman. I wouldn't cut you loose if you were a sinking boat. But every soul on this Earth needs a refuge. This is my gift to you. Take it and use it. Like your life depends on it. It does, you know. 'Part-time bogus librarian' is not your calling. You have a terrific self to get to know. Now, get out of here before I cry too."

"Wow." I laughed to hide how touched I was. "Yoda. All this time I didn't know it was you." The tears kept spilling over. She handed me her box of tissues one last time and gave me a number I could call in an emergency. Plus a few tips on how to identify one of those. We hugged and said goodbye. I was on my own. Flying solo. Breathing as best I could.

Last summer, I called her for a consult. At least these days I could pay my way. That conversation was interesting but not all that shocking to Ruth. "No, Allie. Based on what you've told me, you do not have a so-called split personality. Lee Ann is a well-integrated part of your self-image. A strong, resourceful part. She's—spontaneous like you. She pops up and shoots off her mouth when you need access to the more...let's call them extemporaneous qualities of your younger, less-civilized self. She says the things you need to hear. She helps you be a powerful advocate for yourself. Listen to her sometimes. Only not in the cosmetics section of the drug store."

Tonight was an emergency. She said it was good to hear my voice which I doubted. It was late and she sounded tired.

"How can I help, Allie?"

"I need you to tell me what brand of crazy a guy is."

"Would you ask Lee Ann to give me a break. It's been a long day."

"Sorry. But this is actually for me. I think."

"Girl, you do know that 'brand of crazy' thing was a disaster in about a thousand different ways? Okay. Start over. Be specific. And, while you're at it, don't denigrate my other clients. And possibly yourself."

I was chastened. "Sorry, Ruth. Sometimes my mouth outruns my better nature."

"Sometime your feet do too, but I'm so happy to hear from you. Now. Rephrase. Start at the beginning. I happen to know I can charge you ten thousand dollars an hour these days so you might want to be concise."

"Okay. First of all, I'd be dead, maybe literally, without that breathing thing. So, thank you."

"Me too, as it turns out. You're welcome. Go on."

I filled her in on the new Tito. As we understood him to be. From the beginning. All the way to his latest message.

"How can we survive his—is it politically correct to call it his personality disorder? What *is* he? Like a sociopath or something?"

"Ah. Allie." She sighed. "This is a talk we should have face-to-face. Come to my office tomorrow morning? Seven or so? I don't have anyone on the books until ten."

"Oh, Ruth. I can't. This is—I don't know how to describe—. House arrest, maybe. There's security, but it's not—I'm stuck here."

"I'll come to you."

"No—You—"

"Allie. Shut up. I'm coming. I'm charging you ten thousand dollars an hour, but I'm coming."

"I'll send Otis. And he'll drive you to your office when we're done."

"I don't need—"

"Yeah, Ruth, you do."

A slight hesitation. "Okay. Have him pick me up at seven. I expect coffee. And probably donuts."

"Make him let you sit up front. It's a giant black Escalade. Leather seats. New car smell and everything. Like a high school make-out rendezvous."

A knowing grin in her voice. "And I thought Lee Ann wasn't around tonight."

Chapter Twenty

SATURDAY, MARCH 3

At six a.m. on Saturday—after a long, upsetting day and a short, restless night—Tom nudged awake me at by sliding his bare arm down over my naked back.

Carpe arm, Allie Harper.

"Want to go take a shower together?" he murmured. "Get this day off on the right foot?"

I skootched around to present my bare front to his naked arm. "Is that a euphemism?"

"I guess you'll find out."

His arm cleverly repositioned his hand. I slapped it. Lightly. "Stop it. Give me a second to mull this over. A lady wouldn't just—"

"Oh? Wouldn't she *just.*"

"Okay. Yeah. She would. Beat you there. Do you need any assistance, sir?"

"Nah. I can do this with my eyes closed."

———

He kissed me under the torrent of our "oversized-square-rainfall-showerhead." It was a fraction of an inch shy of twenty-four square inches. I was amazed the real estate agent hadn't led off her description of the house with that. For anyone who ever fantasized about making love to an irresistible man under a pouring waterfall on—oh, let's say Maui—without a lot of tourists gawking, this was the ultimate getaway.

Tom kissed me more, pulling me against him, letting the rush of warm water close us in. My knees stopped holding me up. I clasped my arms around his neck to stabilize the kissing and bring us into alignment.

"Tom, could we…lie down in here. It's supposed to be seven feet by four, and I want—"

"Yeah, me too. Let's see how it works."

It worked. Every which way. And far beyond expectations. Nobody drowned.

"Tom, it's better than Fiji. It's even better than the old mansion-y mansion."

"Agreed. I can't believe I mocked the former owner's fancy heated shower floor. Talk about blind. Let's stay in here until at least tomorrow."

"Nice try. Otis is bringing Ruth. And you need to wipe that look off your face."

"Is it a good look?"

"Uh huh. And a handsome face." I let my gaze travel down over him. Head to toes, he was perfect. "And a seriously great every-single-thing else."

I stomped on my judgment about how Tom was Italian-master gorgeous, and I was an unremarkable watercolor of an ordinary girl. Wet, frazzled, nothing special.

He had radar for that thought. Stood, smoothly, easily, and lifted me up against him. Buried his face in my tangled-up hair. Breathed me in as if he meant it. "I see you, Allie. Like sunlight." He reached behind us and turned off the rain.

"Go talk to Ruth. Meet me back here in a couple of hours."

"In your dreams, Thomas Bennington III, PhD."

"Always, Alice Jane."

———

No question in my mind, you could count the number of psychiatrists in Greater Cleveland who'd make a house call at seven a.m. on a Saturday on the finger of one finger. I was waiting for Ruth with a fresh cup of coffee. Otis had delivered her first cup—and, in spite of his no-crumb-in-car regulation, her donuts—in the truck. It was an extraordinary moment all around, and I was feeling exceptionally mentally, emotionally— and physically—well-adjusted.

She looked me over. "Better today? You look like—" Comment sidelined. "You look a lot happier than you sounded last night."

"Thank you, Dr. Freud."

"I imagine I'm not the one you should be thanking. Let's go for a walk. It's an amazing morning, and this is a spectacular place you've landed in."

"You sure? We have a sniper now."

"Did you look outside? It's snowing. Big. White. Fluffy. Visibility nil. Otis told me about your team." Concern flashed in her eyes. Quick and gone. "I think we can manage a walk. Let's go."

Outside, Ruth's big, white, fluffy flakes were coating the world. Our pine trees, already rimed with ice, had picked up a new layer. Our boots made a lovely crunch on the path. The trees smelled of pine.

We came out of the woodsy stuff at a line of widely spaced rocks, arranged for lake view appreciation in the warmer months. We brushed a couple off and sat, watching snow meet water and dissolve in a mist.

"Isn't this nicer than your gloomy old office?"

"Gloomy is in the eye of the beholder. You brought yours with you most of the time."

"Yeah. I know." I wanted to re-ask my question of the night before. Politically reword it. I was stalling, examining her face for land mines. The cold had blushed up her cheeks and brightened her eyes. I'd assumed they were brown but out here they matched her hooded wool coat. A sophisticated loden-ish green. The hood framed her hair, the reddish, brownish, gold I'd always admired. I figured Ruth Becker to be Margo's age. Apart from a healthy dose of feisty, she was the anti-Margo.

"What do you put on your hair to make it that color?"

"Genetics. Do you like it?"

"Yeah, it's unique."

"Nope. Look in the mirror. It's a half-shade off yours."

"Seriously. No way. But how do you make it lie down?"

"Professional secret."

"Psychiatric?"

"Cindy's Cut & Curl. You're deflecting, Allie. And the meter is at $4,000. Tell me what you want to talk about. I believe last night you were interested in brands of crazy."

"That was wrong. I'm sorry. We're trying to figure out what the new Tito is up to. What he'll do next. He's threatening to kill me, but Tom laughed."

She chuckled too. I wasn't getting a whole lot of respect around here. "Tom was right. Did he say you're the ace in Tito's hand? Whatever he's up to he's not dumb?"

"Yes. He said almost exactly that. But, given everything I've told you about Tito, what can you tell me about—his state of mind?"

"Almost nothing, Allie."

"But wouldn't it help us to know—"

"It might. And if I knew, I might tell you."

"But you're—"

"I'm what? A mind reader? You're asking me what this

guy—whom I've never met, never laid eyes on—is going to do next. I know this is a disappointment, but I'm not psychic."

"But—" I must have been radiating despair because she softened up.

"I know. You're looking for help and I would love to help you. Allie, I would do just about anything to make you safe. And the people you love. So I'll tell you what I can and you're going to be awfully disappointed."

"No. You—"

She raised a loden-green mitten like the bouncer at a bar.

"Hold up. Here goes. Listen. *You* already told *me* everything you need to know. You understand this Tito better than I ever will." She glanced behind us through the fog of snow. "Allie, is that your guy? With the dog? Like a sentry in a war movie? Patrolling?"

"Yeah. Kinda like that."

"God."

"Yeah. You were explaining what I already know."

"Okay. If I said Tito is bipolar or schizophrenic or whatever—which I am not saying. Not now. Not ever—you wouldn't be a bit safer. This man had a childhood, Allie. He had parents, whether he knew them or not, whether they were kind or cruel. Things happened to him. Terrible. Great. Things changed him. In moments you might not have noticed if you'd been right there beside him, he made major decisions about himself. What he wants and needs. What he fears. Now he's obsessed about you and Tom. He is the sum of all that. All. That.

"As are you. You're the sum of your life's experiences and the thoughts you've had about them, just like Tito. You're at least as obsessed with your Tom Bennington III as he is. In a healthier way. I think."

Her truth hit home. Talk about childish. I'd come running to her in desperation. As if I'd skinned my knee.

"I see. I do now. I'm sorry, Ruth. I—"

She, being an expert, read my voice. "Allie. In my unprofessional opinion, you are way too hard on yourself, and I do have words of wisdom for you. Because you've given them to me."

She turned to get another look at our free-range security dude + dog, making their rounds through the pines. The dog was a big handsome German shepherd, more cop than pooch.

Her expression was troubled. "You weren't kidding about 'house arrest.' This is an armed camp. Sentries. Patrols. What's the dog's name?"

I shook my head. "Nobody but the trainer knows. He's not a dog-dog. They won't even let me ask him, 'Who's a good boy?'"

We watched the man and the dog for another minute. A war movie is not a movie if it's in your yard.

"So Ruth, what were my words of wisdom? I don't remember any.'"

She shivered and brought herself back.

"This man whose true name we do not know, shows himself to us with his alias. Ricci is obvious. Money is huge for him. Tito? Who knows? It probably means more to him than a trendy vodka." Her signature humor snuck into her voice. "And in my professional opinion, he did not name himself after the manager of the Cleveland Indians. Maybe it has something to do with that Yugoslavian strong man. Although how—Maybe his real first name is Josip. It's crapshoot. You may never know.

"You do know he has a gigantic ego. You and Tom hammered it like crazy last summer. He styled himself as a formidable villain and you foiled his ass. He wants to pay you back. Double."

Not an answer I'd been hoping for. She noticed. "Hang in with me, Allie. I believe you nailed it when you told me about the guy he killed last year—sacrificed in front of you. Maybe as a lesson for you. The dead man whose body you told me he wanted to kick, but stopped himself. Too late for a second thought. By now he's had plenty of time for 'this was stupid.' It wouldn't be too far of a stretch—since we're stretching here anyhow—to say he sometimes feels sad about it."

"Huh. I have a hard time, Ruth, picturing him sad. He seems bulletproof to me."

"Nobody's bulletproof, Allie. Regret is the ultimate punishment for our mistakes. It's the bottomless pit that persists after the damage that can be repaired is repaired. And you're so right about the magnitude of his new attack. It's over the top. Clever, ingenious. But, at the same time, risky. Uncontrollable. From what you say, the shooter could have killed Tom that first night. Torn up your Tito's entire blueprint right on the spot."

I recoiled. She put a steadying hand on my arm.

"But that didn't happen, Allie. I'm merely saying that Tito has shown us two different kinds of killer. Ruthless and focused. Raging and—

"Off the rails," I finished for her. Sadly.

"That's one way to put it. Descriptive. You've already worked most of this out for yourselves."

"I suppose. But—"

"I'm going to give you some advice. Possibly against my better judgment, but it's not really a professional opinion. Because you would be figuring it out in about fifteen more minutes."

My "figure-it-out" meter was all the way over on "E." And about to cry. "Go ahead and tell me. Please, Ruth."

She got very still, her eyes tracking the guard and the dog, making the rounds. The snow swirling around them, making ghosts of them both. Her voice, which had been upbeat and gently persuasive, turned troubled. Deep breath.

"No matter what, Allie, don't pay him. Don't give him all your money. Or any of it, as far as that goes. No matter the threat. No matter how personal. The money will not satisfy him. Nobody knows that better than you. Whatever he may say, don't cave to his demands. If he gets it, he will first kill Tom to hurt you. Or you to hurt Tom. But, in the end, he will almost for sure kill you both.

"He now comprehends how killing wounds the living, Allie. That could be a huge part of what's driving him now. Never let your guard down. Keep track of people you're known to care about. Be safe."

"He doesn't know about you, Ruth."

"Never assume there's anything he doesn't know. But don't worry about me. Otis covers his tracks like a bandit. Stay safe, Allie. Circle the wagons. Don't forget to breathe."

A short walk back through the woods. A hug.

Goodbye, Ruth.

Chapter Twenty-One

10:30 A.M.

The past couple of years were a free-for-all of new life experiences for me. Before the Night of the Mondo, for example, I'd never even heard of Thomas Bennington III. I'd never spent an arguably ill-advised spontaneous night of passion with a blind man. The same blind man who had, inside of the previous four or five hours, accidentally won five hundred fifty million before-tax dollars. Back then, I'd never stayed in the Presidential Suite of the Ritz-Carlton, Cleveland. I'd never been shot. Not so much as once.

Hard to believe I'd crossed all that off my bucket list in the space of, oh, the first couple of weeks. It's amazing what hundreds of millions of dollars can do if word gets around.

Since that night, I'd also seen dead people. I'd met people who were about to be dead. I'd even seen people die, but until Saturday, the third of March, I'd never been called downtown to identify a body.

Saturday morning, after Otis came back from delivering Ruth to her office, we were enjoying as upbeat a breakfast of leftover donuts as you can have in a nook under glass with a sniper in town, when Otis got another call. Everything he said after, "Hello" we didn't hear because he jumped up and left the nook. When he came back, all the upbeat was wiped off him.

"Okay." He dropped into a faux wicker chair. "I ain't gonna lie. This is bad."

"Otis. Just say whatever it is." Tom looked like I felt. Trashed by nonstop danger and heinous news. Here was more.

Incoming.

Based on recent events and concerns, my knee-jerk "this is bad" response took me straight to Stacey. We still hadn't located her. "Otis? Stacey? Did he—is she—?"

"No, Allie. This is not about Stacey."

That was good, right? So now. Why was Otis so upset? Tom was right here—

Panic set in. "Not Margo, Otis? Not Tony?

"No. No. Not her. Not them, Allie, but this may be even more personal. I'm afraid this is a message for you."

The suspense is killing you?

"For me? Otis. What? Stop it. Go ahead and tell me. Come on. You're making it worse."

"Okay. Allie, I know you've got mixed feelings but that can be—"

"Otis."

"They found a body early this morning. Down by the lagoon. Almost same spot as Kip Wade, but closer to Euclid. He was covered in snow. Nobody noticed until daylight—Big guy, Allie. Well-dressed. Six-four. Muscular build. No ID. And, I'm sorry to have to say this, no hands. So no prints."

"Big guy?"

A message for me?

"They think it's D.B."

My voice sounded odd in my own ears. Calm. Composed, but removed, as if I were deep underwater and couldn't quite make out what I'd just said. What it meant. *It's. D.B.?*

I was fine. Aware of things: The snow. Slacking off. The flakes.

Getting smaller. Fixing to change over to rain. Any minute. I had
time to see those details because nothing was happening, and I
was fine. A peculiar sensation was building up in my throat. *Not
fine.* Tom took my hand in both of his. His hands were warm.

"Take a breath, Allie."

The lock on my throat released, I could breathe. I could talk.

"I'm—fine, Tom. Otis? They think it's D.B.?"

"Well, Valerio does, based on the description. And the circumstances. And we did believe the note last night was for you."

"'The suspense is killing you?'" My voice sounded normal to
me. A little puzzled. "But—"

"Yeah. Allie."

Otis thought I was someone who could hear and talk. I exhaled
and I was that person.

"So it's a message like Kip was. For Tom? Only it's for me this
time."

What Ruth said. *He now comprehends how killing wounds the
living.*

"Yeah. Maybe. It kinda fits. Who knows what goes through that
dude's head? I'm sorry, Allie. They've tried your old—his home
number. Phone turned off. Cell not picking up either. They'd
prefer someone who would recognize him—Or not. And say for
sure. Timing's important."

"Okay. I'll go."

Honestly? Yes. You bet I'd wished Duane Bradford Harper
dead. On several of multiple occasions when he'd been the jerk
I married by mistake and stuck with due to inertia, I'd casually
entertained myself by dreaming up a few scenarios. I'd even threat-
ened to kill him last summer when he hit me with a double dose
of his unique brand of smarmy cruelty. But I'd never meant truly
dead. Not irrevocably *dead* dead.

So now what?

So now I had to maybe identify the dead him. And say goodbye. Once and for all.

In the way terrible things work, this was beginning to feel expected. Inevitable. I could manage. We stood up. Found our coats. Followed Otis out to the garage, said goodbye to the guys, got in the car, and went.

Tom kept me close. Otis was a silent steady consolation in the driver's seat. A glaze of cold rain, sheeting down the windows, melting the snow away to nothing, soaked the world in gray. I stared out and tried to describe to myself what I was feeling. Was this crushing weight inside of me sadness? Regret? Anger? Yes. On all counts. But Otis already nailed it.

This was bad.

I'd been to the ME's office once before on a library-sponsored "Behind the Scenes" tour of 'Cleveland's Most Interesting Places.'" Back then, I was reading a lot of crime fiction, watching the *CSIs*, and imagining myself as a sassy amateur sleuth. I believed it would be cool to see it close-up. It was not. I fervently wished I'd picked "clean out monkey cages" or "ride a freighter up the Cuyahoga." I'd planned never to go back there.

A person who didn't know better from painful past experience might picture a Medical Examiner's office as a dark, grim edifice. Hovering. Glowering. Whispering mortality. Hopping with ghosts. Not so much. In the cold light of March, the Office of the Medical Examiner could have been an ordinary office building, loaded up with folks in business casual.

I knew better.

The entry was disguised as bureaucratic and unremarkable. It smelled like an Egg McMuffin and a spritz of Pine-Sol. Luckily, we didn't have to go very far inside. The location we were here for was right around the corner. I considered it a mercy that a person wouldn't have to journey deep inside to make an identification and let his or her heart break. I didn't think my heart would break, but I wouldn't know for sure until I knew for sure.

A short wait and I was standing, an ice sculpture of myself, before a large window with a curtain over it. Tom and Otis had my back. Tom's hands were on my shoulders. An attendant pulled the curtain open, and, smoothly, gently, but quickly—like ripping a Band-Aid off—uncovered the face and shoulders of the body on the table.

Big, tall, good-looking, and dead.

Tito Ricci.

Chapter Twenty-Two

Okay. Sure. Good.

Of course, I wanted D.B. to be alive. "Jerk" is not a capital offense. He and I had a small amount of history that wasn't totally dismal. I'd remembered, on the interminable ride to the morgue, how much I'd liked his mom and dad. I hadn't forgotten, either, the shock of believing he was dead.

D.B. Harper was no Tito Ricci. Between the two of them? No question I'd pick Tito to be the one on the slab. I'd longed for Tito to be out of our hair forever. 'Shot center mass and gone" worked gangbusters for that. Tito, dead, was "Tito: Problem solved."

The world was a far better place this morning with Tito Ricci not in it. Any one of the three of us, walking dazed back through the Pine-Sol of the M.E.'s entry, out into the now-driving rain, would have happily pulled the trigger on him. In a heartbeat. Even me, although I knew, from a past experience, Tom was a better shot, and Otis was for sure more accurate than Tom. We were all delighted he was gone.

However.

Maybe it was ungrateful of me, but I didn't feel relieved.

In our new state of free-fall, we were finding no answers. No solutions. No peace of mind. No relief. Tito was brutal, merciless, and consumed by a mad desire to destroy Tom and me.

But he was the devil we knew.

Now what? Now *who*? I was pretty sure the Lone Ranger hadn't shot Tito as a favor to Greater Cleveland. I already had a shooter in mind.

The scariest thing we weren't talking about yet? A brand new devil was here. A killer by definition. My neck crawled with that certainty. Where was he at this moment, while we sat in the M.E.'s parking lot, listening to rain hammering the Escalade, sorting our options? What did he want? The rules had changed, but what was the new game? Even Margo would be disoriented by this abrupt conclusion to the T&A's big new "Catch Fucking Tito" case. Tito was as caught as anyone ever could be, but nothing was solved.

Otis fired up the Escalade. I called D.B.

Somebody should have tried his stupid phone at least twice before dropping me into my forty-story elevator shaft of shock and disbelief. He picked right up.

D.B. sounded slightly disoriented himself. A little tipsy per-haps. In the background I could hear the murmur of upscale congeniality. Talk, laughter, and the chime of fine crystal. An undercurrent of cocktail jazz. All of which ticked me off. I'd been planning to tell him I was semi-glad to discover he wasn't dead. The sentiment was fast reaching its use-by date.

"Where are you? Restaurant? Sounds like a party."

My tone reeked disapproval. His response oozed arrogant self-satisfaction. Ms. Reeking. Mr. Oozing, Esquire. We were always such a great couple.

"Delighted you called, Allie," he smirked. "I'm throwing a little brunch to christen my new digs. With all my friends and associates."

New digs? Ex-spouse curiosity generates a powerful undertow, but I refused to be sucked under. "You've moved."

"Yeah, the Shaker house—you know how it was. Too suburban-housewife for my current lifestyle. I need to be where the action is. More amenities and less home maintenance."

As if you could pick a lawn mower out of a lineup.

Amazing. He'd run through my entire lifetime supply of grudging good will in a couple of sentences. Well aware of my silent wrath, he kept going. "Listen, Allie. I need to get back. To what do I owe the pleasure of this call? Maybe we can talk lat—"

I cut him off. "No, Duane. No need. No biggie. I was checking to make sure you're alive. Since I got called to the *M.E.'s office* this morning to identify *your body.*"

Out-loud italics, mine.

"Wasn't you."

More's the pity.

At least I didn't say that one out loud. The man was my lowest common denominator.

His voice betrayed the jolt. "Allie. You're joking. Right?"

"No, D.B. It was a case of mistaken identity. The guy looked sort of like you."

Dead ringer. I crushed that thought like a bug. And sighed, I hoped regretfully.

"Unfortunately, somebody had *chopped off his hands.* So no prints."

Lowest. Common. Denominator. The impulse to do damage was strong in me. If I'd stayed married to D.B. for another fifteen minutes, I'd have been unfit to live with a cat. And cats don't need all that much.

"Well. Okay. We should probably talk."

"No. D.B. We just talked. This was it."

"Okay. Whatever." He was rebounding. I could hear it. You need at least half a soul to make a human being.

"But hey. You should come up. And bring your blind person. And your—body guard person. The M.E.'s office is right around the corner from here. Where are you?"

Time to hang up. Quick but civil. "Uh. MLK. Almost to Euclid. Goodbye, D.B."

Let's try for 'as long as we both shall live.' Again. And make it stick this time.

"Well, tell you what, Allie. If you can't stop by, just look up. We're in the penthouse. At Atelier 24. 'Where Life Meets Art!' And hey, your friend Lisa Cole is here. She's moving into a one-bedroom a couple of floors down. It's a happening neighborhood."

Oh, yeah right, D.B. Hopping with ghosts. Probably a sniper around here somewhere now too.

I glanced out the window. At ground level, construction, corralled by a chain-link fence, was a work in progress. But up higher, through raindrops congealing on our so-called sunroof, I could see a tall, blurry, gray tower. Lights scattered here and there. From the top it would offer a spectacular view of the lagoon, the museum, the entire circle. And beyond. Probably all the way to the lake. I bet D.B. could almost pick out my house from there.

Time for my parting shot.

"Enjoy your party, D.B. I'll keep working on being glad it wasn't you at the morgue."

———

Tom and Otis knew from experience how to give me room for simmering down post-D.B. We traveled a couple of blocks in silence, while I wrestled with my bona fide horror and my petty fit of pique. It didn't help my state of mind that our route home bordered on the park, the lagoon, the benches, and the crime scene tape—

A drumroll of gunfire. We all recoiled. My phone. Theme from *Hawaii Five-O*. Anthony Valerio. I hoped he hadn't heard about his ringtone. In the driver's seat Otis was shaking his head.

"What's up, Officer Valerio?"

"What's up is you got a call this morning, Allie. I got a call before the call you got. And one for what it's turned out to be. So now I'm calling you—"

"Tito, not D.B. Shocker, huh?"

"Yes. In a bad/good/tiny-bit-sorry way." Tony would get that. He'd met D.B.

"Are you with Tom and Otis?"

"On the way home. Why? I'm putting you on speaker."

"Hey, Tom. Otis. I—we need you guys. At the scene. Detective Wood is here. She called me. I'm calling you. Can you guys come?"

Otis hung a quick right.

"We're already there."

Chapter Twenty-Three

Otis parked on East Boulevard. A cop was standing there to stop folks from doing that, but Officer Anthony Valerio was coming up the steps to meet us. It was colder than Wednesday night and raining lightly. As we walked down, I glanced through spindly, trembling branches to the path by the water. Another day, another tent.

The benches at the edge of the lagoon were stone—spaced well apart from each other along the arc of the shore. On Wednesday night, Kip was killed where the curve of the arc began, closer to the museum. This morning, Tito's body had been found behind the bench at the other end of the curve. I couldn't shake the symmetry. It felt arranged. Planned. A new message?

Not from Tito this time. That was for sure.

My vantage point extended across the water to the United Methodist Church, known affectionately to Clevelanders for nearly a hundred years as the "Holy Oil Can." Its steeple was the shape of the beat up old can my dad kept on a shelf in our garage. The church's bronze steeple, worn to a lovely verdigris, was modeled after Mont Saint Michel. In France. Dad's oil can was a can.

The beauty was weighed down for me by a dispiriting watery mist spreading over the surface of the lagoon. Plus my agitated frame of mind. Kip Wade, who'd walked to meet his killer at the other end of the arc Wednesday night, would have seen none of this. Early this morning, when Tito Ricci sat on his stone bench waiting for whatever he'd been waiting for—the church would have been an Impressionist painting in falling snow.

I was 99.5 percent certain Tito's murder was the work of Kip's sniper. But why *Tito*? Why here? Again? Why would the sniper have lured Tito to the scene of the first attack to take him out? Why had Tito come? What had he been expecting? Besides not this.

Old questions. New questions. We'd been working our theories about why Tito picked the museum as the canvas for his garish message to Tom. Now it looked as if this new killer had deliberately put Tito into his own blueprint.

If this was another message for us, what exactly did it say?

Besides, "Be more anxious, Allie Harper."

Lieutenant Olivia Wood, attired in all the waterproofing a sensible wardrobe could provide, plus big rubber boots, splashed over to us. I pictured my mad-spiked Louboutins hiding at home under the bed, dialing 911.

Otis had a question for her. "Lieutenant Wood, do you know where the shot was fired from?"

"Exactly what we were asking ourselves this morning, Otis. We believe we may have a sniper, right? So, first light, before we even got close to the body, we were calculating the shot might have come from the tall building across the street from the park. High up. Maybe the penthouse. There are at least two on the twenty-fourth floor. Balconies, naturally. We sent people up there, right off the bat. But in retrospect—"

"Up where?" I was uncomfortably sure I knew. "Show me?"

"Sure. Walk with me. Tom? You come too."

We trailed her across the piazza toward the water's edge. The rain was easing off. I was trying to ignore it. Staring where she pointed. Across the end of the lagoon. Up. Into the graceful contour of a big, new, gray building, and a penthouse glittering in the rain. Party going on.

Atelier 24. "Where Life Meets Art."

How perfect.

Lieutenant Wood was disrupting my symmetry, however.

"I was wrong. No sniper there when they checked. Some kind of fancy brunch setting up in the one penthouse. Other one was interesting, though. Emptied out. Nothing but furniture and odds and ends. My team said the apartment looked like it was deep-cleaned by one of those "if you've had a fire, you need us" outfits. Recently. Scrubbed down. Carpet still damp. Another interesting development? Atelier's security video was wiped. Suggests somebody covering their tracks. Or crappy security, maybe."

She gazed back to the building. "Was he ever there? Can't say a hundred percent, but I'm not apologizing. We were all in the mood for a sniper, so I looked up. Excellent line of sight from up there. We assumed too quick, but it was not a complete goose chase. Looks good to be a connection. Maybe. Just not to where the shooter was standing. We'll keep after it.

"Closer inspection, however, it's obvious Tito Ricci was shot almost point blank, Allie. Tom. Handgun. Suppressed, I'd expect. So much for our assumptions. Killing Tito at the bench was easier. Less complicated. 'Hey, Tito?' *Pow!* Outta there.

"Instant access to the hands too. Dude is efficient. Meticulous. Definitely *not* another Tito. Makes no difference to us right now. The shooter's in the wind."

She gave me a wry grin. "Do you have any idea how often we get a criminal mastermind in Cleveland? And now they're killing *each other*? You all are a goldmine of challenging opportunities. Landslide."

I'd heard this before.

"We have time of death between six and seven. Conditions make timing iffy. It helps that he was warmly dressed and the snow was light. Crime scene folks got some photos from before the snow turned all the way over to rain. Evidence too. There should be a lot more than at Kip's scene because the killer was right here. And the hands would have taken extra time. More room for error. I'm not going to speculate about his motive for doing that. But he must have thought he had a good reason.

"Ricci wasn't found until dawn. Woman walking dog. Came from Atelier. Dog's name is Van Gogh. Said nobody can decide how to pronounce it, so she calls him Vannie. I hope the original Van Gogh is not anywhere he can hear about any of that."

Olivia and I were on the same page about a lot of things.

She pulled out her phone again and, before I had time to brace myself, showed me photos she'd taken of the scene. I was grossed out but flattered.

Tito had been knocked off balance by the impact. Fallen backwards off the bench and ended up lying on his side behind it. There was a lot of blood on him everywhere. From the wrists. I swallowed. *His heart was still beating when—*

Olivia said the bullet wasn't anywhere. "Skilled."

The wrists were cringe-worthy but I could stand it. The ground was snowy in the pictures, except where blood had seeped through. Big areas were dissolved in it. There were footprints but melted and muddled. Photos of what was left.

The thought that skittered through my mind, as I stared at Dead Tito again, was "I wouldn't wish this on my worst enemy." But, basically, I would.

Lieutenant Wood put her phone away. "We were lucky we got the canopy in place before the snow changed completely over to rain. Sloppy, but I've seen worse. Lucky it's a Saturday so not much traffic at that hour. Lucky the view from the street down to here is chopped up by shrubs and trees. Tracks indicated that the woman with the dog was first on the scene. She didn't blunder all the way in, kept her dog in check, and called 911 like a good, smart citizen—Tom do you have anything to add?"

Tom was Lieutenant Wood's new secret weapon, for sure. I

assumed he'd been following our conversation. Silent, giving his full attention to every word. He closed his eyes for a moment. Listening. Breathing.

He hadn't worn his dark glasses since he'd tossed them onto the table at the museum. As far as I knew, he'd left them lying there. I'd wanted to ask him about that, but I hesitated. I felt closer to him when he wasn't wearing them. Like he was trusting me, maybe everybody, more. Or maybe it was resignation, a familiar refuge he'd given up as a pointless habit.

I hoped he'd never replace them. I loved being able to see all of Tom's face all the time, but at that moment it was starting to worry me. He hadn't answered Olivia and now I saw he'd gone pale. Worse than pale. Blanched. Gray. Even his lips were ashen. I'd been with Tom when he was scared, shocked, worried, tired, angry—I'd seen every emotion I could think of on his face. This was different.

One of the stone benches was behind us. Tom dropped onto it, apparently unaware that it was cold and wet. His breath came quick and shallow.

Olivia noticed too. "Tom. What's happened? What's wrong?" You look very—Are you—? Do you need—"

Tom's voice was as bleached his face.

"Lieutenant Wood. How did he do it? The sniper? How did he cut—How—"

Both of us got there in the same instant. We both sat down on the bench with Tom. Me on one side. Olivia on the other. I had no idea what to do. Olivia had a decade's worth of hard conversations on me. She started by talking.

"Tom. I'm so sorry. I didn't think. This has to be very upsetting for you."

"You don't have a clue." His voice was thin. Distant.

I put my hand on Tom's arm. He flinched. Pulled away. Olivia Wood reached out and took both of his hands in hers and held them firmly. Her grip was gentle but resolute. He didn't resist.

"What do you need to know, Tom?"

A breath. "I need to know how. Olivia. Exactly. How."

"I understand. Okay. I'll tell you what I was told. You can stop me anytime. Just say stop. Okay?"

"Yes." Barely a whisper.

Slowly, carefully, she placed his left hand on his knee. Took the right one and held it, palm up, in her left. Touched it lightly with the fingers of her right.

"This is what I understand about how that was done, Tom. The bones of the arm and the hand are not directly connected. They come closest together here and here." She touched his wrist, first at the base of his thumb, and then where palm and wrist joined on the other side. "Little knobs. Can you feel that?"

He put his left hand on the spot. "Yes."

Sweet Jesus. This has to stop. I took a deep breath to say so, and Otis touched my shoulder. A gentle squeeze that said, *Not your decision. Trust her. Trust him.*

"The bones of the wrist and the bones of the hand are joined by tendons. Very tough, very strong and flexible. The person who did this to Tito had a sharp knife that slipped, fairly easily, between the bones. The cut was clean. Surgical.

"He was already dead, Tom. Or very close. The sniper would not have wanted him to—to scream. Or struggle. Sorry. Sometimes it helps to know these things."

Tom's breath was slower, steadier now. His color was slightly better. He took his hands back from Olivia and rubbed them together, slowly, like a meditation. Like he'd never had hands before.

"Thank you, Olivia. I needed it to be specific." A shake of his head. "Not a cloud of a thousand fears. I'm not happy. And I'm still scared. Disheartened, I guess. Undone. But that helped." He turned to me and took my clammy hand in both of his, and smiled over my shoulder toward Otis.

"Thank you too."

As Tom's fear ramped down, mine boiled up. Terror. Sorrow. Loss. Jostling around inside me. Competing for room in my over-crowded chest. I supposed Olivia knew what she was doing. She'd grounded Tom in a reality more manageable than the dread he'd been grappling with since—I realized now—Otis said, "No hands. So no prints." Back when we'd thought the dead guy was D.B. I blessed her for the way her down-to-earth wisdom and kindness was helping Tom.

Only now she'd transferred his cloud over to me.

Tom's hands drew me into his world. Brought him into mine. Without his touch on my skin—without my body under Tom's hands, the current of tenderness and passion that was *us,* since the night we met—Before we even knew each other, there'd been love and honesty enough for both of us in Tom's hands. Who would Tom be—*who would we be*—without his hands?

I shoved those fears down, as far as I could. Sat there as if Olivia had raised me up too, and now I could deal.

Tom was Olivia's secret weapon again. A beat. A deep breath. He squared his shoulders and he was back. "Now. Lieutenant Wood. You asked me if I had something to add.

"It's colder today. Rain was steadier, longer, on Wednesday. The smells are different here, closer to the water. Algae in the lake. Not as much as in warmer weather, I'm sure, but it's there. Somebody is smoking, not close. Car exhaust, coming across from the street on the far side. Tito's aftershave."

OMG. I'd missed it. Now it spiked into my solar plexus. It was here. *He was here.* For the last time ever, I fervently hoped.

Tom moved on. "I wasn't nearby this time, thank God, so I don't have sounds the way I did for Kip. But, Olivia, I would say shooting Tito would be harder, more complex. Kip was blind. Tito was sighted."

He grimaced. "In spite of what I said yesterday, Allie, about how pointless it is to try to hide, a sighted person has vision to alert him to danger. Hiding is not something I can do effectively. I'd

have an advantage in a cave or a totally dark place. Otherwise—"
He shrugged. "If I wanted to shoot a blind person out of nowhere,
I could be fairly sure he wasn't looking around for me. Wondering
where I was. Ducking. Tito would have seen this guy coming.
Maybe knew him too. You with me, Olivia?

"Yes, Tom. Kip was easier. Especially for a sniper."

Tom's tone bared its edge. "Yeah, Lieutenant. Kip was a piece
of cake."

He kept going, though. "Tito's a totally different target. He
knew this guy. Knew better than anyone what he was capable of.
And Tito for sure was paranoid. The set-up, the ruse to get him
to sit there and get shot would be different than with Kip, who
politely presented himself to be murdered Wednesday night at
a quarter till eight.

"We believe the sniper pulled both triggers, but this murder is
different. Not only because of the gun and"—I felt him tense—
"the hands. Tito was angry and driven by a wild need to punish
us. Hot. The sniper is unemotional, unreadable, formidable. Cold.

"I'm over my head now, but here's what I'd hypothesize. Tito
trusted the shooter as a faithful employee. Or—and I'm tending
to prefer this idea—he deferred to him in another way. Not from
the perspective of an employer. And Tito last week was different
from Tito last July. Less a kingpin, more a partner in crime with
the sniper. He thought they were in this together.

"Now the threat has changed. Tito's out. New devil. New
game."

He sat motionless, his face composed, his palms pressed
together, fingers laced. "It would be unwise for us to deny that
Tito's hands are this man's message for me."

Chapter Twenty-Four

3:30 P.M.

Our replacement devil gave us an hour and a half before he dropped in, figuratively speaking, to say hello.

His calling card was a bullet.

As is customary for a long-distance projectile, encased in copper and crafted for speed and accuracy, this one in arrived in pure silence—out of the proverbial nowhere—to shatter our illusions and the cupola of our cozy greenhouse by breaking all hell loose. No warning.

The sound of Armageddon blowing up the breakfast nook.

Tom and I were in the kitchen, listening to Otis explain the possibilities of the leftovers he'd saved up in the fridge, so none of us was caught in the deluge of glass down into the room.

The ceiling fan hung on its wiring for a couple of seconds, before it let go and landed with a stunning, disjointed sky-is-falling clatter on the glass coffee table. Which shattered too. I know that part in retrospect because I saw the wreckage afterwards. The fan/coffee table explosion was delayed, like an aftershock, so it stands out in my memory like the last straw of sanity.

The rest is screaming.

Tom on the far side of the island, was crying out "Allie. I can't hear you. Allie. I can't hear you. Allie. I can't hear you." Pure terror.

"Tom!" I scuttled around, hands and knees, and found him—curled up, head down, arms clutching his knees—reliving the devastating blast of last year's case. I grabbed onto him. Held him tight, both of us alive. He was shaking. Me too. "Tom. *Tom.* I'm here. You can hear me. You can hear me."

"No. I can't. I—oh." He exhaled. Almost a laugh. Came back to me. "Oh, Allie. I can. I can hear you. Otis. Where's Otis?"

"I can see Otis, Tom. We're all fine. Listen. You can hear him too. He's swearing like Margo. She would be so proud."

Otis had been trained for combat and had walked a beat in the City of Cleveland, so he was the first to seize control, putting a stop to his flurry of swearing.

"Take a breath, you guys. Nobody's hurt." He was on the floor with us though. Leaning up against the island. Still holding the sandwich he'd just made. It wasn't a sandwich anymore. He hadn't noticed.

"Nobody was supposed to get hurt. This was a warning." He considered what he'd said. "More like 'Hello.'"

The two guys from the garage were standing in the doorway now, putting their guns away. Another minute and the guy with the dog appeared. From the look of his uniform, he'd been flat on the ground out there. In mud. I exchanged glances with the dog. Got a minimal wag.

Whispered, "Who's a good boy?"

The three of us hauled ourselves up off the floor.

Otis had the conn. "Okay. Everyone here is fine. You guys go back to your positions. I'll phone this in so Bratenahl can send somebody to probably not find a damn thing of any use to anybody. And then we're going to need somebody to clean up the breakfast nook and put a tarp over that damn roof before it starts raining again."

For a man of formidable experience and skill, Otis could be

very practical about mundane details. It was one of the things that made him formidable.

He welcomed the officers. They took our information, examined the glassy inside of the nook and paced off the sloppy outside. Found the bullet, based on an informed guess. Put it in a bag. Showed it to Otis. They picked up a few other small items that might have been evidence, or sticks, and took them away. Shook their heads. Didn't share anything except the news of finding the bullet and the head shakes. Told us we could go ahead, sweep up, mop up, and fix the roof. They had no suggestions at all about the fan and the coffee table. They'd see if they could discover where the shot was fired from and look for casings.

"Don't hold your breath."

Otis dispatched one of his men to The Home Depot for the tarp and a ladder and tasked another with the clean-up of the nook.

"Otis. You can't send somebody up on a ladder with a sniper out there. That's—"

He shut me down. "Allie, remember what we all agreed about snipers? I know he's put your confidence to the test here—mine, too, tell you the truth—but trust me, the sniper is not out there anymore. Guaranteed. One thing snipers for sure do is leave.

"Bratenahl'll see if they can figure out where the shot came from. Haystack. Might be a help if they locate that. But, seriously, can you picture this dude with the 'silvery eyes' and the 'hair like Swedish children'"—He made his quote marks in the air. Twice. "Not cleaning up after himself? He's a pro. I'm guessing military."

"Otis is right, Allie. He's gone now."

Tom was getting control again too. At least that's what he was pretending. In the vibration of his touch, I could feel he was as wired up as me. Same frequency as me too. The day he'd already had—even before the ceiling crashed down—would have put me under the covers and incoherent for a month. Seeing him in the ratty, stretched out sweatshirt he'd been wearing first thing this morning when Otis got the call—before he'd even had a chance to shave—was like a glimpse into another epoch. His jaw was tight but in spite of the shock and anger on his face, his voice was calm. Reasonable. His hands on my shoulders were—*God.*

So *hot.*

If half the world hadn't been passing through, I'd have been rubbing my fingertips over the roughness of Tom's cheek, slipping them up under the front of that well-worn shirt—*Huh.* That thing about near-death experiences was true. They did heighten all your senses like I'd always heard. Lee Ann thought so anyhow.

Tom continued, oblivious to my moment of distraction. "At least now we know we don't know this shooter. Or what he'll do next. We may not have much time, and until Olivia gets hard evidence or he takes another—makes another move—common sense is all we've got. Even then—" He trailed into considering the serious impossibilities in our situation and let go of my shoulders. After a long pause, he started up talking again as if he hadn't noticed he'd stopped. Shell-shock is real.

"The new guy is not Tito. Maybe he's the Anti-Tito. But at least we now know he can send a message that's not a body." He stopped himself again.

"And that bullet wasn't angry. Or vengeful. It was clean and controlled. Not much fun though—"

I slipped my arms around Tom, pulled him back to me, rested my face in his chest, feeling his heartbeat—rapid—and soaking up his body's warmth—warm.

"So this one is not as—He's not as off the rails as Tito."

"Not as off the rails, Allie," Otis agreed. "Not crazy out-for-revenge like Tito. 'Man was a forest fire. We can hope this person is at least not—" He sighed. "But from what little you heard from Gloria before he killed her—and if he didn't kill Gloria, I can't imagine who did. My money's on him—From what we've seen, he's is ruthless and always on target. Cold. And steady about it. Serious skills and training—"

"A hired gun, Otis?"

"Trained for it. To the core. Only maybe not hired at all if Tito wasn't his boss. I'm thinking freelance. Self-employed. He's the kind that won't kill unless he gets the order, but once he gets the order, hard to stop. I'm afraid he's giving himself all the orders now."

A last big chunk of glass fell out of the greenhouse ceiling.

Everybody jumped.

Damn.

I watched Otis turn around and notice the refrigerator door. Still hanging open. He closed the door.

"This requires a new kind of careful."

Chapter Twenty-Five

9:25 P.M.

Alrighty.

We were in a peculiar state of mind, Tom and me.

Slouched side-by-side on the wide, cushy, leather couch in Tom's office, tired, but not yet sleepy, frazzled but not still terrified. In the limbo between the "Ghost of Danger Past" and our fresh, new, less-defined, but no less unsettling, "Harbinger of Danger Future." Not yet talking about unthinkable fresh hells.

In between. On the edge. At the brink. Not good.

"You ever go to Cedar Point, Tom?"

"Geez, Allie. You are so—No. I bet somebody, somewhere, offers amusement park experiences for 'Daredevils with Disabilities,' but that's not me. Why do you ask?"

"Because I'm thinking about a ride they had out there."

"Because?"

"Stick with me for a minute. I'm trying to describe to you the nature of my current level of anxiety."

"On the continuum from 'Snoopy Bounce' to 'Millennium Force'?"

"Yeah. It's the ten. The Mach Ten. You're sure you've never been there?"

"I'm blind, Allie. Not ignorant of popular culture, and I'm fascinated to learn where you're going with this."

"VertiGO! All caps 'GO!' With an exclamation point."

"Vertigo? A ride? Never heard of it."

"Before your time. A giant sling shot, designed to sling you almost three hundred feet into the sky. Then fling you back to the ground. You could choose whether it flipped you over on your face on the way down. I rode it. Once. Flipped over."

"And?"

"I did not have time to wet my pants. That's the happy part. But I've never forgotten the moment at the top when it flipped and I saw the ground—It was a heartbeat, Tom, but—"

He nodded. "Eternity. I've had a moment or two like that. Several with you—" A smile touched the corner of his mouth. "And that's you tonight, Alice Jane? Three hundred feet up, flipped over and frozen in an eternity of fear. Staring down a long fall?"

Bingo.

"Uh huh. Thanks for not laughing. That's what I'm feeling right now. All that. And helpless too. The ride strapped you in but didn't clamp you tight. Let you fly around. Jiggle. Wobble. Feel the panic."

I reminded myself, once again, of the No Crying Rule of amateur detective procedure.

The wind howled. Spray from Lake Erie slapped the windows. accentuating the warm and cozy of our couch. Tom pulled me closer. "Come over here. I'll hold you tight." He grinned and whispered, "I could flip you over too, if you like."

"I might like. Maybe later. Could be soon. Keep trying to cheer me up."

"Honey, that is not all I'm trying to do." He shifted closer, gathering me in. One hundred percent Tom. His body bypassed the chatter of my frantic mind and spoke directly to my body. He pulled me more into contact with his chest. "How'm I doing?" Another kiss. He still had not had a chance to shave. Too late now.

I put both my hands on the roughness of his jaw and a current of heat arrowed through me.

Less talk, Alice Jane. More action.

I was tuned in to the Lee-Ann Channel, but now Tom was caught up in my story. He pulled away. "Hey. Did you ever get up the nerve to ride it again? I know you. Tenacious. Some might say stubborn."

"I never had the chance. The first winter a windstorm took out one of the 365-foot posts. That was the end of it. So we'll never know."

I did feel better. Not cured. The turmoil of the last three days and my shock at how we'd swapped one deadly threat for another had fried my circuits. Tough to let it go. Even for a night. But I was willing to give it a try.

I inhaled the smell of leather and the signature goodness of Tom. "This is a nice…couch."

He accepted my change of gears. "Otis picked it out. It's supposed to match the feel and smell of Escalade leather, but he says it's brown, not 'Raven Black.'"

"No special, evocative name? Plain brown? 'Sparrow Brown?'"

"He didn't say, and I don't particularly care, but the smell is—new car." He shifted us so we were lying, face-to-face, front to front. "Provocative."

I inhaled.

Holy Whoa, girl.

Sure enough. I'd been too freaked out to notice the sensuosity of the couch aroma. At that moment, lying on leather with Tom, the part of my brain that controls the blurting of unfortunate information went straight to disengaged.

"Oh, yeah, Tom," I murmured. "I am a new-car-smell addict. A guy I dated in high school would get to drive his dad's new Buick on our dates sometimes—"

Uh huh. I remember that car.

A person can get conditioned to all kinds of stimuli from her formative years. That's a euphemism. Rainy nights. Windows fogged up. A brand of cologne nobody wears anymore. A stray hand, here. Or there—A semester's worth of teenage hormones and pent-up frustration saturated those memories. Mine even had their own soundtrack. *NSYNC's hit album *No Strings Attached* was the only CD in Matt's dad's player those days, but it worked fine. At this moment a memory from that back seat was humming along. "It's Gonna Be Me" was playing all over my body, and right here at my fingertips was Tom.

So profoundly Tom. So totally the Mr. Right I was saving myself for back then. My rational brain with all its terrors and inhibitions shut down. Tom's too. I could tell. He was as susceptible as any guy to the distracting influence of sensual cues and hot, old memories. To about the tenth power. Being a human male, and therefore possibly jealous of Matt and his dad's Century, Tom was a man with a backseat history of his own and something to prove.

Okay by me.

Lee Ann and I were in total agreement.

I let the sniper go and closed my mind to everything but Tom. Here in the backseat of—uh—the couch in his office—I was lost, and Tom was an experienced and capable guide. He put his mouth on mine, and every inch of my body wanted to be his new best friend.

Another kiss.

"So," he said.

"*So?*" Somehow I was not expecting a conversation.

"So. You and Mr. Buick. Fog up the windows some? He play a little background music for—inspiration?"

Damn.

"Yeah, well, *NSYNC, if you must know. You are devious."

"I have an active imagination, and I was plenty young enough when you were in high school. Probably a senior when you were a sophomore? Vulnerable freshman, maybe. That would have been interesting. I had a car too, Miss Smith. And an extensive CD collection. You and me back then. Lordy. We could have—" He brushed one finger along my throat and down to my collarbone, planted a leisurely kiss right in that notch.

I made a sound that sounded embarrassingly like begging. Even with my eyes shut, I could see his smile. That dimple.

"Yeah, Allie," he said. "I'd give a million bucks for the time machine that would take me into that backseat with you for one night. I could have got lucky. Very. Lucky."

"Don't be so sure of yourself. Are you jealous? Am I supposed to be ashamed?"

"May I suggest turned on? I know I am."

"Do you know how to get a girl out of her clothes in a limited space?"

"Watch me."

His *hands*—I shut out a pang.

Not tonight. Dammit.

Agreed. Dammit.

His hands were magicians tonight. Matt should have been so talented. Too bad for him. In record time, the bodies of both of us were one hundred percent touch-accessible, and his mouth was back. Magnetic on mine. As was his skin. All of it.

I made the sound again, and he carried us into his rhythm, moving to melodies from our memories, until even my breathing matched itself to his. I followed the persistent, muffled throb of desire from the long past into this one overpowering moment.

Inside the circle of his arms, warm and close against him, I released my questions and fears, the voices inside me, with their incessant chanting about everything the past had brought and what the future might take away.

Whatever this was, it was enough.

Right here. Right now, Alice Jane.

———

Our satisfied bodies and souls were drifting away.

Tom put his mouth against my ear.

"Alice Jane," he whispered. "It's Gonna' Be Me."

"Thomas Bennington III. You can count on it."

Chapter Twenty-Six

Euphemistically speaking, I was in a very relaxed state. I ought to have slipped from love into slumber in the time it took to whisper, "Good night."

No.

I was missing my aforementioned clothes. I was chilly. I couldn't reach the sumptuous throw, located a mile away, over the couch's arm. My skin had fused to the leather, which made lots of squelchy leathery sounds when I tried to release myself from it. Tom was breathing slow and deep. Lee Ann had wandered off somewhere. As always.

I was on my own.

Alrighty. I peeled myself out of the back of our Buick and, after spreading the sumptuous throw over Tom and tenderly tucking it all around him, I headed for a bona fide bed.

Too bad. Our real bed was more comfortable but also a bust. Now that my body was no longer overruling my brain, I was free to start fretting again: Tito? Dead. Sniper? Sniping at us now. And so on. The message of Tito's hands was too much to address head-on, so I'd sent it to the sub-basement of my mind. I could tell Tom had a sub-basement of his own.

I'd never comforted myself by saying, "Besides, we could all be dead soon anyway." After today that seemed rational to me. I was flipped over and frozen in my "eternity of fear." I gave up.

As I ditched the bedroom and any hope of sleep, I grabbed Tom's roomy robe. A Christmas present from me, this robe cost $378 plus shipping. I liked it better than my own robe which cost $49 from Amazon and shipped free with Prime. The money for both robes came from our joint account which could absorb inconsequential purchases such as those with not so much as a blink. My own, former, not very active, bank account would almost certainly crash under the price of a pack of fuzzy socks.

Tom's robe was crafted of three-ply cashmere from Nepalese goats. Guaranteed warm and soft, it sported a hood which created a shelter over my head, under which I felt inexplicably and, of course, foolishly safer. It was the luscious red of a fine wine from Burgundy, France. What's more—and here was the main reason I stole it as often as I could—It smelled like Tom.

Oh, yeah.

Wrapped in Tom, I headed for the one room in the house I had not yet fully described to him. My dressing room. Every time I opened its door and walked into the loving embrace of its comfort and luxury, I could almost forgive the former lady of the house for being such a pretentious bore. Surely a woman who was this romantic couldn't be all bad.

Everything was perfect, but the premier feature was a vintage chaise lounge, upholstered in rich, warm, red velvet. Margo— who was enraptured to the point of speechlessness when she saw it—had presented me with one of her vast, jewel-toned shawls to throw over it. The shawl snuggled warmly around me and my contraband robe on this miserable night, when, once again, hard little bits of freezing rain were ticking against the windows.

I wasn't all that excited about the closets and built-in drawers. I didn't arrange my outfits by color. They weren't exactly outfits anyhow. I didn't have the guts to wear the one or two with scary price tags and illustrious names. At the very least, they'd need to be dry cleaned. The serenity of that room—the chaise, the warm-scone color of the walls—not its organizational skills, soothed my soul. I had my own desk in here, and on it was a green-shaded lamp I'd downright stolen from my favorite room in the old house.

You can take the girl out of the kleptomania, but you can't take the kleptomania out of the girl.

I trained with the best, Lee Ann.

I turned it on for both of us. The light was gentle, calming. Just the right amount of weak. My night terrors slithered back into their nasty little kingdom. I calmed myself more by reminding myself I'd been saving this room as a secret surprise for Tom ever since we'd moved in. Waiting for the right moment. Tom knew I had a dressing room with its own wine fridge and TV. I'd shown him those. But I'd skirted us around the red velvet chaise. Thinking about all that was soothing too. Mostly.

Too bad there was the TV, so handy, inside the also-vintage armoire that was the other major design focus of the room. Tonight the doors that usually hid it away were hanging open, and the remote was lying next to me on the chaise. Right where I'd carelessly left it a couple of nights before.

So I deserved what I got.

I clicked it on.

Channel 16.

Tom, Otis, and I referred to 16 as The Lisa Channel. I usually had to gag on their tacky, sensational junk and a lot of repetitive local commercials to get to her segments, but she was worth it. A real reporter. Always on the trail of her story. I knew she hadn't yet realized her dreams of being a "nationally respected journalist," but she persevered. If she had something for tonight, it'd probably be on after the opening and before the next round of mattress, used-car, and personal-injury-lawyer spots.

I settled in. I was trying to remember whether there might be an open bottle of wine in the handy in-room fridge, when the anchor said, "And just in. Breaking news."

A banner that hollered *Breaking News!* slashed the screen.

"Investigative reporter, Lisa Cole, is at the scene of two recent shootings in University Circle with a new development in the story. Lisa?"

There she was. Our Lisa. Bundled up against the cold, but undaunted by the gusts assaulting her cute earmuffs and ruffling her blonde hair. Tiny drifts of sleet were collecting around the collar of the weather-impermeable L.L. Bean down jacket I knew she swore by. She was reporting from in front of the benches by the lagoon. In the background was the museum, its sweeping steps and iconic white marble façade misted to enchantment by the wintry mix.

I could see the poor, naked, bronze sculpture of The Thinker crouching out there too. Freezing his buns. Maybe trying to figure out who swiped his pants. Icons have it tough.

I shivered and tuned more in to what Lisa was saying. "—from the scene of the shooting, Wednesday night, of blind Cleveland entrepreneur, R. Kipling Ward, and of an unknown man early this morning, and also breaking news this evening of a note discovered in one of the galleries here at the Museum of Art. Police and Museum representatives have declined to comment on this note, and its specific content has not been made available at this time."

My breath caught in mid-gasp. The camera zoomed to a close-up of Lisa's face. Specks of sleet sparkled in her lashes. Money shot. She paused. Long. Opened her mouth to betray our friendship.

The scene cut back to the news desk guy whose face was now displaying a practiced mix of interest and urgency.

"Lisa. I have been given to understand, by a source I consider reliable, the note itself may have been intended as a message for Cleveland MondoMegaJackpot Millionaire, Tom Bennington III?"

Back to Lisa, shivering. The freezing wind, now teasing her hair out of the earmuffs and swirling it over her face. Game enough to nod and gaze defiantly into the camera. At me, I thought.

"We're awaiting more details, Trent."

A jolt of emotion smashed into me. I wanted to scream. I wanted to cry. Also kill. If Betrayed and Homicidal got married and had a daughter, that was me.

The camera zoomed to a close-up of Lisa's wide-eyed intensity and cut back to the news-desk guy whose face now displayed superficial concern and ill-concealed delight. His face should break.

I gave Ruth's breathing exercise a shot. One round. I breathed and observed my anger. Then I took another calming breath and flipped the TV—and also Lisa and her dumbass anchor—off.

I found myself the opened bottle in the fridge and poured a large glass of decent chardonnay all over my freak-out. It worked. I lay back down on the chaise, enfolded myself in the healing essence of Tom's robe, layered on the solace of my Margo shawl and—not right away but sooner than I might have expected—I was asleep.

My last, drifting thought was, "Lisa Cole. You bitch. You are so screwed."

Chapter Twenty-Seven

SUNDAY, MARCH 4

8:00 A.M.

On Sunday morning we woke up to a Richter-Scale-magnitude paradigm shift.

Tito Ricci was dead.

His sniper was the freelancer from hell. He'd signaled a change of command by executing Tito in a manner that asserted—with shocking clarity—both his icy skill and his ruthless savagery. We were pretty sure he was not now—nor had he ever been—Tito's messenger. He was the virtuoso killer who'd orchestrated the events of the past five days to serve his own ends.

Yesterday morning before dawn, he'd laid out his agenda so we couldn't miss exactly who'd been in charge from the beginning. And who'd been the pawn. The crime scenes said it all. At one end of the arc of benches, Kip's body. At the other end of the arc, Tito's. The murder of Kip had been a heads-up for us. The murder of Tito told us who was the real boss around here. The barbaric removal of Tito's hands was the signature of a fearsome adversary.

Tito's severed hands underscored the transfer of power and did double duty as the ultimate threat to a blind man. Tom's hands fused him to the world. Neither of us was ready to discuss that.

Sometimes, an ah-ha moment is not good news.

Understatement.

I was a hot mess.

So, when the phone rang, at the moment I was pouring my first, conceivably life-saving, cup of coffee of the day, I answered the call in the persona of Allie Harper, Ticking Time Bomb.

"Allie."

It was D.B. Something had knocked all the snotty off his tone. The urgency in his voice disarmed me. At least temporarily.

"What, D.B?"

"Your dead guy? The one you had to identify. Who wasn't me." He caught that one on the way out of his mouth. "Obviously."

Regrettably.

I admired myself for showing an ounce of restraint by not saying that out loud. Lee Ann was gone again. Besides, she still had a soft spot for D.B. If my personality ever got split for real, Lee Ann would claim the sluttier side.

"What about him, Duane? He's dead. Somebody shot him and cut off his hands so he couldn't be identified."

"Well, hell, Allie. I can identify him. His name is—*was*—Tito Ricci."

WTF? The name—however bogus—was not common knowledge. In spite of Lisa Cole's friend-shafting, journalistic efforts—it was still not even being bandied about on Channel 16. In theory, nobody knew the body's identity yet unless they were directly involved in killing Tito. Or were the M.E. Or on Olivia Wood's team, who were supposed to be keeping his name under wraps for as long as possible. Or us.

"How the—? How did you know that, D.B.?" *Chill, Alice Jane.*

"He's—he was—my next-door neighbor, Allie. Atelier 24."

D.B. had trained himself over the course of several years not to listen to my mind screams. So he totally missed my suppressed 120-decibel response to his revelation. His self-satisfaction rolled on unabated. "I'd seen him around, but I never noticed he looked like me—Atelier 24 has two penthouses, Allie. Side by side. Top floor. He was in the other one."

I had enough presence of mind left to be aggravated by D.B.'s callousness. The man was too excited about his "new digs" to stick with "dead neighbor" for a half second. But D.B. was closing the circle on yesterday's clues and suspicions. Moving Tito and maybe the sniper into an apartment on the twenty-fourth floor of Atelier. With a view that encompassed the crime scenes.

"You knew him?"

"Not really. He kept to himself. In the other penthouse. He had a housemate too. Showed up, maybe a month or two ago?" Disapproval reared its ugly head. "I don't think he was gay, but that other dude was…disturbing. Cops knocked on my door looking for him. After I talked to you."

Just to confirm. "Let me take a stab at this one: Fit. Maybe five ten? Way blond—white-blond. 'Like Swedish children.' Pale, kind of silvery, eyes. Wears a lot fitness gear. Quiet, not gregarious."

I added, *Neutral. Like clear water* to myself. I was leaving a lot unspoken in this conversation. D.B. would find the water description "frivolous." I remembered it as the scariest thing Gloria said to me about the man. It scared her too, I'd heard that in her voice. Her fear of his cold blood.

Justified.

"That's him. You know him, Allie?"

"Yes. No. I knew of him. He's most likely involved with—with what's been happening, including Kip Wade, and now Tito Ricci. Is he around? Because—"

"No. Nobody's been around, except a major cleaning crew, according to the manager. Place is emptied out, except for big stuff, she said. She tells me things like that because I'm—She calls me Tenant #1 because I moved in the first month after they opened. To the penthouse. She told me Tito'd been there even before it opened. Signed a waver that he didn't care if he fell down the elevator shaft. But I'm still officially Tenant #1."

I commented to myself about D.B.'s penchant for petty satisfactions. The more bootlicking deference the better. And his *fucking penthouse*. For the fourth time, but who was counting? Delusions of grandeur. I let the second mention of "Tenant #1" hurtle into the dark, empty stillness of AT&T.

I could come up with a more creative title than that. With a #1 in it too. I think he got the unspoken vibration.

"One more thing. How did you figure out my "guy who looked like you" was your next-door neighbor? In the other penthouse? D.B.?"

"Another neighbor. I met her in the elevator. She lives several floors down—" Disdain and satisfaction. The D.B. Harper Deluxe Combo.

I rolled my eyes. The Valerio 360. "And?"

"And she actually discovered the body, Allie. She walks her dog around the lagoon in the mornings. Dog's name's Van Gogh."

Stick with "Vannie," D.B. You kinda butchered Van Gogh.

"And she said?" I applauded the neutrality of my tone. I wanted the damn info so I could hang up on my ex-idiot. Dammit.

"She said, 'D.B., you won't believe this. The dead guy looked a little like you.' But you'd already told me that. It kind of clicked then. I hadn't noticed a resemblance. Even when you called. I mean, he was *okay* looking, but—"

My cue to sign off. "Thanks for the information, D.B. We'll be getting back to you. You can count on it."

Killed the call. Loved doing that.

We would be getting back to him, all right. His prattling was chockful of critical information he didn't even know he had. I bet Cleveland Homicide Detective, Olivia Wood, and Officer Anthony Valerio would soon be calling us about the non-sniper tenant of the twin penthouse. What's more, I had not known, until D.B. blathered on about it, Tito was lurking at Atelier 24 since well before the grand opening. Now we knew where he'd been. At home, at least for the last couple of months, with the ghost who was now our new deadly enemy.

D.B.'s gaydar was predictably defective as a rule, but even a blind pig can find a nut sometime. Tom would get a kick out of applying that to D.B. I hustled to find him and Otis. Otis was nowhere to be found. Tom was running away from it all.

———

Our new, more youthful house featured a higher-tech workout room than the previous one. This one had the treadmill to pass up our old one like it was standing still. It had the same expansive view of multiple decks, a—tightly covered—pool, and the sullen lake. Tom was not there for lake view. He was seeing a route he kept stored in his memory. Dressed for summer in shorts and a raggedy T-shirt, a sheen of perspiration on the back of his neck, he looked a couple of different kinds of hot. His thigh muscles flexed with every step too. He'd shaved, though. More's the pity.

I'd heard all about how he used to do four miles, when he was in grad school at Emory in Atlanta. First thing in the morning, every day. "Like clockwork." Back when he was younger, fitter, and not the least bit blind. Now, pounding along on the exceedingly stable and responsive machine, he could relive the smell of asphalt cooking in Atlanta heat and the percolating green sweetness of trees and grass. Dust. Sweat.

No matter how skillful he might become at reading his surroundings, Tom would never again charge down a new, untried path at a breakneck pace. But the imprint of those moments on his body's memories helped him recreate all that, and the machine gave him the freedom to go as fast as he wanted.

He loved it.

Me? I hated the stupid thing. Loathed its air of upscale, tech-savvy self-satisfaction. Also its metallic guts. Merely walking by it made my calves burn and elevated my desire to lie down and read something. I understood Tom's passion for it, but that only made me jealous. Of an inanimate object. Worse, I had to climb on the thing and run to keep up with him in the fitness department. Abs and calves as fine-tuned as Tom's deserved better than the weak little couch potato who lived in my soul. I reminded myself that I had not been Tom's weak little couch potato last night. In any case, sooner or later on this day, I'd have to grit my teeth and do my thirty minutes. Or less.

Fortunately for me, however, the torture device was occupied at the moment. Tom was under his headphones, reading as he ran. I had to raise my voice above the hum of the machine and the voice in ears, "Tom! What are you reading?"

"*The Curious Lives of Human Cadavers.* It's fascinating."

Our lead detective in training. "I bet. Have fun."

I gave my young, hot Sherlock Holmes one, last, appreciative glance that included his well-toned buns, and those thighs—a glance I was confident he could shrewdly discern all over himself—and went to check on my UPS package.

As I went, I shouted back over my shoulder, "Tom, D.B. called. He and Tito were next-door neighbors at Atelier 24. Sniper Man too."

Tom nodded to communicate how nothing would ever surprise him again, so why was I bothering him with this?

Kept running. Didn't miss a beat.

"Penthouse floor, I assume?"

Chapter Twenty-Eight

It seemed like a smart idea at the time.

On Friday I'd ordered myself a paperback copy of *Long-Range Shooting for Beginners* from Amazon—my source for books I didn't want librarians or bookstore people—or Otis—to know I was reading. A few of my previous selections were a lot more entertaining than the incoming "50 Shades of Sniper" could ever be, but challenging circumstances demand sacrifices.

The person who arrived a half hour later with my package wasn't uniformed in the standard brown. Not by a long shot. Otis's current guard in the gatehouse called me on my cell. "Allie? Rick. UPS dropped a package off. I checked it over. It's not a bomb or anything. It's—Well, I guess you know what it is."

Busted. By an off-duty cop.

"Yes." A humiliated croak.

My secrets were not even safe with Amazon these days. Probably never were. I cleared my throat. "Bring it in when your shift is over?"

"Well. Actually. There's a person here I believe is okay to send down with it. Wants to see you. I've checked him out. He's who he says he is. Tons of ID. And the former owner of your house confirmed he's working for her. Plus I have to say no criminal I've ever seen would drive the vehicle he arrived in." He put his hand over the phone, but I heard him say, "No disrespect, sir."

"Oh, please, Rick. Go ahead. Send him. I can't wait."

The vehicle, flashing playfully among the trees along the drive, could have been the twin of the car I'd driven back in the days before the Mondo. My now-exiled Salsa Red VW Bug convertible, the Flying Tomato. To be candid, that was the car I was not-driving back then because I didn't have the cash for a nine-hundred-dollar brake job/tire replacement/ new set of windshield wipers, and whatever it needed to pass its E-check. New catalytic converter maybe. It got fixed by Tom's money and then stuck in the garage "for security reasons." My little car was apparently too cute, too red, and too me to be safely anonymous.

What Mondo money giveth, it taketh away.

This vehicle differed from the Tomato in one striking way. Somebody had painted each of the distinct sections of this bug— hood, front and back fenders, and both doors, its own unique color. Turquoise, yellow, pink, green, and much, much more.

The guy who jumped out of it with my package was plenty cute enough, and on first appraisal, unthreatening. Given my past experience with likable young strangers, this cut no ice with me. Nonetheless, Officer Rick was a pro, so I figured I could at least let the dude hand me the book I was already embarrassed about buying. He parked and climbed the steps. I opened the door.

"Hi. I'm Allie Harper." I held out my hand. "And that's my incredibly intimidating black and silver book."

"Do you even have a gun?"

"No. But you may have noticed I have licensed gun-toting individuals all over the place. So don't underestimate me."

"I would never. I saw the dog." He handed me the book and looked up at me, standing on my top step with one foot in the door. "Ms. Harper, I'm Jay Sawyer. I'm doing a design makeover for the ponderous mansion now owned by the former owner of your lovely, much more user-friendly mansion."

Flattery and curiosity tipped me over. Plus I agreed with Officer Rick about the car. "Come on in, Mr. Sawyer. Honestly? You're doomed. That woman will never be happy with any place, no matter how—" I fished for the right word.

"Venerable?"

"Exactly. But why are you here? She couldn't get out of this house fast enough."

"She sent me to get something she claims was left here in error. I redesigned her dressing room a couple of years ago and she—"

Ah-ha!

"She wants her chaise back? And you're the one who found it. I knew it couldn't be her. You're the romantic who made that gorgeous room. Aren't you. *Aren't* you? You are. Where'd you get the chaise?"

"Isn't it cool? House sale. Nice lady loved it. Got it from another lady who loved it. Who got it—you know how it goes. Passed along hand-to-hand after funerals, for generations. And I had to go and squander it on her ladyship. I bet the only reason she ever went in there was to get a bottle of Chardonnay out of the fridge and watch the shopping channel. She had her wardrobe headquarters in its own suite with bath. How did you know?"

"Well, I'm pretty intuitive and it clearly wasn't her style."

"You are so right. She didn't give a fluffy fart—sorry—She never even looked at it. She was the sort who'd like the idea of a 'vintage room' but she didn't give a hoot how it turned out. I've heard all about how much she 'didn't care for it,' but now she's discovered how much the chaise was worth.

"I took an invoice over there after work one night and she made me have a glass of Chardonnay with her and told me she'd seen it or 'one exactly like it' in a movie with Jean Harlow or somebody. I had to come on over here and get it right back. To threaten to sue you for it. As if. She hit on me too. So not my type. And she said such provocative things. Like, "Jay, your hair is so blond and your eyes are so blue."

We rolled our eyes to signal mutual solidarity.

Then I shook my head. Mock dismay. "Bad news for you, though."

"What."

"I sold it."

"Did not."

"Did too."

"Honey, they'll sell that one after your funeral. And you know it. Or you'll pass it on to your daughter."

"Uh uh. I don't have one of those."

"You will. Trust me. I know these things."

I couldn't think of a smart comeback for that. "I can't pass it on to anybody. Because, I told you. I sold it."

"How much did you get for it?"

"How much should I have gotten for it?"

"Well, if you were savvy about antiques—At least eight thousand dollars. Which is what I billed her. It has great bones and an iron-clad pedigree. No movie credits I know of. But you'd have been more interested in finding it a good home. And you clearly don't need the money. So, five hundred."

"Who do you think I sold it to?"

"A really nice lady named—uh—Sylvia, whose grandmother had one just like it. Too damn bad you don't remember her last name. Or contact information. You don't, do you?" He wrinkled up his handsome face in a caricature of disdain for my absentmindedness.

I shook my head, spread my empty palms to demonstrate bewilderment. "Sylvia is all I got. And she paid cash. Here, let me get you the five hundred. Tell Whatshername I'm devastated. Just…devastated. And point out there are not enough lawyers in this world to scare me."

I grabbed the five bills out of the petty cash Otis kept in the tea canister on the kitchen counter and handed it over, but I wasn't done hearing what I could tell Jay was dying to tell me. It was tough for me to find a truly delectable catty conversation in our current household. I was entitled to this one.

"Would you like a glass of wine, Jay? If I promise not to hit on you."

"Sure. If you promise."

"Cross my heart. We'll sit in the living room. My bodyguard Otis will protect you. What wine do you like?"

"Anything but Chardonnay."

"I feel like celebrating Sylvia's purchase of what's-her-name's couch. Veuve Clicquot work?"

"Oh yes. Indeed. Lovely choice."

I got the fancy glasses out and poured us both a nice splash. He caught me peeking at my watch. Ten-fifteen. The a.m. version.

He grinned. "No worries. It's Noon:15 somewhere."

I got us situated in the living room. He applauded our new décor and the absence of "pretentious crap."

We clinked glasses, and I settled in for our chat. "So what's she like?"

"Well, to tell you the truth, I think she murdered her husband."

Chapter Twenty-Nine

"Shut *up*!"

"No. I'm serious. He's dead. Somewhere out there. Maybe." A casual wave in the direction of Lake Erie. I reminded myself this lake I loved was not a tame body of water. People died out there, sometimes vanished permanently. All too often the search got called off.

"They quit looking for him at the end of November."

"Her trust fund guy? I didn't like him much, but I thought he was the better of that pair."

"The trust fund was hers."

"No way. Well, that takes the money out of the motive."

"Yes. And no. My theory is they were fed up with each other, but there was a prenup and he'd get half if she divorced him. Nothing if he divorced her. In my opinion she'd married above her pay grade in the looks and younger department and realized, way too late, that Mr. Young & Irresistible was not worth half her fortune."

"And?"

"And I think her young/hot/boring jerk became even more wearing after the move. That's a big, gloomy old house. I figured they were planning to stay out of each other's way, and it turned out there weren't enough square feet in all of Bratenahl to get the job done."

"So what exactly happened? And how did you find out about this prenup?"

He squinted his eyes at me and smiled. "Sweetie, women talk to me. They think I'm safe. Or cute. Or a short-term possibility. It's a perk of being Jay The Decorator. For example, you're talking to me right now."

That stopped me. I checked him out more. Great looking. Nice bod. Warm, sympathetic eyes. Cerulean blue, to be precise. Blond with russet highlights, excellent cut. He was damn adorable, but not my type, which was one hundred percent Tom Bennington. However, I'd automatically assumed he was trustworthy. Playing detective while human is tricky.

But there it was. I trusted Jay. For right now. Plus I was dying to hear what he was dying to tell me. Later, I'd run Jay by Tom. He'd pick up whatever threats I might miss. Anything Tom overlooked, Otis would catch. And I could always set the dog on him.

Jay breezed on. "So they had this kayak. She bought it for him, she says. Lightweight. Nice enough but not your Old Town Castine, if you know what I mean."

"I don't. I know nothing about kayaks except I always thought it would be awkward and mortally cold to fall out of one. Even in August." We both considered the concept of "mortally cold" as a small gust spat another round of sleet onto the windows.

"How did I not hear anything about this, Jay? I met the man. His business card is in my desk. Surely I'd pick up on the name."

"Not that surprising. It wasn't all over the press the first couple of days he was gone. They keep names out, for quite a while sometimes, until they know if somebody's seriously missing or maybe didn't tie up his boat the smart way. At that point, the attention span of the ordinary consumer of headline news has wandered off to check its Facebook page. And there was the time it took to rally the posse and find the boat. She wanted a low profile and had enough clout to get it.

"Your big old lake eats people, Allie. They get lost out there and some are never found. Mostly it's not headline news. At least not for long. Very sad, but not a big surprise. Our victim was well-to-do, but not socially—I guess you'd say 'adept.' Not friendly. Not pleasant. Not a community icon of note. *Not* a good conversationalist. *At. All.* Having talked to him for about a total of five minutes in all the time I worked for them, both here and there, I have to say taciturn does not begin—Good looking and semi-hot was the ballgame for that dude."

I made a mental note of Jay's 'our victim.' I needed to stay awake here and lay off the Veuve.

"How do you think she did it? Where is he now? How does it work?"

"Those are my questions exactly. Here's my theory. They move out of this house *here* and into the venerable estate down the road *there* in late September."

He illustrated the move by pantomiming the transfer of weight from his left hand into his right hand. I could visualize the three big vans it required, even with the stuff they left behind, like the chaise and the breakfast set. But not, unfortunately, IMHO, the thousand-pound contents of the wine cellar.

Unaware of my mental detour, Jay went on. "From what I heard, you guys moved from your old venerable estate into this— What *is* this? Tolkien Victorian? But so *cozy*—in October?"

He didn't wait for my nod of agreement on architecture and timing. "Remember that warm stretch of Indian Summer in late November? Pushed almost to 80? Everybody turning the heat off and the air on?"

I remembered. It was a bizarre, and probably environmentally worrisome, but lovely interval. "And he took the *kayak* out?" I shivered. The water must have been hyperthermia cold by then. "Why would he do that?"

"Why. Indeed."

"You sound like a British detective, Jay. You fit right into my little Victorian Tolkien World."

He acknowledged my admiration with a smug look.

"Keep going, Jay. There was a boating accident? I bet nobody saw a thing. Not many of the regular summer sailors on the water. Once you winterize a boat, that's the season. So he went missing in a big patch of lake."

"Exactly. 'Home came his kayak, but never came he.' It appeared to have been submerged in deep water for a bit, then washed up against the rocks after the first twenty-four hours or so. Easy to find if somebody was looking, and she sent the cavalry. Cops. Coast Guard. A chopper. The works. They found the boat floating upside down on the third morning. His cell was tidy and dry in a plastic bag in a storage compartment. Enough to ID the boat, at least, as him. Prints were his and hers. No clues there. He didn't talk much on the phone either. And that, ladies and gentlemen, was the last earthly appearance of Mr. Patricia Stone."

"Stone? Jay. Tell me she wasn't one of the original Cleveland Stones."

Bad enough to have a Wade on our plate. Venerable Cleveland was the curse of the T&A at the moment. A regular tour of University Circle.

"No. No. Not in the least. As much as it would please her, she's another variety of Stone. Sand, maybe." A grin. "But old-family rich enough. And plenty arrogant enough about it."

"All right." I sorted all the mental pictures I had of Jay's scenario. "Let's say she killed him. Somehow. Disposed of the evidence. Somewhere. Hid his body. Ingeniously. Got the kayak to where it needed to be. Somehow again—"

I broke off the talking and gave him my best, long, slow, inquiring gaze. "Jay. Why are you telling me all this? You and I are not just dishing the dirt here. Are we?

He sat quiet for a minute. A disconcerting departure from all his bright banter. "No. Actually we're not."

My turn. I performed a hasty, emergency, calming breath and fired off the best question I could come up with to flush out a liar. "Jay. Who told you about the T&A?"

He didn't blink. "Your friend Margo."

———

"Margo? My Margo? How do you know her?"

"Well, for starters, she's is not only *your* Margo." He read my face and relented, "Although she did confide in me you two are BFFs."

This made me feel better, but I narrowed my eyes at him anyway. "Is there anyone in Greater Cleveland who doesn't confide in you, Jay?"

"Well. Some guys. If they're wearing a Browns jersey that's been washed a hundred times. Or a hunting hat with ear flaps. Generally, those don't. But I am likable and unthreatening, as you noted."

"I'll give you that. So how?"

"I'm another one of her tenants."

"Not in my former house."

"No. Not yours, Allie. I looked at it back in the day before you, but its charm came from never being touched by an interior designer. I didn't want to ruin it. I guess now you and Margo have decided it should remain an abandoned memorial to the two years Allie Harper, part-time librarian, was in residence there."

That stung. "I'm paying rent. Or the Mondo is. And she keeps raising it."

He chuckled. "She would, wouldn't she?"

"Yeah. That's Margo. So you told her what you're telling me and she shared with you about the T&A. In fact—" I paused for five seconds to consider what I knew about Margo and was jolted by the unmistakable scenario.

"Jay, you've been sitting in Margo's garden, knocking back the old 'whatever's-not-Chardonnay' since before she met me, and therefore you've heard everything there is to know about Allie Harper. Going back two years before I met Tom and the jackpot. And all about—" I stopped myself and did a quick review of everything Margo knew about Tom and me. "Everything else."

"I know a lot. But Margo's Margo, Allie. She's loyal. She gave me none of the prurient details." He rolled the cerulean eyes. "I filled in those blanks for myself."

I took fifteen seconds to reorganize my universe and came back to Jay. "You've heard everything about the T&A since the Lloyd case. At least. So you know how my adorable 'mysteries of the heart' game plan has turned out to be one scary murder after another?"

He nodded. "I do."

"Then you know, in spite of its frivolous name, the T&A is nobody's game, Jay. Our current caseload is full up right now. We've got a murder, another murder, and a subsequent murder-of-a-murderer combo. And much, much more. You delivered my new book from Amazon. There's a sniper out there. And he's capable of—" I shivered. "Go look at our breakfast nook. The ceiling's on the fucking floor. Why would you want to get involved with any of this?"

"She's a terrible person, Allie. I'm about eighty-five percent confident she's done the ultimate bad thing to a merely mediocre person, and she's all set to get off scot-free. I can't let that go. It offends my sense of fair play." He must have read the skepticism around my eyes. "And, in the interest of full disclosure, I might as well say she's been on my last nerve for five, long, *ugly* years and I want to get her back. Okay?"

"Okay. Revenge. I get it. You're wacky. Go home, Jay, and don't do anything about this until you hear from me." I gave him my best imitation of the Margo glare. "I mean it. I'm the local expert on how many ways a so-called amateur detective can get dead.

I've got things to sort out. Give me your phone number and get out of here."

He grinned. "I'll do better than that, sweetie. I'll give you my card." He grinned more. Clinked my glass.

"Hey," he said, "how much are you asking for the armoire?"

Chapter Thirty

While I sat staring at nothing, the morning crept in slo-mo around my couch. Jay gave me the card and showed himself out. Tom passed by on his way to the shower, placed a kiss on the top of my head, and gifted me with a sweaty hug. I kept right on sitting. Otis appeared from wherever he'd been. Disappeared. Came back. Went into the kitchen.

After ten minutes or so a waft of good coffee reached my location and I heard behind me the familiar Otis step. He came around and set the coffee down on the side table, next to the half-gone Veuve Clicquot, the two empty glasses, and my moody black and silver sniper book.

Made no comment.

"Thanks, Otis." I picked up the cup. It was a to-go cup. A spark of hope. Tiny, but warm. "Otis? Are we going somewhere?"

"Time for a road trip, Alice Jane. Just you and me. I told Tom. He said, 'good idea.'"

I wanted to ask if he thought Tom meant "good riddance," but I was training myself to believe in true love and unbridled passion and keep my trust issues in the dark.

"Is it safe to leave here?"

"Nothing's a hundred percent, but you yourself are a lethal

combination of stir-crazy and freaked-out today. You don't think I can feel you simmerin' from all the way down the hall? Come on, girl. You need a break and we need to talk. Let's get outta here."

Otis took the curves of the driveway in a manner that delivered an adrenaline rush. Rick waved us through the gate, out into the real world, and up against the full monte of March. The real world was wet and gray—make that charcoal gray. Chilly rain-lashed, pathetic, quivering trees. Every headlight we met was on. Not that there was much traffic happening on Lake Shore Boulevard this lunch hour. You had to mean business to go for a spin in weather this awful.

Otis meant business. He opened by asking about Jay and he nodded along to how I wanted his opinion and Tom's opinion and probably Oprah's opinion before we signed Jay and his case onto our agenda.

"We're too busy, right? Otis? It's too crazy now. Right?"

"Maybe. Might be what the doctor ordered."

He turned onto Eddy Road, heading for the Shoreway and my spirts began to lift. A fraction. Out of my sneakers and up around my ankles, but it was a start. "Thanks, Otis. I needed this."

Disgusting soupy slush splattered my window. I smiled to myself, and inhaled the leathery smell. I was feeling enough better to submit to whatever interrogation Otis had in mind.

"Okay. What do you want to talk about, Otis?"

A long sideways glance. "What's goin' on with you, Allie?"

"That's a joke, right? A hundred things are 'goin' on' with me but I'm trying to handle them one at a time. In the order of their DEFCON number."

"What's the number for whatever's been making you go around looking worried, confused, and kinda embarrassed. All on your one face."

"A two, maybe? Two and a half?" After thirty seconds or so, I fell into the trap of his silent waiting. I exhaled, forced my shoulders down a notch, and hauled my new book out of my purse where I stashed it as a sign of mental preparedness. Held it up where he could see it and still drive.

"Otis, I don't know anything about snipers."

Whatever question Otis was gearing himself up to address, this one clearly wasn't it. He nodded toward the cover of my book and dismissed it with a shake of his head. "Give thanks."

"But if the T&A is going to be dealing with snipers—"

"Allie." He was now arranging his expression to be respectfully grave over the top of patronizingly cracking up. It was a pitched battle. Brow vs. chin.

"I can read your face, you know."

"That's excellent news. So what are you reading now? Beside the snipers' handbook, which that book you got there is *not*, by the way."

"I can see you don't want to insult me by laughing?"

He tried to suppress a small gyration of mouth and eyebrows. Seized control.

"Very good. Now. You be the detective and explain to me why I'm looking at you like that."

Alrighty. On top of everything else, I was getting mad.

"You're the licensed PI, Otis L. Johnson. How about you go ahead and give me a clue?"

"Allie. What you saw on my face is the look I always get when someone sticks 'sniper' and 'T&A' in the same sentence."

My shoulders sagged the rest of the way. "Dammit. Otis. I hate feeling stupid."

We were doing sixty-five around a massive tanker truck slinging a curtain of muddy water onto our windshield. So far, my view of our road trip along the Shoreway had been blurred vehicles getting passed by Otis, low-slung, dun-colored commercial and industrial buildings on our left, the backside of Bratenahl cowering behind high barriers on our right, and slight variations on the curtain of muddy water. My heart rate was twice as fast as the wiper blades. I was gripping my armrest and holding my breath, but still marginally happy to be out of the house. If Otis noticed any of this in his current state of concentration, it didn't show.

His eyes were on the road. His voice was calm. Matter-of-fact.

"Girl, you are not even in the ballpark of stupid. However, I'm sorry to have to repeat the sad fact that you and Tom Bennington III and I are all of us equally well-equipped to see a sniper's bullet coming. As demonstrated yesterday."

"But, Otis, I can't—A bullet out of nowhere with no warning? Coming for Tom. Or you. Or me. Or Jay, dammit, if I don't run him off. Kip Wade—"

My voice was a microsecond from breaking, and an amateur detective worth her salt doesn't cry. I swallowed and released my death grip on the handhold.

Buck up, Alice Jane.

"How come we don't have our own sniper, Otis? Surely we can afford one."

"And that would make us safer how?"

"Maybe our sniper would shoot their sniper before their sniper could shoot us?"

Now you're talking, Alice. That would be way cool.

"You are listening to yourself, right?"

"Yes, Otis. I just heard myself. Sorry. That was dumb."

Traitor.

"But, Otis, I feel like I'm losing it. I'm even jumpy when I'm asleep. I can't trust myself to—handle anything. A blind woman in a sari gave me a fancy note for Tom and I simply forgot all about it until the next day. How can I—"

"Do you know what PTSD is?"

"Sure. But—"

"Yeah, 'But.' You're right. It's not you. I've seen it. You don't have it. So. Wednesday night while you were at the museum, Gloria handed you the envelope and then—"

"I got the call from Lisa and she said—"

"Right. She told you somebody blind had been shot, down by

Severance Hall. A spot you knew Tom and I could be in. Were in. You ran through that mess we saw on the Gloria video. Out to that balcony—where you could have been shot, out of nowhere no problem, by the way. And about then, I'd imagine, the note got erased off your brain by its built-in survival instincts. Big surprise, Allie, you were scared. And distracted.

"We all were. Me. Tom. Even Tony. The one thing you can't afford, Allie, is to lose confidence in your smart, creative, brave self. She's in there. I know you can deal with the harsh reality that there are things we don't get to control. Tom is dealing with it today. I thought he was going to wear that treadmill out this morning.

"So, Allie, listen. There's no MondoMegaJackpot Winner's Police Academy to prepare you for what you all are handling, day to day. For one thing, there has never in the history of criminal investigation been a so-called detective agency like the T&A. The name alone—" He passed a hand down over his face to straighten it out and went back to breaking the speed limit.

I could make out the skyline of Cleveland now, rising tall and cranky out of the bloom of red taillights. The Terminal Tower scowled at us through the murk. Tough old icon of the city's glory days when the builders of the city were all moving to Bratenahl— just in time to watch the stock market self-destruct. My town. No apologies.

"Look, Allie. When Tom won all that money and everybody within a six-state radius found out? You both stepped into the deep—Nothing deep I can think of is deep enough to describe the mess you were in. Still are. That accidental jackpot of Tom's is one genie ain't goin' back in her jar. You all drew the Good Luck Fairy that smokes weed, drinks Jack Black, and juggles grenades."

He noticed the speedometer approaching eighty and backed off the accelerator again.

"Listen. You guys woke up everybody with those multi-millions. The penny antes *and* the howitzers. It was a crapshoot, shook up and thrown out onto the table. You and I met one of the penny antes in the garage at the Arco Building. Armed and dangerous, no doubt. A screaming wind tunnel between his ears. Worst/best day of my life. So, look, I'm in. I've been in ever since you kicked that dude in the nuts and gave me a shot at him. You've got plenty of what it takes."

"Otis?"

He threw a sideways grin at the bewilderment in my voice. "Some speech, huh. I hope you paid attention because I meant every word. And I don't think I could repeat it from memory. Now hold on for a minute. I got another couple of things you need to know."

Big, rapid deceleration. We'd caught up with traffic and got wedged into the stop and start. He zapped me with his "Zero Bullshit Otis" face. I kept paying attention.

"Here are your real so-called detective skills: Smarts. Guts. Intuition. Commitment. Honesty. Although I wouldn't put much of anything past your Lee Ann." He stopped. Shook his head. "If you ever get into a real jam, I'd give her the upper hand.

"On the downside? Patience. Attention span. Self-preservation. You're still weak on those. That's real unfortunate. Because the worst, most useless girl detective on the planet is the dead one."

"Geez, Otis. Now you sound like Tony."

He snorted. "Tony. He talks tough to you but, Allie, if you weren't busy getting your feelings hurt, you'd have figured him out. All that pushback and put down is a tough, cranky, worried old mother hen. He's seen plenty of stuff to turn him that way. Don't take it so hard. And don't tell him I told you that or I'll swear you lied.

"So, look, you need to stop studying on trajectories and what fancy armor-piercing ammo might be out there with your name on it. There are things you cannot duck. Ducking is damn dangerous all by itself. We need you to rely on your brains and instincts to help us figure out what the fuck is going on at any given moment.

Let Tony and me—and the guys in the garage—keep you as safe as we can. No half-assed end runs. We're in this together. You got that?"

"Yeah, I got that. Otis?"

"What?"

"You hungry?"

"Starved."

"Take me to Arby's? We can drive through."

"Works for me. You better now?"

"Sure. Nice cold, dingy, sloppy drive, dodging tanker trucks and speeding tickets, topped off with a Smokehouse Brisket signature sandwich and fries, which we will actually eat right here in your precious truck? Should do the trick."

"Don't push your luck, Allie."

"Never, Otis."

So we drove to Arby's and drove through the drive through. I got the Brisket, a thing of fries, a mint shake—because nothing says March in Cleveland like ice cream dyed green—and about two hundred extra napkins. Otis got the Fire-Roasted Philly and a Diet Coke. We ate in the parking lot, hidden behind our tinted windows. Otis ate three quarters of my fries. After that we went home.

———

The sugar, salt, and grease helped level out my high-test jittering too, but now I had a virulent case of "Don't Know What To Do With Myself." And the boogie-woogie flu. Our pretty glass house was watertight again and had a new ceiling fan. Nonetheless, Sniper Man had ruined it as a refuge for me at least for today. The repairs hadn't made it chill-tight either. Currents of dank, frigid air circulated in there and kept trying to worm their way into the kitchen.

A drink might have been calming, but Jay and I had already

dismantled the No Booze Before 11 A.M. rule. Not smart to go back there. I didn't feel like reading. Especially I did not feel like reading *Long-Range Shooting for Beginners*. I was never going to learn to long-range shoot, and Otis had disqualified ducking as a solution for high velocity projectile peril.

Otis disappeared into his man cave. The security folks were discretely deployed. Nobody had shot anything around here since the afternoon before. Tom was listening to music and/or sleeping on what I'd come to think of as "our couch." Or "our Buick."

So there I was. No help for it. No excuses. I went up to my dressing room, glared at the TV for good measure, changed into my scruffy workout gear and headed to the treadmill. I found my rhythm. Measured. And my pace. Slow. I sent my mind on vacation, which, inevitably, devolved into a replay of last night. I was playing "It's Gonna Be Me" into my earbuds, and jogging along. Poor Tom. His imaginary runs were all melting asphalt and the smell of kudzu or whatever. I'd have to tell him about my playlist. I smiled.

Smiling was a mistake. When I let my guard down and did that, the phone rang. I picked up and Lisa Cole said, "Allie. We need to talk."

Chapter Thirty-One

"No way, Lisa, I need to hang up on you."

"Don't. Please. You were watching 16 last night."

"I was. Watching you smearing Tom's name all over TV-Land."

"Allie. Wait. It wasn't—I got put on administrative leave."

"Lisa." I turned her name into liquid sarcasm. "Why on earth? I thought you were doing a regular bang-up job last night. Channel 16-style."

She was quiet for minute. "I probably have that coming, but Allie. What did you hear me say last night?"

"That the message left at the museum was for MondoMega-Jackpot Millionaire Tom Bennington III." I admired my snarl.

"I didn't say that Allie. Remember again."

"I don't—" On second thought. What I remembered was Lisa's deer in the headlight expression. Her hair whipping at her face. The cut back to the anchor.

"*He* said it." I rearranged the sequence of my memory. "The dumb ass on the desk. You didn't?"

"Because I couldn't. He read that on my face. Even if you didn't."

"Is that why—?"

"Yeah. That's why I'm on everybody's list at 16 right now. Why

I don't care very much, either. Look, Allie. Let's not do this on the phone. Can we meet somewhere?"

"When?"

"Six-ish?"

"Where?"

"Flying Fig?"

"Works. Otis will drive. We'll have guys following too."

"Good."

———

Lisa Cole and I faced each other across a couple of Manhattans in a booth in the bar of The Flying Fig. Except for a murmur of conversation from the main room, the place was quiet. Otis had selected the booth because (a) it had a high back to hide us from the front windows; (b) the door was marked "Please use other door," which stopped traffic coming in but didn't stop a few folks from trying; and (c) he could sit reasonably close without unnerving other patrons by looking like a bodyguard. Or inhibiting Lisa and me by eavesdropping.

He'd situated himself midway down the long bar and was pretending to enjoy his N.A. beer. I saw the face he made after each sip. A couple of extra guys, hired special for the occasion, were parked out front. I felt like Taylor Swift hiding from my fans. I bet no one would realize I was her tonight.

I'd left Tom home, lying on our couch, eyes shut, listening to the "Chet Baker Sings" album, from 1956. The man had eclectic tastes. Jazz. Classical. Indie. I hoped he was thinking about me, maybe worrying about me—not much, but enough to fuel some plans for another high school reunion tonight. Euphemism.

Lisa Cole gave me what a classic noir detective might describe as "the fisheye" over her Manhattan. The Manhattan was a warm, friendly brown. Lisa was wary, with a splash of offended. I reminded myself I was dealing with a skilled reporter. Lately she'd been a happy ex-officio member of the T&A. Now she was on administrative leave from the T&A. Also from 16. Which put a different light on things. Setting aside her noisy visit to the crime scene Wednesday night—we hadn't spoken since I hung up on her in Gallery 241-B. We had a lot to discuss.

I stared into the depths of my Manhattan. It was lovely, dark, and deep, but I needed to keep my wits about me. Maybe just a taste. So this wouldn't feel so much like an interrogation.

The glass was weighty and cold in my hand. The liquid smelled sweet but authoritative, and somewhere in there was a jigger of lighter fluid. Perfect. It didn't rush non-stop to my head, but the heat of it softened up my heart as it passed by on its way down. When I viewed Lisa Cole through the lens of that kinder, gentler sip of booze, I could still catch a glimpse of my friend.

You always hear how a person who knows she's about to die will get a flashback of her life. Just the high points, of course, because time would be fleeting. Watching a friendship you think might drop dead in the next ten minutes can give you a moment like that.

I saw Lisa, laughing with me over salads and girl talk. Being great to Loretta when Loretta's heart was broken. Eating a whole one-pound Slyman's Corned Beef Sandwich with glee and no apologies. Lisa's horror at the moment she discovered she'd been the unwitting pawn of a serial murderer. Her ambition to be a full-fledged member of the T&A and to realize a dream she still entertained of how a reporter's stories might be worthwhile instead of one reckless, tasteless Channel 16 scoop after another.

I pushed the drink a few inches away from me. "Lisa. We're friends. I want us to stay that way, but we have to talk about how we can be friends and work together and not endanger anybody. Especially Tom. Also Otis, who's over there assaulting his taste buds with an N.A. beer to protect you and me. Margo. Valerio. Everybody. So I need to ask you something."

She scanned my face. Glanced away in the direction of nothing. Said, "Sure, Allie. Ask away."

The question had been tapping me on the shoulder, bugging me, ever since I woke up on Thursday morning: That phone call at the museum. Lisa's Huey Lewis ringtone. Her question, *"Allie. Where's Tom?"* The one that broke open my world and trashed my life for a few endless, terrifying minutes spent running through the museum to the balcony and bullying my way through the crowd to get to Tony.

My body was reliving those frantic moments as I studied her face. I folded my arms onto the table and leaned on them. I could feel my shoulders curling in to protect my chest. And my heart.

She nodded. "I get it. I get what you need to know. I can see it. You want me to tell you if I was standing over the body of a blind man when I called you. If I rang you up from—that—so I could prey on your—on your life. For a fucking scoop?"

I sat up and pressed my shoulders into the hard back of the booth to straighten them out.

"Yes. I might not have put it quite that way, but yes. I'm sorry. But I can't—"

She brushed off my apology. Picked up her drink. Set it back down. Met my eyes.

"Those are two separate questions. I'll answer them both. Was I standing way too close to the body of a dead blind man who from what I could see looked an awful lot like Tom? Yes. I was right there. As close as I could get to the barrier. But Allie, I couldn't see his face because—I couldn't see it. So I didn't know for sure.

"I called you to find out. I wanted you to tell me you were both safe at home. And I promise you, if you hadn't hung up, I would have handed my gear off to the sound guy and come to find you until we knew for sure.

"For, me, Allie. For me, that night, as far as I could see, it was Tom lying on the pavement, shot dead, almost at my feet. That wasn't a scoop." Her face collapsed into that awkward, flushed, trying-not-to-cry-but-too-late-to-stop-it morph. Unraveling into a sob.

"Allie." She choked on my name and grabbed a couple of breaths, trying to get control. "It was a nightmare, Allie. The cops wouldn't let me get closer to—the body—or cross the lawn either. They were hustling me out of there when Tom and Otis showed up. You can ask them. I was a mess and a wreck and my makeup was—I wasn't covering the news. I was falling apart."

I groped around in my purse and passed her a handful of tissues. "I wish I hadn't asked you that, Lisa. I—"

She grinned at me and blotted her face. "You didn't ask me that, Allie. You were about to beat around the bush for ten minutes, blurt out something, and then take it back. Girl. I may never make any kind of detective, but you will for sure never be a hard-ass reporter. Not unless I give you lessons."

She handed half her tissues over and we both blotted around and blew our noses. I pulled my drink back toward me. She got hers back too. We clinked glasses.

"Now," she said, "you and I need to have a serious talk, and we're going to have to figure out our ground rules. I think 16 will work me over and, after a short pause for the brutal brow-beating, take me back. If they do, I can work there until I find something better or they fire me for real. I'll also help you as much as I can from inside. I'll be a detective and a spy. Because, in my soul, I'm done with them. But I need to not look kicked out if I can avoid that. And I still have to pay the rent on my awesome new place."

"One last question. Let me try to ask this one out loud. Who leaked about the note, Lisa?"

Lisa pressed her lips together, thoughtful, as if she was taking both sides in a conversation with herself.

"The protect-your-source thing is gospel, Allie. Sacred. People go to jail. I'm proud to know women and men who've done that. But in the spirit of the rule, I hope, I'm going to tell you. Not because I'm mad at 16. Though I am. As hell. But to protect my source from you poking around and getting him fired."

"Getting who fired? Who—Oh." *Light bulb.* "Lisa? It was Chad? Chad Collins."

"It was. And although he was wrong to talk about it, he's a very sweet man, and he was bamboozled by a clever, treacherous television reporter who was not me this time. Our guy was so earnest and interested. So disgustingly impressed and encouraging. I wanted to barf. Your guy Chad is such a fan of you and Tom and so thrilled about being 'part of the investigation—' He was putty, Allie. It was painful to watch. Especially when he said, 'You aren't going to print this in your paper, sir, are you?' You aren't going to get him fired, are you Allie? Or yell at him."

"No. Of course not. Thanks for telling me. I promise not to yell."

I gave a second thought to what she'd just told me. "That's why you clammed up last night. Not only because of Tom and me. For Chad too. You're a stand-up girl, Lisa Čebulj Cole. I'm sorry I hollered."

"You did not holler, Allie. I'm going to have to teach you the difference between being outraged inside your head and outside of your mouth. It's a skill you could use."

She glanced back toward the kitchen. "Let's see if we can find a waiter and get us snacks. I plan to have at least two of these and I can't do that on an empty stomach. And tell Otis to come over here and sit with us. He has the only level head in this bar."

Otis came over. He brought a bowl of peanuts he'd been using to blunt the essence of N.A. He pretended not to notice the both of us fussing at our makeup, read us the menu, and took our orders.

"Waiters give up on ladies like you two, who sit around talkin', drinkin', cryin', and huggin' after happy hour is over. I'll get us food. Allie hasn't had anything to eat today. Except—"

"Otis."

A bland expression. "A light lunch, Lisa. On the run. With a green shake. Not to mention, Veuve Clicquot with an interior decorator before noon. And Lisa? One of my guys will bring your car, and we'll drive you to Atelier 24." He grinned. "We know where you live."

Chapter Thirty-Two

9:00 P.M.

Standing in front of the shining glass entrance of Atelier 24 on a cold, drizzly, Northeast Ohio evening, craning my neck to take in its many, many stories of living spaces—the top several of which were wrapped in an honest-to-goodness cloud tonight—I shuddered. I hoped Lisa was not well off enough to be living up close to the pinnacle of her new digs. The penthouse lair of Tito & Sniperman. And D.B.

Our best guess was Mr. Clear Water and Tito had been roomies, back in the day before yesterday. Until the darkest hour of yesterday morning. Separate rooms, probably, in spite of D.B.'s homophobic musings. Way separate agenda for Sniperman… as it had turned out.

The thought of all his Machiavellian scheming preyed on me as the three of us rode up in Atelier's streamlined elevator. Building management would have changed locks and canceled security keys by now. At the same time, I was confident a sniper might have other handy skills besides shooting people and breakfast nooks.

He could probably jack a key card with the best of them. Even months later, I couldn't erase from my memory the *Chirp, Click,*

Clunk that popped open our hotel room door for a killer last summer. I was doing an instant replay of this tune as we reached Lisa's door.

I was trying to look delighted and impressed by the news she'd moved here. "On a whim, Allie. Took one look at the view and started packing my truckload of clothes. And the three matching dishes. And the pan."

"Do you feel safe, Lisa? After—"

"No worries, Allie. Security is airtight. Look. How cool is this?" She pressed her thumb into a pad on the door. "Touch ID!"

Her door's latch reprised my most unfavorite three-note tune, in the key of *clunk*.

It was cool. It was amazing. It was—my stomach roiled—another excellent use for a dead man's hands. Hiding Tito's identity and stealing it in one fell swoop. Our sniper maybe could still get in up there. A man with the skills to make effective use of a penthouse view.

I had no intention of raining Tito's missing thumbprint onto Lisa's parade. The coverage of the discovery of his body had not included any grisly details. "Body of unknown man found near lagoon at Art Museum" was sensational enough to dominate this morning's news. 16 needed Lisa to pry the juiciest scoops out of law enforcement for them. They'd realize that soon enough.

"What happens if somebody moves out, Lisa?"

She gave me an evil smile, "Well then. I guess you'd have to turn in your thumbs, Allie." Wiggled hers at me. Pushed open the door. Nope. Lisa had definitely not heard about Tito's hands. Just as well.

Lisa's one-bedroom apartment on the fifteenth floor was both my dream and my nightmare. I followed her straight through the living space, which registered "Wow, *trendy*" on the HGTV of my mind, out into the gusty night, and onto her vertiginous balcony. Otis came with us, angling his body to protect Lisa and me from—drones, maybe. I didn't comment. I was too busy taking it all in.

As noted, I am not a friend of high places. In spite of my unbridled desire to live to be ninety-nine and die in bed with Tom, whenever I get up high, a tiny voice whispers, *"Go, ahead, Allie. Jump!"* As a practical matter, I would never, but it was comforting to know that Otis could tackle like Mean Joe Greene. Or at least well enough to stop me from doing something I wouldn't want to do anyway.

Add to my precarious state of mind the gobsmacker view. Otis was appreciative of this as well. "Holy fuckin' spectacular."

The downside of being able to see all of everything everywhere? All of everything everywhere can see you right back. An equal and opposite risk. Especially if the individual seeing you has a top-of-the-line gun with an expensive you-finder and knows how to use it. Against my better judgement, I'd peeked into my black and silver users' manual before I threw it in the trash. 2000 yards is not unheard of. That's a mile and change. A goodly chunk of change. Somebody is claiming "a success" at three. Dark and nasty might hide us tonight, and I was being paranoid, but—

"This is amazing, Lisa. And I'm freezing. Otis, we need to go."

The inside of her apartment was as warm and cozy as four rooms perched on the edge of a cliff could be. It was stellar, but I didn't think I could ever get to sleep here.

"Lock up, Lisa? You're under the same roof as D.B. Harper."

"He's not scary, Allie. I can handle an idiot. I'm glad I didn't know about—the other guys. Glad they were gone before I knew they were here."

Chapter Thirty-Three

MONDAY, MARCH 5

I woke up Monday morning early. Tom was sleeping next to me, peaceful as I'd found him when I rushed upstairs last night with my thrilling plans for the rest of our evening. Dashed. The melancholy Chet Baker vibe must have knocked him out.

At least I was reminded, once again, of how lucky I was to find this man next to me every morning. I made a few more plans to keep us in bed together from today until 2085, and gave his fabulous back my warmest, most alluring, gander.

Psychic Messaging: Out-of-order. He groaned and burrowed deeper into the covers.

Therefore, between seven forty-five a.m. and ten a.m. my day was bland. This lasted until 10:01 when two unexpected things happened in quick succession.

I might have predicted the first:

One of our guys—not Rick or Adam, the two with names I almost remembered—appeared at the front door with a stack of mail. I rifled through it. A thick, ugly Value-Pack, full of cheesy ads for which I had no need at this time, a handful of bills, which held no terror for me these days, and a letter for Otis.

Tito was dead, dammit. We were supposed to be done with sinister mail. But here it was. Addressed, in hand-written block letters, to Otis L. Johnson. Our address. No vellum. No fancy script. No way I didn't know exactly who sent it.

I hollered "Otis!" in a tone and a decibel that brought him up from the cave, Tom down from upstairs, and an extra security dude in from the garage. Like magic. Not-Rick-or-Adam hadn't made it back out the door yet, so he was still there too.

I'd already touched the envelope with my naked hand. As had the guy, and at least three postal workers, by my count. It was March, however; therefore, no doubt, there'd be heavy-duty gloves on a couple of those. In any case, it was from a person who'd proved himself quite competent at a significant number of things—He would not smear his prints on incriminating stuff. Or use it to poison us before he got what he wanted.

I held our third envelope out to Otis.

"It's for you."

Otis fished in his pocket for the gloves he now carried everywhere and unceremoniously opened his mail.

First of all, this style of envelope was available in packs of 50 or 100 at any Walgreens or Office Depot in town. Second, the stationery was torn from a nondescript pad, folded neatly over. My detective skills said, "This individual is no-frills-serious." A thing I already knew.

The message bore out my theory. More block letters. Nothing fancy, Otis read it aloud.

"NO MORE GAMES, NOBODY DIES."

Got it.

Another calling card, this one streamlined as a full metal jacket. Tito's elaborate scheming, stripped down to strictly business. I wasn't fooled for a minute. This guy wrote his messages in blood.

"I got to call this in. We'll talk. Allie. Tom. Chill out for a minute."

I had one question for Otis that wasn't about people, us in particular, not playing games or dying.

"Otis, what does the L. stand for?"

He kept walking, "Allie, I'd have to kill you."

"Otis. Take a number."

———

The arrival of the note was not a major shock. An informal greeting from a stone-cold killer wasn't a fraction as scary as having that killer shoot your glass roof off. We were seasoned graduates of the school of "What you don't see is what you get." Or "The suspense is killing you." We could handle a note on cheap stationery.

I was congratulating myself on maintaining my—superficial, at least—composure.

However.

The second unexpected thing of the morning was a bombshell for which none of us was prepared.

When the doorbell rang again, I peeked out to see the former lady of the house, a.k.a. The Merry Widow—standing on her former front steps. Snappy black coat. Matching umbrella. Big nasty frown. I needed all my hard-won self-possession not to scream.

Okay. I knew this person had been inspected at the gate. Plus, not long ago, we'd written her a check for 2.4 million dollars. Surely she wouldn't kill me in front of witnesses. One of whom was armed. I opened the door.

"Mrs. Stone."

"Ms. Harper."

"Come in. And it's Allie. Here. Let me take your coat."

I tried to measure her minimal civility against Jay's suspicions. He'd been very convincing. His facts were intriguing. I'd never liked her either.

I dispatched her coat and the umbrella, made note of how her trim figure was 100% encased in black. Mourning her wicked deed, no doubt. Her posture was commendable, if tense. She preceded me into her ex-living room. Seemed barely aware of how charming we'd made it.

I offered coffee.

She waved me away. Strode right past me and straight up the graceful curve of the staircase with its custom bronze-embellished railings.

Alice Jane Smith Harper, go! You're smarter, twenty years younger, and not dressed for a funeral. You can take her.

The moral support was welcome, even if I was the only one who could hear it.

I went up the steps two at a time and caught her as she swept into my dressing room. Without missing a beat, she walked over to the chaise, picked up Margo's shawl with two nitpicking fingers, held it at arm's length, and dropped it to the floor. Sat down, crossed her skinny legs, gazed up at me, and raised an eyebrow.

Red velvet and black dry-clean-only made an interesting contrast. She began stroking the lush upholstery with a possessive hand.

"Now. Is there something you'd like to say to me, Ms. Harper?"

One of the advantages of being in all kinds of danger, due to having a fatal dose of good luck and a subsequent oversupply of cash, is that it raises your kiss-my-ass-attitude to a professional level. I'd faced murderers, kidnappers, and a murdering kidnapper with a gun aimed at my heart. On two separate occasions. To be fair, only one of them pulled the trigger. I could deal with a woman in a posh black suit and sassy little black bootie boots.

Take her down, Alice Jane.

"Yes." I allowed myself a moment to admire the extreme lack of fear in my voice. "As a matter of fact, there is something." I leaned across my desk, snatched up the receiver of the vintage phone and held it up like a symbol of truth and justice. "I can call the guards in our security room. Or the Bratenahl Police

Department. Or just holler out the window for the guy with the dog. You. Choose."

Ha. You said holler. Do you think she knows that phone's not hooked up?

Patricia Stone had come to deliver righteous intimidation and shaming. She'd mistaken her current situation for the high ground. There was nothing in her Junior-League-society-matron arsenal this morning to tackle the famous Allie-Harper-Lee-Ann-Smith-Bring-It-On."

The high dudgeon drained off her, and her angry momentum left town—

Look out Allie, she's thinking about making up.

Dang. Lee Ann was right.

Up closer, with her victory lap over, Patricia Stone appeared distraught. Under different circumstances, I might guess she was scared about something. She stood up, wavering on her teensy heels and folded.

Off-suit deuce and seven meet a Royal Flush.

Yee. Haw.

Okay. This was not about the chaise anymore. Chaise was leverage. Leverage backfired. Too bad.

"Let me see you out, Ms. Stone."

And nail you for homicide.

"Wait. Allie. And please. It's Patricia. I've got us off on the wrong—I'm—sorry about—this. I've been—not myself lately. I need your help. Could we sit back down? Talk? Just for a minute?"

"Sure, Patricia." I pulled the desk chair out and offered it to her. Claimed my rightful place on the chaise.

Huh. Well, look who won that pissing contest.

At this delectably gratifying moment, Otis popped in, set the coffee service down on the desk, and left. He hadn't heard Patricia's rejection of coffee, or hadn't cared. Or maybe he was taking an opportunity to check up on us. I needed coffee like nobody's business. She appraised and dismissed it. Of Otis, she said, when he was barely out of earshot. "*That one* seems competent enough."

"Pray you never have occasion to find out, Patricia."

I was ready to toss her off the front steps without her damn umbrella. Now I was triply committed to nabbing her for the ruthless murder of her worthless spouse. I could put up with her for maybe another thirty seconds, but the clock was ticking.

"Why are you here?"

I searched her face for clues. She looked well-put-together in her black Armani or whatever, but not good. I estimated her at late forties. Early fifties, maybe. Haggard will pile years onto your face. Icing your spouse will do that for you too. Her skillfully faux, jet-black hair was skinned back tight and locked into a punishing bun that made my scalp ache to look at it. No softening for the tired shadows under her eyes, no quarter to the fine lines holding her mouth in check.

Guilt, I bet. All over her cramped-up face. That was it. But that still didn't explain—

"Allie." My name was a sour taste in her mouth. She stopped. Glared at me. Started again. "I need—"

Another hesitation.

"Allie, my husband is planning to kill me, and I need—" She closed her eyes, pursed her lips against whatever she was about to say.

This gave me time to think, "*What? What?*"

"I would like to engage the services of your—agency. Your T&A."

Laugh? Cry? Scream? How do you answer a cluster bomb?

"I'm sorry. Would you say that again?"

"Are you mocking me?"

"Not at all. Patricia. I was unprepared for your—request. I understood that your husband died in a tragic—"

"In a fucking *kayaking* accident? *Steven?* You've got to be kidding me. You met him, right, Allie? At least once or twice."

Well. There was a turn of phrase. I could not even imagine Margo saying "fucking kayaking accident."

"I did. Last fall. But I don't recall—"

"That man would only drown in a—in a kayak if someone knocked him unconscious and roped him in there with a truck-load of rocks to hold it down."

"And that someone—with the—rope and the—rocks—and the, um, knocking out would not be you, I suppose."

"What do you think?" She was squinting her eyes at me now. A parody of skepticism. I hadn't noticed how black and shiny they were. Like insect eyes only not as human. Carpenter ant came to mind. I pictured creepy antennas waving. Needed to get grip here.

She ignored my expression.

"I know you talked to Jay. I knew you were lying to him about the chaise, even if he believed you. $300? Seriously. He's not as smart or as cute as he thinks he is."

Jay. You dog.

"Frankly, Patricia, I believe he's both."

She swiveled in her chair and looked down the hall. "Why is *he* listening?"

Damn. I was starting to fantasize about murdering her myself.

Mrs. Carpenter Ant. In the dressing room. With a—with an unopened bottle of Chardonnay. Are we having fun yet?

"He's our *bodyguard*, Patricia," I hissed through gritted teeth. "And carrying concealed. You might want to rethink—"

"You have a *blind* bodyguard? And he's armed?"

My ears tuned in. Tom, moving confidently down the hall.

"No, ma'am." Tom's Atlanta drawl could resurface without warning, especially when was mad or about to laugh. In this case, it could be either. Or both.

"I'm the T of the T&A."

Chapter Thirty-Four

My dressing room was now officially overcrowded. Its Maximum Occupancy Limit was Two Persons. Four in a pinch, if two sat on the chaise, one at the desk, and one on the ornate stool of the antique dressing table. I was acutely aware I hadn't gotten around to "mentioning to Tom" about the chaise. He sure enough knew now.

He and I were sharing the chaise but not in the way Lee Ann suggested the first time I saw it. He settled himself in beside me and murmured, "Is this a *chaise longue*? How was it not part of our guided tour? It's a hell of a lot more interesting than your teeny-tiny fridge."

"I was saving it," I muttered back. "As a surprise."

Sotto voce. "Well, I am surprised."

"Why don't we revisit this conversation after four or five hundred of us have gone home."

"Gotcha."

Otis returned after Tom arrived and therefore drew the short straw on seating. The dressing table's stool was designed for someone with a less ample derrière than mine and was bordered with carved, gold-leaf curlicues. Cute but not comfortable. Definitely not for Otis. Understatement. I made Patricia trade places with him.

She was giving Tom the once-over. I wondered if she might be considering making a move on his blind hotness. Or plotting to drown him in "a fucking kayak." Tom's blindness could work in her favor, but he'd have full access to the scariness of her voice and the chilling pulse of her frantic aura. Her voice was cold and grating. Crow-like. She was not his auditory type.

Something—no, wait. Every single thing—about this morning was driving me to the edge of hysteria. Precipice of hysteria.

Otis had brought a plate of his killer muffins and put them on the desk within my reach. I did not say, "Otis makes killer muffins" as I often did when there wasn't a putative killer in the room. Patricia, whom I was now calling 'Patti" in my head for my private amusement, eyed him with new respect.

"Otis is armed?"

Otis gazed at her. Allowed "former military," "ex-cop," "current PI," and "all-around badass" to breach the veneer of his otherwise gentle demeanor. It was a thing he did with his eyes. And jaw. I never got tired of watching. Or watching its effect on whomever he fired it at.

Patricia sat up straighter on her gilded seat and swallowed.

Otis continued, with the eye-thing still fully engaged. "I am, Patricia. And you can address me directly. I promise not to shoot you. Let's put your—all this—behind us, shall we?"

I picked up a muffin, tipped it to Otis, bit a big chunk of its top off. This was not my easygoing guy who'd dropped the "g's" off "huggin'" and "cryin'" last night. This was Loaded-For-Bear Otis.

Patti was the bear. She got that. Sat up even straighter.

"Of course, I—Of course."

Tom laid our cards smack on the table. "If you could convince us your husband isn't dead. Ms. Stone," Tom said, "we'd extrapolate you didn't kill him, which we've been led to believe you might have. Moreover, I suppose his not being dead would free him up to kill you. While keeping him from being a suspect. Make him a viable threat."

I relished Tom's sardonic professor voice. So cool it was hot. His hand rested lightly on my neck. He could read my neck, I knew. Neck braille. A friendly offer was sent from my neck to his hand. Euphemism.

Pay attention, Allie.

Something was missing. Something obvious.

Like motive. "What's his motive, Pat—tricia? It can't be money. He can't inherit if he continues to use being dead as his alibi."

Geez.

"Otis? Is there...sherry? Or something?"

I always admired the generous application of sherry in British crime novels to situations of bewilderment and agitation. I tried to remember when I'd ever had sherry. No time like the present.

"Generally not before noon, Allie. At least today. Keep on asking those good questions."

"But Allie," Patricia took a deep, centering breath in order to better address my plebeian ignorance. "He doesn't have to inherit to get all my money."

"How is that possible—Oh." My whole body went quiet. "Who gets the money if you die?"

"My niece. Heidi. My brother's daughter."

"Your brother—?" This was Tom.

"He's dead. My only sibling. I have no children. Heidi inherits everything."

Tom was right there. "This Heidi. And your Steve?"

Lordy. And everybody around here is so buttoned up in the daytime.

We were all right there.

A bitter smile. "Not 'my Steve,' not for the last five years. But yes."

Wait a sec. Ask her—

Stop. I got this.

"Can't you just write her out of your will."

"That would be lovely, Allie, but this isn't common money. It's a trust fund. I was stupid. I could have given Steve his prenup cash to get rid of him. That was a ridiculous idea back when he asked. By the time it started looking like an answered prayer, it was too late. He was angry. Angrier than usual. Still a dolt, but Heidi is nothing if not clever. What she sees in Steve—"

I was pulled off course for a second by "common money." Long enough hear someone say, *Arrogant Bitch*. Inside my ears. But then I thought about Tom's Mondo money. Not common either. And, at the same time, tackier. So I cut Patricia some grudging slack.

"And if Heidi should become—out of the picture?"

That set her off the rest of the way.

"Ha. That's a sweet way to put it. You mean if she got crushed inside a garbage truck. Or eaten by feral cats? I dream of it. But no." She tuned back in to what she'd said. Shook off the daydreams and answered my question. "She's got a younger brother, my nephew, who might be a decent human being, given time and attention. But you can see my situation. Oh. Sorry, Tom, I—"

"No worries." Deadpan. I knew he was thinking what I was thinking and Otis and Lee Ann were thinking too. Which was *Honey, that's the least offensive thing you've said all day.*

Patricia let herself slump against the dressing table, black eyes gleaming dread, not menace.

"I'm scared. The security system is excellent. But Steve knows that house. He sneaks back in sometimes. Leaves...things. A half-finished beer. He's partial to Bud Lite, naturally. A pair of shoes. My size, but from Payless." She said "Payless" the way ordinary folks would say, "LandFill." Only not as generously. The insult quotient of those shoes reminded her to sneak another peek into my closet, which was standing wide open and confirming all her expectations.

I wanted to drag my mad-spiked boots out from under the bed and kick Patti in her bony shins with them.

She continued the list of spooky and inferior things left by Steve. "A dead *bird*. I called the cops and they said, 'Probably flew down one of the chimneys.' It's a nightmare. The house is older than God. It creaks and moans even when there's no wind. And when the lake freezes out back, it cracks like a gunshot. The shadows never—Whenever I start down the staircase, I—"

Tell me about it. Twelve thousand-plus-square-feet is a pants-wetter. I'd spent a long hour cowering in a closet of a house almost that big once, before I fell asleep in self-defense. A part of me was would always be quivering like a scrawny little hairless dog about that.

For a couple of seconds, I tried to empathize, but my better nature tripped a circuit breaker. I wanted to call bad old Steve and tell him giving Patti the bird was a laugh riot.

"Are you staying alone there? At night?" Otis's emphasis was on "alone" and "night." The "what are you thinking?" was understood.

"I had a girl who stayed nights, but I fired her. I tried to get Jay to stay, but he said that would be above his pay grade. He's such a—"

Go Jay.

Tom roped her in. "Has Steve made direct contact with you since he—disappeared?"

She shook her head. "No. Not counting the bird and—. Except I got a text I was afraid might be from him. It said, 'Still here, Patti?' I tried to have it traced but it was a dead end. He ditched his real phone when he sank the boat.

"I did buy a gun," she volunteered. 'It's a Glock something. Expensive. Highly recommended. Supposed to be lightweight, but heavy for me. And I've never actually fired a gun."

OMG.

Otis stepped in. "Please don't even think about using that gun, Ms. Stone. Wait here a second." He took himself out of earshot, phone in hand. Came back after five minutes. Didn't sit. Stood looking down at Patti in a way that caused her to sink a few centimeters deeper into her tiny, golden seat.

'Your story is unusual. But plausible, I suppose. I'm going to send one of my back-up people to you. She'll meet you at the gatehouse in a few minutes. Adam will walk you up. Wait for her there. Monica Cowan. She's smart. And seasoned. Retired from the P.D. but a private investigator now. You'll appreciate her no-nonsense personality."

Sounded like "prison matron" to me. I guessed Patti was wondering too, but she nodded meekly enough. Beggar. Not chooser. A new role for her.

"Give Monica your Glo—gun. That'll be safer for everybody. We'll get together with the other members of our group as soon as we can. We have issues to deal with today, but we'll either put together a plan or refer your case to someone else."

Patricia started to protest but decided not to push her luck. I smiled to myself without moving my lips.

We-the-T&A were now the devil Patricia knew.

Chapter Thirty-Five

By the time Patricia—who was henceforth officially "Patti" in my mind—left, it was early afternoon. We'd already piled up a week's worth of To-Dos. We couldn't start doing them yet, however, because, when I opened the door to hand Patti over to our guy, Homicide Detective Olivia Wood was standing next to him, looking official.

She turned to watch them head up the drive. I noticed the rain was coming down harder and colder—a weather moment that felt transitional to me.

Olivia was trained to ignore that sort of thing. "Who's that with Adam?"

Uh oh.

I suspected the lieutenant had limited time and/or patience for a story as tangled as the one we were sorting out. Convoluted kerfuffle, I'd call it. The bogus murder and death threat combo.

Besides, to be fair, Patti's situation was more a matter for the Bratenahl PD, whose natural response to her story might be to turn back around and take another hard look at Mrs. Stone for the kayak murder of Steve. Or make fun of the bird again. Before I could begin to explain any of this to Olivia, I would have to get my detective head in order and find out whether the consensus of the T&A regarding this case would be, "Are you kidding?"

Valerio would bring Olivia up to date when we knew more. Or Otis could decide to tell her when she went into the kitchen for the note and whatever he had in the oven. Not my call.

That handful of thoughts and rationalizations zipped through my head as Olivia and I watched Patti and Adam disappear up the drive.

"Neighborly visit, Olivia. Come on in. I'll take your coat. It's getting nasty out there. The note's in the kitchen with Otis. There's coffee. And muffins. And possibly pie." TV crime shows got one thing right: As long as nobody's shooting, a cop can be diverted by pie. I'm a little bit law enforcement myself when it comes to pie. I tagged along.

Business first. Otis produced the envelope and the note. They both handled it with gloves in spite of the combined years of experience that said, "Waste of time and gloves."

I got that. Admired it too. I wanted to become that caliber of detective. Skilled. Focused. Dependable. Somebody committed to a dogged, unyielding code, who'd handle skepticism, fear, and plain exhaustion and keep walking the grid.

Miles to go, Allie Harper.

The glass coffee table in the greenhouse had yet to be replaced, so we had the pie, coffee, and conversation in the dining room. When we first moved in, I'd been quite taken with this room. It wasn't uptight and baronially overdone like our former mansion-y dining room. The old-fashioned, many-paned windows of wavy glass offered a painterly view of pines in many sizes and shades of green, plus a slice of lake with its ever-evolving hues of water. Also rolling breakers in different shapes and sizes. And the rain. Looking nastier by the minute.

We'd sorted ourselves. Otis Johnson, PI, and Lieutenant Olivia Woods, Homicide, on one side of the table. Tom and Allie on the other. Pros v. Amateurs. I was trying to read Olivia's expression,

Tom was no doubt trying to listen his way into her mood. I bet we'd agree on "murky."

"Stacey? Is she—?"

"Stacey's fine. Well, not fine, but okay. We're keeping an eye on her for a bit, but, common sense, she's not his concern. From his perspective, she's peripheral. This new one is not Tito Ricci."

All our current hopes, fears, and heartaches, summed up in a simple sentence. The more we knew about "this new one," the more cold and dangerous he looked.

"We've got bits and pieces, but nothing's clear yet. He's the new regime. Tito's out, and this guy appears to be his own boss. Not working *pro bono*, you can count on that. Planning on you guys to make all of his efforts pay. Unlike Tito, he's not interested in holding University Circle for ransom. That was more 'Tito-over-the-top'. He just wants the jackpot." She stopped to clear her throat. Stared at the windows as if she was hoping to see something better than March.

"We're going over that empty penthouse. Not much left after the cleanup—" She paused, reviewing the little she had. "Nothing at all on their in-house cameras until they got them started up again. University Circle CCTV may give us an idea of where he's been, but he's professional, this guy. Let's hope he's as businesslike as he looks. Hope we can be smart and grab him soon."

She looked out the window some more. Under Olivia's buttoned-up appearance, I saw a layer of bone-tired. And, under that, a bunch of worry. The precision of the murder of Kip Wade and the cruelty of Gloria's death belonged to our so-called newer, cleaner guy. The grisly killing of Tito—the horror of the hands—haunted all of us now.

"I wanted to let you know I got a call from Chad Collins, your guard—"

"From the museum. Is he okay? I was just—" Not going to reprise what Lisa had said last night. She'd sacrificed something to tell me about his conversation with the bogus journalist, I wasn't about to betray her. Or Chad.

"—wondering about him. What did he say?"

She smiled at me in an "I know who you are, Allie Harper, and I forgive you for it" way.

"He told me about talking to the 'news guy' who turned out to be from 16. As if that isn't as obvious as one of their cheap—You and Lisa Cole still tight?"

"Jobs come with built-in compromises, Olivia. She told me about Chad because she doesn't want him to lose his job. I hope you—"

"I won't say anything to anybody. He wants to get into the police academy. I didn't discourage him, but I told him not to give up his day job until he knows more about what cops actually do. Big leap from the day-to-day of 'don't stand too close to the pictures.' They don't send museum guards to their posts saying, "Let's all make it home for dinner." He's on the older end of eligible. He's afraid to call you. I thought you should know, but apparently you have your own source."

"Lisa is a friend. And I like Chad. Next steps? What should we be doing now?"

"Not a damn thing, Allie. Your next step is to stop in your tracks. All of you. Sit tight. I don't see any role for the—for you all until—For a while. Except as very careful civilians. The Art Museum—University Circle in general—it's all quiet now. I talked to Cecilia Southgate at the museum. She agrees. Their security is always on the alert. We've got an eye on things. So that lets the T&A"—for the first time in the history of our five-and-a-half-day relationship Lieutenant Wood cracked a smile about the name—"off the hook for now. Stay alert. Let Otis and his team keep you safe. The next move is your new guy's. I don't believe you need to worry about it being another bullet out of nowhere. He wants something. He'll let you stew until you're irrational and then make a demand.

"Grab a breath. You guys sit tight. Read a book. Binge some Netflix."

Or take on a small, quick, new case.

Chapter Thirty-Six

TUESDAY, MARCH 6

10 A.M.

Sometimes you have to throw caution to the winds and go to a funeral. First, however, I had to stonewall a wannabe attendee.

"No. Tom. No. Not a chance. Not a prayer."

"Allie, I'm going. I have to. I have a responsibility to Kip's—"

"Send them a nice note. Make a donation in his memory. Visit his grave someday. You cannot show up at his funeral. Think again. This whole thing got started because Kip Wade was almost a dead ringer for you."

"That's not funny, Allie. He's dead because he looked like me."

"I didn't mean to be funny. Listen to what you just said. Think about what it would be like for his family and friends—"

He let this sink in. "Okay. I get it, but you can't go either."

"That's where you're wrong. As much as you can't go, I have to."

"And why is that?"

"For starters, I'm not a...a look-alike."

"Okay, but surely you'd be a painful reminder."

"Tom, you have never seen me, so you don't understand how completely I'll blend in. In a black dress, I'm invisible. Everything about me is nondescript. I cut him off before he could say what I saw on his face.

"Thank you. Your kind disagreement is noted in advance. I have an outfit that makes me essentially invisible to anyone who doesn't know me as...well as you. I'm going. I need to find out stuff. Kip had a brother."

"Robert Frost Wade. I've met him. He's the brother who's not blind. Kip always referred to him like that. Hyphenated. My brother-who's-not-blind."

"Robert Frost? Wow. They—That's—Never mind. I'm sure Robert's sad about his brother, but I think he might talk to me. I can scout around. See who else shows up. Tom, what you said about Kip looking like you is true, but we don't know why he died. Not really. Maybe not at all."

"I would be happy if we could find out what Kip Wade was planning last Wednesday night. There had to be something in it for him, a reason to go out there alone. He believed somebody would meet him. Give him something. Tell him something. I'm hoping important information will show up when I talk to Robert. Something unexpected."

Yeah, Alice Jane. Like a bullet out of the dark. I threw her and her redneck twang off her spot next to Tom on the red chaise. He and I had taken to meeting in the dressing room. Just to chat. We both had plans about that we weren't discussing. Yet.

I'd now ransacked my closet for black and frumpy and turned up quite a bit of frumpy but not a lot of black. I had two dresses to choose from. I gave up and picked the one that would cover my knees. *Funeral, Lee Ann.*

I threw the dress over the back of the chase and sat down next to Tom. "I want to know how Tito got to him, Tom. What Kip had to gain by going down to the lagoon. Whether the scene at the door was a complete coincidence or a part of a strategy we've only got a piece of. Kip is dead because of—we don't know exactly what. Critical information is missing."

He exhaled and unwound himself maybe a half turn. "Okay. You're probably right. I don't like this, but you should go. Take Otis and his security. Wear your frumpy disguise."

———

Church of the Saviour in Cleveland Heights is a magnificent house of worship. Gothic in design, it fronts on the full block between Bradford and Monmouth Roads and reaches toward heaven with a tower chock-full of bells. Forty-seven to be accurate. Weighing thirteen tons. I loved everything about those bells.

For the five years of my unfortunate marriage, this church was my Sunday morning haven. When I sat in my customary spot, steeping my sad crankiness in the glow of the stained glass, the rolling chords of the big pipe organ, and the welcome, reaching out from the membership, I felt as if I'd arrived safe home.

This afternoon, as Otis and I slipped into a pew midway back, in the shadow of the stone arches, I felt as if I'd never left. It reminded me of my Buddha. My Buddha reminded me of it. There's a place in the heart recognizes a home when it finds one.

The church wasn't jam-packed with mourners for Rudyard Kipling Wade, but it was a respectable showing. He hadn't been nice, but his family went all the way back in the history of the congregation.

His father was there. And his mother. He'd had a mom and a dad. On this occasion they were the wreckage of a handsome, well-to-do couple. His brother—Older? Younger? No clue—was sitting next to the mom. They'd been ushered in as the service was beginning. The dad carried a white cane.

The cover of the little program ushers were handing out showed a Kip several years younger than I'd seen him last Wednesday evening, walking with a big brown guide dog. The dog made me like him more. I was prepared to discount the only five to seven disagreeable minutes we were ever going to spend together. Except for Tito Ricci and his shooter, nobody could have dreamed a week ago that Kip would be here this afternoon on a carved pedestal in a tasteful urn. I'd been next door to his last half hour and it was still hard for me to take in.

I drifted along on the familiar current of the service. A lovely solo of "Take My Hand Precious Lord," by a man I'd not seen there before, the appropriate scripture readings by a couple of young cousins. After that there was a hymn and then Robert got up to talk about his brother. I noticed the Frost part of his name was omitted from the program.

At first, he seemed more nervous than sad. I guessed he wanted to do a good job, comfort his parents, make his brother-in-absentia proud. He was smart and well-spoken. He told a little story about how his kid brother had created major disarray in his confirmation class by expressing serious reservations about, "well, just about everything. He was like that. Always doubting. Always battling. Always at odds. He was so brilliant, so tough. I thought he'd mellow as we went along."

He paused for a long moment as the bones of the old church clicked and shuffled like they do. "So. We're here for him today and we're very shocked and sad he won't have the time to find the joy he had coming to him—"

His voice broke. I'd forgotten to bring tissues. Otis passed me a clean hanky.

The minister was a new guy since my time. He was young and radiated intelligent kindness. He didn't make me feel terrible about myself. He said things that would comfort a sad believer. And he told Robert that he believed Kip would find the joy he had coming to him. It was hard to tell if people were encouraged by this. Attendees of funerals are almost always polite and undecipherable.

When the service was over, everyone headed to the parlor to shake hands with the family and have refreshments. Methodists excel at refreshments. After all, they get a lot of credit for the invention of the potluck. Little sandwiches, meatballs on tooth-picks, and rafts of cookies. Lemonade and coffee. I wasn't hungry so I queued to express my condolences, figuring Kip's people wouldn't have a clue who I was. I was right about everyone except Robert.

I shook his hand and said, "I think your brother would have liked what you said about him."

And he said, "You're Allie Harper. We need to talk."

———

The chapel was empty so we ducked in there. I could tell Otis was pleased to get me into an enclosed space with doors a bodyguard could stand guard over and see both of.

We picked a pew and sat sideways, facing each other. Robert resembled Kip without the hard, angry edge, and the dark glasses. Also Tom somewhat. I knew from experience that a warm under-standing is possible without eye contact, but it helps. We sighted humans believe we can figure out a person by looking into his eyes. It's all guesswork.

"I didn't get to know your brother, Robert. I only…met him… for a few minutes Wednesday night. He was…outspoken. But I could tell he was very intelligent."

He smiled. It wasn't a happy smile but there was a spark of humor in it.

"He was a royal pain in the ass, Allie. You want to know the whole story about the membership class? He totally blew up the discussion of heaven and hell. Said you'd have to be a—expletive-deleted since this *is* a chapel—moron to believe any of that crap. And he didn't say crap either. Nobody there would have beaten him up for what he did or didn't believe but he took himself out of the discussion by dismissing faith in anything as being naiveté. Stomped out. The next time he came to church was this afternoon. In a vase.

"What happened, Allie? I know you're on the inside of this somehow. You must know something. I won't tell my parents anything they can't bear and I certainly won't be quoting you, but they need some kind of explanation. Kip had been talking about a genius business guy he'd run into at The Happy Dog on Euclid. He hung out there a lot. Ubered to get around town. Uber was a godsend for him. Anyway, guy's name was Tito, I guess. Like the vodka. I never got a last name. Was he—was Kip—really murdered because he looks—looked—like Tom Bennington? Is that possible?"

Possible? The first time I ever kissed Tom Bennington, we were interrupted by a woman's voice, reciting Tom's winning lottery number. How could I tell Robert Wade I could trace a line of cause and effect from that moment to his brother in the vase?

Straight up, Allie.

"It's possible, Robert. I'm so sorry. Actually, It's probable."

"So, your Tom is responsible for…this?" Angry color bled onto his face.

"No. He's not, Robert. My Tom is responsible for buying a Mondo Mega ticket to show a kid in our neighborhood that gambling doesn't pay. To protect him from it. The odds were— You have an idea, I'm sure."

"I don't get it."

"Don't even try. The day I met Tom, he was an associate professor of English lit at Case. A handful of hours later he was 'The Blind Mondo.' No chance for anonymity. Not even on that first night. Because of the way the news got out. And where it got spread to. Which was all over Greater Cleveland. The MondoMegaJackpot is the devil's own game.

"If I hadn't seen it up close from the beginning, I would never have understood how the simplest thing can create a chain of events you'd never predict. You can't stop it. Or control it. All I wanted that night was to kiss Tom. All Tom wanted was to say to the kid, 'Look, Rune. We didn't get even one right number.'"

Saying Rune's name out loud brought it all back and spilled the sadness of everything that had happened into my voice. How we'd planned to adopt him. How I'd pictured us as a family. How we were too dangerous to even see him now. Before I could shove it back into place, I was sobbing. At least I still had Otis's hanky. I used it for the mopping up.

"I'm sorry, Robert. I'm so sad for you and your folks. I've been watching this for almost two years. So much violence. So much greed and ugliness. So many people have died—"

"So, Kip was at the wrong place at the wrong time? Mistaken identity?" At least he didn't sound so mad.

"No. We don't believe so. It was more than that. We think Kip was set up. We don't know how or why. We think the…person was waiting for him. Specifically."

"Money." He shook his head. "It had to be money. Kip was on fire about a new treatment. Expensive. Experimental. Maybe a pipe dream, but he could never give up on seeing again, and he believed people like him and my dad were… *are*… getting their vision back. Dad would have helped him but he'd lost a lot when the economy fell apart. And he's realistic. He's been blind a long time. This Tito person? Why would he want to kill Kip?"

I could see it better. Tito had preyed on Kip's oversized ego and his terrible loss. Offered him his sight back. Didn't have to deliver the money to pay for his chance at sight, because, from the beginning, he was planning to kill him. As a power-play message for Tom.

Here was at least a partial explanation for Kip's outburst that last night. *How come you're not a big philanthropist, you sorry son of a bitch?*

No way on God's green earth was I going to tell Robert the truth about the why of Kip's murder. "Nobody knows for sure, Robert. The investigation is ongoing."

Well, that sounded like a lame police briefing. "We're pursuing all available leads." Giving him zilch. Robert shot me a look loaded down with skepticism, but he didn't press. A person can walk the perimeter of something he doesn't want to know and never step over the line. I do it myself.

"What will happen now?"

"The police will continue their investigation."

"They'll tell you what they find?"

"At least the high points."

"Are you working with them. I heard—"

In spite of my opinion that Tom's money was well-used trying to solve "mysteries of the heart," I was not going to discuss the T&A in the chapel of a United Methodist Church with a guy who'd already invoked, "expletive deleted" to spare the empty chapel's delicate ears.

"Tom provides funding for investigations sometimes." Strictly speaking, this was true. Patti Stone fluttered through my mind like a bat in a black dress. I waved her away.

"Robert, we'll tell you whatever we find out that isn't restricted by legal stuff. And you can decide what to share with your parents."

"Promise? Even if you think I can't handle it. I can."

"Promise."

I offered him my hand, and he held onto it for a moment before he let it go, capturing my gaze with his. Then he reached into his coat suit pocket and pulled out a card. "Call me when you know something. Anything at all. And I'm sorry I lashed out about Tom."

I shook my head. "No worries, Robert—" I glanced at the card. "You dropped the 'Frost,' huh? I dropped the 'Alice Jane.'"

He smiled a little, his eyes looking somewhere far away. "Yeah. And Kip always said he'd dropped the 'udyard.'"

Chapter Thirty-Seven

7:00 P.M.

In spite of our circumstances—unstable, unpredictable, and probably dire—it was fun to watch Jay Sawyer on Tuesday evening arriving at the realization we'd been coming to terms with since yesterday.

His face matched the dazed incredulity in his voice.

"Allie? You're telling me she didn't hide his body anywhere? Because it's not—*he's* not—*dead*? Patricia is not the murderer? *He* is. But nobody's dead. At all. Yet."

"Uh huh. He's one of those wannabe murderers, Jay. Our specialty."

Margo, Bright & Bouncy.

The T&A was her natural habitat. From her perspective it was mostly gossip, thrills, and parties. Any memory of terrible discoveries, terrifying fireworks, or a party better described as a wake, she would suppress. Tonight she had us exactly where she wanted us.

The T&A met in Margo's atmospheric living room last summer for a quick detour from our main, inaugural, Lloyd case. It didn't appear to be an opportunity for disaster, but somebody died anyway. The blast from that detour deafened Tom for a long day and night and still re-echoed in my chest. Not loud. Not over. An ordeal can end without being healed. The plan we devised in Margo's living room that warm June evening, blew up in our faces, and did major damage to my cute, sassy spirit.

, Tonight was supposed to be another minor detour for the T&A. Our most recent case was in scary limbo, a waiting game. The sniper had our attention, but he hadn't outlined next steps. Olivia had freed us up for reading and Netflix, but I couldn't sit still for more than three minutes. Time for a diversion. I felt curiously relieved to have something—anything—new and different to focus on. Numb, maybe. At least I wasn't wearing my funeral dress tonight.

Present and accounted for: The full, unabridged complement of the T&A Detectives. In the order of our tenure, Tom & me, Otis, Valerio, Margo, Lisa, and, due to his pivotal role in our new case, Jay.

Except for Margo and Princess, Margo's vast, black mastiff, and Valerio, whose car was already here for some reason, we'd arrived together. The T&A now totaled seven. For tonight, at least, we were The Full Escalade.

Three of Otis's security team had preceded us and were now in strategic positions. I didn't know exactly where, but I was sure they weren't staked out in Margo's garden tonight. This was prudent because Margo's garden had been cancelled tonight. On account of snow.

One can never over-emphasize the staying power of the phrase, "March in Cleveland." Or how it can be applied to a full spectrum of weather options, ranging from "seventy-six degrees and sunny" to "WTF?" The word "Armageddon" comes into play, in the company of modifiers not found in the Book of Revelation.

However, even the national weather folks were caught off guard when a late-winter storm they'd promised would merely "batter the East Coast" took a spiteful turn and came battering on in across our great lake. Winds gusting to forty-five. "Snow, up to twelve inches."

Peek. A. Boo.

"Lake effect storms" usually hauled their excessive inches on up to Shaker Heights and dumped them there, but this one was an equal-opportunity dumper, borne on the full force of an icy wind.

Margo's cottage was cozy-warm, wrapping us in its lush, comforting glow. The house shuddered in the wind, though, and, from the base of the cliff at the end of her property, waves thundered and growled. Their collisions sent tremors up from the foundation to the soles of my feet. Tough to ignore.

Margo's big, weathered kitchen table must have served a family of Vikings back before Vikings were only a football team. It accommodated the new, expanded T&A comfortably with no elbowing. Margo was at the end closest to Mabel, her vintage Maytag oven, so she could supervise whatever was bubbling in there, and dominate the discussion as much as possible.

Valerio sat at the right hand of Margo. I was tucked in between him and Jay. Otis got the other end, Lisa and Tom the other side. The Princess Vespa didn't require a chair as long as she could rest her head somewhere on Tom. I shared that sentiment.

Jay was grappling with his new reality.

"But Patricia's such a *bitch*," he moaned, "and I've hated her for so *long*. Allie, you've met the real her now. Was I right?"

"Yeah, painfully right. But, Jay, this is your case. If Steve is clever enough to kill Patti so Heidi can inherit—

"Oh, well. *Heidi*." Jay's expression gave up maybe fifty percent of its skepticism. He rolled his eyes. "Heidi's in on this? Now you're telling me something I can work with. On the evil scale from Steve to Heidi, Patricia is a four. Steve is now a six. And Heidi is a fifteen. The two of them as a team? Off the charts.

"Steve is a human bludgeon. Blunt but useful. Heidi's a unprincipled, over-indulged babe. Steve is putty in the clutches of a babe. We should consider Steve to be 'The Pawn of Heidi.' And therefore 'Heidi's Human Bludgeon.'

"You make it sound like a cheap thriller, Jay." Lisa was wearing her combative, detail-oriented-reporter face, and her eyes were on target, the way they got when a juicy headline might be in the room.

"Way cheaper now that I know Heidi's on board. *Lisa.*"

Jay was making eye contact with Lisa in a way that made me reassess my first impressions of him. Margo was checking out her old Chardonnay-swilling bud, Jay, as if a new day were dawning on her horizon too. This signaled the imminent arrival of an unscripted and bound-to-be-memorable Margo-ism. I sat back and waited. Tom, blind and psychic, waited with me.

"Jay. Aren't you gay? You know I like to fix people up but you always—"

"Yeah, Margo. I love you too, and you always, *always* like to fix people up. How many stories have I heard about who would be perfect for whom? And 'how kismet' is it Allie and Tom are so right for each other? And blah, blah, blah. I've witnessed how your matchmaking works out when it self-destructs. I figured I was better off letting you cling to your inaccurate assumptions.

"So, look. It's no big deal. I'm an interior designer with a well-developed sense of style. Also a pragmatist. It doesn't hurt my credibility—or my feelings—if my clients assume I'm gay. It helps me fend off awkward advances." Jay and I exchanged an episode of eye contact that spelled out P-a-t-r-i-c-i-a in the air between us. "If you have someone in mind for me, Margo, I might be grateful. My dad would thank you too."

Otis and Valerio were managing their expressions for opacity. Lisa was looking over at Jay like he hadn't shown up on the Lisa-Meter and now he was at least preregistered. Margo was taking offence at the "And blah, blah, blah," but almost over it. New possibilities were arising. She was observing Jay and Lisa with an expression that needed its own cable channel.

I couldn't see Princess, but I could tell Tom was rubbing her ears, so I figured her mighty mastiff head was driving his leg, slowly but surely, into the floor.

Just another ordinary evening with the T&A.

Lisa. Businesslike. "What happens now? Do we vote? We agree that this woman, this Patricia-Patti, is a bi—has a lot of undesirable and unlikeable traits. I'd like to go on record that many men have those as well, except we talk about guys differently, but I'm prepared to let that go. For now. Sounds like your Patti is in real danger, Jay, and none of us wants her to be murdered. How do you usually proceed?"

Tom shifted in his chair. "Last time, Lisa, I bought a house." Those of us who'd been there shared a moment of silence, remembering the assorted traumas of Tom's detonated house.

I was right next door to Valerio's mixed emotions, which included three or four different flavors of agitation. Otis, at his end of the table, was making guarded eye contact with Valerio.

"Tony?"

"Yeah, Allie. Otis and I talked this afternoon. I drove by and looked. That's one very big house your Ms. Stone is in. Way too many exits and entrances. Way too—" He broke off, remembering.

"She's a sitting—She's vulnerable in there. Otis and I think this Heidi, being the one with a brain, is hoping for a fatal accident. Tidy. A fall. A little breakdown in the carbon monoxide detector. An overdose of sleeping pills if she's taking those. Which I bet she is. I would if I was her, trying to get a decent night's sleep in that joint—Anyway, something that fits."

"Or suicide," Otis added. "She's murdered her husband. She's all alone, in the coldest, darkest end of winter. Guilty, jumping at shadows."

To punctuate this theory, the thud of a heavy wave jiggled the house under our feet.

Sitting duck. I was beginning to wonder if Patti would survive the night.

I reminded myself about the unexpected snow storm. Car tracks. Boot prints. Muck trailing all over. Not optimum. Somebody up there was watching over Patti, and her new housekeeper Monica, for us this evening. Maybe the complications of crappy Cleveland weather had saved Patti up until now.

Things got quiet. We were all sorting our ideas about who killed, or didn't kill, or was about to kill, who. I was watching Jay who had more opinions about Patti to rearrange than anybody. I figured he was out of his depth. Poor Jay.

"I'm the newbie here, right—Lisa, were you in on this party last year?"

"Nuh uh. Ex officio. Not invited. Not as newbie as you, though."

"So I'm new, but I know that house, Lisa. Top to bottom. And I can go there any time without anybody getting antsy. Steve definitely assumed I was gay. He has a stereotype for everything. He believes all women are hot for him—"

He pulled his phone out and started poking and swiping. "I'll send you the house plan, Otis. Tony. Give me your emails. I have window measurements. I know what's installed everywhere. I've even been in the basement. It's a rat's fantasy."

He raised his shoulders and dropped them. "I cannot stand that woman, you guys. She appalls me. She insults my friends. I hate her guts. No remorse about that for me. But brace yourselves. This is the worst thing you may ever know of me."

We waited.

"Okay. I kept taking work from her even while I thought she was a murderer. She's paid me a barrel of money over the last five years. And because she has such conventional taste, and her new house is so wonky, the work is still a fun challenge. Like when I put your dressing room past her, Allie. That chaise—"

Chaise.

Tom, without his dark glasses these days, had much better access to his eyebrows for a private communication. I ignored him as best I could. But Margo said, "Heh."

Fortunately, Lisa picked that moment to respond to Jay's confession. "Oh, stop that, Jay. You think you're the only one who ever took a slutty job for the money and the challenges? You ever watch 16 News?"

"Every once in a while. You're the best thing on it. Your sports dude doesn't suck either. I play a little game where I chug for the commercials. That helps."

This earned him points, I could see. Lisa squelched a giggle and salvaged her dignity by glaring at the memory of 16.

Whoa. Jay was not nearly as out of his depth as I'd supposed. He rolled on. "From what I'm hearing, our first job is not to nail Steve and Heidi, even though that's where the most fun would be. It's to keep Patricia alive and protect your guard, Monica, until we can locate Steve and flush him out into the open. We do this, we've won and nobody gets shot or kayaked or anything. If we can prove he's alive, we've got him."

"Got him for what, Jay?"

"It must be a crime to fake your own death, Lisa. I mean at least he'd be in trouble about the helicopters and the Coast Guard. Not to mention cops everywhere for several days.

"And our goal here is not justice. It's keeping Patti alive long enough to die a mean, lonely old bi—person. Look. If I were trying to decide who the world would be better off without, Steve, Heidi, and Patricia would be neck and neck. Once we have Steve alive again he should stop being a threat. Patricia won't be a suspect in his murd—my bad—his disappearance anymore. She'll be the victimized, exceedingly wealthy taxpayer. Steve would be done. But—Heidi." He stopped to catch his breath.

Otis stepped up. "Yeah, Jay. When all this dies down, Heidi's still a threat. It'd be good if Steve rats her out. Excellent chance of that once he finds out he's in big, awkward trouble and not going to be rich again. He'll realize he's been set up to be Heidi's murder weapon. Disposable too. If he doesn't figure that out, someone—possibly a cop—could explain it to him. He'll blink a coupla times and start incriminating her.'"

Tom was nodding agreement. Around the table the nod-rates indicated considerable sign-on.

Jay was a hit.

I was dazzled. Jay had a wonderfully devious mind. Also, I nudged myself, he'd fooled Patti and filched my two hundred bucks. We'd need to talk about that. I couldn't have this guy thinking I was a pushover.

"One thing?" Valerio.

"Jay's right, we have to keep Ms. Stone alive until we flush Steve and Heidi out and catch them at it. The problem is they've been patient a long time. The longer it takes, the more danger she's in and the harder it will be for us to protect her. Monica will be slowing them down now. Which is good and bad all at the same time."

While the rest of us were spending probably sixty percent of our focus on our eyes, Tom was alone in the dark with his unique skills. True, he could be distracted by the bubbling aromas from Margo's stove and the warm, affectionate proximity of Princess, but I understood how, as he listened to Valerio, he was watching a woman—alone and vulnerable—in a house exponentially more treacherous than the mansion we'd survived last summer. We'd put Monica in there with her too. Tom was our expert at appreciating the danger that comes in the night. "We need to flush them out faster."

"And we gotta have some really huge caliber ammo for the flushing!"

Tom grinned, "Margo? You have some huge ammo in mind?"

She was off and running. "How about this? How about we get *Patti* to tell *Heidi* she, *Patti*, is going to take a nice, long vacation. Someplace warm and not even slightly Cleveland. A fancy-ass resort with palm trees and tiki drinks, handsome half-naked guys bringing the tiki drinks. Whatever. That'll wake Heidi up. Then we pull Monica out. That should flush 'em *good*."

Tony shifted in his seat. He didn't want to get crosswise of Margo, but he had a question. I'm Tony's friend so I asked it for him. "Margo, once we flush them. How do we make sure we stop them from actually killing her?"

"Huh. Dunno. Gimme a minute."

"I have a plan for that, Margo."

She yawned. "That's good, Jay. My ace detective brain needs a break."

"I'm The Designer. I'll 'convince' Patti that 'since she's going to be away for a while,' I could set up 'a few projects we've been discussing: HVAC, painting what's not already been painted, painting over what's 'not working.' Whatever's not 'been done.' Or needs 'doing over.' You know. 'The usual.'"

Jay could do fingerless finger quotes professionally if there was any market for that. I thought his current profession might be that market. I was getting large, colorful mental pictures for everything he was not actually planning to do.

"We'll have to pretend to get estimates from the home improvement hoards but I could 'email them to her.' If Steve and Heidi are watching and listening—and how can they not be?—they'll see vans and 'design professionals.' And me. The service entrance is through the garage and the garage is around back and under the house. Otis, you can put a vanload of your folks *very quietly* inside. There's a 'lovely servant's wing.' Of course. Where they can hide. Lots of bathrooms. Stakeout heaven."

"*Then*," He was rocking along with his drama now. "The decorating hoards go off 'to put together their estimates.' Things quiet down. Patti is leaving town "early next week," after all. It's Tuesday night. We could be set by Friday night.

"Estimates are in. Patti is packing. She 'lets Monica go.' We've done everything we can. If nobody tries to kill her, we'll regroup and fine tune. Or let them kill her. Kidding. For the most part."

"Downside?"

"Surveillance, Tom." Downside was Valerio's specialty. "Are

they watching the house? Listening? How could they not be? We should be doing this in 1993, it'd be a hell of a lot easier. We'll need to make sure they're aware of the opportunity opening and the door closing. Observing, but not too close. How competent would this Steve and Heidi be, Jay?"

"Medium. Steve could have got electronics put in place before he headed out to drown. Heidi has money for that sort of thing. Neither one of them is what I'd call systematic about anything. Wildcards."

"Anyone involved in this caper a heroin addict who'd overlook a gas leak?" Tom couldn't let go of the T&A's wildcard of last summer."

Otis jumped on that. "No stakeout at the scene for you guys, Tom. Not this time. All we need is to find Steve—with or without Heidi—I'm betting both—in the house and it's over. They're nailed. Steve-alive is almost for sure all the evidence we need to save Patti."

"One more thing. Money." Jay raised a hand. "I'll need a couple of high-end suppliers out on short notice with their logo-identified vans. Can't do that unless you bribe the living daylights out of 'em. Not," he eyed Tony and Otis, "not a bribe-y bribe. A bonus for good, fast service."

"Keep talking, Jay. This is so cool." Margo had been silent but Margo-alert. All this talk of high-end everything and bribe-y bribes was front and center in her wheelhouse.

"I'm about done, Margo. The thing is, Patricia Stone is in danger but she is the same cheap…individual I've worked with for years. She knows about the T&A, obviously. I bet she'll expect you all to pick up the tab. It could be a good bit."

"Allie."

Tom's tone was the ultimate power play. I remembered yet again how unforgivably hot he was. "Explain to Jay the one advantage the T&A has over all other detective agencies."

"No need, Tom. I believe he got the drift when you said to

Lisa, 'Last time, I bought a house.' Is there anything else we're overlooking?"

Valerio was wearing his standard grumpy Valerio face. "Bound to be. Otis, what are we missing?"

"Something. But this sounds pretty solid. If I can get four or so guys in there by Friday night we'll be set. Steve and Heidi come in, we'll be waiting. I'll think more about this and we'll go over details tomorrow. Can we eat now?"

Margo's dinner was pasta fagioli, salad, and her tiramisu. We had a plan so fabulous it almost took our minds off the sniper problem we had no plan at all for at the moment. This case would be handled by the weekend.

If we could have reached across the Viking's table, there would have been high fives all around.

Chapter Thirty-Eight

10:30 P.M.

Otis dropped Tom and me back at the house on his way to deliver Jay and Lisa to her place.

Lisa had tuned into the many new possibilities of Jay—*As a designer, Allie*—her glare telegraphed to me as she pounced on him. "Jay? Do you do discounts for the T&A? I just moved to Atelier 24 and I need to make it more, you know, me—"

Jay pounced right back, "Say no more, Lisa. I'm your guy. I have been dying to get in there. Maybe a photo spread in *Cleveland Magazine*. 'At Home With Lisa Cole.'"

Those two were meant for each other. Opportunists, the both of them. They agreed that if Otis were kind enough to take them both to Lisa's place, Jay could Uber home.

I'd follow up on that last part. Tomorrow. Or the next day. I was a Margo-In-Training.

The snow continued as if it hadn't been informed its "up-to" was twelve inches. It kept burying the world in more sodden, slippery inches-per-minute as the Raven Black vehicle carved its way down around the twists and turns of our driveway.

Bless you, four-wheel drive.

We said good night all around. The garage detail welcomed us in. The door closed behind us.

———

We hung up our cold, wet coats, and turned, as a single conscious entity, to press our still-shivering bodies into each other. For the sharing of warmth. As solace for the sorrows and challenges of the day. As a reward for choosing to help old wretched Patti, instead of sitting around being scared. Also in honor of the one thing I'd had in mind since we climbed into the leather backseat of the Escalade at Margo's.

"Tom," I murmured, the awe of a new realization beginning to warm me from within. "It will take Otis at least a week to get to Lisa's place and back in this snow. Security is deployed. We are all alone in this giant house. Which is, as you know, a large, very private—twenty-nine-dollar-an-hour motel. We could do—anything—anywhere. The possibilities are—"

"Alice." Tom's tone was stern.

Stern?

"What?"

At least he hadn't let go of me. If anything, I was feeling a little smushed. And much, much warmer in the electricity of his embrace. A consolation for the severity in his voice.

"I thought we shared everything, Allie, and you—you were supposed to give me a complete picture of our environment. In detail. For my safety. And enjoyment. You always say that's part of your job description."

Puzzled now.

Oh. Wait.

"Tom, is this about the chaise?"

"It is." He was still holding me tight against him. I couldn't see his expression, but I could read his body. Like braille. He wasn't nearly as offended as he was trying to sound. "It seemed a very comfortable place to sit. Is it a true Victorian or a fake vintage thing."

"True, Tom. In every respect. True."

"And you saw fit to exclude me from the knowledge of this. Until yesterday?"

"You're so sexy when you talk like a professor. Or a PI."

"Don't even think about trying to distract me."

"I told you I was saving it."

"Saving what I now know is a red velvet, authentically Victorian chaise?'

"Our chaise. For a surprise. As I mentioned yesterday."

I may have been seriously imprisoned in his arms, but I had unabridged access to my hands. I put them to good use. He pretended not to notice, but I read the little hitch in his chest. Like braille.

"Okay. I'm game. Go ahead. Take advantage of our rare opportunity for doing anything, anywhere. Surprise me."

"It would be my pleasure."

"Oh, honey. You have no idea."

Understatement. The room was toasty and romantically lighted by my favorite swiped lamp. The chaise anticipated our every move and even proposed a couple. The wind raged and icy sludge pounded the windows, but we were so warmed by our—everything, we didn't need Margo's shawl.

It was the perfect storm. All the Victorians in Heaven were fanning themselves and blushing tonight. This was their chaise after all.

"Tom."

"Mmm?"

"I don't think we should fall asleep here."

"Because of not being able to walk tomorrow?"

"That's my concern."

"Mine too. But while we're so—completely together, describe this room to me again, Alice Jane. And don't leave out anything this time."

"No problem." I pulled him back down to me and kissed his handsome mouth. "It's 'The Victorian Snow Globe of Hot Sex.'"

Chapter Thirty-Nine

WEDNESDAY, MARCH 7

7:00 A.M.

Last night's snowfall was collapsing under its own soggy weight. After clogging up roadways, bending a lot of fenders, freeing lucky kids from school, and maybe—wild surmise on my part—shutting down all the Ubers in town on behalf of Lisa and Jay—the potential multiple feet of "white stuff" was turning to mush. Slinking away in embarrassment.

That's another thing about March in Cleveland. Nothing lasts.

The morning light was wobbly at best, but the mounds of snow melting onto Otis's deck sported a few dazzling patches of sunlight. Waves from the storm were roughing up the shore. The wind was down but not out.

I ran through my Sniper Risk Assessment: Challenging weather for a sniper. No workable spot for a sniper to set up between here and Canada—I hadn't read more than a few bone-chilling pages of the handbook, but I knew that much. Team Otis would fend off any sniper who showed up with a regular old handgun. All was well.

When I'd wandered into the kitchen at six-fifteen, feeling perky and generally satisfied with life, Otis invited me down to his place for coffee and waffles. Warm syrup too. I was good with that, but my guard was forty percent up.

"You're wondering why I invited you down here."

I was. An invitation to the man cave was a hot ticket, but this felt like a bribe-y bribe. "Yeah. You don't get the urge to feed me waffles down here at seven a.m. Very often. Ever."

He rubbed at his eyes. Tired and worried. It was early, and Otis already had trouble in mind. Part of that had to be our brand-new case. The rest was probably the not-dead old case. I empathized.

A couple of weeks ago Otis had given up and shaved all the gray off his head. In my opinion, this actually made him look younger and more badass, but I figured it was a small surrender for him. Now he massaged the top of his head. Winced. Taken off guard by the bareness, I could tell.

In the beginning, when he told me he'd make us the good bodyguard we were about to need, Otis underestimated the scope of that job description. And the magnitude of the disasters in store for us. I knew this for a fact because none of us had a clue about that back then. Good thing too.

Tom and I sensed we'd "probably need a little protection for a while." We'd witnessed how big lucky money could capture the twisted imagination of anyone who could spell M-o-n-d-o—even if they had to copy it off a ticket. But back then we believed those folks would wander off soon and forget the whole thing.

Naive-R-Us.

We were clueless babies about the dogged persistence five hundred million before-tax dollars inspires. We pointed to people who'd been way richer than us for generations and lived their normal, wealthy lives unthreatened. My research on former lottery winners was disconcerting, however. A jumbo jackpot could trash your life over a weekend. Or end it. And we didn't foresee the bigger, smarter, more competent killers in the wings. We knew better now. Tom and I couldn't envision life without Otis.

"Allie, a couple days ago, I made fun of you for suggesting our sniper might shoot their sniper."

Why does everything come out of left field?

Because it never left. Get used to it

Our Sniper versus Their Sniper? We'd both mocked me. I swallowed hard. Didn't help. The molten heaviness in me was dread and hopelessness about the dread. Unflappability was never my strong suit. The day they covered that, I must have been out practicing how to be cute and sassy.

"Yeah, Otis, that sniper/sniper thing. I heard how dumb it was and took it back."

"Now it's not looking so dumb."

"Because everything's changed. Since—" I counted. "Since Saturday?"

No kidding? Only Saturday? If I kept a diary—which, *note to self*, I definitely should—Saturday, Sunday, and Monday would get a whole extra month of pages. The shocking conclusion of the Epoch of Tito was at least a decade ago in whimpering dog years.

"Yeah. A lot's changed, Allie. Since then."

"Otis?"

"Allie. Things are not ramping down the way we thought they might."

"No. Duh." Bitterness. I heard it. Sarcasm too. "You think there's somebody out there with a nuclear agenda?"

"Yeah, maybe, but I'm not worried about that right this minute."

"Sorry. It's just—I'm scared, Otis." My voice wavered. "Sorry. Damn."

"Everybody cries, Allie. It's how you can tell somebody's alive in there. And scared is a sign of intelligence. This ain't easy. You're doin' fine." His voice was a hug. Otis was talented at that.

Back to the sniper conversation at hand. And the new T&A case now on the front burner.

I got up and poured us more coffee and we carried the mugs to the couch that offered the best view onto the decks. The morning had layers. A layer of freshly washed blue, high above, then a lower layer of puffy white clouds, and under them, the gray-green of deep-cold water. The whole thing was sprinkled with hundreds of bonehead gulls. Being gulls. I breathed that in. My panic backed off.

"You're talking about Shadow Man, Otis. I'd be fine with him. That was him at the back of my mind when I asked my stupid sniper question. He'd be our first choice, wouldn't he? Since I guess Batman isn't real. But you have got to tell me his name. He made fun of me when I called him—that."

"Ah, Allie. He kinda enjoys you calling him 'that.' He likes you. And Tom. He doesn't show a lot of—You could ask him yourself, but I suggest you think twice—"

Ah, Shadow Man. Another mysterious, fit stranger. In black ripstop.

"He's a sniper too."

Otis was retired from at least three careers, and he'd accumulated many interesting friends. Understatement. I used to be a part-time librarian. My only friend from that career was Lorretta Coates who worried all the time and cried a lot.

"Otis? I thought he was the tech genius. You told me he was an expert in 'the new domain of intelligence.' I assumed that meant hacker. Hacker and sniper don't mix. Do they?"

"He's a lot of things. The training for what he did—in the Navy and after? It's intense and multi-intimidating. Sniper isn't his main skill. Not anymore at least. None of us from back then are as young as we used to be. He's older than me—he sure doesn't look it—He mostly makes his money with his hacker skills now."

Hacker skills. A man who could make your security system unlock all its doors and let all your money run free. Set your house to eavesdropping on you. Move freely in the "domain" I pictured as a scene out of *Ready Player One*. Shadow Man had out-hacked that brand of hacker for us last time.

I nodded as if I knew all about it. Otis forged on.

"You've seen what he can do. Savant with it, Allie. Nobody gets how it works for him. Not even him. But he's versatile and that's critical for us. We don't know what all our sniper can do. He shot Tito up close, no problem. We know he's skilled with a blade—"

We both flashed back to Tom's pale horror.

"So we'll need our guy's knowledge and expertise, all of it. I don't think he could outshoot the—the new guy for the big distances. I'm counting on him not needing to do that. I'm not expecting, 'O.K. Corral at two thousand paces.' But your 'Shadow Man' can tell us a lot. Maybe outthink the dude when the time comes. He's high-test, high-caliber, Allie. We need him now. Plus, he can help us with the Patti case."

For one mean second, I got a kick out of "The Patti Case."

Re: Shadow Man? Let me go on the record here: I'm not as brave or as smart as I'd like to be, but I'm an excellent judge of hot and, from what I'd glimpsed of him—under the cover of moonlit darkness, out of the corner of one eye—Shadow Man was hot. Fit. Buff. Black. Radiating "takes no prisoners."

However, the cruel-eyed-dark-and-handsome impression he'd made on me last summer was mostly fabricated by me because I'd never snagged a good look at him. A professional vanisher. Shadows 24/7. "Shadow Man" fit him fine for now. My address book was overrun with aliases these days. No biggie.

"You're head of security, Otis. I'm with you. Tom will be too. Did you talk to him? Is he available? Is he coming? Is he here?"

"He's willing. He's in the neighborhood. I probably should have checked with you and Tom before—He doesn't come cheap you know."

"Cheap has never been our game, Otis, and you know it. Light up the bat signal."

Chapter Forty

What with one thing and another, I'd never given Patti and Steve's mansion any serious consideration once they'd moved out of their old one—which was our new one—and into their new one which had been "the old one" of many well-to-do Clevelanders, quite a few of whom were now residing in Lake View Cemetery.

Casa Patti was on display from Lake Shore, of course. It's tough to camouflage a twelve-thousand-square-foot fortress. From my quick, drive-by impression, it was another one of the upscale crowd lining the north side of Lake Shore Boulevard. Set well back from the street behind appropriately embellished gates, on the inevitable aesthetically-pleasing landscape. End of story.

Until we picked up our new case, I certainly never expected to go inside that one.

Right after Otis and I broke off the waffle-fest so he could get Shadow Man going, I went upstairs to tell Tom about our shadowy new plan. Right after Tom succeeded in luring me back into bed with my clothes on—"My specialty," he murmured, getting all deft with the shirt buttons—my phone buzzed.

The screen said, "Jay." He needed a ringtone.

I said, "Tom, it's only Jay."

Tom said, "Don't answer that."

I said, "Keep working on my shirt. This will only take a minute."

I needed to hear what Jay was planning at Patti's Place. Also, I hoped to deftly grill him about what went on at Atelier 24 last night. Tom wasn't the only deft one. I was aiming to pry every scrap of the info I wanted out of Jay, hang up in five minutes or less, and get straight back to Tom.

Too bad.

Jay was full speed ahead and all business this morning. "Allie? Are you up? Are you dressed?

Yes. No. More or less. Less all the time—

"What do you need, Jay?"

"You. I want to swing by and pick you up so you can take a look at the Stone place. Get a jump on this thing."

He didn't hear Lee Ann think

Damn

but Tom did. He stopped with the shirt.

Jay breezed on. "We can't take Tom over there. He's a dead giveaway because he's...him. But anybody sees you going in, you could pass as a design consultant. Wear something sorta design-y. No worries. Patricia and Monica are the only ones there now. You don't have to fool them."

"Give me a little direction on 'design-y.' Pretend you're gay."

He paused and I imagined him mentally reviewing what he'd seen of my wardrobe, pained by my questionable fashion sense.

"I don't suppose you have leather pants?"

"No. For more reasons than you have time for right now."

"Jeans, then, maybe? Distressed could be good. Not too distressed. Boots. Surely you have a good pair of boots. After all, you're with—" Another pause while he mentally assessed everything he and Margo didn't know about the fiscal details of my relationship with Tom.

He abandoned protocol.

"Allie. You're a woman who can definitely afford good boots.

And a woman who can afford good boots knows her boots. That's the law. I figure you've got a pair. Or five.

"Margo told me about the great shawl she gave you for the chaise. You know the shawl. She loves that chaise as much as you and I do. I bet that shawl would be a nice fashion-y touch. I'll show you how to tie it when you get in the van I'm going to pick you up in. If you like."

Oh yeah. I knew that shawl. Intimately. Remembered its silky farewell caress, as it slid over Tom and me on its way to the floor last night, abandoned in the heat wave of the moment. How the glow from the lamp had burnished Tom's shoulders as the silken fabric fell slowly, soundlessly away. How deliciously *Tom's* I'd been in that moment.

This memory made me want to grab a time machine, ride it three and a half minutes into the past and not answer Jay's call. But this was our case. The one I'd jumped on. Tom's bare hand was lying quiet on my bare front. I picked it up and gently kissed it goodbye.

———

I stopped by the kitchen to apprise Otis of the outing. He said, "I know. Jay called me before he called you. You're covered."

"Thanks, Otis." As I turned to go, I noticed someone, not anyone from our usual detail, sitting at the island.

Cup of Otis's coffee. Thousand-yard stare—*Holy Shadow Man!*

Sitting at our kitchen island. In full daylight. As if he weren't an enigma wrapped in my one million unanswered questions. Although I'd been trained to avert my eyes from his covertness, this morning I didn't bother to pretend I wasn't staring at him.

He looked to me like a well-toned black man with smooth-chiseled features, close-cut graying hair, and a semi-fierce expression. A skim coat of gray stubble on his jaw. He was the guy from a war movie, having his morning coffee and assessing opportunity and risk. Every minute of every day. A little older than Otis. A little fitter than anyone in Bratenahl this morning. Sleek, black pants and a standard-issue white T-shirt. Well-worn gray sweatshirt. "Navy" on the back.

Black and white and "Seal" all over.

In spite of the general intimidation of his bearing, our history of him always disappearing, and me not having the nerve to follow up, I was no way backing off this time. I was going to look right at him. Talk to him too.

"You're back. Or still here. Whatever. I'm glad."

"I'm your semi-permanent fixture."

"Does that mean we'll see more of you?" I was picturing pizza on the deck on the 4th of July. Eggnog at Christmas. Shadow Man carving our turkey—

"Not really. It means I'm on your payroll. If Otis needs me, I'm here."

"Okay."

"Yeah. We are. We're okay."

He stood up. One smooth motion, as if his body was the servant of his indomitable will. He could even set a coffee mug down with authority. "Those are excellent boots, Alice Jane," he said.

Gone again.

———

Ten minutes later I climbed into Jay's nondescript van. I assumed the weather was too barbaric for his insouciantly decorated bug. I was wearing my favorite jeans, black turtleneck, and the LL Bean jacket I'd copycatted off Lisa Cole before we were deadly enemies for eighteen hours and then back to friends again. It was rated "warmest" and "to −35 degrees." Lisa's coat was a TV reporter's professional khaki. Mine was the unruly "Cayenne." The color that broadcasts "Sizzlin'!" I'd described it to Tom, as I kissed him goodbye. He appreciated knowing my coat was trying to hit on him, but he'd given up on me for now.

My excellent boots were plenty expensive enough. $598 at Saks, and there was sales tax too. Not as overpriced as "Ms. Mad-Spiked," but these were leather combat boots. Born to kick butt. Not what Jay had envisioned, I didn't think. But Shadow Man said they were excellent. He understood the lay of the land. I climbed in and scooped up the sample books occupying my seat.

"And the look you're going for is?"

"Take no prisoners."

He nodded. "Shawl didn't work for you?"

"Too big."

Too still smoldering.

"I need to be me, Jay. I distress my jeans by eating Otis's waffles."

"Always be you, Allie. The boots are awesome. 'Kick-ass' comes to mind. Literally."

Yup. That's the consensus.

The gate house was empty. Since the thirties, from the look of it. We called the mansion. Monica answered, very crisp. Buzzed us through.

If I thought I was about to get a good look at the approach to the house, I was wrong. With the warming earth, the no-longer-freezing water temps, the melting snow, and the dying wind, conditions had hit the mysterious dew point for one of Lake Erie's "localized weather events." Visibility on the boulevard was fine. By the time Jay got us half-way down the long, shrub-lined drive, I couldn't make out the shrubs anymore. Patricia's mansion was up to its venerable ass in dense fog.

Jay parked as close to the front steps as he could without scraping off a fender. Through the soupy mist I could barely make out the baronial front door and the feeble glow of the bronzed light fixture above it.

If this were an airport, it would be closed by now.

Alrighty.

I hopped out with our sample books. As I turned to nudge my door shut, a slight movement in the way back of the van snagged my attention. Adam was wedged in there. He wiggled his fingers at me. *Thank you, Otis Johnson.* My phone vibrated and a text message from Adam with a number in it popped up. "I'll be out here. Call me if anything seems off."

Chapter Forty-One

"Off?" As in spooky? Freaky? Cold as an icy finger on the back of my neck? Check. Check. Check.

Everything about the place felt off. I thought it had probably been at least slightly out of sorts since October of 1929. Monica, our reliable off-duty police officer, sensibly layered in warm sweaters, could have played the role of The Homicidal Housekeeper in that environment. Dour and dangerous. Her hair was dark and her eyes were too, but then she smiled and the friendly version snuck out. She was waiting for Jay and me in the hand-carved entry hall, on a large expensive rug. The rug reminded me of our former mansion. Last summer I couldn't imagine anything over-the-top fancier than that place. Clearly a failure of my *newbie-riche* imagination.

Wooden nymphs peered at us from a swirling pattern of vines and flowers carved out of the polished columns like they were hoping they'd found the escape route. Their expressions were sad but composed. Maybe they were waiting for someone to break an evil spell and set them free.

Sorry, ladies.

The grand staircase, also embellished up the wazoo, loomed behind Monica. Foggy daylight illuminated a giant many-paned stained-glass window at the top of the stairs. Barely enough to bring out the reds in a pattern that appeared to feature bloodstains.

Monica responded to the look on my face. "It's not this bad all the time. The fog—"

"Yeah. And the low wattage. And the chill. And the eyes of those ladies in the carvings. Is the furnace broken?"

"No. It's going. Set to sixty-five and killing itself trying to get up that high. The heating guy showed up at the crack of dawn, and took a look, but he needed a part, so he left. He's out there somewhere, I suppose. Stuck maybe." She waved toward the blank whiteness pressing silently against the sidelights of the door. "I expect to die here."

I was good with Monica. We were on the same semi-hysterical wavelength, but we had it contained. I had another thought: *Heating guy?*

I believed the heating guy was last seen drinking coffee in our kitchen. But then he didn't really need to fix the furnace. He had other fish to fry.

"I'll just keep my coat on, Monica. It's rated for thirty-five below."

I turned to Jay who was wearing the expression I could feel on my face. He and Monica and I were a matched set.

"What part of this is your work, Jay?"

"Oh. None of *this*. This—" He waved his arm to take in the staring eyes of the maidens—"this, we're *preserving*. Because it's—" He swept his eyes heavenward and saw Patricia Stone staring down the stairway at him. "Priceless."

It was too.

I made note of how fiercely Patti was gripping the bannister. The stairs were so steep a person could almost tumble out into space without tripping. I guessed she'd recognized the staircase, early on, to be the Widower-Maker it was. Buyer's remorse is a bitch. Suited her somehow.

"Allie, thank you for coming." Her tone was polite but cool. "Your furnace man told Monica the problem he was most concerned about didn't affect most of the house. Only my study and my bedroom. And the house phones. So I guess it's electrical. He needs a part. Says just to choose different rooms to talk in, for now. And to be grateful for small favors. He's kind of…odd. But pleasant enough."

An ah-ha moment. Otis had lighted up the Shadow Signal sometime in the dark hours of the night. I was this morning's rubber stamp. Fine. I was happy to be the stamp. Shadow Man made me feel safer. Edgier, but safer.

Patti gave me a tour. Monica followed along as far as the cavernous living room which had an authentic wood burning fireplace you could play cards in and a raging fire you could roast a pig over. But not both at the same time. Jay and Patti sat down close to it. I walked Monica to the hall.

"He swept for bugs. Found a couple. Left them alone. He says there are things we'll want the suspects to know about. Says they'd trust what they don't know we know they're overhearing. Does that make sense?"

"It does. He's the best."

"Well, he found no video, except outside. Which is a blessing. When he drives the heating company van back here this afternoon, there'll be a swap. In the garage. After that, he'll stay until it's all done. I'm glad. He's not very approachable but he seems to know what he's doing."

True. And true.

Just to be sure. "And you'd describe him, Monica—?"

"African American. Six-two, a hundred-seventy, all muscle, alert as hell. Strung up tight. Older than me, but hard to say how much. I wouldn't try to sneak up on him in the dark, if I were you."

"Good thinking."

"What's his name?"

"He didn't tell you?"

"No."

"He's secretive. By design. For now, let's leave it that way. You don't need to call him anything. I think of him as Shadow Man."

She nodded. "Fits."

A couple of minutes later Jay joined us and handed me a couple copies of a document. "Lisa and I drew this up last night. It's a contract that describes in detail the work we're going to do here this week."

My eyes said, "No it's not."

His eyes said, "You're right, it isn't."

"It's brilliant, Jay."

"Patti has her copy. We need to take it with us. So make sure she reads it more than once. Monica this is yours. Shred it, burn it or eat it when you're done. I have to transfer something from the van into the garage. Then we'll go."

Jay was all over his new undercover detective role. I assumed the "transferred something" was Adam. "Call me if anything's off." Adam would wait for Shadow Man in the garage which would surely be warmer and less of a back-breaker than the rear of the van. After a reasonable time for furnace fixing, Adam would drive Shadow Man's vehicle away.

The Shadow Man would be embedded here for the duration. Once the house was asleep, Monica Cowan, PI, would smuggle him food in the servants' quarters. And books of poetry. And bourbon. Their eyes would meet. The sweaters would slip to the floor—It was a romance novel. I shredded it.

My Shadow Man would have brought freeze-dried jerky and his own bourbon.

I took my copy of Jay's document and joined Patti in the living room. The fire had died. The room was clammy cold. The fog was still jammed up against the windows.

Jay's fake contract idea was brilliant. It explained our plan, quickly and clearly, so that nothing needed to be said out loud. Even though we now believed the bugging was minor, it was good not to try to explain everything in that big echoing room. What we'd do. What Patti needed to do. She got it. She was mean but she wasn't stupid.

"I understand. It's a good plan. I can do this. Allie?"

"It is. You can."

"Should I change the locks?"

Well, yes. Back in November.

I didn't have to say this out loud.

"I know I should have. I didn't after—at first. And then, once I figured it all out, I was afraid it would tip him off."

"He has keys."

"A full set. She has the front door. 'In case anything should happen to me.'" Patti could do irony and finger quotes with the best of us.

"Don't change them now. It helps to know for sure he has them. And if he's made copies, she's got a set too. We want them in here once we're ready for them. Then we'll get them."

She was giving me only a quarter of her attention. Staring in to a distance I couldn't see. Distracted. I could relate.

"I hope so. That furnace guy of Jay's? He's kind of scary."

Oh, my dear. "He's here to protect you. He's the best."

"Expensive?"

"As they come." That was cruel, but she had it coming.

She considered arguing but stop considering when she translated my expression into a lot of swearing.

I was messing with her. The furnace guy was on our payroll.. Otis would handle the details for Tom.

Jay reappeared. "We can go."

The van was back where Jay parked it when we arrived, and the fog had broken down into unraveling wisps. Here and gone. That's fog for you. The day was drab and dank, but the snow was going fast too. Big swaths of lawn were exposed, and they were almost green.

I wasn't about to be disarmed by a half-inch of naked grass.

We had full two months to go before we could count on more than two consecutive days of spring. But it made me feel chirpy.

"You and Lisa put together that document for Patricia?" I paused, letting the silence evolve. "That must have taken all night."

I watched Jay out of the corner of my eye. He didn't actually smile, but there was something—

"Not quite."

Chapter Forty-Two

8:45 P.M.

A Millard Fillmore Presidential Library could be just about any-thing. It might even have books. But the only one I know of—the only one I've actually been in—is a bar where a person who's had a trying day can find a good selection of craft beers, regu-lar performances by local music groups, and memorabilia and photographs of the former president himself. Who upon close examination bears a disconcerting resemblance to Alec Baldwin. The women's bathroom is labeled "First Ladies" and the front awning quotes President Fillmore's last words, which were, "The nourishment is palatable."

It was too.

For the first time since early that morning I had a free moment and a place to savor it. So I was savoring being able to sit in here with people I loved and/or liked a lot. Like a normal person. Who'd escaped from jail. Still wearing the ankle monitor, but happy to be temporarily free. Tonight's band was Maura Rogers & The Bellows. Rich and soulful singing, served up with a shot of moxie and an accordion. Fire and honey.

Breathe, Allie. It'll do you good.

I inhaled. The big room smelled like a bar in a building with decades of bar history. A breath of fresh beer. The scent of old wood, ancient brews, palatable nourishment, and, tonight, wet wool, permeating everything. Wet wool is a classic Cleveland fragrance at least six months out of the year. "Eau de Mitten."

Mmm. Mitten.

Tom had been easy to seduce into a short road trip. Otis was more of a challenge, but he shared our belief that nobody would benefit from killing us tonight. We were worth more alive and in touch with the money than dead. Our new adversary presented himself as a pragmatist and not a raving loose cannon. Cold comfort was better than no comfort at all. The past week was a no-comfort zone.

Otis put together a minimal team for our trip to the Library. He was at the table Wednesday night, carrying concealed, and stone cold sober. With guys on the front and back doors—one of whom was Adam—and Otis and Valerio sitting at our table, I theorized President Fillmore, whose tenure in office predated the Secret Service, would have thought himself lucky to be protected by Otis's detail.

So far it was a reprise of last night's T&A meeting, without nearly as much tension and more booze. I was hoping for merriment enough to offset my awareness that tonight was the one-week anniversary of the murder of Kip Wade. Almost to the hour. A cold-blooded killing, I forced myself to admit, commissioned by a raving loose cannon, and executed at the hand of our pragmatist. I was doing everything but singing La-La-La with my fingers in my ears. But for that moment it was working.

Lisa and I were continuing our tour of Manhattans. We agreed that the Fillmore Manhattan—featuring shots of Grand Marnier and Jägermeister and legendary in our small corner of Ohio—stood up well to the Flying Fig's. Lisa and Jay arrived together, but there were so many feet around our improvised table I didn't dare try to kick Margo about that. Margo was subdued anyway.

Valerio was there, I assumed to protect her, although he'd allowed himself a beer. After a while she traded places with Tony to sit by me. *Margo advice, incoming.* When Margo was wearing her current face, she was all about advice. Also warnings and rantings. Followed by swearings. I braced myself.

She stole a sip from my glass. Swallowed. Made a face. "Well, that's interesting. Allie, I'm—"

The noise level ramped up. People were scraping their chairs around and hustling to the bar for fresh drinks and palatable snacks

"Allie. I'm worried."

A party of five blew in the front door. Their friends who were already here hollered a welcome and started rounding up stray chairs. I leaned closer to Margo so I could hear what was bothering her. She was a freestyle worrier, but I respected her intuition. This could be entertaining. Or serious.

"Worried about what?"

"About I'm not sure we should trust—"

Three things happened.

1) The band hit a few test chords.

2) Another bunch of bar-hoppers came in and slammed the front door.

3) One of those hoppers broke away, came over, wedged in yet another chair, and sat down between Tom and me. Plaid flannel shirt. Leather jacket. Indians hat. Right hand in pocket. *Pale eyes. Very composed. Neutral.* Like Gloria said. *Clear water.*

Here—at our table—was the man who'd killed her. So close I could see his chest rising and falling with each measured breath.

I wasn't looking at Margo, but she leaned in close and spoke into my ear. "Him. I'm not sure we should trust him."

I glanced over to Otis who was making a move to rise from his place across the table. Tony was on the alert too. The man froze them with a look and raised his voice barely enough to cut through the din, but sharp and precise enough to get the job done.

"Otis. The only dangerous people in here right now are you, your cop friend, and the guy who's coming our way from the back. Stop that one." Otis turned and with a quick gesture that could have signaled, "We need another round over here" sent the man back to his post.

"And Allie, how about you look happier to see me?"

The band started up. I wrenched my face into something I hoped didn't look like the mix of terror and suppressed rage it was.

"Hello, you son of a bitch. You murdered Gloria."

"I shot Rudyard Kipling Wade too. I also took out the roof of your greenhouse, Allie. And I killed Tito Ricci and cut off his hands. I get it. I'm a murdering son of a bitch. By vocation." He took the bite out of his tone. "I understand. It's hard to imagine me as the answer to your prayers, but if you can chill yourself out enough to be smart, you'll see I am that. You can stop trying to smile now. You're creeping me out."

"Allie?"

"Margo, it's okay. Allie and I are talking for a minute here. That's all."

"Allie, how does this man know my name?"

"It's okay. It is. He's only going to be here for another couple of minutes. Let's listen to what he has to say."

"Huh. I can't hear a fuckin' word."

Praise the Lord.

"I know. It's fine. I'll listen for both of us. And report back."

I'd spoken too soon. The band launched in to the first couple of bars of "I Am an Animal." In this moderate-sized, one-hundred-percent-hopping space, we were swimming in music and mayhem. I was going to have to read his lips.

Tom slid his hand along the table and found mine where it was death-gripping the edge. Cold. So cold. The hands of both of us. The sniper moved closer and locked my eyes in his pale gaze.

Mouse. Snake. I knew which one was me. I was desperate for a quick trip to the First Ladies Room. Also Fiji.

"Your other guy? The one who could pass for your ex? In a pinch?"

Shit. TMI. My eyes were welded to his.

"Your Tito. So-called. He wanted it all. All the money. All the glory. And you, Tom, and everyone you care about—" He let his glance slide around the table and linger on Margo. "He wanted all of you dead. He told me so."

I kept my eyes trained on him.

He could read my mind, I could tell. He knew fucking everything.

"That was Tito, Allie, not me. I don't especially want anybody else dead. Here's what I do want. I want to let this die down until people forget recent events. Shouldn't take long. Everybody has a short attention span these days. I want you to go ahead and take a break. Keep working your little case."

Was there anything this guy didn't know?

He continued. Business-like.

"Tito was a maniac. I am never out of control. Never." His emphasis on the word bared his teeth which were white and even. I couldn't take my eyes off his mouth.

He continued as if he weren't reading the disintegration of my mind on my face. "My only job at this point is to keep track of you. I'm extra talented at that. Tell Otis good work, though. Your place is locked up pretty tight. Margo's? Not so much. Think on that, but don't worry. I'm happy to see you occupied.'

"What do you want?"

"Money, of course. Clean and simple. Tito lured me into this gig with information about a chunk his boyfriend cut away from the herd last summer. It's still there. Not available but vulnerable. I'll have more information shortly. You'll barely notice. I'll give you the details when it's time. So you can have things in place."

"And if we refuse to pay?"

I was hearing Ruth's warning. *No matter what, Allie, don't pay him.*

Did that apply only to Tito? I didn't know much psychology

but I could tell this guy and Tito were cut from different cloth. He was the chain mail of that twosome.

His silver eyes chilled ten degrees. "Think extra carefully and don't go there."

He stood up, gave everybody at the table the well-trained sniper's once-over and left the building. Adam, Otis's guy on the front door watched him turn and go on down the street. I'd seen Otis's almost imperceptible head shake. So had Adam.

Another handful of seconds and a woman wearing a funny wool hat with tassels hanging off it and a big neighborly smile was there asking, "You guys mind if I steal this chair?"

Otis and Valerio and I shared five seconds' worth of eye contact. The man was wearing winter gloves. On his left hand, at least. And his right hand had stayed in his pocket the whole time. We also could see the metal chair the young woman had both her hands all over at the moment.

Prints? Sure, right. Thousands. From back when Millard was still in office. That last thought was probably Valerio's, but I could hear it.

"No. Not at all. Help yourself."

"What the fuck just happened here?"

Tom shook his head. "Not sure, Margo. I believe a lady swiped our extra chair."

"Dammit Tom."

"Hang on a sec, Margo. Otis, should we leave?"

"No point, Allie. I'll check with the guys, but it looks like we're all good. Nothing to be done about this right now. I think you guys should have another drink. I certainly plan to one of these days."

Chapter Forty-Three

FRIDAY, MARCH 9

11:10 P.M.

Now was the waiting.

"I thought we agreed no more stakeouts."

"We didn't have to be here tonight, Tom. Shadow Man could have sent the video straight to the monitors in our own cozy garage. He's handy like that. You're the one who was determined to do this. And it's is a good, safe stakeout."

"Yeah, I especially like how it's about half a mile from the action. Should be far enough. Although you can never be too pessimistic about these things."

His tone was light. I wasn't fooled. Things blow up.

Many of the mansions on Lake Shore had gatehouses, often mini copies of the main residence. Little architectural offspring. These days they were in demand as rentals for young professionals who lust after the neighborhood and the proximity to the lake. Patricia and Stephen had neither renovated nor rented theirs. It was rundown, chilly, and had a smell that said *Rats were here* to me. Maybe earlier today. Maybe now.

Jay had announced, loud and clear, in one of the bugged rooms, that he was going to "store stuff" in the gate house. The stuff was us, carefully disguised as a couple of cramped moving boxes, and Shadow Man's spy equipment disguised as a box of paint cans. Wheeled in by Shadow Man disguised as your almost-average hot delivery guy.

Tom and I been here since we were delivered late this afternoon. Enjoying the ambiance. The windowless, meticulously blacked-out room we'd been stuck in since dark fell was rundown, chilly, and rat-smelly, but it now provided us a link into what I was guessing was the highest-tech communications network in Bratenahl on this Friday night.

When it came to tech, Shadow Man ruled.

"Face it, Tom. Shadow Man rules."

His grin flashed in the half light from the video screen.

"You've not been talking about how crazy good looking he is. So I figure he's extremely good looking and you're sparing my feelings. Didn't he steal Julie from our security team last year?"

"She went of her own free will. It was a career move. She's working for a government agency now. I'm guessing one that ends in and "I" or an "A." Otis won't say which. Or where."

"So he's not hot?"

"Oh, he's crazy hot, Tom. And also an expert at listening in on his stakeout team. I'm interested to find out how he feels about this highly-not-protocol conversation."

The grin faded.

"Allie, look. We had to be here. For better or worse, you and I are the T&A of the T&A." Another flash and a glimpse of the dimple I couldn't live without.

"We're in this now. We didn't have Patti in mind at the beginning. Or Lloyd even. I assumed we'd help folks find their lost dogs. One or two afternoons a week. But the Lloyd case—We made a big difference for Loretta. For a lot of people. It was worth it and I'm not sorry. Not willing to give it up.

"Look how Valerio and Olivia and Ms. Southgate at the museum came to us—okay, us and the money—to do something good. Worthwhile. Even though they don't need us and the money to save them after all. This new guy wants us to ransom ourselves. Museum looks to be home free."

I breathed out. Surrendered. We were committed to the T&A. The T&A was committed to saving Patti. Gears were turning. If Steve and Heidi didn't show up tonight, we were screwed.

The flurry of so-called HVAC and general home improvement experts who'd cycled in and out over the last forty-six hours had been for the most part a smoke screen for the installation of surveillance, and the embedding of Otis's troops.

Plans for this operation got coordinated in "non-surveilled" locations, via the most burner of burner phones. Jay had been in and out, nonstop, prattling about color ways and window treatments and smoothing the path for all the comings and goings and embeddings.

Patti did her part. She got on the compromised house phones and talked up her planned vacation with travel agents. She interviewed posh resorts about the amenities she was insisting upon. She declared she "absolutely had to" get out of town first thing Saturday morning and, at the same time, stubbornly refused to make a solid reservation. I suspected the number of people who were ready to kill her this morning had increased exponentially. I also figured the T&A was going to be on the hook for significant penalties on any actual reservations.

Tonight was the perfect setup from Steve and Heidi's perspective. Heidi would realize the scheduled vacation might make it a week or more before the body was even discovered. She probably had to point this out to Steve.

Patricia Stone was as prepared as she'd ever be. Stoked by her vision of Steve and Heidi in cuffs, I assumed. She'd gone up to bed at ten. I was super confident she wasn't asleep. Otis would alert her when they came into the house. She'd go to her assigned spot in the upstairs hall and give her best, quavering performance of, "Hello? Is someone there?"

Our setup might not have fooled Shadow Man or Sniper Man or Otis or even security freaks such as Tom and I were these days, but we were confident it would outsmart Heidi and Steve. If they showed up tonight.

"Do you think they'll come, Tom? Tonight? I can't wait for Patti to be safe and sound and out of our lives. I hope she goes to Fiji and stays for months. And sends no postcards."

"You'd wish that on poor Fiji?"

A few minutes past midnight, it started to look like Steve and Heidi were about to be outsmarted.

I watched the screen as a car crept along Lake Shore, doused its lights, and turned into the drive. A moment's hesitation and the gate swung open. As we figured, Steve had his own set of open sesames. He drove on in, slowly. The car purred. We could barely hear it pass us by. It glided around the oval and parked, facing out. The doors opened. Interior light was off. Steve was not a complete fuck-up. Or maybe Heidi was in charge of even the smallest details. Two shadows disembarked and stole up the front steps. The door opened. The alarm got disabled before it could sound.

I was describing it all to Tom. The switch from outside to inside camera was flawless. We had a perfect view of the empty stairway. So far so good.

A moment passed. Two.

"Hello? *Hello?*"

Patti's voice was shaking realistically. She was doing fine.

"Who's there? Monica, is that you?"

Nice little extemporaneous wrinkle. Monica had left in the afternoon. She'd asked for the evening off. Patti had given an Oscar-winning performance of "Patricia kicks Monica Out" for the benefit of anyone listening in. "Sure, go ahead. Don't bother to come back. I don't know what I'm paying you for anyway." A practiced kicker-outer.

Now she now she appeared on the landing, wrapped in a heavy throw such as she might have snatched up in a hurry, looking down the precipitous staircase. Smiling.

With good reason. Otis's team would be closing in on Heidi and Steve. Shadow Man would be his own shadowy self. The camera was entirely focused on Patti so I couldn't see Steve and Heidi's expressions, but they had to be there, at the bottom of the steps, looking up. I could picture the flood of doubt washing over them, the moment of indecision, looking left and right. Seeing only darkness but sensing trouble. Maybe already turning away.

Thinking, *Something's not right here.*

Too late.

Something wasn't.

"Tom, there's something—Something's wrong. Tom. It's Patti. She's holding a gun. She's—"

Two quick shots. Sharp and loud. Tom and I both jumped. Two more.

Shouts and running feet.

I was still staring at Patti. Trying to see—I fumbled, frantic, with the controls.

She eased herself down onto the floor at the top of the stairs as if a thoughtful gentleman had pulled a chair out for her. She laid the gun next to her on the floor. Based on my sketchy gun research, it was the "Glock something" she'd mentioned the first day we met.

Patricia Stone. Smug. Defiant.

Still smiling.

Chapter Forty-Four

SATURDAY, MARCH 10

12:24 A.M.

This was not the game plan.

Hearing chaos getting unleashed is an anxiety provoking experience. I was torn between fussing with the camera and looking at Patti. The explanation had to be in one of several conclusions we were jumping to. Patti had shot at Steve and/or Heidi? Were they both dead? One dead? One or both merely wounded? Severely? Slightly? Had she missed? Where was Otis? I stopped dithering and stayed with Patti. The damn resolution was excellent.

Her smugness was less smug now.

When she fired, Tom's hand was resting lightly on my arm. Now his grip was progressing from painful to bruising. "Allie, what happened. Who's been shot?"

"I can't see that either, Tom. The camera only shows Patti. She aimed down the staircase. I saw the flashes. She looked really pleased with herself, but now she's just sitting there. Staring."

I fumbled with the video controls. This time I located the one that should have been labeled *"Duh, Allie."*

Bingo. The bottom of the stairs was on screen—an indecipherable scrum of jostling bodies. A struggle. Confusion. No answers.

Our burner phone went off in Tom's non-arm-crushing hand. "Otis. What did—Oh—Okay. Yeah. We'll be ready."

He clicked off. "They need us. And a car from the Bratenahl PD is going to pick us up on their way in. Otis says nobody's dead. Yet."

———

I felt a trifle uneasy about scooting into the backseat of a squad car. The officers were polite enough. Reserved though. As their training required. Especially in Crazy Town. Where we now appeared to be.

I knew someone high-up at the Bratenahl PD had been pre-apprised of the circumstances by Tony and talked into standing back until we could get everybody in one place. I was pretty sure he'd encouraged them to believe there'd be no shooting. No promises, I'd bet. Tony did not do optimistic.

What were the cops expecting to discover when we arrived? Simple B&E? Attempted homicide? Justifiable homicide? Merely intended homicide? Unexpectedly complex situation? All of the above.

Tom and I could picture Steve back from his watery grave only to be heading to his actual one. Heidi dead for the first time. Steve and Heidi under arrest? Treated for shock? The possibilities were multitudinous. I thought even Tom and I could land in jail before the sun came up. We rode along in a silence I'd describe as tense. Holding hands again. Both of our palms were medium clammy.

By the time we got there, the situation was sorted out if not clarified.

Nobody was shot dead. Nobody was shot at all. Nobody was in cuffs. None of the three principals was looking particularly satisfied. In fact, they all three looked anxious as hell.

Steve and Heidi were finding themselves in a situation that gave new and colorful meaning to the phrase, "a lot of 'splainin' to do." As the cops ushered them out, Heidi halted in front of Tom and me. "Who *are* you? What *is* this?" Her expression was an oscillating mix of rage, fear, and bafflement you don't often see on a human face. I could almost empathize. Up close and glaring, she was as I'd imagined her: An expensive veneer of "Heidi has it all" spread over the deep disappointment of "It'll never be enough."

Otis's team had shown up in the front hall—a crowd out of nowhere—while Steve and Heidi were busy not-murdering Patti and getting not-shot. Although, for a handful of long seconds, I bet those two were checking for bullet holes all over themselves.

After that, Otis and Valerio popped out from close by to grab them both. Now here was Bratenahl PD, plus the tall hot blind guy and me. Confusion had to be reigning inside Heidi's head. I was savoring the moment.

Steve's expression mirrored the blank, hopeless faces of the maidens still trapped in the hall's woodwork. It was going to take him years to figure out what happened to his foolproof plan. I could have saved him time by explaining how he was the fool, but I figured he'd be needing something to ponder for the rest of his almost-sure-to-be-less-privileged life.

Otis told me he'd taken custody of Patti's gun. He answered my raised eyebrows. "Blanks. Just in case. I'd met Patricia Stone, so I asked myself 'what would Patti do?' Our specialist took care of the swap. Looks like she knew how to handle her Glock just fine."

All in all, the resolution of our case was unexpected for everyone involved, but from the T&A perspective, the plan had produced the desired result. Steve was now outed on faking his own death and breaking into his own house to—circumstances suggested—murder his own wife. He'd probably spend the rest of the night and a few days answering tough questions and facing anything that could be made to stick. At the very least, I could look into his future and see an uncontested, unremunerative divorce. The consequences for Heidi probably depended on the conditions of the trust. And how much shade Patti could throw on her. Some, I thought, but not enough.

For right now, Patricia Stone was scheduled to make an official statement tomorrow, and, I figured, not leave for Fiji. At least for a week or two. I bet Tom would let her handle her own reckless penalties on the travel arrangements.

Someone had relieved Patti of her blanket, beneath which she was well-and-expensively-dressed, except for no shoes. I could see this footwear *faux pas* was gnawing away at her sense of herself as an impeccably-attired and fashionably-shod wealthy person of unimpeachable social standing. She wasn't grateful we'd stepped in to save her life as she'd begged us to do, not even five whole days before. No. Not in the least. She'd glommed onto our plan and, as a clever twist, added the righteous slaying of a couple of people she had good reason to hate. Maybe that was her dream from the get-go.

"You! You've screwed up everything." Her face was drawn and angry. Not a good look. "I'm going to put your T&As out of business."

Tom busted out laughing. I was right there with him. Maybe it's not as awful as I thought to have a business name that cracks you up when you hear it spat at you by an ungrateful client. "We should be so lucky, Ms. Stone. Let me warn you, though, if you tell anybody about any of this? You'll end up looking stupider and more reprehensible than your limited imagination could comprehend."

She squinted at him. Not a great look either. "What is that supposed to mean?"

"Think about it. It might do you good. And 'reprehensible' is in the dictionary. In the Rs."

I loved him an extra lot right then. He looks so hot and handsome when he's kicking somebody's ass. Figuratively speaking, of course.

Patti turned on her—bare—heel and huffed up the stairs.

Steep as they were, she didn't falter. She was fit. That was the only positive thing I could give her. Coming from old lazy me, it wasn't much.

Otis and I watched her go. "Guess she could handle that Glock okay after all," he said. "No real surprise there. Given the givens, she should thank us for those blanks."

"What's going to happen to her?"

He shrugged. "She's going to spend the rest of her life being who she's always been. That's probably punishment enough. According to Patti's Rules, they were intruders. She meant to kill the both of them. It didn't work out. Too bad for her."

"What's going to happen to us?"

"Something new and different every day."

"Is that an ancient Chinese curse?"

"I'm afraid so."

Chapter Forty-Five

THURSDAY, MARCH 15

5:45 P.M.

In the wake of our episode of disorganized crime prevention, the T&A's were feeling good about ourselves. We'd wrapped our small, quick, secondary "Save Patti" case. We'd saved her, all right. All her wishes came true. Except for the really big one.

Hah.

As we'd hoped, Steve and Heidi got subjected to considerable uncomfortable legal scrutiny and a righteous pummeling in the press. Many Clevelanders had been alerted to the news of the weekend's "mystifying events." I took particular satisfaction from a Plain Dealer headline that screamed, "BRATENAHL RESIDENT 'MISSING' IN LAKE ERIE FAKED OWN DEATH." Heidi's name came up a lot in unofficial discussions as "heir to the family trust." Not in the best possible light. She and Steve both ran for deep cover. As far from one another as the restrictions of the formal investigation would allow.

Patricia Stone was treated more circumspectly. Nobody beyond the small inner circle of police officers, a few amateur detectives, a PI, and a former Navy Seal knew the facts of what happened in the front hall of her venerable mansion. Firing blanks at theoretically unidentified intruders coming up your stairs in the middle of the night is not a crime the law anybody can hang on anybody. Those present—and/or monitoring from the safety of the gatehouse—knew she'd shot with a wholehearted intent to kill.

On a more satisfying note, earlier in the week, Patti recklessly agreed to an interview with Lisa Cole, newly returned to Channel 16 after a "brief illness." Patti's complete ignorance of Lisa's T&A status rendered her vulnerable to a number of questions designed to make her appear vaguely guilty and, for sure, paranoid as hell. Also mean, rude, and unattractively snobby. Not a good look. The black-widow coiffeur and couture and her angry, hardened glare didn't play well to the camera either.

We tuned in. Tom said, "I guess she forgot to look up 'reprehensible.'"

Olivia Wood gave us a moderate amount stink-eye about the whole thing when she heard from Tony about it and realized she'd crossed paths—or at least our front steps—with Patricia Stone on the first day of the case. Then she said, "Thanks for keeping me out of the loop on this one. So many things a person is better off not knowing." She thought about that for a second. "But don't get carried away. Watch more Netflix."

On the evening of Thursday, the Ides of March, we convened the entire agency—T&A+O,V,M,L& J—to celebrate our small victory. True, it had not gone precisely as we'd planned, but the case was our most satisfactory so far, *i.e.*, no one had died. Our client was now on her own. That was my favorite part.

An extra bonus was the weather. The highs, with almost no warning, as usual, were pushing seventy degrees.

Clevelanders, even imported Clevelanders such as Tom and me, know how to maximize the gift of modestly warmer temperatures. We would all say, "This can't last." Nobody cared.

Everybody was all, "Carpe spring. Carpe baseball. Haul out the boat." I figured if the sniper was out there tonight, he'd be wearing Bermuda shorts and flip-flops and holding a Great Lakes Brewery's Edmund Fitzgerald Ale in his non-gun hand.

Our fabulous veranda, conveniently accessed through French doors, ran the full length of the house and overlooked the lake which—pay no mind to Channel 16 Weather—was an open refrigerator door that afternoon. Never you mind. We had sweaters, coats, a shawl, and Veuve Clicquot. We'd uncovered the deck furniture at least until tomorrow. It was a party.

All in all, we were pretty laid back, even for us.

To quote Jay, he'd been "permanently, utterly, and screechingly" fired from his twelve-thousand-foot mansion project, and "happier than I can express to be done with all that. Particularly the Patti part." His only regret, he said, was that he'd never been able to "liberate those poor girls from the woodwork in the front hall."

Lisa, in her words, was "luxuriating in the multipurpose revenge" of her scoop interview with Patti. "I'm a secret investigative reporter working behind the scenes for the T&A. My dream is coming true."

Valerio was off duty. We were all technically off duty. It would have been a full-bore vacation from the detective business if not for a few nagging loose ends and unanswered questions now bullying their way back to front and center. That other case.

Margo drained her second glass. "He's messing with us, isn't he? Your sniper? He's—whaddya call it—'gone to ground.' He's not going to do anything for about a month and then whammo."

"Yeah, Margo. The whammo is definitely the problem." Jay refilled her glass. We all understood, no comment, Valerio would drive her home.

"And what *is* the whammo? I worry about the whammo." Margo was pursuing her line of questioning. "He is a fucking sniper, right? So fucking sniper whammo?"

Nobody was willing to address the fucking sniper whammo of it all.

"Fucking Sniperman." She took a sip that reduced the level in her glass by about fifty percent "We need to call him something else. We've already got a 'Shadow Man.' More than one 'Something Man' is overkill—Crap. Sorry. Never mind. 'Shadow Man' is a workable name. For example, I have not yet seen him. According to what I hear from Allie, it fits. Right?" She caught my eye and mouthed "Hot." In my direction.

"I heard that, Margo. Don't start reverse-matchmaking Allie and me."

"Never, Tom. But we do need to call that dude something that doesn't include the scariest thing he can do. A code name. Like in a war. Or in spy stories. 'Dark Star.' 'Armored Tank.' 'Artichoke Heart.'"

"That's a lovely idea, Margo." Tom was amused, but her point was well-taken. "I'm putting that in your court. Make us a short list. We'll vote. I'm favoring the artichoke one for now."

The Margo wheels were turning already, I could see. I was glad Tom had specified 'short list.' She brightened more. "But right now we don't have to worry, right? It could be at least a couple of months before you hear from him about the money? Make it three. That'll be June. We'd be hanging out in the deep doo-doo, waiting for another shoe to drop, but at least it would be June."

We all sat quietly. Looking into the future. Soaking in the warmth of the sun. Summer on the horizon. I could almost taste it.

"Margo, that is the stupidest thing I've ever heard you say, but I can't believe how much better I feel."

"Thanks, Tom."

"You're welcome."

Chapter Forty-Six

TUESDAY, MARCH 20

4:11 P.M.

On the first official day of spring, my phone rang. The ringtone was for the gatehouse number. Theme from "Law and Order" Just because Otis preferred plain vanilla didn't mean I couldn't spice up my own phone calls.

"Allie. It's Adam." He sounded faintly amused. "Somebody dropped a kid off up here. He won't tell me his name, but I frisked him and he's clean. Okay to send him down?"

"Sure. I guess."

We didn't get much door to door soliciting but I supposed even in Bratenahl school kids were bound to be raising money for a bus trip to DC. "Send him along, Adam. Make sure he doesn't wander into the woods. Or the lake."

Less than three minutes later the doorbell rang. Kid must have run all the way.

I opened the door. A boy, not tall but getting there, good-looking, black, maybe ten or eleven, wearing a warm, quilted silvery jacket and clutching onto the backpack slung over his shoulder, stood on the steps. He looked profoundly uneasy and—I blinked—a lot like Rune Davis. Our Rune.

"Rune? *Rune*? Where did you come from? How did you get here?

"Pittsburgh, Allie. Bus. And Uber."

"Uber? And, like, a Greyhound Bus? Seriously? They still have those? Is it okay with Iona? Are you all right? Rune. Get in here. Let me look at you. And hug you."

He submitted to my looking and hugging—and he spared a moment for a "Wow. *Sweet*." as he glanced around at the house—but I could tell he was scanning for the person he'd really come to see. I subdued my questions, and a twinge of rejection, and called up the stairs, "Tom? Can you come down. Someone's here to see you."

There it was. The happy ending scene from a tearjerker movie. Tom coming down the stairs. The look on Rune's face when he saw Tom. The look on Tom's face when he realized who had tackled him, crying, "Tom! Tom! It's me." Now that was a hug. Everybody cried except Otis who was making supper and missed it.

I moved the three of us into the kitchen and introduced Rune to Otis. They'd never formally met, but Otis had heard everything there was to hear about Rune. Rune knew nothing of Otis but he liked what he saw. He'd never experienced Otis's formidable bodyguard-PI skills but he could relate to the baking. As soon as they all started talking at once, I left. A phone call had to be made.

I hurried up to the master suite and called Iona. She and I had a polite working relationship, based on the fact that we both loved Rune and wanted him safe and happy. We'd only met once at what was the end of our time with Rune. We never got a chance to become friends, but I wouldn't rule out the possibility.

She answered the phone. On a Tuesday, she should have been teaching her classes, but she was at home, on the straight-edge of panic.

"Iona—"

"Allie. Oh. Allie. I was just going to call you. It's Rune—He's—

"He's here, Iona. He's safe."

"What? Oh, Allie. Oh. I'm so—We were so—" She turned away from the phone and called out, "Clarence! He's okay. He's safe. He's with Allie and Tom." She came back to me. "When? *How?*"

"He showed up on our doorstep ten minutes ago. Greyhound to Cleveland. Uber to us. I didn't even know he knew our address. Iona—"

"Yes, Allie." She was coming down from panic to her next inevitable state of mind. Another minute and she'd be furious with Rune and none too happy with us. Human nature.

"Iona, we're going to get him back to you as soon as we can do that safely."

"Safely? Allie, are you still—Is it still so—I heard something—"

"No, Iona. It's been bad, but now I'm starting to think we might be getting out of the woods. I've got someone in mind to bring Rune to you. About as capable as Secret Service, and he might be a good influence on Rune regarding his recent behavior."

"I need to talk with Rune."

"He needs to talk with you. I'll get him for you in a minute. He's sorry and scared. You might wait to start the major yelling until you have your hands on him. You'll be able to shake him then too."

She exhaled a tiny laugh and I could hear fear seeping away. Not all of it by any means. The boy had hollering coming. I was betting no video games until he was forty-five, but that would be my response. Iona was a real mom.

"I promise to hug him first. Oh, Allie. We were so worried."

I walked downstairs and into the kitchen and said, "Rune." He dropped the cookie he was holding onto the island and slid off the stool. He took the phone away from me and walked with it, out of our sight. I heard him say, "Iona, I'm—"

After that it was mostly her talking and him listening.

Busy evening. Between the painful phone conversation and the wide-ranging dinner conversation, my head was spinning. Tom told Rune he was wrong to scare Iona and Clarence who loved him and were frantic about him, and Rune said he'd known he'd made a mistake by the time the bus rolled across the Fort Duquesne Bridge. "It was too late to go back. I was going call her. And you. But my phone didn't have bars and then it was too late. I'm sorry, Tom. I screwed up."

"Big-time. You'll need to make it up to her. I'm glad none of us knew you were on your own between there and here. Anything could have—" He stopped himself. "But you're here now. And I intend to enjoy every minute. We'll get you a ride back to Pittsburgh tomorrow, but let's make the most of the time we have. It must have taken planning. Why'd you decide to come now?"

"It's my spring break. I figured I'd call Iona and you after I got on the bus, and she'd be mad, but you'd meet me and it would be okay. I was worried, Tom. I saw in the paper about that blind guy—and about how maybe somebody shot him thinking he was you. I know the lottery's my fault—"

"Rune." I could tell by the way Tom's face froze this was a thought which, in all his anguish about Rune's safety—from those first awful days right up to this moment—had never once occurred to him. "Rune, do you blame me for buying the ticket?"

"No. Tom. You did it for me. To show me. To help me not turn out like my mom. I understand that now. I said I wished I had a dollar for a ticket. I lied about my true age for the Mondo Ball number too. If I hadn't—That's what started everything. It's all my fault."

I was back in the chapel with Robert Wade, relating the chain of events that led inexorably from Tom's well-meaning purchase of the ticket to Kip's murder. Cause-and-effect was a killer every which way. I was supposed to be a grown-up and it made me want to stare off into space until the sun burned out.

Rune was a kid, and all this time he'd been blaming himself for his mother's death. For the danger that came to all of us because of the jackpot. How could Tom—whose well-meaning impulse was a source of his perpetual guilt, fear, and sorrow—free Rune from it? What would he say?

"Rune. That summer, you were a lit—very young boy. I've had no idea you were thinking that. That you've believed it all this time. I'm so sorry. It's not true."

The two of them were sitting, side-by-side, on the couch in the newly restored greenhouse. Under the clear evening sky the lake was winking at the sun. Seeing them together like that brought me back to the moments right before Iona appeared and all our hopes for adopting Rune ended. The sorrow of it—especially for Tom, who loved Rune, but also for myself, just beginning to imagine us as a family—knotted itself tight around my heart.

Allie Harper, do not let that kid see you cry.

"Rune," Tom was wrestling with his fear of saying the wrong thing, I could see, but his voice was rock steady. "I need to tell you something that's tricky to understand. Complicated. I can see how smart you are. You always were. How grown up you are now, but this is something many grown-ups never get. And even when you get it, it's hard to—hold on to. Hard for me too. So pay attention."

Tom was right. The "seven-and-three-quarters-year-old" who'd told Tom his age was eight—the winning Mondo Ball number—wasn't a child anymore. He was taller, stronger, more composed. His serious face and deep, troubled eyes were not a little boy's face and eyes. He was fully focused on Tom, waiting for this adult thing Tom believed he was old enough to understand. Which, I was painfully aware, Tom and I grappled with every day.

"First of all, that day, it never occurred to you any of the bad things were going to happen. You didn't mean for it to."

"I know what 'well-meaning' means, Tom. It doesn't cut any ice with anyone."

Tom smiled in spite of himself. "I believe I hear the voice of Iona."

Rune made a face. "You got that right. Nothing gets past her. Clarence, either."

"One day you'll thank her. Your college graduation would be a good time. I hope Allie and I are there for that. But Rune, we're talking about who's to blame for something bad happening. Right?"

"Right."

"Okay. Suppose a mean guy—You must know some mean guys, right?"

"Uh huh."

"Well supposing this mean guy, let's call him—?" He waited for Rune to fill in the blank."

"Andre."

"Good. Thanks. Supposing Andre throws a rock at you, but you're quick—I can tell you're quick—so you duck. And the rock goes over you and breaks a window. Who's to blame?"

"Andre." Even though the case was hypothetical I detected a note of satisfaction in Rune's answer. "His fault. Not mine."

"But the window is still broken."

"And my mom is still dead."

Rune's quick answer caught Tom off guard. He didn't bother to try to hide it. "You're right, Rune. But intention is important when it comes to blame. You didn't start out to break the window in my example. Or to hurt your mom by wishing you could win money. I never dreamed we'd win, or she'd be anything but happy if you learned to avoid something that was causing her a lot of problems. You wanted to do good things with it if we won. We thought—you and I both of us thought that day—good could come from the ticket. It's not our fault that it went so wrong. But my actions and my friendship with you caused all of it."

Rune's face was a mask of sorrow. He was trying his best not to cry. "That's very sad, Tom. I feel very sad about it. Almost every day."

"We both feel very sad about what happened. We always will.

But at least we don't have to feel like we were bad or did it on purpose to hurt people. Everything we do has a consequence. Big or small. Bad or good. We tend to notice the bad ones more. But, Rune. If I hadn't crossed the street to buy our ticket at Joe's, I wouldn't have met Allie. Or Otis. We wouldn't be living in this beautiful place. You wouldn't have your Aunt Iona and your Uncle Clarence and four cousins who are like your own brothers, I bet. I'm glad about Allie And Otis."

Otis winked at Rune. "I think maybe he's a little gladder about Allie, Rune. But I can deal."

"I'm glad about my family too, Tom. And Allie and Otis. I just—" Rune pursed his lips to puff out a shaky breath. "Thanks, Tom. I feel better about everything, but I need to think about it some more."

He'd understood what Tom said more logically than I would have expected, but I could see we'd missed part of what was bothering him.

"Rune. Something's still on your mind."

"Yeah, Allie. A little. You guys let Iona take me. I thought maybe you didn't want a—me."

"Rune, that's because you didn't see us both crying after we left you. You're almost ten. And you were one smart almost-eight-year-old then."

I stopped, considering how much to say. "Okay. You can handle the facts. Listen, Rune, we were hoping to adopt you. We came to Elaine's that day planning to take you home with us as soon as we could. But, Rune, Iona is your mother's sister. Your own aunt. Her family is your own family. And her boys—You and Damon were almost brothers already when we met him."

Tom found his voice again. "And we'd already seen how the lottery money blew up everything. People got hurt. Nothing was safe here. We couldn't protect you enough. And suddenly you had a chance to be with family in a safe place. We couldn't argue with that. Even now, we're finding out this big house is not a safe place. Not yet. But why did you leave Pittsburgh? On a bus, for cri—for goodness sake?"

"They don't talk about my mom, Tom. Not ever. Or my real dad. I know she's not coming back. Duh." He shrugged and I got a peek at the teenager he would be in another ten seconds. "But my dad? You think Damon is my family. And Iona. And Clarence—They are. But your father is—I thought you guys—In your letters you talk about being detectives."

A grin broke through and right there was the kid we'd planned to make our own. My heart stabbed me.

"Iona says the name of your 'so-called agency' isn't nice. I had to ask Eric, my biggest cousin, what that was about." The grin widened. "I told him it was really for Tom & Allie. He said you should have put your initial first, Allie."

"Yeah. I've heard that. Elsewhere. Like nine hundred times. Tom, I believe this kid needs your detective advice. Since you're the 'T.'"

"Rune. I'll talk with your aunt and if it's okay with her, we'll look into your case. Maybe she knows something she thinks you're not ready to hear. Dads can't be with their kids for all kinds of reasons. You know that. I trust Iona, don't you?"

"Uh huh. She's great. Really nice to me. She and Clarence are family. I guess I want to stay with them, but you said I could come and visit."

Tom laughed. "I did. I wasn't thinking Greyhound and Uber, though. Rune. I promise that as soon as we can sort out our current situation, we'll invite you for as long a visit as Iona and Clarence feel okay about. Deal?"

The boy was gazing out over the lawn to the lake, shimmering at the edge of the shore. "You guys have a real pool?"

"We do. It's huge, Rune. You'll love it."

"I hope it's summer when I come back."

Otis had been observing the conversation without much comment but without missing a word.

"I hope it's this summer, Rune. In the meantime we should all go down to my quarters. I manage the ice cream collection."

———

For about a thousand reasons, we got Shadow Man to drive Rune back to Pittsburgh. He was the next best thing to an armored division. Rune took in the "Shadow Man" of him without ever hearing it spoken. He was black rip-stop everything today including the attitude. He looked the kid over and stuck out his hand.

"Hello, Rune. My name is—" I held my breath. "Everett."

Rune shook the hand as if he got introduced to the Badass of the Universe every Friday. "I'm glad to meet you, Everett."

Iona was getting the job done. The kid always had presence. Now he had polish. It made me happy and sad at the same time. I wanted Rune here. I wanted him safely away.

I hugged him more than he considered reasonable. "Come back soon, Rune. I haven't been in that pool yet either."

———

"Otis, is 'Everett' Shadow Man's real name?"

"One of 'em, Allie. Maybe."

Chapter Forty-Seven

FRIDAY, JUNE 1

9:57 P.M.

The sniper put us on hold.

Left us to mark time in the uneasy limbo of his silence. Sent no messages, postal or lethal. For the rest of March, all of April, and May, Margo's wish came true. The sniper—Code Name: Mercury—left us alone. We were grateful not to hear from him. Afraid to relax. Trying to forget he was out there. Not thinking, for even one minute, he was gone.

The inevitable result? We were on pins and needles from one end of spring to the other.

Mercury had set it up that way when he walked out of the Millard Fillmore Presidential Library on the evening of Wednesday, March 7, and took himself off to put the finishing touches on his big, deadly, avaricious plan. I gave us credit, however, for not spending that stretch of hard time locked up indoors. To quote Margo, "It's bleeping spring, dammit. I have no intention of wasting it on that evil, slippery guy. Especially since I have friends with a water park."

She did too. The rains melted the snow. The lawn crew—all vetted by Otis—removed downed limbs, trimmed away the dried-up remnants of perennials, and extricated the snowdrops popping up under the pine trees from the debris of winter. The air quit smelling like iron and auto exhaust and warmed to the fragrance of pine and thawing water.

We, the T&A, presided over the grand opening of the pool, the patios, and the decks, and dragged out the assorted tables and reclining furniture. Jay and Lisa raised the umbrellas, bright gestures of defiance, barely twenty-four hours after the last flake of snow evaporated. Valerio showed up and shook his head. Well into April, we still had an occasional day under forty degrees, and we didn't see seventies worth a darn until May, but Margo pronounced any high above fifty "temperate."

"Besides, the pool is heated. So who cares?"

As she frequently reminded us, this was the "deep doo-doo" she'd predicted, but the snow had more or less stopped, and we'd all survived this far at least.

We discussed Mercury, naturally. We agreed Margo's choice of his code name was spot on. She found it on Wikipedia. "Listen to this, you guys. He's 'the god of messages, trickery, and thieves?' If that doesn't fit that fucking rat bastard—with those icky, creepy silvery eyes—I don't know what would. Gives me chills to think about him."

'Yeah, Margo," Jay agreed, "And any name that doesn't include 'our' or 'sniper' is an improvement. Plus 'Fucking Rat Bastard' is too many syllables."

Otis was particularly inspired by the kitchen on the patio with its massive grill. He reported it to be good as brand new. "I don't see Patti cookin'—especially outdoors—and I assume Steve never figured out how to turn it on."

I searched Otis for indicators of his state of mind. It was set on "Alert" all the time, in the zone between Orange for "High" and Yellow for "Significant." He never stood all the way down.

He'd assessed our current state of affairs as the lull before the killer's next offensive, and although he was always calm and steady, he never let us forget how ruthless the man could be. He kept the security team on their toes, even as he delivered their barbecue to the garage, but I took it to be an encouraging sign that Shadow Man wasn't so much a fixture these days.

In spite of our determination to wring every warming breeze out of April and May, the feature of our outdoor recreation area that saw the most action on the days when a faint breeze off the lake could take your breath away was the firepit.

A feature of the lawn nearest the lake, it was Jay's pride and joy. He'd wheedled it into the budget by telling Patti it would be her beacon on the shore. "Like a lighthouse." He said she'd only half bought into that notion. "Whatever." He shrugged. "She paid for it."

A ring of hand-hewn stones surrounded the inner circle of seating, which encircled the fire pit itself. The full "concentric installation," as Jay liked to call it, might easily accommodate twenty or thirty tipsy Clevelanders singing "Kum Bah Yah." That had not happened during our tenure, but it could. More important, the circles—which Jay referred to as "Ohio Stonehenge"—included plenty of room around the fire for the eight red Adirondack chairs of the T&A. Including a chair for one guest, usually Olivia.

At the beginning of May, Tom and Jay engineered the positioning of Predacious, the metal sculpture of a bird of prey poised for flight on the lake edge of the stones. We'd brought it from the former mansion with all its attitude intact. It brooded over its new perch, gazing hungrily out to the horizon. Fierce as the young artist who'd created it. Tom had chosen it in spite of, maybe because of, its many sharp edges. I hoped the installation meant we'd stay here for a while. Be all together here for a while.

The seven of us were sprawled around the firepit on the first night of June. A line of red-orange flared along the horizon, underscoring the navy blue of the sky and the first spark of Venus, coming in for her landing. We were debating the differences among the "astronomical," "nautical," and "civil" twilights when Otis got a call.

His face, relaxed and burnished by the light from the fire, froze as if it were trying to ward off a cascade of unwelcome emotions.

"Yes. Okay. No. Fine."

"Otis?"

"Sorry, Allie. Tom. That was the Bratenahl P.D. They got a tip a couple of hours ago. Man said, 'Check on Patricia Stone. I'm afraid she's had a bad fall.' They broke in. Found her dead at the bottom of those stairs."

My phone binged. Text incoming.

Happy June. I closed your case.

———

"He's sent us Patti as another "Dead-Human-Being-As-A-Fucking-Message?" What is wrong with these people?"

So many emotions. So little time.

Margo, who'd be an alien impersonating the real Margo if she didn't freely speak her mind, covered several of our bases in that distinctly Margo-esque pair of questions. She wasn't expecting an answer. Good thing. None of us had one.

Each of us in the circle around the fire was freaked out for a different reason:

Tom was furious because once again the T&A's "big win" had turned out to be, in his words, a "pyrrhic victory." He was smart and educated like that, but I knew he was feeling both defeated and frightened to death by this news.

Otis was dealing with the fact that he would never in a million years have predicted Patricia Stone's murder. He hated being caught off guard.

Valerio was annoyed. He saw the logic, but the cruelty of it pissed him off anyway.

Lisa was frustrated because here was another groundbreaking story with angles and twists she'd never be revealing on the six o'clock news. Or talking about with anyone but us. Ever.

Jay was feeling guilty about how much he'd hated Patti. How he'd led us to her out of spite. Her death was making him despise himself a little.

I was stabbed by an image of Patti crumpled at the foot of her precipitous staircase—all of her hard, vindictive energy erased. Shocked by the sorrow of that picture. But the driving emotion for me, before I could reject it on humanitarian grounds, was "ticked off." Whatever happened to justice and gratifying endings? To getting it right for once?

Patricia Stone would have been disappointed to learn my second reaction to news of her demise was "WTF?" And my third reaction was "I wonder if Heidi's going to get it all?"

The fire died. Nobody got up to poke it. Venus was sinking in earnest, her glittering trail reaching across the water for the horizon as she fell. Darkness rose up all around us. I shuddered. We could see our enemy better now. Track his path too. Like a sharp-edged iron bird blocking out the sky. Predatory.

I satisfied my urge to psychoanalyze without a license by saying, "Just because he's not Tito doesn't mean he's well-adjusted. And he sure as hell is not a nice guy."

In their duel to the death, we'd drawn the winner.

Chapter Forty-Eight

SATURDAY, JUNE 2

Skip Castillo, our friend, lawyer, and trusted adviser was present and fully accounted for on the day Tom and I first met Otis in the basement of the ARCO building—the top floor of which was occupied by Skip's law firm. That was the day I started thinking of him as "my big & tall mama duck." He'd also arranged for the return of some ransom money we'd not had to pay, and brought his lawyerly gravitas to a meeting we'd held with D.B. at the Cleveland Clinic after D.B. got beaten up by a couple of guys for being my idiot ex.

More relevant to today's news was the call Skip had made to me at lunchtime on a Thursday morning last July to explain how someone had tried to hack into Tom's jackpot.

Skip and I had in common the fact that neither of us was screamingly tech-savvy.

His description of hundreds of doorknobs stealthily turning to open the doors of the money was not high-tech, but it worked for me. He was bringing that visual back, here and now in living color. His voice was ashes.

"The money's gone, Allie. I'm sorry. We've—" He started over. "We've not been able to—It's just—Gone."

I took his call from my spot under an umbrella at a table on the deck. The sun was shining. The umbrella was luffing in a stiff breeze coming in off the water. Skip's news wasn't a punch in the gut. Not exactly. Not yet. I'd gasped when he said, "Gone." I was letting go of a breath Tom and I been holding for almost two years. I knew there was a financial asteroid out there, coming to crush us like bugs later in the week. But for now I was—

Alrighty.

"So. Skip. How broke are we?"

Well," he considered for a long moment, "you still have a savings account at KeyBank that doesn't appear to have been touched. It's a decent amount, but not rich-person decent. As I recall, Tom wanted an account with a year's worth of his teaching salary. Enough to live on for a while. He hasn't touched that. You paid for the house in full, right?

"We did. Against advice of legal counsel, as I recall."

"Not all of counsel's advice is smart in all circumstances. As I'm painfully aware today."

"And this is one of those circumstances?"

"Yeah. Tom was smart. You'll have a roof over your head. I suggest you consider putting it on the market before your tax bill comes due—"

He sounded way more upset than I was at the moment.

"Allie. I don't have to tell you how—awful I feel—calling you up like this. Where's Tom? I tried his cell but—All of us here are in shock. We'll do everything we can to get the different—everyone who had the money—to cover your loss—They'll have to acknowledge the obvious security breach, but those inquiries take forever. An amount this big, and this well-distributed—Years. I'm—"

"Skip. Listen to me. I'm sure I'll be upset about this once I've thought it through. I may have to reconsider my recent addiction to pricey boots—But you know what we've been through because of this money. If we can have it stolen from us and live to tell about it? Cut down on casualties—" Patti Stone skated angrily through my mind, but I brushed her away. "—I'll remember this call from you pretty fondly. Maybe not tomorrow. But soon."

———

I called Tom. "Where are you? We need to talk about something."

"You sound funny, Allie." Thomas Bennington III, master of the unspoken everything.

"It's been a strange morning. Where were you and Otis?"

"Buying a gross of burner phones. Why?"

Too late on the phones. We probably wouldn't be getting as many unwanted calls from now on. I wondered if Code Name Mercury was planning to ring us up and say goodbye. "Thanks for the $200+ million."

I guess Patti was his lovely parting gift, huh?

Shh.

"Come home. Tom. Nobody's dead. Nobody today, at least. As far as I know. I need to tell you something, but it'll keep for another—?"

He filled in the blank. "Fifteen minutes or so. We're almost there."

"Fifteen then." I hung up.

I sure hope they kept their receipt for those burners.

Shh.

I eased my phone down onto the table as if it were a partially defused bomb, and sat waiting for Tom and Otis. When they showed at the door of the greenhouse, I waved them out. They brought beers. I stalled until they were seated, and I'd had my first major glug of beer. Then I told them.

We finished our beers.

The facts were simple and direct, but there was a lot of ricochet in the conversation. We'd be picking up fragments for the foreseeable future. Some things are too big to fit into a coherent thought, but we tried. Sharp exclamations. Long silences. In there, jumping up and down and demanding my attention, was a question I'd been asking myself since ten seconds after Skip said "Gone."

"Otis? Where's Shadow Man? We need him here. Today of all days. Last summer he was able to un-hack all the work of Tito's guy in twenty minutes. Is he monitoring the accounts? Does he know, do you think? Have you heard from him?"

I searched my own mental date book. Shadow Man had been more shadowy than usual lately. Had I seen him at the island for morning coffee yesterday? The day before? Now that the decks weren't covered in heaps of slush, he often came into Otis's cave through the lower level door. There had been precious little chatting between us—ever—but I couldn't remember speaking to him at all this week.

"Otis?" I was trying to stop the bottom from dropping out of yet another fortress of trust. "Otis? Where is he?"

Otis's eyes were locked on the far horizon.

———

Back in May, when life was not quite so World War III, I did some research on the physical properties of two hundred million dollars. Not its value in the market place, not its ethereal presence in the form of Apple Pay, nor its invisible magnetic attraction for death and destruction. The question I asked myself—and the Internet—was "How much space would that amount of money take up if, let's say, a truck pulled up and dumped it onto your living room floor? Could we, for example, still access the couch?

I'd hoped it might help both Tom and me if we could consider The Money in the form of an actual, solid object. Bigger than a bread box.

Maybe we'd be better able to subdue it, manage it, give it away in a sensible, orderly fashion if we didn't keep imagining it as a ghostly death threat. Or electrical impulses speeding along the pathways of commerce. Flashes of lighting in a dark—deadly dark—cloud.

Here's what I found out: one hundred million dollars in hundreds fits "neatly" on a standard size pallet. And, not counting the pallet, it would be roughly four feet by four feet by three feet, so two hundred-plus million would be double that, with a few extra thousands sloshing onto the rug. Big. But not all *that* big. If we shoved our pallets between the two couches in our living room, they'd be way too big to make a functional coffee table, but not Washington-Monument-over-the-top.

This afternoon, however, as I wandered from room to room of our about-to-be-former mansion, I meditated on the new reality. Our two palletsful of money had gone "poof" out of our world in a ghost-like instant. They were in the wind. With Mercury. And his brand new partner, Shadow Man.

Chapter Forty-Nine

SUNDAY, JUNE 3

If it's not a syndrome, it should be.

Pretend for a second you're starting your diet on Monday. It's time. It's past time. You're committed. In a possibly perverse way, you're looking forward to it. It's Sunday morning. Someone has gone out and brought home a dozen donuts. There's are four still in the box on the kitchen counter. One of them is a Boston Cream. You could get a head start on virtue and self-denial by having an egg-white omelet right now. Or you could have the Boston Cream and take a full thirty minutes to savor every last, precious bite.

Or you could eat all four in seven minutes or less.

Or maybe that's just me.

Does this compare in any way to having two hundred million+ dollars in a—as it turned out—not-safe location on Friday night and waking up on Saturday morning to discover it's time to put your budget on bread and water? For me, the answer was yes.

But. First.

You need a really nice outfit for the last big, fancy party you'll probably ever be invited to—and given free tickets for—because of how rich some people foolishly believe you still are.

That was me on Sunday morning, the third day of June.

Otis found me at the kitchen island, not with four donuts but with a bunch of VIP invitations to the Solstice Celebration at the Cleveland Museum of Art, on Saturday, June 23. Tom, Otis and I plus all the members of "our agency" were invited to celebrate the coming of summer in exuberantly lavish, artistic style.

The other item in front of me on the island was my laptop. When Otis showed up I was surfing fashion sites for dresses about five to twelve hundred dollars above my pay grade. Not including shoes—which I was learning were stunningly expensive, even though you could probably get a hundred of those insubstantial strappy sandals out of one cow.

I was considering those mind-boggling prices might be a crime—or possibly sin. My mother would definitely say they were. I could almost hear her saying that all the way from out-of-state.

Do not listen to that voice, Alice Jane. We're entitled to one last big fling before you go back to your bogus part-time librarian gig. Carpe vanishing fortune.

Otis poured us each a cup of out of the bottomless Otis pot. "Seems like you might be a little bit late to the shoppin' bus, girl. Especially that bus route you're checkin' out there. Louboutin is not for the recently financially demoted."

There was a lot to ponder in that sentence. I sipped my coffee and pondered it.

Otis, you know I would never consciously stereotype anyone, particularly not you, but I would not have expected you and Christian to be acquainted.

This was true. I began again.

"Otis. I am reminded that you are a man of many surprises. So are you a fashion maven?"

I would have expected him to laugh. Or look offended.

He smiled that slow Otis smile I'd come to recognize as the presence of the True Otis. "Not what you'd expect from an overweight—*formerly* overweight—black, retired Cleveland cop?"

"Otis—"

"Allie. Cut that out. I know I'm the most unlikely fashion maven you ever met."

I was nodding while trying to assimilate "fashion maven" into the vocabulary of the Otis who lived in my mind. I was picturing him at the first moment I ever saw him on the day he saved me from kidnapping and almost certain death.

To be perfectly candid, at that moment I was so busy watching my life flash in front of my eyes Otis registered mainly as a big, black, blue-uniformed blur. Truly, though, "fashion maven" would not have occurred to me, even if I had full access to my brain.

He brought his coffee around to my side of the island, sat next to me. Started scrolling, absently, down through the strappy sandals. Remembering.

"It was my mom got me interested in all that. She was smart, Allie. She wanted college so bad, but it wasn't in the cards for her. My dad was Army because Army was a good, decent job for a guy like him in those days, but he ended up in 'Nam after a while, and he didn't come home from there. Not even in a box. MIA for a long time and then presumed dead."

A tiny sympathetic sound got away from me, but Otis wasn't having any. "Don't. It's not so sad anymore. I don't remember him. He'd be in his seventies. She's been gone a long time now too. Nobody is missing my daddy anymore."

"That's sad of itself, Otis."

"I know. But I don't dwell there. I don't think he'd want me to. And I know she didn't because she said as much."

"Okay, then. Tell me more about how you got to be a fashion maven."

"Yeah, well. My mother's life was on hold for those MIA years. She went to beauty school so she could feed the two of us while we waited for him to be dead or be found, and eventually she had her own shop.

"I used to go there after school. Hang out until she was done for the day. That's where I saw my first copy of *Vogue*. And *Harper's Bazaar*. There were *GQ*s too—though the few guys who got their hair cut there were not the GQ type—more *Sports Illustrated*. And there was always *Ebony*.

"I got to hand it to my mom, Allie. If I was interested in something and it wasn't guns or drugs, she'd support me. She did not say 'everyone will think you're gay.' She did say, 'best not to discuss this with your friends at school.' But I was already aware.

"She made a decent living, and I guess she had a good life after a while. She always was a big reader. She turned me onto all kinds of books and didn't give me hard time, ever, about my choices. Even when I told her I was going to the Police Academy, which was really hard for her." He paused, remembering, I assumed.

"Anyway. You can't judge a book by its cover, Allie. You know? But my cover is a little more misleading than most."

"What was her name, Otis?"

"Mae."

We sat with that for a long moment.

He switched gears. All business. "Allie, you sell yourself short and you tell yourself that's a virtue. Ain't. You actually believe it's a good thing Tom can't see you. It's time you gave that shit up.

"Okay. Let's shop. We'll do it online here. Then I'll have Nordstrom pull the outfits and the shoes and the what-all you decide you like and then you can go try them on. I'll lurk around in the "gentlemen's waiting area" outside the dressing room and raise my eyebrows and nod my head, like they do."

"Cool, Otis. The Nordstrom folks will think you're my Sugar Daddy."

He shook his head. Dropped his vowels down somewhere south of Birmingham.

"No, honey. I believe y'all already got yourself one of those. He'd sell the house to buy you some shoes. Now. Let's go shoppin.'"

I believed the look on Otis's face was relief that we all could dress up and go to a party without wearing bulletproof vests.

The dress we picked out was totally the prettiest, sexiest, twenty-five-hundred-dollar dry-clean-only dress I'd ever owned. From Day One, I thought of her as "Dry Clean Only." The shoes didn't suck either.

Chapter Fifty

7:05 P.M.

Light. Color. Music. Solstice!

Tom, Otis, and I walked out the south entrance of the museum into a lush June evening at the center of a kaleidoscope. Projected geometric designs—shifting shapes, changing colors—chased themselves around the building's Ionic columns and marble façade. Towering eerily-human balloon creatures swayed, hovering low to search the faces of the crowd with large, round, wistful eyes. The steps leading down to the main outdoor stage—where a band was blazing Latin *rock y alternativo*—were jammed with partygoers. Sitting, standing, dancing in place, all of them caught up in the wild beat of frenetic energy. Electronic. Exotic. Erotic. Hypnotic.

I couldn't see the rest of our party at the moment, but they were all here, eating, drinking, smiling. Lisa, Margo, and Jay all admired my outfit before they drifted off for more eating, drinking and smiling. Olivia and Valerio were "semi on duty." I breathed in the magic moment unfolding below us and slapped down my unwelcome awareness of Atelier 24, hovering over the far end of the party, a small bank of thundery-looking clouds at its back. Not raining on my parade tonight.

Done with all that.

Deep breath, Allie Harper. Stop borrowing trouble.

Party on, Lee Ann!

Tom was missing out on the light and color but I could tell his other senses were fully engaged. The sultriness of the sun caressing us. The smell of fresh-cut grass, mingling with a thousand carefully chosen fragrances in the heat of a thousand bodies. The seduction in the beat. His close proximity to me. He put his warm hands on my bare shoulders and his mouth against my ear.

"We invested quite a bit of our working capital in this dress, Ms. Harper, and I notice there's not much dress here. I'm wondering if it was a wise choice."

"I wasn't going for wisdom."

"Ah. Excellent. What would happen if I undid this little bow at the back of your delicious neck?"

"Just to be clear, Dr. Bennington. You're blind and no doubt haven't realized we're in a huge crowd on the front porch of a venerable institution. Or that Otis is standing three feet over."

"Maybe he could be bribed to look the other way."

"Which brings us back to our money problem."

"No babe. I think our money problem has been solved." He abandoned the tiny knot that stood between me and total top-lessness and pressed closer. "I feel I'm missing a lot here, due to my being a person with a disability. Describe all this for me? Can you?"

Could I? This magnetic mix-up of melody and chaos? The strange and yet unmistakable yearning of the luminous balloon beings. The shared spell of "your pulse is my pulse" in the insistent drums. The flush of euphoria. Oh yes. I could describe all this to my blind man.

"Uh huh." My Louboutins had raised me up to his level. I turned under his hands so I could whisper.

"It's the Twenty-first Century Confetti Globe of Hot Sex."

"Thought so. I bet you have never danced with a blind man in such an globe as this."

"True. I bet you've never danced with a woman wearing almost three thousand dollars' worth of not-much and perilously tall shoes. Will I require any special instruction?"

"Nothing to it. See if you can get us to the dancing without stepping on anyone with those lethal shoes. Find us a small space to bob around in. No worries. These people are intoxicated by the beverages, the music, and the pheromones. The only person I need to impress with my dancing skill is you."

With one hand on my back, he let me guide him. I picked our way down to the dancers. Found us a spot, wrapped my arms around his neck, and gazed into his beautiful eyes. Seven hundred seventy-five dollars' worth of shoes raised me four inches closer to his mouth. "I'm impressed already, Tom. We're here. We have a dance floor big enough to stand up in and wiggle around. We've got this."

He pulled me tight against him. Positioned his hands on my hips. Cinched me in tighter. "Indeed, we do." For a blind man in a cramped space with a girl wearing "lethal shoes," he moved us with perfect confidence and skill.

So we danced. Celebrated the coming of summer and our wide open future in which the streets would never again be paved with gold. I let myself revel in my one fabulous dress-of-a-lifetime, and closed my mind to any awareness that we were dancing a stone's throw from the Wade Lagoon, Severance Hall, Atelier, the Holy Oil Can, and the benches by the water. We earned this night.

Let the past be past and the future be free.

I was still savoring the moment and remarking to myself that—no surprise at all—Tom could move his body with compelling grace and sensuosity even when he was standing on a two-by-two-foot square in the midst of thousands of strangers, when Otis tapped on Tom's shoulder. Tom said, "Hey, Otis. Cutting in?" I opened my eyes.

"Not this time. Sorry to break it up, but there's a young lady up there who says Ms. Cecelia Southgate, Deputy Director of the Cleveland Museum of Arts would like to see you all. In the Armor Court." He raised his eyebrows. "Command performance. Time to pay for the tickets."

Tom winced. "I hope she's not looking for a big bunch of cash."

———

Even the horses wore armor.

A setting dominated by knights and their weapons, the Armor Court stood at attention. The knights—mounted and on foot—waited like statues, frozen into a state of perpetual preparedness. The big room's sky-lit stone walls, the soft luster of its floors, and the subdued beauty of its tapestries lent it an aura of quiet order. The weapons told a different story: broadswords, small swords, half-handed and two-handed swords, rapiers, daggers. Crossbows. A battle-axe. And much, much more. These people lived in a continual state of DEFCON 1.

In spite of the festive spirit of the evening—the noisy presence of happy museum-goers, dressed to the nines, saying "What's up?" to the knights, and the musical turmoil bleeding into our lofty space from the lawn below—a somber state of readiness prevailed in here.

Or maybe that was just me. I wanted to get back to the party. ASAP.

Otis had scanned the knights and was now focused on the doors in and out. He'd positioned himself at the edge of the rotunda with its figure of Terpsichore holding her lyre. I figured she was waiting for some knight to ask her to dance, secretly tapping her marble toes.

Cecelia—"Oh, please. Call me Cece."—Southgate waited for

us in a less-traveled spot beneath one of the tapestries and next to a plume-hatted guy on a horse. Her dress was ivory. Matching shoes. I estimated her ensemble to be twice as pricey as mine. It was a sculpture of the perfect dress. I bet she couldn't sit down in it. Worth it though. Flushed with the exuberance and the tension of a massive evening, she looked like a goddess.

A long-haired man wearing trendy owlish glasses and one of those many-pocketed vests every woman should own at least three of stood by with a camera. Cece embraced us both.

"Thanks for taking time to do this. We like to get photos of honored guests. Allie, that is a fabulous dress. Who?"

She goes by 'Dry Clean Only.'

I blocked Lee Ann and answered the question.

Ms. Southgate nodded approvingly. She spoke quietly. "Off the record, we're marking the happy ending of everything that happened—and didn't happen—in March."

I bet Kip Wade would be tickled pink to hear her say that.

Cece either read my face, heard the same voice I did, or brought herself back to a hard memory. She sighed and shook her head. "Not everything, of course. You know what I mean. Anyway, Tom, one of the PR guys wanted us to get a photo with you in the armor court. Because you've been 'our knight in shining armor.'" She smiled at Tom, a well-orchestrated mix of amusement and admiration.

Tom heard the finesse of the smile and chuckled appropriately. "Sounds fine." He raised our clasped hands. "May I bring my lady?"

"Oh, of course. I meant to say you and Allie. Come stand together right over here—" The photographer was clicking away. Not good. "Candid" is not my best side.

She was interrupted by the sound of someone rolling a bushel of potatoes out onto the skylight above us.

"Oh dear. I certainly hope that storm passes us by. I've been checking the weather every fifteen minutes since last week and they *promised*—" She cast a look of dismay around the room, which had darkened noticeably. A flash illuminated the skylight. Another clap of thunder came close on its heels.

"Oh. I've got to—We always put together a plan for fitting everyone inside but we almost never—Tom, Allie, let Simon get a couple of nice shots of you two. Oh. And stand close enough to get the Mercury tapestry in the picture. The PR guy thought that would be appropriate—Allie?"

I was looking up at the woven scene on the wall above us. A figured floated in midair above a downcast-looking man. "That's Mercury? What's he doing? Who's the other guy?"

She was walking, wanting to play the good hostess, but needing to be gone. "The god, Mercury, is telling Aeneas he has to get out of Carthage. Story ends badly, but it's a great tapestry. Have a lovely evening, Allie. Tom."

The camera guy was carefully packing up his gear as if death hadn't entered the room.

"Allie? He's here?" Tom's voice was a miracle of self-control. "This is not just a crazy—"

"Coincidence? No. It can't be. We have to get out, Otis!"

I raised my voice, but he was already closing the distance. "I saw her take off. What is it? The storm—?"

"It's him, Otis. It's Mercury. Shadow Man must have told him about the code name. The tapestry above us. It's the god Mercury delivering bad news. Telling somebody to leave. He's playing with us. We need to go. But where?"

Otis pointed toward doors at the far end of the room. "Out through there. Upper walkway. The rain is starting. People will pour in from outside—Let's move."

"Otis. We'll never make it—We have to—Where can we hide?" Tom's face was rigid with fear, but his voice was steady.

"We'll make it up as we go. I have my gun but it's worthless in this crowd. Come on."

Chapter Fifty-One

That was how I found myself once again on the walkway above the atrium, even more heavily flooded with the museum's guests than it had been on the last night of February. This time I was traveling in a river of people who were not the least bit scared. Laughing, hanging onto their drinks, jostling casually in the spirit of adventure. *"Remember that Solstice Party at the art museum when it stormed? Craziness!"*

The atrium floor below us was jammed. End to end. Edge to edge. Wall-to-wall dancers had barely room enough to bob up and down. The indoor band's music was as insistently driving as the one outside. Patterns of light raced bright colors along the marble front of the vintage building, the entrance of which was spilling more happy guests into the mob scene.

I was plenty scared enough for all up-to-5,000 of us. Dizzied by panic. Above the skylighted arc, thunder rolled more potatoes. Drops of rain, or maybe a scattering of small hail, pinged its surface.

This time, at least I was not alone. Tom had my arm. I had Otis's arm, and I could feel him putting the brakes on, slowing us down, melding us into the unhurried pace of the lighthearted mob. Leveling out my panic. Setting our rhythm to "going with the flow." I didn't bother to look back.

When we made it to west end of the atrium, he bypassed the route Gloria had taken to the restroom that first night. At the next opening off the walkway, though, he made a quick right and led us into a hall with absolutely nobody in it.

"Elevator back here. For staff, mostly. Safer than an escalator, that's for damn sure. We'd only be able to hide ourselves in this mess of folks for so long before we'd get stuck. Or seen. We're a danger to bystanders. He won't care who he shoots. We need to not forget that."

We'd come to a halt in front of a big, tall elevator door, "Fee-Fi-Fo-Fum." Giant-size. It loomed.

"They bring stuff up and down back here. Heavy stuff. Big. I'm gonna take you all the way down to the lower level. See if we can find a spot for you to disappear while I start looking for him. Alert security. Get Olivia and Valerio. As soon as we can figure a way to take you out of here without getting you or anybody else hurt, I'll come back. It could be a while. You're going to need to stay put. Like it was your job."

Even for its size, the elevator was painfully slow. We rode, vibrating tension but without speaking as it clanged and thumped its way past the first floor without stopping and then down to the lowest level. Slowly. If a snail were an elevator—I used the time to lean against the wall and remove the Louboutins. My feet were on fire. I thought about tossing them into a corner of the elevator.

We shall live to dance in those shoes again, girl. Hang on to them. Besides that would be seven hundred seventy-five dollars' worth of litter. How much does a bogus part-time librarian get paid these days?

She had me there.

After a groan, a small jerk, and a micromanaged touchdown, the big doors slid open. "How did you know this was here, Otis?"

Terse. Tense. Grim. "Security dude, Allie. My job to know." He glanced out and around. "Okay. Let's go."

We stepped into a murky hall. I was checking everything everywhere. One thing moved.

As quietly as I could I murmured, "Someone else down here, Otis."

He swept his jacket away from his gun, released the strap holding it secure, rested his hand on it, said, in a moderately interested, conversational tone, "Hey, anybody out there?"

A voice came back. "Otis. Is that you?"

A punch to my chest. *Not good.*

Otis didn't answer. We waited, calculating.

"Otis? Otis *Johnson*. It's me. Chad. Chad Collins. Is that you? Are Tom and Allie with you?"

Careful. Wary. "What are you doing down here, Chad?"

Exasperation. "Whaddya *think*? I'm the guard they stake out where nobody in their right mind wants to go tonight. Big thrill. They said they'd bring me food. And a beer too. Not so much."

We breathed again. Otis dropped his coat back over the gun. Moved out into the hall where Chad was standing, having abandoned a folding chair against the wall. The lights were low here, but this was definitely our Chad. Definitely, seriously, aggrieved.

"What are you guys doing down here? Where nobody in their right mind wants to be?"

"Chad. I need a place to stash Allie and Tom for a little while. A really good hiding place. There's a big storage room, right?"

For a guy who'd appeared to have missed out on violence and crime for his whole first thirty-plus years, Chad spent no time mulling this over. "Sure. Great. Storage vault. Runs all the way under the atrium. Big. Dark—"

"Locked?"

"Oh yeah, Tom. But I have keys." He held them up and jingled them. Hurried past us, stopped in the dim light, and inserted one into the lock of a very large door. It swung open into a vast, gloomy space. Except for a corridor running through the middle, it was overflowing with shapes that could be odds and ends or art or both. I made out objects lurking in big caged areas too.

Figures. Furniture, maybe. I assumed they must be the serious second-string art stuff. "You have keys for the cages too, Chad?"

"No cage keys for me. Too low on the totem pole."

'How dark is this space, Chad?'

"Pretty damn dark, Tom, but Allie will be able to see enough so you guys won't trip over anything. Security lights are on. Overheads are off now. The staff has to get around down here."

"Needs to be darker. Can we shut it all down?"

"Sure. There's a circuit breaker, but that would make it totally—Oh. I get it. 'A place to hide.' I can do it. No outside light comes in here at all."

"Allie," Tom said, "Walk on in and look around. Try to identify the landmarks. Look for a good place for us to disappear into. Make a mental note of stuff we might trip over, if you can. Stay where it's open until I douse the lights. You'll need to talk me to you after it's done."

"Chad, take me to that circuit breaker. Then I want you to get yourself out the door. Lock it. Stash the keys somewhere. Not on your person. For when Otis comes back. You remember Officer Valerio and Lieutenant Wood?"

"Yes, Tom."

"Don't give the key to anyone but Otis or one of those two."

While Tom talked to Chad, I walked and looked. And listened. All hell was breaking loose above me. "Chad? What's that racket? The storm?"

"No, Allie, that's the party. We're underneath the atrium. You've got probably a thousand people dancing on your head."

Great. At a life and death moment when Tom needed his hearing, there'd be two thousand shoes' worth of interference. My lovely, expensive, Louboutins wouldn't be among them. I found a place for them next to a box marked "Fragile. This side up." Told them, "Stay right there. I'll be back."

Optimism can't hurt.

Chad left us. As he was going Tom said, "Chad." Stern, allowing no discussion. "The man who'll—who may come looking for us is a killer. About your height. White-blond. Unusually light eyes. Don't get in his way. If he comes in, he comes in. If there's a place to sit down, sit. Cross your ankles. Act like you don't especially care where he goes. Complain about not getting your beer. If he wants the keys, tell him you're "too low on the totem pole.""

A quick smile. Back to stern. "Don't confront him. No matter what. Otis gave me his gun. We both know how to use it. Be safe. You have a family to think of."

When Tom said "family," the memory of Rune's worried eyes came into my mind. Young. Hopeful. Watching Tom with all his heart. I gave thanks for Iona and Clarence. Waited for the lights to go out.

Chad called softly, "Good luck, you guys."

———

The door clunked shut and the lock caught with a click. I heard that much. At least the sound from upstairs was dampened now. Tom was waiting at the circuit breaker.

Counting down.

Shadowy objects intruded onto the expanse, but the center of the corridor was unobstructed. Farther along the aisle one of the cages appeared to have people crouching in it. My scalp tingled. Spooky Town.

After not nearly enough time, Tom said, "Allie, stay where you are." Complete darkness fell on me like a weight. A cavern. Under a mountain. Like that. Only darker.

I spoke into the blackness, my best eye roll in my words. "*"Both of us know how to use it?"*"

Tom. Closer than I'd expected. Zeroing in on my voice.

"I figured if I told him I'm the one who'll be handling any shooting, he'd refuse to leave us alone in here. Or take away our gun."

We verified Tom's burner phone had no signal whatsoever. No emergency call in our future. I'd left mine at home, because it was a burner and not imprinted with my personality. He shut his all the way down. "How many times have you seen some yo-yo's phone go off like a bomb at the worst conceivable moment. Who says there's nothing worthwhile on TV?"

Otis was in charge of whatever was happening outside. This was our world now.

"Will you know if the—If Mercury comes in here, Tom?"

"You'd know first. There would almost surely be light from the hall. He'll close the door once he's in. What sniper worth his salt doesn't have night vision? And we might as well accept my hearing is not going to be our biggest asset until everybody upstairs goes home after midnight. We'll be—out of here by then."

I noticed how smoothly Tom had segued from "if" to "when." Otis had surveyed this building in preparation for tonight. Now we understood Mercury had too. Tom's next words confirmed it. "I don't know how he found out we'd be here tonight, but he did. He's planned for this. Clearly, the money wasn't his only target. After all.

"When the door opens, you'll see light, Allie. I might feel a draft. Sounds will rush in. Then we'll know. Our best defense is invisibility and silence. We need to be as dead-like as possible to stay alive. That's my whole game plan." I read his smile in the words—pictured the dimple. "I'm good, but I can't outshoot a sniper. Not sure what Otis was thinking, giving us the gun."

We went as fast as we could toward the far end of the room. Both of us blind. No cane at all for Tom this evening. I was supposed to be his seeing eye girl for the party. Not anymore. I put my hand on his elbow and let him lead. It was awkward and scary. Trust was never my strong suit.

You might want to start working on that one, Alice Jane.

I'm busy working on not screaming.

My Buddha upstairs would counsel, "When time is short, proceed slowly." Tom was the master of Zen calm. Me, not so much. He'd figured out the arrangement of the cages and was walking along them. Patient. Careful. Finding their doors. Testing the locks.

"Yales. Lucky for us. Maybe."

I struggled to keep up. Tom moved patiently. Finding the locks. Jiggling each one. Toward the back of the hall was a cage door with a lock someone had neglected to click completely closed.

He laid it on my palm. "See. We're lucky. You got a pocket for this? My pockets are full of gun. And a spare clip."

"Sorry. 'Dry Clean Only' has no pockets."

"Not much of a top either."

We were speaking to each other in the range between normal talk and a whisper, relying on the mayhem above to provide cover for our voices.

I checked the time. Disconnected from my phone, my watch was a mere watch. "It's 8:52, Tom."

We were going to miss the sunset. 9:04 p.m. Tonight and every night for the rest of the month. Summer pausing on the brink—

"*Allie*. Turn off your watch."

Against a black background, a tiny spotlight is a still a spotlight. We both turned them off. We now had access to the exact same number of electronic devices as the knights upstairs. And not a single damn broadsword or crossbow. He described everything as we went. Softly. I listened and stumbled. Disoriented by my blindness. Slipping along an unmarked ledge above a cliff. Quietly missing my Louboutins. If I hollered, "ouch" every time I stepped on a nasty little sharp thing down here, even the people upstairs would know exactly where we were.

Tom pulled us into the cage. This one turned out to be full of—people?

"Allie. Hang on. There's a…a *head*? About waist high on me.

It's a sculpture of a guy. Kneeling, feels like." He knelt down too. "Naked guy. Big shoulders. Muscular arm—Ah. Hand to *chin*— It's The Thinker? Not regular size. Smaller."

He moved further in, dragging me with him. Excited. "Here's another one." He inhaled. "Can you smell that? It's paint. And something else. Glue maybe?"

I sniffed. Papier-mâché. *Even a blind pig, Allie—*

"It's 'The Thinker Tic Tac Toe', Tom. They had a serious exhibit for the Rodin Centennial, but this was for kids. Neon colors like the Warhol Marilyns. They had miniature sets for the children to play with. Sold them in the gift shop. There should be nine in here, three in a row. Can we crouch down in among them?"

"I don't think so. They're not big enough. And if he has night vision, we'd still—You're right, though. This is the third one in the row—" He stumbled. "Something on the floor back here. Feel this. It's a heavy—Drop cloth. Big. This could work. These shapes might divert him from us. If we lie down under this, back in here, flat as we can—It'll have to do, Allie. We need to—If he makes it in before we get set—catches a glimpse—"

We hit the floor behind the last row of Thinkers. Lay down side by side. Pulled the sheet—big, heavy, and smelling of paint and dust—over us. We bunched it up to make it look carelessly cast aside, checked to make sure we were completely under.

Tom skootched closer to me. "Wanna make out?"

"Let's wait and see how this goes."

The floor of our makeshift hidey-hole was hard and cold. My heart was clattering *"They're here! They're here!"* in Morse code for anyone within a five-mile radius. Plus I now really, really had to pee.

Dear sweet baby Jesus. I hate hide-and-seek.

If we had to wait in here for hours—

Stop twitching. Even I can hear you.

From outside the door, the muffled *chuff* of a shot. A thunderbolt. *Chad.*

Chapter Fifty-Two

The door snapped open.

Light.

Slammed shut.

Night.

Sniper in the house.

So much for the lock. Lying next to Tom under the drop cloth—the two of us interred, side-by-side, still as mice, in spite of the choking paint smell, the throat-tickle of dust, and our ridiculously bleak situation—I tried to screen out the rumpus above our heads—and the one inside me—and isolate any minuscule, insignificant, *nano*-sound.

Where in this vast dark space was he?

Swift. Stealthy. His vision enhanced to catch our slightest movement. A feather-light scrape? *There.* The subtle tap of a strategically placed foot? *Here.* Prelude to that final, suppressed cough—the one I might not hear coming. Closer. Close *Now?*

For crissake, Alice Jane. Buck up. Don't just lie there and die.

No kidding, Lee Ann. Shut the fuck up.

The unknown is a demoralizing enemy, and my optimism had gone over to the other side. Mercury had the edge. He had all the edges. Night vision would alert him the instant we moved. If he had thermal, he'd find us by reading our body heat. I knew squat about all that but I had a kick-ass imagination. And, of course, his aim was Certified Grade A. He was a warrior. We were civilians. Hell. We were blind rats in a cage. Under a sheet.

Second by second, my mind multiplied its own fright. His silvery eyes, narrowing to slits. Taking aim. Focusing his shot. His smug satisfaction. "Mission Accomplished."

Was Shadow Man here too? They were buddies, after all. Colleagues.

I struggled to square the picture of my Shadow Man—sitting in our kitchen, drinking Otis's coffee, wearing his Navy hoodie—with the terror racing through me now. Was he here with Mercury, silently stalking Tom and me. Tall, hot, and corruptible. One last devil.

The two of them together would be an elite special operations unit all by themselves. Betrayal and death, times two. I lay as quiet as I could. Hating them both.

Tom and I were frozen in place, hands welding us together. My fingers were numb. My pulse was galloping. Tom's too. Our shared fear pulsed in our palms. Being frantic is extra-bad when there's nothing to do for it—Tom had Otis's gun in his other hand, I could smell it. Metal and oil.

Maybe we should—?

Not a chance.

With all my experience of Tom's well-honed talents and occasional near-supernatural skills, I couldn't come up with the scenario in which either Tom or I—both of us in the dead dark—could make the exceedingly awkward move to get out from under the sheet and off the floor, and then aim that gun—let alone fire it—without getting shot.

C'mon. Do something, Allie. Flight or fight. Pick one.

You pick, Lee Ann. Flight? We die. Fight? We die.

Girl, your options suck.

Stony despair pinned me to the floor of our cage. One gun. Both of us blind.

Alice Jane Harper Smith. Are you guys going to just lie there like dummies and let him shoot you. For fuck's sake?

Oh, please. Go for it, Lee Ann. Let me know when you have a scheme that doesn't involve free nail polish.

Tom moved ever so slightly to put his mouth against my ear. Spoke hard words, softly.

"Allie…Done what we can… This…best chance… Maybe Otis…so sorry."

Lee Ann heard him too.

The storm of possible options faded away. I relaxed my body into his. Letting it answer him for me, once again. *Don't be sorry. You're right.*

In spite of what you read in popular fiction, every once in a while "lie there like dummies" is your best option. Also the bravest. And the cruelest. In the end, none of it would make a molecule of difference, and this way I'd be here with Tom. Still terrified. Still holding hands.

From somewhere in the dark silence the sniper fired his voice at us. Good as a bullet. We both jerked.

"Oh, c'mon. Tom. Allie. You know you can't hide. I've got night vision. Not using the thermal to be sporting. But if I'm going to be sporting, you have to play along."

A quick flash of an opening door, and a new voice broke into our shared blindness. Cool. Calm. Familiar.

"Mercury?" Like it was a joke they shared.

"Everett. Or should I say, "Shadow Man?""

Despicable lying, cheating, stealing, betraying, bastard.

Well said.

"Do you have them?"

"Not quite yet, Everett. Waiting for you. Like we agreed."

Let's go ahead and say, "Despicable lying, cheating, stealing, betraying, fucking bastard."

Let's.

"So. Everett? Friendly little wager? Who bags the first one?"

"That is not what we agreed, Mercury. We both get to hunt, but she's mine. You get him. Optimum damage. I wouldn't mind a small wager, though. Say one hundred thousand dollars for whoever locates them and brings both of them out for us to deal with. Night vision but not thermal. Sound good?"

"Done. I'm about to get plenty of cash. Thanks to you. And you'll have quite a bit. Thanks to me. You start where you are. Work your way to me. I'll start at the far wall. Work my way in. No thermal until I say. Deal?"

"Deal."

Deal? Rage was diluting my fear. Tom's grip was a vice.

Shadow Man's real name is Judas.

Back at the beginning, Gloria pegged our silver-eyed devil as colder than Dante's ninth circle of hell. We were there now. Underground nightmare. Mercury. Shadow Man. Betrayal everywhere.

Our Judases wouldn't appreciate the Dante thing. This wasn't hell to them. They were playing "special ops on maneuvers in the jungle with live ammo" tonight. Big game hunters. Stalking their prey.

Them, the hunters. Us, the quarry.

Otis. Where are you?

Down the corridor, maybe two or three cages away, the sound of metal on metal rattled the wire grid. The music of a kid with a stick and a fence. Only this was a sniper with a—

"Oh. Tom?" His words were casual, but they fell on us like stones. "I thought you'd appreciate hearing—I brought the knife."

Chapter Fifty-Three

For Tom, time had died. He let go of me, but not before I read a flash of animal terror all over him. I was unraveling too. Out of ideas. Out of guts. Out of time.

Otis? Now would be good.

And here was the sound I'd been straining my ears for. The sole of a shoe, brushing over concrete. Barely there, but right here.

Mercury.

"Sorry, guys." Pause. A musing, almost philosophical, tone from outside our cage.

"I lied about the thermal. You need to come out here." Matter-of fact. "Now.

"Tom. I can see you both. I know which image is you. And which one is Allie. She just moved her arm. Hey, Allie. Wave—or don't. Makes no difference."

He was looking directly at me.

"I'm going to count to ten, and if you're not making a sincere move to get up out of there, Tom. I'm going to shoot Allie. Not the kill shot. But enough. I'll let you lie there with her until she dies. Then I'll take your hands and leave you here. If you don't bleed to death, you'll have the problem you've been concerned about since Tito. And I'll have a couple of trophies. Let's go. One. Two. Three—"

Bull's-eye. Both targets annihilated. Tom sat up. Threw the drop cloth aside.

"Good. Now come on out."

"That was cheating, Mercury." Shadow Man. "The thermal. Seriously cheating."

"You should pay closer attention to the guy you're betting with, Everett. All's fair in war. End of story."

Tom stood up and raised me to my feet. Ignored the "you cheated" spat going on outside our cage. Held me tight. Put his hands on my face, pressed his forehead to mine, and spoke as if we were alone somewhere lovely.

"No matter what happens, Alice Jane. You and I—" His voice broke. "We've been lucky. Let's get out of here. This place gives me the creeps."

He led me out, skirting us around the crouching shapes. So many Thinkers. Not a single bright idea. When we arrived at the door he stopped. Waiting. One of our two Judases opened it for us. Gallant.

Mercury. "Come on out." I couldn't see him. Not even an outline. Or smell him. Or hear him breathe. But his voice, so close, was a punch, dizzying. My knees gave way for a second and I braced myself against Tom. The man snickered.

"Now that we're all together, we have time for…closure. To be clear, I have a Beretta PX4. Suppressed. As if any of those noncombatants upstairs would recognize a shot. Or believe it could actually be a shot. On such a festive evening. This means I'm in charge."

I wondered what Shadow Man thought of that. He'd never struck me as anybody's second-in-command.

Mercury continued. "You looked quite lovely tonight, Allie. Nice dress. Those fancy shoes I happen to know you really couldn't afford anymore. Glad I captured you for posterity in the armor court. I took the liberty of emailing a copy to Ms. Southgate. You're in it too, Tom. Her 'knight in shining armor.' You might say that was the first time I shot you both this evening."

Of course. A camera-zoom behind my eyes: Tom and me with Cece. Beneath the tapestry of "Mercury Delivering Bad News." *Of course.* The long-haired, owl-eyed photographer in his damn vest. With an all-access pass to get him and his "equipment" past security. *Of course.* A great wig to hide his hair and funky glasses to disguise his eyes. *Of course.*

Our guard had been so far down.

I concentrated on my ears. The crowd noise from upstairs had diminished. The storm must have passed over. The brightly-dressed partiers would be emerging into the sparkling night. Pretty people. Dancing with balloons. The contrast between Tom and me up there then and us down here now—lead in my chest.

Cry. Or Whine. Pick one. Stop feeling sorry for yourself.

———

"Allie." Him again. "I believe Tom has a gun in his pocket. Tom. Give Allie the gun. I know you blind folks have magic ears to help you aim a shot. Like Mickey Mouse."

I was wondering about the mental competence of the sniper. He sounded a tad manic to me. This made me think of Ruth. I could use her calming influence about now. I closed my eyes, exchanging Mercury's darkness for mine. *In/Out, Deep/Slow, Calm/Ease.* As usual, I got hung up on the smiling part.

Tom moved closer and put the gun into my hand. Handed me something else. The spare clip? No. The Yale lock. Locked tight now.

Brass knuckles. I knew some stuff. The lock was warm.

Mercury said, "Excellent. Now. Tom. Come over here and stand by me. Yes. Right there. Now Allie. Go nuts. Shoot anybody you like. You don't have magic ears though. Maybe you'd hit me. Maybe Tom."

I enjoyed the weight of my useless weapon. Otis Johnson's gun felt like a friend.

The sniper moved very close. Uncomfortably close. I could hear him breathing now. Smell him too. Sweaty. Traumatizing people was demanding work. I held my ground.

"Tom handed you something besides the gun, Allie. Show me."

Well, it was worth a try. I held out the lock. He took it.

"Nice." He slapped me across the face. Hard. The force of the blow made me stagger. For a split second he'd been point-blank close, but I heard him dance away long before I could un-jolt my head. My TV heroes would be so disappointed.

"*Allie.*"

"I'm okay, Tom." My cheek stung. My eyes were watering and for sure out of focus but who cared? Where was Shadow Man in all this? If he wasn't close to Tom, maybe I could shoot *him*—A gun in your hand can mess with your common sense. But the idea was appealing.

Mercury's voice was ice.

"That was stupid, Allie. Go ahead and try something else. Next time, I'll have that lock in my fist. Assuming you live that long. Your minutes are numbered.

"And Tom. Extra stupid for you. Stand still. Hold out your hand. Left or right. You choose. Or maybe I'll just do all your fingers."

He came close to me again and put the tip of the blade at the notch in my collarbone. I didn't even think about raising the gun. A tiny, sharp sting. A warm trickle of blood. "You need to exercise extreme self-control for this part of our adventure. Got it?" I nodded and the knife stung me again.

"Good."

I was now officially frantic and utterly optionless. In my fog of horror, I wondered what had happened to Otis. And if I'd find out before—

Every now and then, your burning question gets answered in a blinding flash of light. For real.

Shadow Man, from right next to me, shouted, "*Go for it, man. Now.*"

With a sudden metallic screech from the far end of the room, all the lights came on.

Otis Johnson was back in the game.

My eyes flew open, and quickly closed in self-defense. The unnerving brightness was a surprise for me, but the sniper yelped in pain. For a man using night vision and thermal, the sudden light was a few seconds of blindness. Those few seconds were enough.

Before I could focus my eyes, another gun made the *chuffing* sound.

Shadow Man was back too. I was glad I hadn't shot him.

Chapter Fifty-Four

Three of us stood over the dying killer. I'd seen Tom angry. In fact, I myself had made him pretty mad, but I'd never seen him like this. Not this fierce cold.

"I want to kill him. I want to personally make him die."

His mouth was a tight line. His handsome face was dead white except for the flush of color high on his cheeks, seeping upward into his temples, pulsing his heartbeat under the skin.

Margo loved to say anger was the top level of fear. I was grasping at last how Tom's fear of the sniper had built up over the past four months, like sediment making rock. Since the final night of February when he killed Kip Wade, I'd tried to ignore the many layers of threat the sniper had laid down in Tom's mind. The chaos he'd constructed, one cruel and terrifying deed at a time.

Kip. Gloria. Tito and, God help us, Tito's hands. The clash of glass cascading down into our greenhouse while we huddled on the kitchen floor. The murder of Patricia Stone and the mockery it made of our attempt to use the money for good. His every act undermining Tom's determination to make a worthwhile life. Right up till tonight's attempt to utterly destroy Tom and me. Both of us. Together. The love.

Shadow Man had shot Mercury in the chest. The bullet hole

in the many-pocketed photojournalist vest was not all that big, but his blood—what looked to be all of it—was spreading out around him on the floor. Mercury's eyes had lost their silvery glint, but he could still talk. He reached over, grunting with the effort, and picked up the knife from where it had fallen. Shadow Man moved to take it from him, but he laughed and held it fast.

"Tell you what, Tom. I can see you're…unhappy with me… Take my knife… Finish me. Keep your hands. Cut my throat… You'll feel better."

He folded the knife to hand it up, and Tom, with his unerring sense of where things were, took it from him. I wondered if Tito looked up at Mercury the way Mercury was watching Tom. Taunting. Sneering.

Mercury answered my unspoken question. "Tito… He knew… Couldn't talk or…scream…but…wasn't dead when I cut into his wrist… Hated me…more than you do, Tom."

"Hard to imagine." Tom stood over the dying man and opened the knife. It was jet-black and as hateful as an inanimate object can ever be, its angled tip impossibly sharp. The blood on it was mine. I wanted to say, *Don't*. But Shadow Man shook his head, a warning. Tom's life was at stake. He was on his own.

Out of the corner of my eye I saw Otis open the door into the hall to let somebody in. Music rushed in too. An exultant dance beat celebrating joy on a distant planet. Tom ran his fingers along the blade, and the moment shifted.

He spoke to the man at his feet. "Thanks, whoever you were. I think I'm good."

The sniper's eyes stared at nothing.

Tom folded the knife and held it out to Shadow Man.

Otis, behind me, said, "Allie?"

I turned. Chad was standing with him, covering his arm with his nice museum guard jacket. "Hey, Allie. Tom." His voice betrayed considerable pride. "Look. I got winged."

Chapter Fifty-Five

We were alive. My worldview was slowly reassembling itself for the better.

Even the corpse was not turning out to be the sticky wicket I expected. Shadow Man made a call. Apparently our "Mercury" was a "national security matter in some context." The M.E.'s van was not going to show up on Wade Circle tonight.

"People are coming."

Nobody had covered the body yet, and it was unsettling to see. I searched my soul. *Gratifying too.*

Cecelia Southgate, Deputy Director of the Cleveland Museum of Art, entered the storage vault under the atrium and surveyed the basement of her kingdom. The lights were up. Except for the body, we were leaving this room—and virtually everything else in the building—the way we found it. Once again, it appeared we'd not broken her museum.

Her eyes widened when she noticed the trail of drying blood on the front of my formerly merely floral Caroline Herrera. I shook my head and glanced at Tom. She nodded. Didn't ask.

After a confused and awkward bit, she sighed and said, "I think I've seen everything I need to. I'm glad everyone—you and Allie are safe, Tom. Maybe we could talk next week." She glanced at

Shadow Man. He was his usual deadly, hot self and totally black-rip-stopped for the part. He shook his head at her too.

"Or perhaps not." She left, but as she went, she paused to rain congratulations on Chad Collins, patched up and incandescent. I'd never seen a man so delighted to be shot. He'd fallen back into the wall, stunned, and "played dead like you wouldn't believe."

Otis was right up against Tom and me. Unremitting bodyguard observation. Valerio and Wood were both here, out of their jurisdiction maybe, but rock-steady in their support of us. Olivia put her hand on Tom's shoulder. "You told me back in February you wanted to be there when the sniper went down."

"It wasn't as satisfying as I imagined, Olivia."

"It never is, Tom. But you had a major role. I'm so happy you're okay. You're a good man to know."

I examined Tom for residual damage. He looked like a tired, brave, blind man wearing a dirty, wrecked outfit. But whole.

I was avoiding reflective surfaces. I could cope with a dead body on the floor, but I hadn't confronted the demise of "Dry Clean Only" yet. Baby steps.

Shadow Man gave the big space a comprehensive parting glance, let the glance graze the dead man.

"You all shouldn't have to be here. Let's sit down for a second over there." He pointed to a spot that offered no view of Mercury's remains. It had folding chairs too. Tom, Otis, and I followed him. Tom slumped into his chair and went to silent running. When I sat down, the room swam around me like a school of minnows, sparking in sunlight. I closed my eyes until it stopped.

"Shadow Man?" The query in my voice covered many bases.

"You have questions for me. Not going to say much but you and Tom deserve—It's simple, actually. He was a man of many skills. Excellent at long range. Unparalleled close-up. Experienced with poisons and unexplained accidents. Bloody hell with a knife, as we know, or a garrote, according to people I spoke with.

"But—" He made the "tsk, tsk" sound with his tongue, and

amusement tugged at the corner of his mouth. Sardonic. "He was an excellent killer, Allie. But, beyond rudimentary surveillance equipment, and being *almost* able to erase somebody's in-house video, not all that—"

Ah. "Tech-savvy?"

"Too bad for him. He put out feelers with mutual contacts. Described a situation I recognized as $250 million distributed in a manner I was familiar with. He needed a hacker. Irony there." The mouth tug again.

"Serious luck for us. I played along. Helped him out by wiping the security video at Atelier to 'prove my capabilities' and show I wasn't afraid to bend the law. Nothing on it worth saving." He shrugged. "I saved it all elsewhere, just in case."

———

My scariest, most troubling question was so tight in my chest I could barely breathe around it. "Otis? Were you *in* on this? Did you know everything? From the *beginning*?" Otis stayed silent. Staring at a moment I couldn't see. Vibrating with an emotion I couldn't read. I was aware Tom was back with us now. Waiting to find out what we all might have lost tonight.

Shadow Man answered me first.

"You both need to understand. I've known Otis for—hell… for decades now. And I've never seen him face down anything this hard. The night you all heard about the money, I came to see him in his quarters downstairs. I believed there was a decent chance he'd kill me. Or at least try. For your sakes, I needed him to be as shocked as you were when word about the heist came down that morning, but then—that night—he had to get 100% on board with a plan I knew he was going to hate."

Tall, dark, tired, and uncompromising, Shadow Man gave us the gift of hard truths. "Allie. Tom. You're alive tonight because over the past three weeks Otis has done things *he would not ever do*. He lied to you. He accepted a risky, unpredictable situation for you. He put your lives on the line, because, as far as either of us could see, it was your only chance. Only. Chance.

"That guy was bound to wipe the slate. He told me so. You, Allie. Tom. Anyone who had the slightest link. Including Otis. Otis wasn't even interested when I told him about that. *And I led with it.* Remember that, please."

I looked at Otis. He was hunched over his knees. Hands clasped. Beyond silent.

Tom could talk just fine.

"*You* told them about the Solstice tickets, Otis. *You*—helped him arrange tonight. It could have gone—"

The ground under Tom had crumbled. Tom needed Otis to still be our solid ground.

Otis came back to us. Sat up straight in his folding chair. Looked me straight in the eye. Spoke directly to Tom. "Yes, Tom. No kidding. We could all of us be dead right now. Like as not, they'd have found us Monday morning. Like as not, he'd make sure even Chad was dead.

"No matter what lies he told us, that man would never have let you guys live. We had to stop him. Tonight. If we hadn't, he'd be out there. Taunting you. Stalking you. Targeting you. Up close or 2000 feet out. Everywhere. Anywhere. Anytime. And you'd have no security or peace—24/7—while you waited for him to get you in his sights. And I would not have been able to protect you from that. Tonight was risky, but it was our best shot as we saw it. As controlled as it ever gets. This room was just the right amount of "out of nowhere." We knew we had a decent chance to stop him here.

"But you both have always trusted me to be straight with you. And the last three weeks, I've been everything but that. I'm sorry."

My face spoke for itself.

Emotion choked Tom's answer. "I'm insulted that you'd think you needed to apologize being willing to lay your life down for

Allie and me tonight, Otis. But I'm going to overlook it. This once."

All this fellow feeling gave me courage to bug The Shadow about something else.

"So. You stole all our money."

A brief nod.

"Geez. Did you put it back?"

The shadow of a smile. "Most of it."

I blew right by that. "How did you get that obviously unprincipled man to trust you not to run off with the cash."

"You'd be surprised, Allie. All I had to do was make the assurances and guarantees sound really complicated. It was the clown car of checks and balances. Something like, Mercury and I would have to go to a bank in the Bahamas. Handcuffed together. In our underwear. With matching pass keys. Never would have worked. But, again, he wasn't very—"

We all recited the words like a benediction.

Tech. Savvy.

He shrugged. Matter-of-Fact. "All's well that ends—"

I'd heard that before. "With only one dead guy."

Tom grinned. "You got that right, Allie."

While everyone was all smiling, I went for one last question.

"You and him. Mercury. You ran in 'the same circles?'"

I made finger quotes. The occasion seemed to merit them.

"It's a large circle, Allie. Population of a nice-sized town, Saints, five percent. Villains, forty-five percent. Mixed, fifty percent. And the who's-who varies, day to day. Like a town."

"And you? You in the Saintly Five Percent?" Now I was seriously pushing my luck, but the Universe owed me answers tonight.

"I try, but there's a shitload of temptation in my line of work. Hacker powers are so very—seductive."

Dead serious now. "And you all should know, I would have taken your Mercury out myself, no question. No remorse. In March. But once we had the setup, the bastard made himself scarce. One burner phone after another. Never gave me a clean shot. Until tonight. I took the first one I had."

"So is it 'Everett'?"

"You put way too much importance on names, girl. Ask quite a few too many questions also."

"So it's not Everett."

"Hardly. If I could put 'Shadow Man' on one of my passports, I would." He stood up. "I need a vacation. And I've got the extra cash. Besides, it wouldn't hurt to make myself scarce for a while."

I turned to see if Otis was following along. And okay with all this. He was. He grinned and Otis Johnson, Fashion Maven, gleamed out of his eyes. "Give me some credit. I knew you were going to be able to pay your Nordstrom bill."

When I turned back, the shadow had vanished.

My Louboutins were next to the "Fragile. Keep Right Side Up" box by the door. My purse was there too. I put the ensemble back together without much confidence. I checked myself out in the window of an deserted office as we took the back door to the parking lot. "Dry Clean Only" was twenty-five hundred dollars' worth of flowery dust rags. With a distinctive bloodstain.

Good thing we were rich again.

Chapter Fifty-Six

Last summer, at the end of our first T&A case, I cleared the slate of my never-going-to-be-answered questions with what I liked to think of as a "creative hypothesis."

I used the mix of things I knew for sure and the ones I never would to imagine key moments I wasn't present for and would never have accurate knowledge of. Especially since key players weren't talking, due to being dead.

I had my own head movie for this case too. The creative answer for a question I'd kept at the back of my mind since the morning after Kip Wade's murder. *Where would a man like Tito meet a man like Kip Ward?*

I had an answer: The Happy Dog.

I pictured a pivotal moment, maybe in the late fall of last year. After July's foiled jackpot grab. After it became clear to Tito that an accomplice discarded in the heat of a moment had never been as disposable as he'd imagined. After Tito fled with his rage into an empty, unfinished high-rise apartment building, and before his hunger for revenge opened the door to a deadly alliance that turned him into his own collateral damage.

How one rainy autumn night he might have taken himself down many flights of stairs and out into the wet-tobacco fragrance of leaves piled up in gutters. Music would have been seeping out of the Happy Dog. Somebody reading a poem or a short story over the insistent buzz and clink of the bar. Lisa could have been there that night. D.B. too. It was my damn scene, I could set it however I liked.

Besides, they would all be neighbors before winter was over. D.B. and Tito Ricci in a bar or an elevator together was another scene I could imagine. That one was the official Allie Harper Nightmare. Surely they'd met. Said a semi-cordial hello. Sneered at each other. I shook that one off. I could ask D.B. to tell me more about it if I ever spoke to him again.

The Happy Dog was Kip Wade's official hang out. His brother told me so when we had our little talk in the chapel after his funeral. So Kip might have been there that night when Tito arrived. At the bar drinking. He'd Uber home. It wasn't far. He'd never had the chance to drive a car. That pissed him off. He'd made it a practice to be royally pissed off by anything or anyone that made him sad. His brother told me that too. I felt as if I understood Kip now.

"Human being" is the answer to so many "whys".

The moment unfolds. The door opens and lets in the damp, leaf-perfumed breeze. Traffic sounds rush in too. Cars hum and roar. Tires fizz along the wet street. Footsteps. A voice. Puzzled. Slightly hostile. Asks, "Tom? Tom…Bennington?"

A flashpoint for Kip Wade. How might he have reacted to being mistaken for a man he both envied and hated. On a whim he could have lied. Claimed Tom's identity, his good fortune, his story, Added his own pinch of arrogance. 'Yeah. What's it to you?" Lied and died outside on the street later. Maybe. But he said the magic word.

"No."

It would have been the fatal meeting nonetheless. He and Tito having a chat that evening. Sharing a couple of drinks.

Kip would want to tell Tito what an ass that Tom Bennington

The *Third* turned out to be. All that money. All that luck. Maybe he told Tito about the new technology coming along that might give people back their sight. Or something like it. How it cost a fortune. And here was that SOB Bennington with money to burn but no interest in helping anybody but himself. Perhaps right there, sitting at the bar, Tito began concocting his plan. Baiting his vengeful trap with the dream of restored sight for Rudyard Kipling Wade.

Bare bones that night, but the rough sketch of a design. *A message for Tom Bennington.* To set it all in motion.

They would have exchanged info and Tito would probably have put Kip into a car and settled up with the driver.

I wondered if, later that night, Tito stood on his scarcely finished balcony in the damp, blustering dark, feeding his ego the bile it craved. Looking down over the lagoon to the pale gleam of marble in the distance, nursing a wild dream of sweet revenge and a huge payoff. Seeing all the death he would make.

In my imagination he gazes down on the path by the water and pictures Kip Wade there, walking with his white cane to meet his fate.

Seeing it all wrong, backward, and upside down. Not noticing a second dead man, right there at the bench.

What you don't see is what you get.

Chapter Fifty-Seven

SUNDAY, JUNE 24

On the evening after the summer solstice party, the sun set over Cleveland, Ohio at 9:04 p.m. The sky was a clean, uncomplicated blue and gold. Everything glowed. The lake. Tom. Otis. Me. Even the gulls—bragging raucously about how smart they were—glowed as they soared. Tom, Otis, and I lolled by the pool, drinking Great Lakes Burning River Ale, talking about everything except death and destruction. Both our devils were dead. All was as well as it was ever likely to get.

We agreed we'd stay put, for now, in this, our less-mansion-y-but-still-fairly-mansion-y mansion. We'd stand down the troops, say goodbye to "Who's A Good Boy?" and rely, like run-of-the-mill multi-millionaires, on a high-quality security system—vetted and maintained by Shadow Man. He'd be back. And, always, Otis would keep us as safe as humanly possible. And be Otis. Tom would turn our attention away from self-preservation to philanthropy as we intended all along.

"No Ducking" was our new work in progress.

I was delighted not to have to move out of our Hobbit cottage. Tom said it would be pleasant not have to learn a new floorplan every fifteen minutes. Otis said transporting his ice cream collection would be a logistical challenge. "We'd have to eat it all. That might get burdensome. After a coupla weeks."

I'd quizzed him about how he'd got in last night without the light from the door giving him away. "Chad and I killed the lights in the hall. He was hurting when I found him. He's a stand-up guy. If he really wants to be a cop, I'll encourage him. I think the museum appreciates him more now, though. He's the first guard they ever had take a bullet for a patron."

Otis stood for a minute, his gaze fixed on the tug Dorothy Ann Pathfinder, trundling a barge along the horizon. She was painted as brightly as the gulls in the light from the setting sun. "Great night to be on a boat headed somewhere." He shook the wistful note off his voice. "Fine night to be alive. Good night, you guys."

Tom and I lingered. The evening breeze was warm. I was musing about the money. Vanishing. Reappearing. $250 million. Give or take. Not the fortune of a billionaire's social media empire. I'd seen diagrams of a billion dollars. You'd need quite a few more coffee tables to do that many millions justice. Our modest stacks of bills paled in comparison, but those millions had changed our lives.

"Tom. I need to tell you something."

"Is it something I'll appreciate hearing."

"It's about a major character flaw. So probably not."

"Does it have anything to do with you and Shadow Man becoming a couple?"

"This is serious."

"That would be serious."

"Okay. Here goes. Tom. I like being rich." I searched his face. In the dying light of one of the longest days of the year he looked quietly composed. So far, so good.

"I hate the horrible things that happened because of the jackpot since Tuesday, August 18, two years ago—"

"Our anniversary," he murmured. Trailed his awesome hand-some fingers over my bare arm. He didn't seem to be repulsed by my confession. Yet.

"Maybe you didn't hear what I said."

"I heard. Don't be disappointed. I guessed."

"When?"

"The night you helped me verify the numbers on the ticket. You were jigglin."

"The first night? You've always known?"

"It hasn't been a secret. You saw the possibilities of the money. I only saw the—"

"The reality. Tom. You saw—"

"Bad things. And there have been many." His fingers found the patch of gauze covering the small cuts in the notch of my throat. "So many. But good things too. Both realities. Your brilliant object lesson the other day helped me see what I'd missed."

"My unworkable coffee table?"

"Maybe Jay could make a suggestion—"

"Stop. I don't see—"

"Yeah. You do. The money has always been two pallets' worth of wonderful and terrible. Good works. Terrible evil. Joy. Love. Hate. Death. Moment to moment. It took people's lives. It brought me you. It brought Otis to us. I would never have met Margo, and I cannot imagine life without Margo. This is the conversation we had with Rune. The one you had with Robert Wade after Kip's funeral. Cause and effect. Luck and its consequences.

"No worries, Allie. We'll deal with your shameless attraction to the money. Share it and use it for good and keep enough so we can be in this house and Otis can stay forever. And you can replace Dry Clean Only. From what I understand the shoes are good to go."

He stood up and found my hand. Pulled me to my feet and held me close. "Alice Jane Harper, last night I would not have placed a dollar bet on the chance of our living to see today. Today is what counts. I'm ready to embrace our two—and no doubt soon— three pallets of cash. For every fine thing they can be. And keep funding the T&A until we get it right. Okay?"

"Uh huh."

Back inside the house, he kissed my forehead, lightly—too lightly. Too forehead. And murmured, "See you upstairs."

I showered. The room gleamed with marble. The fixtures shone. The rain storm fell on me in all its glory. The shower floor offered to warm my feet or whatever else I might want warmed. I paid it no mind. I was soapy, rinsed, clean, and toweled off before the steam even got going. Tom's robe was hanging by the door. I wore it to the bedroom and let it fall to the floor.

He was lying back against the pillows in the lamplight he always turned on for me. His headphones were covering his ears. His eyes were closed, the sculptured contours of his face were relaxed, and his handsome not-so-smoothly-shaven jaw was unclenched. Dozing, maybe, or chasing his rich visual memories through the voices of a novel.

He'd told me his dad was a rockbound New Englander, trapped, sweating, in Atlanta but his mother was Italian, fierce in her love of sun and warm weather. Tonight, with his bare skin a warm contrast against crisp white sheets, he was a Tintoretto saint spilling headlong out of a cloud. Like a lightning bolt. Electric. Hot.

He smiled and slipped the headphones off. "Alice Jane, you can't sneak up and take advantage of my vulnerability. Maybe I didn't hear you, but you just got out of the shower, and you smell delicious. And irresistible."

"Don't even think about resisting me." I climbed up onto the bed next to him, sat back on my heels, and stared down more. "You look very handsome, Dr. Bennington III. But too covered up."

I slipped my fingers under the edge of the top sheet and billowed it out all the way to the foot of the bed. He grinned. "I feel a breeze."

"Oh no. Are you chilly?"

"Not. Even. Close."

I put my face to his chest and inhaled. Breathing him, as if I could make him part of me forever. Sat back again, still admiring. He came up onto his elbows to meet me, but I gave him a gentle push into the pillows.

"Shh. Lie there for me. We're always so busy. I never get a chance to look at you."

"I like busy. Busy is one of my favorite things." He settled back and reached up—unerring as always. My skin hummed her answer to his touch, but I grabbed his hand and pinned it back to the pillow.

"Stop that. Just. Let me stare at you for one damn minute."

A smile twitched his mouth. "Then it'll be my turn to have a look at you. And you know what that means."

"Uh huh."

Carpe stare, Allie. Carpe braille, Tom.

I let my gaze drift down over him. A body is a mystery that contains an entire person. A mystery within a mystery. His breathing had quickened. I could see his heartbeat stirring his chest. It reminded me of the angry pulse in his temple last night, right before he gave up the knife and stepped away from the brink of revenge. That narrow escape. I touched the patch on my throat again, remembering.

So much darkness and so few guarantees.

Before I could grab it, a tear spilled onto his shoulder. He put his fingers on it. Rubbed it into his skin. And pulled me closer.

"Shh. We're here now. We're alive. We're fine. But more important, we're super-extra-fine at the moment, and it's my turn to look you over. Come closer. I plan to be very, very conscientious about this particular investigation."

I moved to make as much of myself available as humanly possible.

"Promise?"

"Promise."

I wasn't done wooing him. "You're kind of the blind Sherlo—"

He put his fingers over my mouth. "Stop it. You're trying to seduce me by talking detective trash."

"Uh huh. Succeeding too, I'd say. But no, really, you've got that analytical, honed senses thing going all the time. If he'd been blind—"

"He had a cocaine habit, Allie. If he'd been blind he'd have gotten high and fallen down Mrs. Hudson's stairs. DOA."

"Or over a waterfall," I agreed. "You'd beat him in the blind detective department because of no cocaine. That's very sexy."

I relocated myself on his chest and brushed my lips over his. Not even a real kiss. Not yet. Teasing. Tom's world deserved a long, respectful exploration. Sweet time.

"About the money?"

"Shush yourself, Alice Jane. You are the least material girl I know. You have the very expensive habit of giving cash, food, and dog biscuits to anybody within reach. Also, we are running your detective agency at a massive loss. I'm aware of how much you enjoy not having to balance a checkbook but forget about all that. We're good."

He yawned. It had been a strenuous less-than-forty-eight-hours.

I insinuated my head into his shoulder. "Are you beginning to tire of me, Dr. Bennington the Third?"

"Does any part of me seem at all tired, Ms. Harper?"

This was more promising.

"Let me check. Mmm. I'm going to have to answer no to that question. I only thought—"

"You think too much. That's a problem with you. Sometimes you also think too stupid."

I poked him in the middle of his chest to communicate indignation. He picked up my hand and planted a kiss in the center of its palm. To communicate, "This is my mouth on your hand." Which had the effect of waking up more parts of me. Even the soles of my feet were aroused.

I could still talk, though.

"So you don't think I'm smart enough for you? Or reliable enough? Or something else enough?"

He rolled away from me and lay back, moving his head side-to-side on the pillow. Consternation. With a dimple. "What did I say? Only a moment ago? About thinking stupid?"

Ah, God. This was a step in a very wrong direction. I scrambled for the words to change it back.

"It's only—I don't want you to be disappointed, is all. Or bored." I leaned up and touched my tongue to the favored, delicious, sculpted indentation right next to his ear.

"Ah. That's…so…kind. Do I look bored to you? I can't see my face."

"No. Nothing about you appears bored. Or tired."

He sighed somewhere midway on the scale between satisfaction and exasperation and rolled back into his place like the heat-seeking missile he was born to be. Every part of my body said, "Welcome Home, Heat-Seeking Missile." He smiled. It was a smug smile, but I didn't care. I'm not the sort of girl to hold a grudge at such a moment. Not stupid either.

I gave my full attention to bringing as much of the available surface area of my skin into contact with as much of the available surface area of his skin as I could.

"So? You're not bored? You don't want to do…this…or possibly this…with another girl?"

"Not at all." A tiny pause. "Well, maybe there's one other girl—"

A shiver poured down over me. I would have pulled away but he had me securely immobilized.

"One other? Who?"

"Well, someday—" he murmured, moving with inexorable grace to carry us to our moment of total, uninhibited, spontaneous combustion. The last thing I heard, as I let go all of my cognitive functions and cast my whole being into to the fires of Tom Bennington, was his voice.

"I don't know. Someday, I might like to get a little better acquainted with Lee Ann."

Author's Note

When I dreamed of writing a mystery series set in Cleveland, I found inspiration and encouragement in the success of Cleveland author Les Roberts, whose seventeen mysteries featuring a Slovenian private eye take place in *my places*. So, when I decided—with considerable temerity—to set key scenes of *The Devil's Own Game* in and around The Cleveland Museum of Art, I turned to something Les Roberts said about writing Cleveland.

When someone asked him, "Don't you know the Cleveland Orchestra never plays on Wednesday, you dummy?" Roberts answered, "*My Cleveland Orchestra* plays whenever I tell it to."

Like Allie Harper, I love the Amitāyus Buddha in Gallery 241-B. But my plot depends upon the bench in front of him. *Not. Really. There.* I also obscured and misdirected descriptions of things I thought might be sensitive to security or disrespectful in any way to our city's magnificent and venerable art museum. So when I hear from a knowledgeable reader who says, "You dummy! There's no bench in front of the Amitāyus Buddha," I plan to hide behind Mr. Roberts and answer, "*My Amitāyus Buddha* has a bench. You got a problem with that?"

One of my greatest pleasures in writing a series which features Tom Bennington, "nice, hot, smart guy" who's also blind, is the friends I have made at The Cleveland Sight Center. Thanks to them I have walked with a white cane, sat in on the Sight Center's rowdy book group when they discussed *Too Lucky to Live*, and volunteered at a Touch Tour like the one featured in this book. It was on last summer's White Cane Walk around the Museum of Art's lagoon that I realized what and where the first scene of this book would be. I am grateful to Alicia Howerton, Community Relations Specialist, who led me on my first tour of the Center, Melissa Mauk, Manager of Volunteer Services, who "turned me into a volunteer," Larry Benders, President and Chief Executive Officer, who's been forever gracious and welcoming, and to "my CSC book group!"

The Cleveland Museum of Art and the Cleveland Sight Center are both institutions dedicated to uplifting the human spirit. Treasures.

On an unhappy note: Time passes. Things change. The Happy Dog on Euclid Avenue, lively setting for all manner of entertainment, enlightenment, and a scene in this book, is no more.

Acknowledgments

Much gratitude to:

At Poisoned Pen Press, now the new mystery imprint of Sourcebooks, I owe all thanks and my sanity to my editor, Annette Rogers, who is my stalwart source of courage and my unfailing common sense when both are lacking. And, as ever, unlimited appreciation for Barbara Peters, Rob Rosenwald, Diane DiBiase, Holli Roach, Beth Deveny, Suzan Baroni, Kacie Blackburn, and Michael Barson. And for my fabulous, intrepid PPP Posse—every writer should have a posse so generous and remarkable.

My agent, Victoria Skurnick, for her insight, and patience. And those wicked-fast response times. Speed of light, Victoria. I am so grateful for everything you do and who you are on my journey.

My Sisters in Crime, more than ever, my tribe.

Tina Whittle, my lightning strike of luck and my constant supply of blessings. Without you, no this.

Thrity Umrigar. The 100 percent friend.

Stacey Vaselaney, of SLV Public Relations, for smart PR and abiding friendship.

Meredith Pangrace, of MAP Creative, for keeping AnnieHogsett .com ever-fresh, alive, and pretty—and Bill Hogsett, for web-mastery with swearing.

My experts:

Our neighbor, Dr. DeRoss, for his keen insights into matters surgical.

Elaine Martone, fashion consultant, partner in Veuve Clicquot, and BFF.

For footwear wisdom, Stephan Moody, artist/designer, shoe guru, and self-described "hunka hunka burning love."

Joe Valencic. (Jože Valenčič.) For keeping me up on the "čič" of my Slovenian characters.

Laura Starnik, for inspiration and commitment. You know exactly who you are.

Steve Gluskin for the braille and the laughs.

The Usual Suspects—Douglas Bunker, Thomas Moore, Elaine Martone, and Bob Woods—for state-of-mind repair.

Mary Lucille DeBerry and Joe Sigler for morale unfailing.

Vicky and Chet for being our daring in-law duo.

John Farina for offering himself up as "murder victim" multiple times. Be careful what you wish for, John.

I am fortunate way beyond deserving to have so many wonderful, kind, and patient friends and family whom I've ditched and deserted multiple times as I wrote and rewrote this story. You know who you are. I promise I'll be back! And while we're talking neglected friends, my wonderful, forgiving book group who have supported me unfailingly, even when I turned ghost and didn't hold down the cupcake end of our meetings this year.

And last, because this is the true bottom of my heart, Bill and John for being the epicenter of my world. And Cujo because his love can be bought with treats.

About the Author

Annie Hogsett, the author of the Somebody's Bound to Wind Up Dead Mysteries, lives and writes in the city of Cleveland, ten yards from the shores of Lake Erie. She has never won a $550 million lottery jackpot. *The Devil's Own Game* is the third in her series.

Photo by Dan Milner